Scar

Book 5

Mariah Dyer

Chapter 1

Aurora tucked her handgun in the back of her jeans and made sure her sweater concealed it. She adjusted her crossbow to correctly secure it to her hip along with the arrows. She took a few deep breaths to steady herself before she carelessly started wandering though the woods. It went against her most basic training. She couldn't help but flinch when she purposely stumbled over a tree root while making as much noise as possible.

She'd never been a double agent before. But neither had anyone else in the rebellion, besides the shapeshifters. The idea of someone trying to trick the enemy into thinking that they were on their side was something that none of them had been crazy enough to try. Until she had to be stupid enough to volunteer herself as a guinea pig.

She would never forget how angry everyone had been at her for suggesting that she voluntarily join forces with her sadistic father. It was shortly after the magical explosion that almost took out their whole community. She hadn't been in any shape to participate in a council meeting, let alone suggest going undercover, but she had anyway.

It took some convincing, especially for Riley, to let her do it. Demian had even tried to close the meeting before they decided on whether they would go with her plan or not. Riley had brought up Wade, and what happened to him after being a double agent, to convince her not to do it. Aurora had to remind him that he had effectively kidnapped Rebecca and succeeded in his mission even if he did die in the end.

She understood their uncertainty, but she was a rebel leader. She had demanded that they treat her as such no matter how severe her injuries were. It didn't help that she still had them, weeks later, but it couldn't be helped. Pain had never been something she feared anyway.

She couldn't help but think of Gabriel. He was more furious with her than anyone else; which was saying something.

There had only been a handful of times in their entire existence that he had been truly angry with her. Gabriel got angry at Marcus all the time, but hardly ever at her. When Gabriel was angry with his brother he would usually grumble about it, or hit him if he was furious enough. When he was angry at Aurora he gave her the silent treatment.

She wished he would just hit her instead.

Her mind wandered to the conversation she'd had with her brother before she disappeared into the woods:

"There's nothing I can say that will make you reconsider this insane idea, is there?"

"So now you're finally talking to me?" She tried to keep the hurt out of her voice, but she knew he'd heard it when he winced. "Right before I'm about to leave?"

"I'm sorry about that," he grumbled.

"Don't worry about it," she said nonchalantly.

"What if Carvolo kills you the minute he sees you?"

"He won't."

"How do you know that?" Gabriel asked in a desperate tone that he rarely used.

Gabriel didn't show fear very often.

"I'm about eighty-five percent sure."

"That is not okay with me," he said as he defiantly folded his arms across his chest.

"Well, tough," she said with a hint of her own defiance. "It's not your decision to make. If there's a chance that we can pull this off, we have to take it. If everything goes according to plan we could take out two of our most dangerous enemies."

"Do you have any idea what it would do to Riley if you died? Or Marcus and I for that matter?"

The fear in his voice made her hug him. It took a moment for him to hug her back, probably because he didn't want to cause her any discomfort. But when he did he held onto her with a vice-like grip. She ignored the pain.

"I will do whatever I need to do to survive," she whispered to him. "I'm coming back, I promise."

The brush in the woods was getting thicker. It made it easier to make a lot of noise, but it wasn't ideal for escaping if that's what she ended up having to do. She wished she knew where Carvolo was. It would've been easier if she could be in control of the situation. That way she wouldn't have a chance of being caught off guard.

There was also the chance that she would run into Arothor or Zalina. She fervently hoped that wouldn't happen. Carvolo she could deal with, but fairies were her worst nightmare.

She made sure to rub her arms against a few trees and bushes so that any werewolf would be able to smell her easily. If one of Carvolo's followers picked up her scent they would certainly tell him that she was wandering around the woods.

Eventually she decided to stay in one spot and map out an escape plan in her head. After she killed Carvolo she'd have to escape somehow. No doubt he would be surrounded by werewolves and it was likely that Zalina would be there.

Suddenly, she heard a soft rustle behind her. She was willing to bet it was an untrained skinwalker. Even untrained werewolves didn't make any noise when they prowled around. Silence was instinctual for werewolves and a skill that skinwalkers had to learn.

She reached for her crossbow.

"Why don't you come out so we can talk?" she called out to the dark woods. "I need to speak to your leader."

There was silence for a few minutes. There wasn't even a rustle or the sound of breathing. It made Aurora nervous and she kept a firm grip on her crossbow.

"I have orders to shoot rebels on sight," a small voice whispered from behind the trees.

"I'm not a rebel tonight," Aurora replied sternly. "It's an urgent matter. I need to speak to Carvolo."

A girl emerged from behind the tree and Aurora had to swallow her anger. She didn't look much older than thirteen. She had dark unkept hair and her clothes were ragged. She couldn't have looked more homeless if she were found camping

4

under a dark bridge. Aurora made sure her face remained neutral so the girl wouldn't decide she was lying and put a bullet in her.

"I should shoot you," the girl said in a quivering voice. "The leader will have me punished if I do anything wrong."

"What's your name?" Aurora asked in an authoritative voice.

"Kate," the girl whispered in reply.

Her eyes widened and it looked like she was trying not to cry. She raised her gun and pointed it at Aurora with a trembling hand.

The poor girl was so scared.

"You aren't going to shoot me, Kate," Aurora said in the same commanding voice. "Lower the gun and take me to Carvolo. Now."

Aurora didn't even have to threaten Kate with the crossbow. She lowered the gun hesitantly and beckoned for Aurora to follow her. She followed Kate for a few minutes before stopping the girl.

"You're going to walk behind me," Aurora said. "You'll make it look like I'm your captive instead of the other way around. That way Carvolo won't think that I threatened you."

Kate looked at her in confusion, but did what she was told. That was the trouble with Carvolo's soldiers. They were so abused that the ones he used as pawns would listen to anyone that seemed to hold authority. All the fire had been beaten out of them at young ages. It made obedient soldiers, that's for sure, but also intimidated ones that could be manipulated easily.

"Are we close to where Carvolo is stationed?" Aurora asked.

"Yes," Kate's voice was shaking with fear. "I really should shoot you."

Aurora turned her head sharply and saw that Kate had aimed the gun at her again. The girl's hand shook violently and her breathing was erratic. Aurora worried that she would shoot her as a result of a twitchy trigger finger.

5

"If you shoot me Carvolo will kill you," Aurora said as she glared at the girl. "I am his daughter and he gets to claim my life. Not you. Lower the gun."

A hopeful spark ignited in Kate's eyes.

"I've heard of you," she whispered as she lowered the gun again. "I've heard stories. Are you here to save us?"

Aurora managed to keep her face neutral despite the stabbing pain that ripped through her gut. This was the problem with what she had to do. She had to be a coldhearted person in front of this poor child. She really did want to save her, to save all of them, but it wasn't possible. It was one thing to set aside feelings and do what had to be done. It was another thing to look at an abused defenseless child and tell her that she couldn't be saved.

"No," Aurora said as she pivoted away from the girl quickly. "I don't do that anymore. You better hope that I don't tell Carvolo what you just asked me."

The girl let out a soft whimper as they continued through the brush. Aurora stomped down the guilt and avoided meeting Kate's eyes again. Sometimes she really hated the fact that she could be so convincing.

Aurora heard voices and recognized one as Zalina's. She grimaced and took a cleansing breath. Carvolo's deep voice came from the same direction and the ball of anxiety in her stomach threatened to burst.

She gestured for Kate to come closer to her.

"Call out and tell them you have captured Aurora Ryder," she whispered to Kate.

Aurora didn't want either of them to get shot by showing up unannounced. Kate did as she was told and someone growled angrily, probably Carvolo.

Suddenly, Zalina appeared next to Aurora and immobilized her with a binding magical spell. Aurora had to stifle a gasp when the fairy turned her angry gaze at the young skinwalker girl. She really hoped Zalina decided to leave Kate alone.

"She told me that she wanted to talk to the leader," Kate whispered meekly.

"I'll deal with you later," Zalina said harshly to the girl.

Aurora didn't miss Kate's terrified flinch when Zalina muttered a torture incantation. A burning pain ripped through Aurora in a matter of seconds. She would have screamed in pain if she could, but the fairy's magic cut off her oxygen.

"Enough, Zalina," Carvolo chuckled darkly. "You can have fun later. For now, I'd like to find out why Aurora decided to so carelessly forfeit her life. She could have easily killed the skinwalker girl and moved on."

Zalina's torture spell faded quickly. Aurora fell to her hands and knees with a small gasp of relief. She didn't have time to recover before a strong hand grabbed her hair and roughly pulled her head back. She stared into Carvolo's yellow eyes with as neutral an expression as she could muster. His hand gripped her hair harder, but she refused to wince.

"Why are you here, Aurora?"

"I've come to warn you," Aurora whispered in a sincere voice. "Arothor is planning on betraying you."

Carvolo threw back his head and laughed. He took her crossbow and arrows from her as he chuckled in amusement. He handed the weapons to a terrified Kate. The girl held them as though she thought they would explode in her hands. Two werewolves that Aurora recognized from when she was a young girl came into view. She couldn't remember their names, but she knew that they were leaders. One was tall and thin with long blond hair that almost reached his hips. The other was short with cropped hair and broad shoulders.

"Just kill her, Carvolo," the blond one said absently. "She's a rebel. She will lie."

"You aren't the least bit interested in what she has to say, Edmond?" Carvolo asked humorously. "I know this skinwalker isn't stupid. Surly she has something up her sleeve besides attempting to turn us against our ally."

Carvolo pulled Aurora up by her hair and lowered his face closer to hers in a threatening manner.

"You have thirty seconds," he said with a glare in his werewolf eyes. "This better be good."

"Arothor tried to kill Riley at Dur Den Thome," Aurora explain neutrally. "He tried to kill him with a magical bomb that he created in our community. He's here to try to kill him again. I came to you because I love him and I want to save him."

Carvolo laughed and tightened his grip on her hair so hard that Aurora felt chunks of it pull out of her scalp.

"Why would you come to me?"

"Because you can stop Arothor," she continued. "You can stop this battle from happening today. You can change Riley on the full moon before Arothor can kill him. I can lure Riley here for you. Just call off the battle."

"Why would you betray the one you love?" Carvolo asked skeptically.

"Because I'd rather see him as the werewolf leader you want him to be than a dead wizard."

Carvolo stared at her for a moment in thought. The two werewolf leaders waited impatiently for Carvolo to decide if he believed her or not.

Standing this close, Aurora couldn't help but notice the similarities that Gabriel had with Carvolo's appearance. They both had dark wavy hair and soft features while they were in thought. She never would point this out to Gabriel, though he probably already knew that he resembled their sadistic father. At least none of them had inherited Carvolo's brown eyes.

"I don't believe you," Carvolo said with a smirk. "You're here to try to gain my trust so you can kill me, correct?"

Aurora kept her face neutral and didn't say anything. She knew he wouldn't believe her. Not without some kind of test. Something that she would regret doing later. To her surprise, Carvolo handed her back her crossbow and a single arrow.

"If you want me to consider trusting you," Carvolo breathed into her ear. "Kill the skinwalker girl for me. Or you are welcome to put that arrow into my heart. Although, I doubt it will do you much good."

8

Aurora stared into her father's eyes. He guided her hand to point the crossbow at his heart. She quickly shoved him back angrily and he stepped away from her with a dark smile. She pointed the crossbow at the blond werewolf, Edmond, and fired the silver tipped arrow into his heart. The werewolf dropped lifelessly to the ground instantly. The other werewolf leader stared at his companion's body in shock for a moment before his eyes flashed werewolf yellow.

Carvolo laughed as he clapped his hands slowly in a demented applause.

"You still remember," he said happily. "You were just a child, but you learned the art of betrayal so well. How did you remember I despised him?"

"You were a good teacher," Aurora said quietly. "But I believe I am better. You need me to train your young soldiers. If you save Riley I will gladly be your daughter again."

"Will you take care of my other friend for me as well?"

"With pleasure."

Aurora took another arrow from Carvolo's outstretched hand and fired it into the remaining werewolf's heart before he could disappear into the trees. Kate stood as still as a statue while she stared at the dead werewolves at her feet. Aurora thought she must've gone into shock because she no longer was trembling in fear.

"Why are you still here, girl?" Zalina asked Kate harshly. "You're on guard duty."

Kate's eyes widened for a moment.

"No," Carvolo said with a shake of his head. "Aurora, you still need to kill her for me or I won't trust you."

Aurora gritted her teeth and clenched her jaw slightly. This was the part where she knew she would fail. She saw this coming, but was stupid enough to try to kill Carvolo anyway. If Riley had killed Arothor she would've succeed by now.

Unfortunately that hadn't happened yet.

"I don't waste things that could be of use later," she replied a little more sternly than she meant to.

9

"That is not your decision to make," Carvolo said. "I can't trust someone that won't kill for me without question."

"I just killed two werewolves for you without question."

"But you knew they weren't innocents. Kill an innocent for me and then I will know for sure that you aren't a double agent. That you aren't lying to me."

Aurora stared into Carvolo's psychotic eyes. She had told Riley and Gabriel that she would do whatever she had to do in order to survive. In that moment, she knew that she had lied to them. There was no way that she could kill the poor girl that shook violently from sheer terror right in front of her.

"You know I won't do that."

"Of course I know," Carvolo said as he took the crossbow from her. "You have a soft spot for the young and helpless. That will be the death of you one day."

Carvolo roughly pulled up the back of her sweater and took the handgun out of her pants. He cocked it and aimed it directly at her forehead.

"Why do you think I make most of my soldiers young and helpless?"

Aurora couldn't help it. Her cover was blown anyway. She glared at Carvolo with all the hatred that she could muster. If he was going to kill her she wanted him to know how much she despised him.

"It's because I knew it would hurt you, dear girl," Carvolo said with a sadistic laugh. "And I just love to make you miserable."

An explosion sounded in the distance and Carvolo smiled cruelly.

"That, Aurora, is the sound of your precious rebellion killing my army of young and helpless soldiers."

Carvolo adjusted his aim and squeezed the trigger of her gun. She collapsed to the ground without making a sound when the bullet entered her leg. Another explosion came from the community, but she didn't pay it any mind as she tried to staunch the bleeding from the wound. Everything was right on schedule. The only thing that was going wrong was her part of the plan.

"You," Carvolo said as he gestured to Kate with the gun. "Restrain my daughter with the silver chains. Quickly."

Kate sprung into action as though her life depended on it; which it probably did. She secured the chains around Aurora's arms and feet as quickly as she could. Aurora felt lightheaded and she glanced down at the hole in her leg. She was bleeding profusely, but she couldn't use her arms to try to stop the blood flow. It hurt, but it was nothing compared to the panicky despair she was now feeling. She had failed her mission. She could only hope that the others didn't fail theirs.

"Now, get back to your post," Zalina said to Kate. "Before Carvolo decides to kill you himself."

The girl stood up quickly and hurried off into the woods. Carvolo knelt down next to Aurora and glanced at her bullet wound with a small smirk. Other than that his face showed no emotion.

"I'm sorry about that," he said. "Couldn't have you running off now that I got you back."

Aurora met his werewolf eyes with a defiant glare. The yellow werewolf glow had left them and she could see his brown irises glare back at her. He smiled slowly with a hint of sadistic madness behind it.

"We are going to have so much fun together."

"Carvolo," Zalina said abruptly. "Something is wrong."

"What?"

"Jenina is going off the plan," the fairy said quickly. "From what I can see…she is planning on killing the chosen one."

"How do you know?" Carvolo asked angrily as he turned around to face her.

"I caught a glimpse of them when I did a location spell," she explained solemnly. "They are in a field on the outskirts of the community."

Carvolo turned to look at Aurora and she saw the yellow glow was back in his eyes. She had to breathe through her

11

panic. Riley was in danger and there was nothing she could do about it. She didn't understand why everything was going so wrong. She knew her mission was a hit or miss, but Riley and Rebecca should've been able to take out Jenna and Colette together with ease.

Unless, Riley didn't have it in him to hurt his mother. They all should've seen that coming.

"I wasn't lying about Arothor wanting Riley dead," Aurora told Carvolo in a broken voice.

"Shall I go and investigate?" Zalina asked.

"No, I'll go," Carvolo said hastily. "See if you can get more information out of her."

"Certainly," the fairy said with a nod. "But you must hurry. Riley Hanson didn't look like he was faring well."

Carvolo disappeared and Aurora's heart sank. She had a feeling that Carvolo would come back alone and with bad news. Tears stung her eyes, but she refused to let them fall. Not in front of a fairy that was about to torture her.

"What information can you give me?"

The fairy walked in circles around Aurora as she ignored the question.

"One useful thing you can tell me is where the rest of your communities are hidden."

Aurora didn't say anything as she stared at the leaf covered ground.

"I don't want to hurt you, Aurora Ryder, but I will."

Aurora couldn't help but laugh humorlessly.

"You want nothing more than to hurt me," she said as she gave Zalina a hard glare. "Why don't you get on with it? Nothing will be more painful than the thought of Riley's death. No matter what you do I won't tell you anything."

That's when the pain started. Aurora didn't scream at first, but the pain became more intense as the torture proceeded. Her screams pierced the night air and Zalina smiled cruelly as she watched her writhed on the ground. The torturous agony seemed to last for hours and Aurora screamed until her voice became hoarse.

Suddenly, the pain ended and Aurora laid in the dirt, dragging in labored breaths.

"The wonderful thing about torture incantations is that it does absolutely nothing to injure the body," Zalina said as she walked around Aurora in circles again. "All the pain in is your mind. I could literally do this all day long without you dying. You will talk eventually just to have a release from the mindless agony."

The fairy raised her hand again and uttered words in a language that Aurora didn't understand, but Zalina was cut off by the sound of Carvolo growling furiously.

Suddenly, the angry werewolf picked Aurora up by the collar of her sweater and threw her into a nearby tree with supernatural strength. Before she could fall to the ground, he grabbed her in midair and smashed her into the tree again. The scars from her burns burst into pain, but she remained silent.

She was done screaming.

She knew why Carvolo was attacking her and her insides had gone completely numb. Grief embraced her in its relentless grip a split second later.

"He is dead!" Carvolo screamed into her face. "I blame you! If you would've proven I could trust you then I would've believed you! Stupid girl!"

"You decided to trust Arothor even though you knew Riley was supposed to kill him with the wand," Aurora said in a broken voice. "You knew there was a possibility that he would want Riley dead to save his own skin. You ignored the red flags. You have no one to blame but yourself."

Carvolo's rage made his face change into something more wolfish. It could only happen to a werewolf when they were enraged close to the full moon. His smooth face became slightly scruffy with wiry fur and his teeth became a bit more fang-like. Aurora hadn't seen this happen to a werewolf for a very long time. She knew she was in danger of him killing her right then, but she didn't care. Riley was dead and her emotions went from devastation to pure fury.

13

"I hope the ancients kill you slowly for what you have done," she said in a dangerous whisper.

Carvolo took an animal-like breath and closed his eyes. His features went back to human and he let Aurora fall. She laid on the ground and felt a tear run down her cheek. She had half-hoped that Carvolo would kill her. She didn't want to live with this kind of lose, but she knew that he wouldn't do her the service of putting her out of her misery. Death would be an escape and Carvolo knew it.

"Let's get out of here," Carvolo said to Zalina. "We need to regroup and find a safe place to keep Aurora. I'm sure her brothers will be looking for her soon."

14

Chapter 2

Riley sat up abruptly; making everyone around him jerk in surprise. He glanced at his arm and saw that an IV was hooked up to his wrist. Apparently, the wand hadn't put a protective barrier around him this time.

Jackson, Rebecca, Gabriel, and Marcus were sitting in the tarp tent that someone had hastily constructed. He looked around for the wand and noticed part of it sticking out of the satchel that Rebecca had kept it in.

"How long was I out this time?"

"Twelve hours," Marcus said as he looked at his watch. "Give or take an hour."

"At least it wasn't three days, right?" Riley said as he pulled the IV out of his wrist.

"Could you at least tell us what you saw before you put the wand down next time?" Gabriel asked in a clear attempt to hide his frustration.

"What did you see?" Jackson asked him timidly.

"Before I passed out," Riley said thoughtfully. "I saw that she was alive in a den prison. I don't know which one, but at least we know she's alive."

"Is that all you saw?" Marcus asked.

"Yes…" Riley began, but then he remembered the dream he had.

He gasped and stood up quickly; making everyone jerk in surprise again. His stomach plummeted when he remembered the pain that Aurora went through. She had been tortured and captured with no one to help her.

"Riley?" Rebecca asked as she stared at him warily. "What's wrong?"

"I think the wand gave me another vision while I was sleeping," he said. "Holy crap. She thinks I'm dead."

"Aurora?" Gabriel asked quietly.

"Yes, and so does Carvolo," Riley said with a nod.

15

"We could use that to our advantage," Jackson said. "That's good news."

"It means that the community is safer than it was before, doesn't it?" Rebecca asked and Gabriel nodded.

"It won't be as valuable a target now that they think Riley is dead."

Riley sat down again from a sudden dizzy spell. His wife thought that he was dead. He couldn't get the agonized look on her face out of his mind. Anger surged through him when he remembered how Carvolo had blamed her for his supposed death. His anger mixed with pride as he recalled how she threw it back in Carvolo's face and wished him a slow death at the hands of the ancients.

He loved her so much.

"Riley," Rebecca said. "Can I get you anything? Are you hungry?"

"We need to get going," Riley said as he shook his head. "I can eat later."

"You're face is as white as a ghost, man," Marcus said with a raised eyebrow.

"Fine. I can eat on the road, but we need to go. We've waited too long already, thanks to me. Which community has the map of the werewolf dens?"

"The one that Veronica and Demian are visiting in Idaho," Gabriel said. "Let's go."

Riley tried to stand up to follow Gabriel, Rebecca, and Jackson out of the tent, but the dizziness hit him again. He felt nauseous and he had to put his head between his knees to keep himself conscious.

"Maybe you should sit this one out, man," Marcus said as he studied him carefully.

Riley looked up at him with determined eyes.

"Not on your life," Riley said. "But I wouldn't be opposed to a little help."

Marcus nodded in understanding and held his hand out to him. It was awkward, since Marcus ended up practically carrying him to the van that was parked outside of the tent.

16

He sat down in the backseat while the rest of them packed their bags into the back. He leaned his forehead against the window and tried to ignore the hunger pains that shot through his stomach. He didn't want to complain too much about needing to eat since he knew that time was of the upmost importance. Luckily, the IV they gave him was able to keep him hydrated.

He closed his eyes and tried to think of where Carvolo would be hiding Aurora. He really hoped that she wasn't in the Ancients Den since they had no idea where it was. They had a map that showed where most of the dens were in North America that had been extracted from the Leaders Den before they destroyed it. They kept that information in a different community. It was foolish to keep all the rebellion's information in one place. So they made sure to divide up their secrets between the communities. That way, if one was ambushed, their enemies wouldn't learn all of their secrets.

Jackson climbed into the driver seat and started the engine. Marcus got into the passenger seat and placed a handgun, with a few boxes of bullets, in the glove compartment. Gabriel and Rebecca slid onto the seat he was sitting on with Rebecca squished in the middle. It wasn't the most comfortable way to travel, but they had to take the third row of seats out of the back to fit all of their gear.

"Everyone ready?" Jackson said as he strapped his seatbelt on.

"Did you bring enough blood bags?" Riley asked.

He noticed that Jackson had looked a lot better than he had a week ago, but he couldn't resist the temptation to mess with him. It helped him take his mind off of Aurora for a moment.

Jackson turned in his seat to give him a glare.

"I have survived on my own for almost four days without you or Karven shoving blood down my throat," Jackson said sternly. "I think I'll be fine."

Riley gave him a smirk and Jackson rolled his eyes before putting his foot on the gas pedal.

"That's because I've been doing it for them," Rebecca chimed in. "Did you even bring a cooler?"

"No," Jackson replied. "There was no room. I don't need blood bags anyway. If I get hungry I'll just take a bite out of Marcus."

"Very funny," Marcus said with a chuckle.

When Marcus realized that no one else was laughing he grew silent for a moment.

"Wait. You were joking, right?"

Jackson laughed in response, and Marcus eyed him warily.

"Seriously, though," Jackson said to Rebecca and Riley. "I'm very fast. I can catch a rabbit or squirrel if I get hungry. No big deal."

"I've seen you drain four bags of deer blood in seconds," Riley said in concern. He hadn't realized before that Jackson hadn't brought any blood with them at all. "A rabbit or a squirrel isn't going to be enough."

"I don't need to do that anymore, buddy."

Riley glanced at Rebecca for some kind of confirmation on that. Thankfully, she gave him a quick nod and he relaxed.

"When did that happen?"

"A couple of days ago. It's kind of nice not having to drink all of the time."

They drove in silence for a few minutes. Riley noticed that Jackson was driving more erratically than he used to when he was a human. Probably because he didn't think about physical safety as much now that he was invincible. There were a few times that Riley's stomach clenched from how fast he was going around the sharp turns in the road. It wasn't helping with his nausea and he felt like he was going to vomit.

"Um," Riley mumbled quietly. "I don't want to be a backseat driver, but there is one person in the van who could potentially die in an accident."

Jackson immediately slowed down and apologized.

"Are you okay, Riley?" Rebecca asked as she studied his face. "You look a little green."

18

"I'm fine."

"No, he's not fine," Gabriel said to Rebecca. "He needs to eat something."

Riley actually didn't know if he could eat with how nauseous he felt, but there was also the possibility that food would help settle his stomach.

"Tacos or burgers?" Jackson asked Riley as he pulled onto the highway.

"Um, I don't care. You choose."

"I won't be eating it," Jackson said as he glanced back at him in the rearview mirror.

"Oh, yeah," Riley mumbled tiredly. "Sorry."

"I vote burgers," Marcus said enthusiastically.

The drive to Idaho didn't seem as long as Riley had expected it to. It was probably because he fell asleep for most of the trip. He didn't know why he was so tired after sleeping for basically three and a half days. All he knew was that he was exhausted and every time he closed his eyes he had nightmares of Aurora being mistreated. He couldn't tell for sure if they were dreams or visions. He hoped that they were just dreams, but something inside him told him that they weren't. It made him feel desperate. He almost wished that he could go back to not knowing what was happening to her, but he knew it still wouldn't help him feel better.

When they entered the community, Riley noticed that it was almost an exact replica of the one they lived in. But instead of a warehouse they had a couple more houses. Jackson parked the van in front of a green house with yellow trim. The colors reminded Riley of the bouquet that Aurora had carried down the aisle on their wedding day. He flinched at the emotions that the memory caused him. He tried to hide it, but he knew that Rebecca had noticed his reaction. He was grateful that she didn't say anything.

Riley wasn't surprised to see Veronica hurrying toward him when he got out of the van. The last time she'd seen him he was in a coma-like-sleep. Rebecca had told him that she was having a hard time with everything that had happened recently. It was probably because their mother had almost killed him. She left four bloody marks on his abdomen with her magical knives that Riley had, unknowingly, been using for a few years. If it wasn't for the wand he would have died. So Demian had taken her to visit her werewolf step mother and her half sister.

Riley tried not to wince when she gave him a tight hug. It was a common occurrence for his werewolf sisters to hug him a bit too tightly. Normally he was used to it, but his abdomen was extremely sore from his wounds. He ignored the pain as he hugged her back. He was so worried about Aurora that he didn't realize how much he needed the hug.

He didn't let go of her for a while.

"I'm so glad to see you," she whispered. "It was really scary seeing you sleep like that. I'm sorry I left, I just-"

"You have nothing to apologize for," Riley interrupted her. "So don't, oaky?"

Veronica nodded unconvincingly.

"I'm having a hard time dealing," she told him quietly.

"Me too," Riley said in understanding.

"Demian keeps telling me that I need to talk about it, but I don't really know what to say."

"Well, if you ever need to talk you can talk to me."

Veronica laughed humorlessly. It sounded weird coming from her.

"I should be telling you that. You're the one Jenna almost killed."

Riley gave her another hug and a swift kiss on the cheek.

"I'm fine," he lied.

Veronica glanced at him for a moment in concern

"We heard that Aurora is being held in a den somewhere," she said in an attempt to change the subject. "Is that true?"

20

Riley nodded and told her about the visions he'd had. He followed her into the house and stood awkwardly in the doorway. Everyone else sat on the couches and sofas in the living room. He knew who was temporarily staying in this house and he wasn't all that excited to meet them. In fact, he was terrified. He had always wondered how Teresa would react to meeting the person who killed her husband. Unfortunately, he was about to find out.

Teresa appeared from the hallway and she stared at him for a moment. She had long dark hair and was about average height. A couple inches taller than Veronica. She was very skinny, but Riley knew she had werewolf strength despite her lack of muscles. She wore a yellow sundress with white flats. From the looks of her, Riley assumed that she was very fashionable.

Behind her stood a girl who looked to be a year or two older than Pearl and Tanya. Jasmine had the same dark hair as her mother and same build. Something about her face reminded him of her father, Bill. When Teresa noticed Riley looking at her daughter she deliberately stepped in front of her.

"Riley, this is Teresa," Veronica said awkwardly. "Teresa, this is Riley."

"Pleased to meet you," Riley said politely.

He wasn't surprised when Teresa glared at him with a hint of yellow in her eyes.

"I will not say the same," she said harshly in a french accent. "I can not."

"Mama, what's wrong?" Jasmine asked as she tried to get a look at Riley.

"Come, Jazzy. You will not talk to this man."

"Teresa-" Veronica began, but Riley grabbed her arm.

"Don't. Let her go," he said quietly. "I was expecting that."

"You didn't deserve that," Veronica said fiercely.

"I'm the reason Bill isn't here. It's okay for her to feel how she feels."

Veronica looked like she wanted to argue, but she didn't say anything else. Riley knew that he had to be careful how he handled this situation. Teresa was a follower. That meant Veronica could potentially command her to tolerate Riley. That wasn't something he could live with. He didn't think that Veronica would purposely try to control Teresa's feelings. But there was the possibility that the follower would catch on to her leader's discontentment about the situation. He didn't want Teresa to feel pressured into tolerating him. Besides, if Teresa didn't want Jasmine around him then they should respect that.

"I'm sorry, Riley," she said with a sigh. "I guess she doesn't understand what happened like I thought she did."

"Even if she does understand I don't want her to feel like she has to hang around me."

Veronica nodded and led him into the living room. They sat down on the vacant sofa and waited for Demian to bring the information that they needed. He came down the stairs carrying a battered cardboard box. Riley stared at the box with curiosity. It didn't look like something that would be trusted to contain important information.

Demian pulled a lockbox out of the cardboard one and took a key out of his pocket. He unlocked the box with the key and opened the lid. The werewolf pulled out the map and a ratty old book that had a different language written on the cover.

"What's up with the nasty cardboard box?" Rebecca asked in confusion.

"The last place our enemy would look for hidden information is in a worn out box in the attic," Demian explained. "At least that's the idea. It's not a perfect hiding place, but it was the best I could do for now."

He laid the map out on the coffee table for everyone to see. There were random red X's and green circles scattered around the map of North America. There were a lot more red X's than there were green circles. Riley assumed the X's were dens that had already been destroyed and the green circles were the ones that the rebellion hadn't conquered yet. He

22

hadn't realized how many dens the rebellion had conquered in the short time they've had the map. It was impressive.

"Since we don't have much to go on from Riley's vision we need to decide if we want to search the closer dens or the ones further away," Demian said as he stared at the map. "With everything that happened this full moon in Seattle I would assume that Carvolo would want to get as far away from Washington state as possible."

"I haven't been caught up with what happened in Seattle," Riley said.

"We kicked some serious butt," Marcus said with a half smile. "Only a few casualties too."

"We successfully stopped the werewolves from taking over the city," Demian said with a nod. "With Arothor dead, the enemy didn't have nearly as much magically protection as they've had in the past."

"Do you think that Carvolo could get far?" Gabriel asked. "He's had a few days head start."

"It looks like there's only two or three dens close enough for him to get Aurora to," Jackson said as he stared at the map. "Within the time period."

"We could split up and look into all of them," Marcus said. "We could take out a few more dens that way too."

"Or I could try the wand," Riley said.

Everyone stared at him and he shrugged.

"What? It's the best way to find out where she is."

"Have you looked in a mirror lately?" Jackson asked him. "I don't think that you can physically do it."

"Last time you held the wand for about one minute and you had to sleep for twelve hours," Rebecca said in concern.

Before Riley had a chance to reply, Veronica stood up from her seat.

"You're not touching it again for a while," she said sternly. "You're no good to Aurora when you're exhausted, or dead."

"I doubt it would kill me," Riley said dryly.

"You don't know that," Gabriel said with a shake of his head. "You were asleep for three days with no food or water. You could've died if you slept any longer."

"Wouldn't it be worth it if we could know where she is?"

"No," Demian said with a shake of his head. "It's not worth it, Riley."

Riley slumped back into the sofa in defeat. He could argue with them all day, but he knew it would be pointless. Everyone was against him using the wand anymore for a while and they weren't going to budge. The only one that stayed silent was Marcus, but he knew what it was like to have his wife captured and tortured by Carvolo.

"So what do we do now?" Riley asked impatiently.

"I think we should do what Marcus suggested," Demian said. "We have enough soldiers that we could potentially take out any den within the radius that Jackson pointed out."

"What if she's not in either of those dens?" Riley whispered.

"Then we'll look elsewhere. We have to start somewhere, Riley."

Everyone nodded in agreement and began making preparations. Riley struggled to stay awake during the planning. Veronica gave him a sandwich and juice, but it didn't seem to give him energy like it should have.

"I think I'll go take a shower."

Veronica nodded and pointed out where the bathroom was. Before Riley could reach the door handle, it opened. He stepped back to make room in the narrow hallway for whoever was coming out. He was surprised to see that it was Jasmine. She smile at him when she saw him.

"Hi," she said brightly. "I'm Jasmine Hanson."

Riley nodded his head in greeting, but didn't say anything. He didn't want Teresa to hate him anymore than she already did. He took a quick glance around to make sure she wasn't nearby.

"I know who you are," she whispered with a small smile. "You're my step brother."

24

Technically, that was true. Bill had been his step father the whole time he thought he was his biological father. His family tree was seriously messed up. It seemed like he was gaining sisters left and right. But he had a feeling that Teresa would be very upset if Jasmine thought of him as her step brother.

"Don't tell my mom that I know that," she said conspiratorially. "She'd be super mad because she doesn't like you."

Riley was slightly surprised by the young girl's blatant honesty. She reminded him a little of Pearl, but not as damaged.

"But that's okay," she whispered. "I've heard a lot of stories about you and I like you. Don't let whatever my mom says make you sad."

Jasmine gave him a bright smile and hurried off before he could say anything. He stood in the hallway for a moment as he watched her disappear into another room. He doubted that she knew he had killed Bill. If she had known she wouldn't have been nearly as friendly. He shook off the thought and went into the bathroom.

Riley had hoped that a shower would help clear his head and it did a little bit. He felt more awake, but his energy was still zapped. He found it hard to even lift his arms and he didn't know why. He looked at himself in the foggy mirror and noticed his bloody wounds. They were still tender to the touch, but other than that they seemed to be on the mend. He had other various bruises and blisters all over his skin. Maybe his injuries where the reason for his complete lack of strength.

He quickly pulled on a shirt to cover up his wounds. If anyone saw how bad off he really was they'd probably try to bench him; which wasn't happening. He was going to find Aurora no matter how wounded he was. He knew that there hadn't been any time for Demian and the fairies to create healing elements. So he would just have to push through it.

His face was extremely pale. Even his lips almost looked white. He wondered if that would go away soon. He hoped it

25

would. Another dizzy spell hit him and he had to hold onto the bathroom counter to keep from falling down. He waited for it to pass and was relieved that he didn't feel nauseous like he had before. He turned on the sink and splashed cool water on his face to try to clear his head.

There was a sharp knock on the door and a string of French words that sounded like cursing. Riley had only taken one year of French in high school, so he didn't recognize anything that Teresa was saying. He had a feeling that she'd found out about the encounter he had with Jasmine in the hallway. She sounded upset. He didn't want to open the door, but he knew he had to face Teresa and get it over with. He pulled the door open before she could knock again.

"You speak to my daughter," she said angrily as her eyes flashed with a yellow glow.

He thought about telling her that Jasmine was the one who did all the talking, but he didn't want to get the girl into trouble. He mentally cursed his protective streak he had when it came to his sisters. If Jasmine had refrained from pointing out that he was her step brother he wouldn't have felt the need to protect her from her mother.

"We met unexpectedly in the hallway. It won't happen again."

"You take too long in bathroom," the werewolf said disapprovingly in imperfect English. "Other people need it too."

"I'm sorry," Riley said as he stepped past her. "It's all yours."

Teresa didn't look at him as she shut the bathroom door. Riley blew out a frustrated sigh and walked to the end of the hallway. He noticed Rebecca leaning against the wall as she eyed him with concern.

"What's up?" he asked her tiredly.

"You don't have to take that crap from her," she said as she folded her arms across her chest. "I can talk to her if you want me to. I won't force her to do anything, but I can ask her to leave you alone."

"No, it's okay," Riley replied with a shake of his head.

26

"You don't deserve that."

"She thinks I do," he replied with a shrug. "I'm too tired to worry about it anyway."

Rebecca studied his face for a moment. Her brow creased worriedly.

"You think you deserve it," she said so quietly that Riley barely heard her. "Why?"

Riley was about to deny it, but he couldn't. Deep down he felt like he could've tried harder to save Bill. He hadn't realized until he met Teresa and Jasmine that he felt guilty about it. It didn't help that Aurora was probably being tortured by Carvolo and they didn't know where she was. He knew he was close to having a breakdown. He hadn't had one yet and he knew it was coming. His emotions were all over the place. Meeting Teresa and Jasmine hadn't helped with that.

"You've got enough on your plate right now without dealing with that," Rebecca said sternly. She wave her hand at the bathroom door where Teresa was probably overhearing their conversation. "I'm going to tell her to back off."

"No," Riley said as he grabbed her arm. "Please don't. Her reaction to me is normal. I'd be worried if she acted otherwise. I don't need you to protect me."

"I'm not trying to protect you."

"You're stressed, just like we all are, and your werewolf instincts are kicking in. You feel the need to protect me because I'm... Well, I don't know exactly what I am right now. But I don't need you to protect me from Teresa. I can handle it."

Rebecca stared at him as she realized that what he said about her instincts was true. It didn't seem to change her mind though, so Riley changed the subject.

"When are we leaving?"

"I'm not sure yet. Mom, Sammie, and the girls are coming over," she said reluctantly. "I guess this is the community they came to. I didn't know that until a few minutes ago. Oh, and Sara's here too."

"Sara?" Riley asked in surprise.

"I guess Sammie escaped with her and the babies before the community was invaded," Rebecca explained. "I think that Demian told Sammie to take Sara with her, but I don't think he expected Sara to stick around. Apparently she has."

"I don't like that," Riley said with a shake of his head.

"Same here. I don't think Marcus does either."

"What if she decides to kidnap Leigh and Elizabeth? I wouldn't put it past her."

"Then Marcus would hunt her down and kill her with Sammie's encouragement," Rebecca said. "Sara's stupid, but I don't think she's that stupid."

"Do we have teams put together yet?"

"Karven is going to take a team to the den in Nevada."

"He's recovered from the fight with Arothor?" Riley asked incredulously. The vampire had been torn apart by the powerful fairy.

"Yeah, he woke up shortly after you did. Apparently, vampires need a few days of sleep after their arms are dismembered. Anyway, Naomi is going to take a team to the Southern California den. We are it for the Montana den. Demian and Veronica are going to check out a few dens further east while we are taking those ones out. I think they are just going to observe to see what information they can get."

"Sounds good," Riley said as he tried to keep a positive tone.

Rebecca gave him another concerned look and hugged him.

"We are going to get her back," she whispered encouragingly. "She's going to be okay."

Riley could feel himself getting closer to that breakdown he had yet to have. He hugged his sister tightly. He took a deep breath to calm himself before he let her go.

"I know," he replied quietly. "It's the waiting...it's killing me."

She was about to say something when the front door opened and their family crowded into the house.

28

"R-Riley! Rebecca!" Tanya exclaimed as she hurried over and hugged them. "You're o-okay!"

"No," Pearl said sarcastically to her sister. "Riley's not okay. He looks sick, or something. Not that we would know, though. Mom won't tell us anything."

"Pearl," Rachel said warningly.

Riley normally would've teased her, but he didn't have it in him.

"Were you injured?" Pearl asked him pointedly.

"A little, but I'm fine."

"We heard about Aurora," Rachel said tentatively. "Do you have any leads?"

"Not really," Riley replied in a whisper. "All we have are guesses."

Rachel hugged him and he had to blink back the moisture in his eyes. If people didn't stop hugging him he was going to end up crying in a corner somewhere. He needed something to do. Sitting around and talking wasn't something that he could handle anymore.

"I want to help get Aurora back," Pearl said stubbornly. "I don't want to stay here while everyone else goes to find her."

"You haven't been trained yet," Rebecca said as she ran her fingers through the girl's long blond hair.

"Yes, we have," Pearl replied tersely. "Riley taught us how to throw knives. I've been practicing a lot."

"So h-have I," Tanya said with her arms crossed. "I want t-to help."

Rachel gave the girls a disapproving look. Riley had a feeling that an argument was going to start. Normally, he would've cut in to take care of the situation before it got out of hand. He was definitely not acting like himself.

"Pearl, Tanya," Rachel said. "I know you want to help and that's very brave of you. But you are too-"

Riley cleared his throat to interrupt when he realized what Rachel was about to say. She was going to tell them that they were too young. That would only make things worse. Pearl hated it when anyone pointed out her age.

29

"I think what mom is trying to say," Rebecca explained. "Is that you are still inexperienced in a fight. Especially with knives. You'd also have to learn how to shoot a gun and fight in hand to hand combat before you can handle a mission like this. We also don't want you to have to go back to a werewolf den ever again."

Tanya visibly shivered when Rebecca mentioned the werewolf den. Pearl's face hardened, but she didn't argue. She glanced at Riley with an ashamed look in her eyes. She was angry at herself for being untrained and just a child. She felt useless. That was too much of a burden for a young girl to feel. Riley hugged her and kissed her forehead.

"You are so brave, little sis. Thank you for offering to help. But Aurora would kill me if she ever found out I let you risk your life for hers."

Pearl nodded in understand and pulled out of his hug. He hurriedly wipe a tear from his cheek before she saw it. He didn't think she would appreciate the fact that she'd made him cry. He had to take a few breaths to hold it together.

"Why don't you girls go find Jasmine?" Rachel suggested. "I'm sure she would like to play for a bit."

"Yeah," Pearl said with a shrug. "Okay."

She and Tanya hurried off down the hallway.

"When did they start acting like normal kids?" Rebecca asked in bewilderment.

Rachel stared at her daughter with wide brown eyes for a moment.

"You think this whole scene was the behavior of normal kids?" Rachel asked with a raised eyebrow.

"No, I mean, since when did they play?"

"Jasmine has been teaching them how," Rachel explained. "It's been kind of nice. Except the other day I found them playing with army men that Jasmine gave them. It wasn't pretty. They came up with some rather disturbing deaths in the war they created. I think I need to find a child therapist."

"You can't do that unless the therapist knows about the supernatural world," Rebecca said. "Or else they would have the girls committed-"

Riley snuck away into the living room. He couldn't listen to the conversation anymore. He needed to find something to do. Jackson had just gotten done talking to Demian and was hurrying over to Rachel. It had been a few days since they'd seen each other. Rebecca joined Riley in the living room to give them some time alone.

"Is there anything I can do, Riley?"

"What do you mean?"

"Could you talk to me? Please?"

"About what?" Riley asked a little more aggressively than he meant to. "I feel like all I've been doing is talking. I want to get in the van and go."

"We will," she said reassuringly. "We are just regrouping for a bit. No one has seen their families since before the attack on the Washington community. We'll leave tomorrow."

Riley looked out the window and saw that the sun had gone down. He already knew they wouldn't leave until the next day, but it was driving him insane. He shouldn't take his frustration out on Rebecca and he tried to reign it in.

Another dizzy spell hit him out of nowhere and he sat down before he stumbled.

"Riley, you're scaring me," Rebecca whispered worriedly.

"Why do you always say that? Do I look like a killer clown or something?"

"Stop trying to deflect the conversation with humor. It isn't going to work. I saw you cry when you hugged Pearl."

Riley didn't say anything. He stared at the floor instead.

"I know you're hurting. You don't have to pretend like you're not. You don't have to talk about it either if you don't want to. Just don't shut me out, okay? Gabriel is going to stay with Sammie and Marcus tonight, so I'm staying with you."

"You don't have to do that," Riley said as he gave her a sideways glance. "I don't need a babysitter. Besides, if I do have a meltdown it's not going to be pretty."

31

"So?" she said as she gave his arm a light punch. "You've seen me have plenty of meltdowns before. You've babysat me at my worst. I'm just returning the favor."

Riley gave her a light punch in return and mumbled a quiet 'thanks'. They sat there in silence for a while. It wasn't awkward, but there was a sad stillness in the room that made Riley's chest tighten. He wasn't sure if he could handle the silence either. He was relieved when Rebecca finally spoke.

"Do you remember when we'd camp in my backyard?"

Riley looked at her in confusion for a moment, but he nodded. They only ever did that when they were young kids. When Riley got older Jenna eventually forbad campouts with his friends. Especially with Rebecca.

"My..our dad, would tell us ghost stories right before leaving us outside for the night. He promised that he'd give us twenty bucks each if we lasted the night without coming inside."

"I'm pretty sure we cleaned him out that summer," Riley said with a smirk. "I think I took home about a hundred dollars before I wasn't allowed to camp out with you anymore."

"I miss those days," Rebecca said with a sigh. "It's crazy that we ended up like this."

"Growing up is a crapshoot."

"I wouldn't change a thing, though."

"Really?" Riley asked as he looked at her. "You wouldn't change a single thing?"

"If things hadn't turned out this way then I probably wouldn't be with Gabriel. My mom wouldn't be here and neither would Pearl or Tanya. A lot of bad stuff has happened, but a lot of good has come of it."

Riley nodded absentmindedly. He wasn't sure where Rebecca was going with this.

"Good things will come again, Riley," she said as she rested her head on his shoulder. "Even though we lose sometimes; things always seem to turn out fine."

Except for Jake, but Riley was sure that she wasn't talking about him. Or Roy, but at least he was still alive.

"Your positive attitude is inspiring, sis."

"I'm not trying to be inspiring," she said with an exasperated sigh. "I'm just trying to make you feel better. It's not really working is it?"

He shrugged. The only thing that would make him feel better was violence and maybe a dead body, or two. He knew that sounded like the ramblings of a psychopath, but his wife was missing. The only way to get her back was to take Carvolo out.

"Would you want to go visit with Sammie and Marcus?" she asked hesitantly. "I think they're staying in the house across the road."

"No, I'm not very good company right now."

"Well, I know you don't want to sleep in the same house as Teresa."

"Not particularly," Riley said with a small grunt.

"We have a tent and sleeping bags in the van," Rebecca said with a grin. "Wanna take a trip down memory lane."

"Definitely," Riley said with a nod. "No ghost stories from dad though. I'm pretty sure we're too old for that."

Rebecca chuckled as she followed him outside.

"I feel like a pansy watching you do that without helping."

"With how lovely you smell, Riley, I really don't think you resemble a delicate charming flower."

"Very funny, sis."

Riley closed his eyes against another dizzy spell as he rested his head on his knees. He had been too weak to help her set up the tent. He wouldn't have been able to see very well anyway. They didn't have a flashlight and they didn't want to use their magic to create light since it could illuminate the whole community and disturb people. So Rebecca was relying on her werewolf night vision to prepare the tent.

It didn't take her long to get the tent set up. Riley was able to help her get the sleeping gear into the open door of the tent. They hastily kicked their shoes off and zipped the door shut. Spring time was in full swing and the bugs had appeared with a vengeance. They didn't bother werewolves much, but wizards were a different story altogether. Mosquitos seemed to especially like Riley's magical blood.

"And to think she could've been sleeping on a bed, in a house, with her husband," Riley said with a tsk tsk.

"I know," Rebecca said as she rolled out her sleeping bag. "Seriously, who came up with this idea anyway?"

"Um, you did."

Rebecca laughed as she shimmied down into her sleeping bag. Riley did the same and stared up at the tent ceiling. It had been a long time since he had slept in a tent. It really did make him feel like a kid again. It was oddly comforting. He let himself relax for a moment and not think about what was happening to Aurora. Which he immediately felt guilty for and, just like that, he was panicky again. If Aurora knew how much he was beating himself up she would be furious with him. But she didn't know because she believed he was dead.

That thought just made it worse.

Rebecca must've noticed how anxious he had gotten because she glanced over at him. He was still staring at the ceiling to avoid looking at her. He could feel her concerned gaze wash over him like a cold shower. He tried not to let it bother him because he knew she was just being the amazing friend that she was. The last thing he needed was to be alone.

"Are you going to sleep at all tonight?" she finally asked him.

"Probably, but it won't come easily."

"You still have nightmares every night?"

"Yeah," he said with a nod. "Ever since Dur Den Thome I've had one every time I close my eyes."

Rebecca didn't say anything. She just listened. He realized that was what he needed so he kept talking.

"She thinks I'm dead, Rebecca," Riley whispered as he kept his eyes glued to the tent ceiling. "And she's being tortured. I really hope she doesn't give up."

"What do you mean?"

"When Gabriel thought he lost you last year." Riley swallowed a lump in his throat that formed from the memory. "He became suicidal. I really hope that doesn't happen to her. If we don't get to her in time…I will not be able to live with that."

"She promised Gabriel that she will do whatever it takes to survive."

"She promised me the same thing," Riley said with a tight grimace as a tear leaked out of one of his eyes. He didn't wipe it away. "But she lied."

"How do you know that?"

"While I was asleep for those twelve hours I saw what happened after she entered the woods. There was this girl named Kate. I think she must've been a skinwalker. She let Kate capture her and take her to Carvolo. From what I could tell in the vision this girl looked terrified. She definitely wasn't trained for combat. Anyway, Carvolo wouldn't trust her if she didn't murder this innocent girl."

"Which she didn't do," Rebecca said knowingly.

"She wouldn't be Aurora if she did."

"So that's when her cover was blown and Carvolo took her as a prisoner. Which left her without a weapon and defenseless."

"I shouldn't have let her do it," Riley whispered angrily.

"None of us should have," Rebecca said in a tight voice. "But hindsight is always twenty-twenty. I thought it was a good idea when Aurora suggested it, but we should have known that Carvolo would've demanded the impossible from her."

"I tried to convince her a few times to reconsider," he said with a shake of his head. "But she seemed so confident in herself that it must have rubbed off on me. I should've tried harder to convince her…"

"It's not your fault, Riley," Rebecca interjected.

"Yes, it is."

"You can't take the blame for everything that goes wrong," she said softly. "Blaming yourself is the only bad thing that you're really good at."

"I really want to grab the wand and see what it can tell me," he said as he rubbed his tired and wet eyes. Rebecca looked at him sharply. "Don't worry. I'm not going to. The physical toll wasn't something I was expecting. Roan actually told me that I wouldn't get tired."

"He was sorely mistaken," Rebecca said gruffly. "At least using it didn't kill you. Now we know to be more careful with it. Maybe you can condition yourself? Like you did when you were learning to expand your pure magic."

"That's not going to help Aurora, though."

"You never know and it might help us find the Ancients Den eventually."

"That would be nice," Riley sighed.

"How does that work anyway? When it talks to you?"

"It depends. Sometimes it's a voice in my head, or visions. It's weird to experience. It's hard to think of it as an object when it's got a mind of it's own."

"Why do you think it's not trying to control you anymore?

"I don't know for sure," Riley said with a shrug. "I let it control me when it took Arothor's magic from him. It was weird to not be in control of my own body, but it was the only way to stop him. I was actually surprised when it gave me back control after it was finished. Maybe we have a mutual trust now."

"Does it still scare you?"

"It terrifies me," Riley whispered. "It's the scariest thing I've ever encountered. I'm glad that it's on our side."

"Do you think you'll ever destroy it?"

"I'm not sure why I would when it's helped us out so much already. Besides, it probably wouldn't let me."

They laid in the tent without talking for a while. Rebecca had closed her eyes, but Riley knew she wasn't asleep. She wouldn't go to sleep until he did; it was part of her protective streak. She wouldn't leave Riley alone until she knew he was okay. He wasn't. Their conversation hadn't helped him feel better at all.

"You should probably try to get some sleep," she whispered with her eyes still closed. "You don't want to be tired tomorrow."

"Yeah, because nightmares always make for a good night's sleep," Riley said sarcastically as he sat up.

Rebecca opened her eyes and watched him closely for a moment. Riley ignored her and pushed his fists into his watery eyes. He had tried to cover up the eventual breakdown with sarcasm, but it didn't do any good. Tears came from his eyes no matter how hard he tried to stop them.

He didn't know how long he cried while Rebecca hugged him. Eventually, they both fell asleep; which only ever made matters worse for him. He could only hope that the wand would give him another useful vision while he slept.

Chapter 3

Aurora stood in the den prison with her hands chained at the wrists above her head. Her back jerked against the cold stone wall as she shivered uncontrollably. She wasn't sure how long she'd been standing there. Her hands and arms had long ago become numb and the rest of her body was slowly following suit. It was so cold that she could see her breath every time she exhaled.

The journey to the den had been unpleasant. She didn't even know where she was because she had been tied up in the trunk of a car with a hood over her head the entire trip. She attempted to draw a map in her head, but the journey had taken about a day and a half. After a while her mind had shut down and she wasn't able to keep up with the turns and counting estimated miles. Shortly after the miserable trip she ended up chained to the prison wall. With nothing but her depressed thoughts to keep her company.

Aurora jerked her head upright when she heard footsteps in the prison hallway. So far her captors had left her alone. It was far more preferable to the alternative. Not that being chained against the wall wasn't it's own form of torture, but she would much rather suffer alone than with an audience. There wasn't much chance of them getting any information out of her that way too.

The cell she was in had no bars. It was made of stone walls and no windows. The door was carved out of mahogany; which was odd. Aurora would be able to knock the door down easily. Unless there was a bit more to it than just wood.

The mahogany door opened slowly. Aurora strained to see who it was, but her vision was fuzzy. It must've been nighttime because she felt exhausted and weak. She hadn't been fed or given any water since her capture. It was no wonder why she couldn't see very well.

The door closed with a loud slam and her vision finally came into focus. She wasn't surprised to see Carvolo leaning against the opposite wall with his arms folded. He stared at her for a moment without saying a word. His expression showed a hint of exhaustion, but mostly he seemed like the normal psychopath that he was.

"I see you're awake," he remarked. "How delightful."

"Why are you here?" Aurora asked hoarsely. "I was enjoying the peace and quiet."

"I knew solitary confinement wasn't something that would break you. I've given you enough time to think."

"What is it that you believe you can do to me that would make me break?"

"Everyone breaks, my sweet daughter."

Carvolo smirked arrogantly.

"Don't call me that," Aurora spat out angrily.

Carvolo laughed.

"What else am I supposed to call you? That's what you are."

Aurora mentally cursed herself for falling for the bait. She had never been good at mind games. She got angry easily and that made her aggressive. That was probably why she didn't have much of a sense of humor.

"I had no idea that you cared so much about that," Carvolo continued. "I should've known. You've always been such a sensitive little girl."

Aurora rolled her eyes and had to bite back an aggressive retort. Carvolo paused for a moment before speaking again to see what her reaction would be to his verbal jabs. If he was disappointed by her silence he didn't show it.

"You know," he said. "I remember the desperately tragic look on your face when your boyfriend, Jeremy, was killed. Yes…I cared enough to remember his name… Anyway, there is something that I have felt guilty about ever since that day."

Aurora stared at the ground as her body shook. She was no longer shivering from the cold, but from pure fury. She would've killed Carvolo with her bare hands right then if she wasn't chained to the wall. She managed to clench her numb fingers into tight fists as she listened to what he was saying.

39

"I'm shocked that you seem disinterested in what I have to say about Jeremy," Carvolo said with a shake of his head. "Maybe it'll peak your interest to know that I lied to you about what happened to him."

"What did you do to him?" Aurora's voice was filled with such rage that it barely came out as a whisper.

"He's not dead," Carvolo said with a heartless chuckle. "That's what I've been feeling so guilty about. I must be going soft. I knew you cared about him, so I tricked you instead."

"I swear, I'm going kill you!" Aurora shouted angrily. The rush of anger suddenly zapped the rest of her strength. Her knees buckled and her bodyweight strained her shoulders and arms. It took her a moment to find her footing again. Carvolo watched her struggle and laughed.

"Yes! That, right there, is why I've always loved you more than your brothers," Carvolo declared with a wide grin. "You have such a beautifully short temper that reminds me so much of myself. All I have to do is get you to break and then you'll be mine. Forever."

"That's not going to happen, Carvolo," Aurora whispered menacingly. "I'll die before I become yours."

"We'll see," he said with a chuckle. "I'm never going to kill you. You'll either stay in prison for eternity, or you can join me. Since your newest boyfriend has recently been killed it's only polite to give you back your old one, right? Think of this as a gesture of goodwill."

Aurora was at a loss for words. Carvolo was messing with her. Jeremy had died right in front of her. She had watched the life leave his body. She didn't know why she let Carvolo work her up into such a furious lather. It took her a moment to realize that it wasn't Carvolo that made her so angry. It was Riley. Her pain over his death had been replaced with anger. Carvolo was using that to his advantage.

"I kept him alive," Carvolo said smugly. "I'm sure this comes as quite a shock to you."

"I don't believe you," Aurora muttered.

40

"I knew you wouldn't. That's why I planned on showing you."

He rapped on the mahogany door with his fist and stepped back. The door opened and a man was shoved inside. He had semi-short curly blond hair and his clothes were ragged. He looked thin and unhealthy. His scent took Aurora by surprise. He was wearing cologne and she briefly wondered why a prisoner would have access to something like that. The thought quickly escaped her when the prisoner looked up at her. She couldn't help but gasp.

He looked almost exactly as she remembered him.
Jeremy.

His brown eyes widened when he recognized who she was and her heart skipped a beat. She had to stop herself from gasping when all those feelings she had for him came rushing back. He'd been her boyfriend for five years. Even if she didn't love him the way that she loved Riley, he was still important to her.

At least his memory was. She had no doubt in her mind that Carvolo was trying to trick her.

"I'll leave you two lovebirds alone," Carvolo said sarcastically.

He dropped a tiny metal key on the stone floor next to Jeremy before he knocked on the door. It opened and he paused to look at Aurora before leaving.

"Rest assured," he said with a smirk. "This door is impenetrable, so don't try anything rash. Have fun catching up."

Carvolo closed the door behind him with a loud thud. Jeremy stayed where he was for a few minutes; probably to make sure that Carvolo wasn't coming back. Aurora stared at him for a moment before tearing her gaze away. She couldn't keep looking at him if she expected to keep her sanity.

Jeremy grabbed the tiny key cautiously and slowly stood up.

"How'd you get here?" he asked in a broken whisper.

Aurora didn't reply. She kept her eyes away from his. Her mind had gone completely blank. The anger she felt only

41

moments before was replaced by shock. There was no way that Jeremy was actually alive and she didn't want to talk to this imposter.

"I think this will unlock those chains," Jeremy said as he moved toward her.

Aurora had almost forgotten how tall he was. He was at least as tall as Marcus, who was a few inches over six feet. He towered over her as he worked on removing the chains from her arms. It made her nervous having him so close. She instinctively tried to move back and was stopped by the cold wall behind her. There was something off about him. There was a slight difference in the way he held himself and it freaked her out.

This isn't Jeremy. It couldn't be.

"Stay away from me," she said through chattering teeth.

"I'm just trying to help you," he said gently as he kept fiddling with the key.

"I don't want your help."

"I'm gonna chalk that up to exhaustion and ignore that statement," he replied calmly. "Whether you want my help or not, you definitely need it."

Aurora clenched her jaw shut and felt her skin crawl as his warm fingers brushed her hands.

"You're freezing."

"How very observant of you," she replied sarcastically.

The cuff fell off of her right wrist and she realized that she couldn't hold her weight with her legs. Pain shot through her left shoulder as she slumped lower to the floor. He quickly grabbed her around the waist and lifted her up with one arm while he worked to unlock the last cuff. She could feel body heat radiating off of him. The warmth would have been a relief if it had been someone else. When the last cuff fell from her wrist she struggled weakly against him.

"Let me go!" she exclaimed in a hoarse voice.

ι   He made sure that she was sitting before he moved away from her. He took off his ratted hoodie so all he was wearing was a torn and stained t-shirt. His arms were thin, a lot

42

thinner than she remembered Jeremy having when he was alive. He used to be in good shape and healthy. This man was anything but that. He held the hoodie out to her, but she batted it away feebly.

"I don't want anything from you."

"Aurora," he said gently. "I have no idea why you're acting like this, but you're freezing. Just take the stupid hoodie."

"You are not him," she replied furiously. "You're not Jeremy."

He sighed as he sat down cross-legged in front of her. She tensed through her shivers and glared furiously at him.

"It's been a long time since I've seen that glare," he said quietly. "Didn't realize how much I've missed it until now."

Aurora momentarily forgot her discomfort as anger surged through her.

"Shut up! I know why you're here. You're not getting any information from me. So if you're going to torture me just get on with it."

He stared at her with bewildered eyes for a moment. He blinked a few times as though he was trying to process what she had just said.

"I'm curious...who exactly do you think I am?"

"You're a shapeshifter."

Jeremy chuckled humorlessly.

"I really wish that were true, but it's not," he said darkly. "Not that I'll be able to convince you of that. I've never been good at persuasion, especially with you."

"Shut up!" Aurora shouted angrily.

"I will if you take the stupid hoodie."

"I'm not taking anything from you."

"And I'm not going to sit here and watch you freeze to death," he replied sternly. "So either you take it or you'll be sitting on my lap to share body heat. And trust me...you won't be able to stop me."

Aurora stared at him in shock. If shapeshifters didn't have the ability to tap into other people's personalities she would've thought her first assessment of him had been wrong.

43

The more he talked, the more he sounded like the guy she used to love. Jeremy had always been stern and assertive. Which made them clash a lot, but they had always came to a mutual decision to agree to disagree whenever they argued.

Jeremy swore under his breath and abandoned his attempts to give her the hoodie. Despite her ferocious struggles he pinned her down on his lap and hugged her tightly to him. Her healing burns screamed in agony and she didn't have the resolve to hold in a pained cry. His arms loosened almost immediately, but he didn't let her move away from him.

"Are you hurt?"

"Let me go!"

"No," he replied matter-of-factly.

He gently patted her arms and legs to look for any sign of injuries. She winced as he moved over her burns, but she was too stubborn to tell him about them. It didn't take him long to find a burn mark that wasn't covered by her clothes. He swore when he rolled up the sleeve of her sweater. He stared at the scarring on her arm for a moment and swore again.

"What happened to you?"

The growl in Jeremy's voice made her look him in the eye and what she saw broke her soul. Yellow glowing eyes stared into hers for a moment before he blinked a few times and his brown eyes reappeared.

She stopped struggling against him and let him share his body heat. It made sense now how he could be so warm in such a cold room. How he was so strong despite how weak he looked.

"I told you I'm not a shapeshifter," he mumbled.

"How…?"

"It's a long story," he said. He wrapped his warm arms around her again and shuddered. "Jeez, it's like I'm holding a human-sized ice cube."

"Are you going to tell me? We're gonna be here for a while."

"Tell me how you got those burns first and I'll tell you my story."

44

"You aren't a follower."

"Nope," Jeremy said. "Much to Carvolo's disappointment."

"I need to make sure that you're actually on my side before I start spilling my guts to you."

"Well," Jeremy replied with a sigh. "I'm definitely not on Carvolo's side."

"How am I supposed to know that for sure?"

"If you thought you couldn't trust me you wouldn't be asking me that question."

"Fair enough," Aurora whispered. "But why did you put cologne on to disguise your werewolf scent from me?"

"I didn't do that. One of Carvolo's henchmen doused me in it before he shoved me in here."

"Why didn't you tell me?"

"I knew you'd figure it out eventually," he replied in that deep voice she had missed so much. Tears filled her eyes and she had to blink them away. Jeremy didn't handle crying women very well and she didn't want to make him more uncomfortable.

"Have you been in this den all these years?"

Jeremy sighed and leaned his head back against the stone wall.

"It's your turn to answer my question," he said. "It's not like you're going to give away any rebel secrets by telling me how you got those burns. They only look partially healed. I've never seen you heal slowly before."

"A fairy bomb almost killed me a few weeks back," she answered pointedly. "Apparently, this particular bomb prevents supernatural healing."

"That sucks."

"Yeah," Aurora agreed. "But it'll heal completely eventually."

"How are your brothers doing?" Jeremy asked quietly.

He had always been fond of her brothers. Most people were.

"I'm sure they're angry and worried right now. Probably wondering if I'm still alive."

"Why are you wearing a wedding ring?"

It was then that Aurora noticed that he had been holding her hands in an effort to warm them up. She had been so engrossed in their conversation that she hadn't thought about what his reaction would be to her relationship with Riley. If he had been a prisoner this whole time he probably still felt the same way he did for her when they were together. They had discussed breaking up a few times in the past. But only because she was a skinwalker and he had been a human. It had been hard on him and he didn't like that side of her. Mostly because his entire family had been killed by Carvolo's skinwalkers before she met him. The only reason they stayed together was because he had no one else to turn to.

"I got married the day before I was captured," she whispered. "The day before…"

She couldn't say it out loud. She tried to tell Jeremy that Riley was dead, but her mind went blank. She couldn't find the words.

"He's a very lucky guy; whoever he is," Jeremy replied with a small smile. "I'm glad that you moved on. I've always worried about you."

Aurora kept quiet. She was barely listening to what he was saying. He must've taken her silence as a bad sign because he sighed in mild frustration.

"Seriously, Aurora. I'm not mad or anything. You know that, right? You thought I was dead and it's not like our relationship was heading in the right direction. I always thought we'd be better as friends anyway because I was such a prejudiced jerk."

Tears fell down Aurora's cheeks and Jeremy quietly swore. He opened his mouth to say something else, but she beat him to it.

"It's not you," she managed to blurt out. "He's dead."

"Who?" Jeremy asked with a concerned look on his face.

"Riley…his name was Riley Hanson."

46

"The guy that Carvolo's been after?" Jeremy asked with wide eyes. "You married him?"

Aurora couldn't reply, so she just cried into Jeremy's shoulder. He hugged her and tried to murmur comforting words into her ear, but it didn't help. She eventually dried her eyes and took a shaky breath.

"I'm sorry," she said quietly. "I haven't really adjusted yet."

"You have nothing to apologize for," he replied. "Are you sure that he's...gone?"

"That's what Carvolo said."

"Carvolo hardly ever tells the truth."

"He was this time. I've never seen him that angry before."

Silence fell between them for a while. Aurora's extremities were becoming less numb and her shivering had subsided. The room was still very cold and Jeremy was her only source of heat, so she stayed where she was.

"I really want to know what happened to you," she whispered. "If you're willing to tell me."

"Sure," Jeremy said with a shaky sigh. "There's not much else to do...it's weird though."

"What's weird?"

"I haven't talked to anyone in six months. I know this because I've kept track of the days on my cell wall. It's just weird to talk to someone."

"I'm going to kill him," Aurora said angrily. "He's had you here for six months in solitary confinement?"

"He's had me here for almost five years," Jeremy said with a shake of his head. "Ever since he turned me."

Aurora remained quiet as she waited for him to continue.

"Carvolo mauled me," he said as he shivered at the memory. "I thought that he had killed, or captured, you and your brothers because when I woke up after the stabbing I was surrounded by werewolves. That's when he mauled me. The next thing I knew I was stuck in a stone cell with fangs, claws, and an even shorter temper than I had before."

47

"I swear, Jeremy," Aurora said sadly. "I thought you were dead. You had no pulse. You weren't breathing and you'd lost a lot of blood. Even Sammie thought you were gone. I didn't want to leave your body there, but we had no choice. I am so sorry."

"I already told you," he said sternly. "You have nothing to apologize for."

"Yes, I do," she said firmly. "I should've known you weren't dead."

"I was almost dead," he said with a sigh. "I think my body went into shock. Something must've made my vitals hard to read."

"So, naturally, Carvolo turned you into a werewolf hoping that you'd be a follower that he could rub in my face later," Aurora said with a snort. "He didn't know you very well. You're the most dominate alpha male I've ever met and that's including Marcus and Demian."

Jeremy rolled his eyes at that before continuing with his story.

"I don't know why he didn't kill me when he realized he couldn't control me."

"I think we are living that reason right now," Aurora said with a grimace. "He kept you alive to use you against me if he ever captured me."

"He's going to torture us," Jeremy said with a nod. "But it's nothing we haven't experienced before. Nothing is worse than six months of solitary confinement anyway."

"So you've been in this den prison the whole time?"

"Yeah." His arms tightened around her involuntarily, as though he subconsciously needed her to ward off the bad memories. He quickly loosened his grip when she grimaced at his strong hold. "I made a few friends, but they're gone or dead now. So, it's all been bad."

Aurora studied his face for a moment, but he had a neutral expression besides a small furrow of his eyebrows. She wrapped her arms around his neck to give him a comforting hug.

"I've tried to escape many times. It's landed me in solitary confinement a few times, but mostly they just physically punished me for it. They quickly found out that I wasn't going to give them any information. Not that there was much to tell them anyway. After a couple years they stopped interrogating me because by then the information I could give them would be invalid anyway. You and your brothers would've relocated many times."

"They probably stopped asking you questions because Carvolo found us a couple of years ago when we first met Riley."

Aurora rested her head against Jeremy's shoulder and he let out a small sigh. She had a feeling that it had been a long time since anyone touched him like this. Luckily there was nothing awkward about the situation since she was so happy that he was actually alive.

"Oh, that makes sense then," he said in a husky voice. "Anyway, I've just been chilling in this den prison. I've had some really low lows. Solitary confinement really messes with your head. It's a good thing that they keep anything silver away from me."

Aurora lifted her head and glanced at him sharply. He knew what she was thinking and he quickly shook his head.

"I haven't contemplated that for a while now," he reassured her. "I made a friend, Mary. She saved me from that crap. We were in a cell together for one month. They took her away for the full moon because I change into a rage monster. I haven't seen Mary since, so she's probably dead."

Aurora rested her head on his shoulder again so she wouldn't have to see the pain in his beautiful brown eyes anymore.

"What do you mean you *turn into a rage monster*?" she asked quietly.

"Even after almost five years of being a werewolf I still have no control on the full moon. If I were to shed my skin right now, you'd be a dead girl."

"I don't believe that," she said with a snort.

49

"Well, believe it," Jeremy said sharply. He lifted her chin with his finger so that she was looking at his face again. "It's happened before to my cell mates."

"I'm sorry," Aurora said again. The pain in his expression was more intense. This conversation was making him relive every single horrible moment that he'd gone through since he'd been taken from her. She couldn't even image the kind of pain he'd experienced.

She tightened her arms around his torso and rested her head on his shoulder again.

"Quit apologizing," he said with a sigh. "It's only gonna piss me off."

"Carvolo targeted you because of me," she said as tears fell from her eyes again. She was glad that Jeremy couldn't see them, but she was sure that he could smell them with his werewolf senses. Luckily he didn't comment on her emotional turmoil.

"Carvolo targeted my family before we even met," Jeremy growled. "You guys showed up *after* I watched his skinwalkers kill my entire family. It has nothing to do with you. He just thought a fatherless family would be perfect target practice for his soldiers. So, no, you aren't responsible for any of this."

"We'll have to disagree on that. I left you for Carvolo."

"Whatever," he said with a frustrated sigh. "I'd forgotten how stubborn you are."

"Some things will never change," she replied with a smirk.

"Thank goodness for that..." He paused for a moment and leaned the back of his head against the wall. "I heard some of the werewolves talking a while back; did you guys really find Demian?"

"Yeah," Aurora said with a nod. "Only took us a few centuries."

"Sorry that I wasn't there to help."

"If I'm not allowed to apologize then neither are you."

"Sure," he said with a sarcastic nod. "What's up with the werewolf prophecy nonsense I've been hearing about. I heard about your…well, I heard about *him* being killed and that his witch-werewolf-hybrid sister, Rebecca Singer, is still alive. But I don't know much other than that. I only hear bits and pieces of conversations with my werewolf hearing."

"You probably only know what they wanted you to hear," she said cooly. "Just enough to pique your interest and drive you nuts."

"Can you fill in some blanks for me without revealing any sensitive information?"

Aurora told him all about the prophecy that Sarai told the ancient werewolves centuries ago and how they had rescued Demian in Romania. She also told him about how Carvolo had attempted to control Rebecca after changing her.

"So that's why Carvolo's been after them?" Jeremy asked incredulously. "Because of a prophecy given by some weird fairy? That's how they think they're going to dominate the world?"

"It hasn't worked out so far," Aurora said. "Thankfully."

"Especially since they trusted Arothor when they shouldn't have. If they hadn't then maybe Riley-"

"Do you have any idea how to get out of here?" she asked as she swallowed a lump in her throat. If they could steer clear of Riley as the topic of conversation she'd be better off. "You know this place better than I do."

"I quit trying to escape years ago when I realized that I couldn't control the monster inside of me," he said with a shake of his head. "Everyone is safer if I stay here, but I have no objections to helping you out if I can."

"Well, if you won't leave then neither will I."

"No," Jeremy said with a shake of his head. "You don't deserve to be here."

"Neither do you."

"I killed innocent people," Jeremy said vehemently. "I'm a monster that should never see the light of day."

"You aren't a monster, Jeremy."

51

"Yeah, I am."

"Have you ever thought that maybe you don't have control during the full moon because you've been locked in a cell the whole time?"

"That's no excuse for attacking and killing my cell mates."

"Even if you can't control it outside of the den prison," Aurora said gently. "I know someone that can help you."

Jeremy didn't reply, but Aurora could tell that he didn't believe her. She had a feeling that she'd have plenty of time to convince him to escape with her later, so she let the conversation fizzle out. She would tell him about the tamer, Raya, when he was less angsty.

His heart beat rapidly against her shoulder while he talked about the cell mates he had killed. No matter how crass his personality seemed; he really did have a tender heart. Killing someone that he viewed as innocent probably weighed heavily on his conscious.

In time, Jeremy's heart rate went back to normal and Aurora was able to relax enough to fall into a much needed sleep.

Chapter 4

"That is impossible, man," Marcus said as he paced the living room floor. "Jeremy died right in front of us. Carvolo's skinwalker stabbed him repeatedly in the chest. There was no walking away from that."

Riley rubbed his eyes as he tried to ease the headache that the vision had given him. He wondered if he would have a vision of Aurora every time he slept. It was worse than his usual nightmares because of how exhausted they made him. He didn't know if his fatigue was due to his debilitating fear for Aurora, or if that's just how his visions were going to effect him. It didn't help that he kept being reminded of her agony over her belief that he died. He wished he could magically send her a message to let her know that he was alive, but he knew the wand didn't work that way.

It worried him to see Jeremy in the vision. Not because Riley was the jealous type. He was very happy that someone Aurora knew was there with her. But it did make him want to rescue her even more, which he didn't think was possible. If Jeremy were to shed his skin with her in the cell he would probably kill her. Riley didn't know if this was Carvolo's plan, but it wouldn't surprise him if it was. Carvolo would probably use the threat of the full moon to get Jeremy to convince Aurora to talk. Or he would torture Jeremy in front of Aurora to get to her.

Riley watched Marcus as he continued pacing the room. They were sitting in Teresa's house as they tried to figure out what to do about Riley's newest vision. Gabriel was eyeing Riley curiously, while Marcus seemed agitated by the whole thing. Samantha and Rebecca sat on the sofa holding the babies. Veronica and Demian had lounged in silence on the floor while Riley explained his vision to them.

"Can you describe Jeremy to us?" Gabriel asked quietly.

"He has brown eyes, curly blond hair, and he's about as tall as Marcus…maybe taller? I can't be sure though. I was seeing the whole thing through Aurora's perspective."

53

"That's him, Marcus," Samantha told him firmly. "That's Jeremy for sure."

"No, it's not," he said with a scowl. "It can't be. There has to be another explanation."

"How would Riley be able to describe someone he's never seen before?" Gabriel asked. "He's not lying."

"I know that," Marcus said gruffly. "I'm sorry, Riley. I believe that you had a vision, but I'm just concerned that it's been falsified somehow."

"The wand wouldn't do that," Riley explained. "And I'd be able to tell if it tried."

"How?"

"I can't really explain it," he said with a shrug. "Ever since it helped me kill Arothor its like we are connected telepathically."

"Are you sure it wasn't a shapeshifter?" Marcus asked again.

"Marcus," Samantha said gently. "Riley already told us that he's a werewolf. You don't have to feel guilty about this."

Marcus stared at her for a moment before he glanced at Gabriel; who stared back at him wordlessly. They both had grim expressions, but Marcus seemed completely ticked off while Gabriel was just plain sad.

"He was our responsibility," Marcus said to his brother. "And we *literally* left him to the wolves."

"Don't forget that you and Sammie were both captured that day as well," Gabriel said quietly. "It's not the best outcome we've ever had on a mission."

"I don't care about that," Marcus said sternly. "Jeremy trusted us and he's been living under Carvolo's thumb for almost five years. I thought we were a bit better at our job than that."

"Marcus, please," Samantha said soothingly. "Don't be too hard on yourself about this. It's not going to do Aurora or Jeremy any good."

"She's right," Demian said firmly. "Don't dwell on the past, Marcus. You too, Gabriel. We need to follow through with our plans to eradicate the dens. We just have to adjust the plan to save Jeremy as well."

"What if he doesn't want to be saved?" Rebecca asked hesitantly. "From what Riley told us he seems pretty adamant about staying."

"I'll knock him out with welhum and carry him if that's his attitude," Marcus replied sternly. "He and Aurora aren't staying there any longer than they have to."

"That won't be necessary," Gabriel said. "If he can't control his werewolf instincts after all these years it's probably because he hasn't had the chance to learn. I'm sure Raya will be able to help with that. She could convince him to leave."

There was a stunned silence in the room as everyone considered what Gabriel had just proposed.

"I don't think we should send Raya into a den," Veronica said cooly.

"That's not necessarily what I am suggesting," Gabriel replied. "It would be her choice, of course."

"Why shouldn't Raya go into a den?" Riley asked in confusion. "Couldn't she force our enemies to calm down?"

"She could for the sane werewolves, yes," Demian said with a nod. "But some of Carvolo's followers are crazed to the point that she wouldn't have much effect on them. They will listen to their leaders over her."

"How do you know that?" Rebecca asked.

"I've been alive a long time, Rebecca. I have seen what happens when a tamer's charms don't work like they should on werewolves. Yes, she is very powerful. But she can also be killed easily since she has no instinct to fight. If she was a better fighter than maybe she would stand a chance."

"She's been training for months," Riley said incredulously. "She's a skilled fighter compared to Carvolo's followers."

Demian grew silent for a moment as he considered it. They had all seen what Raya could do in training. She was more capable of handling herself than some of the skinwalkers that they had trained. She was anything but helpless. Riley wasn't sure why the werewolves were against her going.

"It's not that they don't know she's a skilled fighter, Riley," Rebecca said as she eyed Demian with a disapproving look. "It's because they want to protect her. Tamers are rare and leaders generally want to protect them if they can."

"You guys don't want her to help save Aurora just because you want to protect her?" Riley asked.

He was trying not to get angry, but he was already at the end of his rope by the fact that they weren't on the road yet. Gabriel twitched slightly and Marcus glared at Demian. Samantha took the babies out of the room in case an argument ensued.

"It's not like that, Riley," Veronica said hesitantly.

"What is it like then?" he asked forcefully.

"We-" Veronica began, but Demian interrupted her by grabbing her hand.

"It is like that," Demian said with a sigh. "Rebecca is right. We want to protect her because that's how it's supposed to be in the werewolf hierarchy. I didn't really realize I was being overprotective until now."

"Let's leave it up to Raya," Rebecca said. "I don't want her to go either, but we have to look at the bigger picture here. Raya could potentially help us win this war."

Demian nodded reluctantly, but Veronica stared at Rebecca angrily.

"What happens if she dies?" she asked vehemently. "Would you be able to live with yourself?"

"Of course not!" Rebecca exclaimed. "But I also wouldn't be able to live with myself if Aurora and Jeremy died and we didn't let Raya help!"

"I think we are done here," Marcus said in a severe tone. "I'm going to contact Raya and see what she wants to do."

Marcus left the room briskly. Gabriel was staring at the floor with his fists clenched, which was similar to what Riley was doing. He was about to burst at the seams. They were wasting time and he was glad that Marcus was calling Raya. If they

56

could get her on board it would be easier to deal with Jeremy. If she didn't want to help, which he doubted, then they'd do what Marcus had suggested. He had no issue with poisoning Jeremy to make sure Aurora got out safely.

No one said a word as they waited for Marcus to finish the phone call. Riley couldn't hear the conversation through the walls, but the others were listening intently. After a few minutes, Veronica's face had paled and Demian grabbed a hold of her hand again. Riley took that as a sign that Raya had agreed to help them.

"She said she'd help us out," Marcus confirmed when he entered the room. "She and Raven will be flying in with Naomi, so give them a couple of hours. We need to decide which group she should go with."

"Does anyone know of a den that is made up of stone walls and mahogany doors in the prison section?"

Everyone stared at Riley for a moment. He had forgotten to describe what the den prison looked like. He mentally kicked himself for not describing it earlier. Now that he thought about it, the mahogany doors where very unique. The other den prisons he'd been to had silver bars.

"I've never heard of such a thing," Gabriel said. "Is that the room Aurora was in?"

Riley nodded.

"I haven't seen anything like that," Marcus said. "Which probably makes sense. Carvolo wouldn't have Sammie or I go near the den that Jeremy was held if he wanted to keep him a secret."

"So which dens have you been to?" Riley asked.

"I'm not sure," he replied with a grim expression. "I've been to quite a few, but Carvolo never let me know where we were."

"We will just have to guess then," Rebecca said. "I think we should have Raya come with us to Montana. If they turn up at a different den then they'll have to poison him if he refuses to leave."

"That sounds so harsh," Gabriel said gruffly. "He's already been through a lot."

"We'll just have to hope he's in Montana," Marcus said. "Or that he comes to his senses."

"Wait," Veronica said suddenly.

They all looked at her as she stood up slowly and walked over to the map that was spread out on the coffee table.

"I think I know which den they're in."

"Have you been there?" Riley asked her.

"Yes," she said with a nod. "I think so. It was when I was first changed. Carvolo took me there because he knew that I was a leader and he wanted to beat it out of me. I decided after a few days of torture that I would be better off doing what he wanted me to do. He let me see where we were when we left. By then he viewed me as his follower with no mind of my own. I remember a lot of pines and mountains."

"Mountains?" Marcus asked thoughtfully. "Probably Montana. The dens in California and Nevada are in the flat lands."

"Don't quote me on it," Veronica said with a shake of her head. "I was in a really bad place back then and a lot of my memories of that time are fuzzy."

"We trust you," Riley said. "If you think it's Montana then we'll have Raya come with us."

"It's definitely possible," Veronica said with a shrug.

"So everyone is good with their assignments?" Demian asked.

They all nodded. Riley breathed a sigh of relief that the meeting was adjourned. He hated just sitting there. He needed to do something besides talk.

He stood up and left the house as quickly as he could without seeming like he was in any kind of a hurry. He planned on taking down the tent since he and Rebecca hadn't taken the time to do it yet. After he woke up the first thing on his mind was to tell everyone about the vision he'd had during the night. Taking down the tent was something that still needed done and he needed something to do. He got to work as carefully as he could. His body was so sore that he could barely move.

Riley heard footsteps behind him and turned to see Marcus. He had Leigh in his arms and he looked exactly how Riley felt. Exhausted.

"Why did you sleep in a tent last night anyway?" Marcus asked him as he watched Riley unzip the tent door. "Veronica said there was a guest bedroom in Teresa's house."

"I didn't want to intrude on her territory."

Marcus stared at him in confusion. Apparently, he didn't know their history. It wasn't surprising since he and Samantha weren't with them when he had killed Bill.

"I killed her husband in Romania a couple years back," Riley explained. "It's understandable that she doesn't want me around."

"Wow," Marcus said with wide eyes. "Why would Veronica want you to stay with her then?"

"Um, because Teresa is her step mother."

"You killed Veronica's dad?" Marcus asked incredulously. "Dude, I'm so sorry. I think your family dynamics are more screwed up than mine."

"Tell me about it," Riley said as he gingerly pulled the sleeping bags out of the tent. "Did you really come over here to talk about my family drama?"

"No, I actually came to see how you're holding up."

"I could ask you the same thing," Riley replied gruffly.

"Yeah, I'm worried about her because she's my sister," Marcus said in a low voice. "But I think we both know that it's completely different when it's your soul mate."

"I'll be better when Raya and Raven get here and we can hit the road," Riley said as he tossed the sleeping gear out of the tent.

"I can't imagine what it would be like to see visions of her all the time and not be able to do anything to help."

Riley didn't say anything as he continued taking down the tent.

"I don't mean to be uncomfortable," Marcus said hesitantly. "But I'm sorry if I seemed weirded out by the vision you had of Jeremy and Aurora. I didn't mean for it to come off that way."

"It's fine," Riley said with a shrug. "You thought the guy was dead. Completely understandable."

"Yeah, well, I didn't need to be a jerk about it."

"You're anything but a jerk, Marcus."

Marcus chuckled humorlessly as he situated Leigh in the crook of his arm.

"You wouldn't say that if you knew me a few centuries ago."

"Well, Sammie did marry you," Riley said with a smirk. "So you couldn't have been that bad."

"She just couldn't see past my good looks."

Riley would've laughed, but he just didn't have it in him.

"What are you two talking about?"

Samantha came around the corner of the house with Elizabeth snuggled in her arms.

"Marcus says you think he's hot," Riley said as he raised his eyebrows comically.

"He's not lying," Samantha said with a small laugh.

She handed Marcus baby Elizabeth. Riley watched with wide eyes as he held his babies in both arms. It looked a bit overwhelming.

"No fair," he said to Samantha as he shook his head. "I don't have a free arm now."

"At least they aren't crying," she replied optimistically. "I need to talk to Riley in private. Sara is ready to help you feed them at the house."

Marcus blinked at his wife for a few seconds and he exhaled in annoyance.

"I don't want to do that," Marcus groaned. "Why can't Rebecca help me?"

Riley stopped taking down the tent for a moment and watched Marcus complain. He'd seen the skinwalker uncomfortable before, but this was borderline hysterical. Riley would've normally laughed at Marcus's reaction.

"Because Rebecca is busy and Sara knows what she's doing."

"That woman hates me," he complained as he stared at his wife.

"Well, you hate her too," she said with a smirk. "So you're even."

"That is true," Marcus said with a sigh.

He gave his wife a kiss before walking toward the road. Samantha waited for him to get out of earshot before she turned to Riley.

"Rebecca told me I should have a look at you."

"Why?" he asked with a shrug. "I'm fine."

"I'll be the judge of that," she said with a shake of her head. "Take off your shirt."

Riley sighed. He took the time to finish zipping the tent bag shut before standing up. Samantha folded her arms patiently while she waited for him to do what she'd told him to. It didn't seem like it most of the time, but she was a very stubborn person. Especially when things became medical.

He took a deep breath before pulling his shirt over his head. The movements hurt and he had to concentrate on not wincing. He didn't want to give away how much pain he was in.

Samantha studied his wounds with an expressionless face for a couple of minutes. He glanced down at the four stab wounds while he waited for her verdict. They looked a little more raw than they had the day before. He inhaled slightly when she touched the skin around the wounds with the tips of her fingers.

"Does that hurt?"

"A little," he said as he refused to grimace.

"I've never seen anything like this," she said quietly. "It doesn't look like it's healed much at all, but there's no bleeding. It shows signs of infection and that's not good."

"I think my insides are still healing too," he said nonchalantly. "The wand saved me from dying, but it didn't repair the damage."

"You shouldn't even be standing," she said sternly. "Let alone going on a mission."

"I'm not staying here," he said firmly. "There's not much to do anyway. All of the medical supplies are gone."

"I know," she said in a disheartened tone. "No one has had a chance to replenish our supplies. It would be nice if the fairies would hurry up and get us some guresh, or at least hemioc."

Samantha's eyes moved to the blisters on his hips and her brow furrowed.

"What happened here," she asked as she touched the skin around the burns. He twitched involuntarily and she moved her hand away.

"The knives burned me before they stabbed me."

"Wow," she said with a low whistle. "You gotta tell me that story sometime."

She took his wrist and felt his pulse while staring at her watch. Riley pulled his hand away and looked at her indignantly.

"I'm fine, Sammie."

"Actually, you're not," she replied sternly. "There's no way to find out if the stab wounds are healing correctly without taking you to a hospital. Your pulse seemed a little erratic to me and you're complexion is still very pale. Not to mention your shaking a lot. Have you been experiencing any dizziness?"

"No," Riley said, but then decided against lying to her. "Well, not today."

Samantha met his eyes worriedly.

"I can't let you go, Riley," she whispered. "You're not in fighting shape."

"That's unfair to say," he said as he crossed his arms over his chest. "And you can't stop me from going."

"All I have to do is tell everyone how serious your condition is and you wouldn't be going anywhere."

Riley's jaw clenched and he forced himself not to scream at her.

"Do I feel good? No. Do I hurt? Yes. But I can't sit here while Aurora is with Carvolo. It would kill me more than the wounds would. Besides, the wand won't let these injuries get any worse."

"We need to wrap them," she said. "I don't have the supplies here, but the first thing you guys need to do when you leave is stop at a pharmacy. I don't have any prescriptions with me right now, but you should be able to stop the infection from getting worse with topical over-the-counter ointments. I'll make you a list. I would suggest that you have someone else get the supplies for you since you shouldn't be seen in public looking like a walking dead man."

"Aw, come on," he said with a small smile. "I don't look like that."

Samantha stared at him with a raised eyebrow as he struggled to put his shirt back on. She ended up helping him when the painful movements caused him to break out into a cold sweat.

"Just be careful, okay? Don't overdo it. If Aurora finds out I let you go after her in this condition she would kill me."

"I wouldn't let that happen," Riley said as lightheartedly as he could.

"The only reason I'm not ordering you into bed right now is because I know what she's going through," Samantha said quietly. "I don't want to stop you from getting her back. Just don't kill yourself doing it either."

The thought of Aurora going through the things that Samantha had gone through was almost too much for him to handle. Thinking of her being stuck with Carvolo for as long as Samantha had been made him nauseous. He hoped that Aurora wouldn't have to deal with that.

He thanked Samantha before she hurried toward the house Marcus had taken the babies to. He stood there a moment and shook off the uneasy feelings. He had to stay focused or he would lose it again like he had the night before.

He couldn't let himself cry anymore. It did no one any good, especially Aurora. He had his breakdown and he was determined not to have another one.

He picked up the tent and sleeping bags. He was in the process of organizing their supplies in the back of the van when he heard someone clearing their throat behind him.

He finished what he was doing and shut the back hatch. He wasn't surprised to see Teresa standing behind him with an impatient look on her face. He briefly wondered what he had done now to deserve that look.

"You told my daughter you are her step brother?" She snarled angrily as her eyes glowed yellow.

"No," Riley said with a shake of his head.

"Why does she say you are?"

"I'm not sure," he said in confusion. "I'm sorry if that bothers you."

"You are nothing to her," she replied vehemently. "You killed her father."

"Does she know that?"

He didn't want the situation to get worse, but he needed to know the answer.

"You think I would keep that from my daughter?" Her voice was so loud he was sure the whole community could hear her. "She knows."

Riley was stunned for a moment. He wasn't sure why Jasmine would tell her mother that she knew he was her step brother. Maybe she was trying to get him into trouble. It would make sense if she hated him too for killing Bill.

"Stay away from Jasmine."

"I assure you I have been," he said calmly. "We're leaving soon so you won't have to deal with me anymore."

"Not true," Teresa said in a low voice. "I deal with what you did all the time. With you gone, it is the same."

"I wish there was something I could do to fix that," Riley said apologetically. "But it was self defense. He kidnapped me."

"You didn't have to do it," she snarled. "He had to do what he was told and so do I. You are free. You had choices."

"You're right," he said quietly. "I'm sorry."

Teresa's glare intensified into something more loathing. Her yellow eyes glowed brightly and she growled deep in her throat. Riley was surprised she didn't attack him. He could feel hatred radiating off of her. He couldn't take the look in her eyes anymore so he stared at the ground.

"I hope you fail," she said dangerously. "I hope you die."

"It's okay for you to wish death upon me," he said patiently. "But don't say that you hope I fail. Aurora's life is at stake and she didn't do anything to you. She is a good person who doesn't deserve what's happening to her."

"She is the daughter of the werewolf that destroyed me," Teresa said angrily. "She married you. She is not good."

Riley had to stop himself from calling the woman a very unkind name. The insult was on the tip of his tongue, but he managed to swallow it like a bitter pill. He was beginning to understand why Teresa and Bill hooked up. They were both rigid people and he suddenly felt very sorry for Jasmine. He wouldn't be surprised if she had a similar upbringing as he did. He hoped that Teresa was a better mother than Jenna had been.

Something about the way the follower looked at him made him feel uneasy. He didn't trust her by a long shot, but he was beginning to think that maybe Veronica shouldn't trust her either. There was no way to know where her loyalties were. Carvolo had changed her and she seemed to hate him, but it could all be an act. They had been tricked before by a doubt agent. He didn't want to say anything though. He was too biased. Regardless, he still needed to tell Veronica about this.

"Mama!" Jasmine called as she rounded the corner of the house. "What are you doing out here?"

Teresa started talking to her daughter rapidly in French. Jasmine folded her arms across her chest and jutted her chin out stubbornly.

"Mama," the young girl said defiantly. "You can't talk about him like that. He's nice and he's saved lots of people. Veronica told me."

65

Teresa stopped babbling in French and her face paled a little. Her eyes darted to Riley in a glare and she walked away. He was surprised that she didn't insist Jasmine follow her.

"Veronica told her that she should leave you alone," Jasmine said with a sigh. "She usually does what Veronica says, so I don't know why she's still being mean to you. I'm sorry."

Listening to her apologize for the idiocy of her parent reminded him so much of himself as a young kid that his hands clenched into fists involuntarily. It made him even more furious to know that she was apologizing to the man that killed her father. He took a deep breath and sat on the bumper of the van.

"Jasmine," he said softly. "You don't need to apologize to me. Neither does your mom. I did something horrible and I'm the one who should be sorry."

"No," Jasmine said as she shook her head stubbornly. "I know what you did and it was the right thing. My daddy was a bad man."

Riley didn't want to know why she thought Bill was a bad man. But he felt like it was his responsibility at that moment, so he had to ask.

"Why do you say that?"

"He was mean," she whispered. "And he hurt me sometimes."

Riley closed his eyes as memories of his childhood flooded his mind. He really hoped that Bill hadn't been as hard on this girl as he had been on him. He was suddenly very concerned for her wellbeing and he had to press some more.

"Is Teresa a good mom to you?"

"It's better with daddy gone."

He didn't miss the fact that she hadn't exactly answered the question.

Riley couldn't help it. He hugged her. He knew he shouldn't have, but she hugged him back tightly. She seemed like such a sweet girl. She shouldn't have to go through a sad childhood. He really hoped it was better for her now. He would

66

make sure that Veronica knew about this. He was okay with forcing Teresa to be a good mother.

"If you ever need anything," Riley whispered to her. "Ask Veronica. She will help you, okay?"

Jasmine nodded and gave him a small smile. She said goodbye and hurried to the front door of the house. Riley took out his cell phone and texted Veronica that he needed to talk to her immediately.

"That's not possible, Riley," Veronica said quietly. "Teresa doesn't have the mental capacity to be a double agent. Especially for Carvolo. She hates him."

"I'm not saying that she is," he said quietly. "I'm just saying that we need to be careful with how much information we let her know."

"I have been," his sister said with a nod. "So has Demian. Rest assured, followers can't lie to leaders. I believe her when she says that she hates Carvolo."

"Have you asked her if she's a double agent? Because if you haven't you probably should. Besides, Jasmine said that you told her to stay away from me and she didn't listen."

"I'm still not sure how that's possible. Maybe her dislike for you trumped my order."

"Are you certain that she is truly a follower? I understand her hatred for me, but today was different. For a moment, I thought she was going to try to hurt me. If Jasmine hadn't shown up I don't know if she would've attacked me or not."

"I'll keep an eye on her," Veronica promised. "Just worry about finding Aurora. You don't need this drama right now."

Riley knew she was right, but he couldn't let the subject drop just yet.

"Did you know that Jasmine was being mistreated by her parents?"

Veronica's face paled and she looked at the ground for a moment.

"I had suspicions," she said quietly. "But I wasn't sure."

"Take it from someone who knows what that's like," Riley said gruffly. "If you ever have suspicions you need to look into it."

"That's why I wanted them close to me," Veronica said. "Jasmine seems happier now."

Riley nodded in understanding.

"You need to keep it that way. Even if you have to command Teresa to be a good mom."

"I already did that."

Riley nodded again in relief and Veronica gave him a hug.

"I'm sorry that you had to deal with this," she whispered. "I was hoping that Teresa would've ignored you a bit more."

"It's no less than I deserve," he said. "She was right about one thing; I did have a choice."

"No, you didn't. I don't want you to say things like that. You don't deserve that kind of crap. You're hurting right now and it's making you vulnerable. Don't let her make you feel like a bad person."

Riley nodded, but didn't say anything. He was hoping that he'd never have to see Teresa again. Now that he was sure Veronica knew Jasmine's situation he felt a little less responsibility toward her. Now he could focus all his efforts on finding Aurora. They would be on the road soon and he could put all of this behind him.

Chapter 5

"I'm sorry I tattled on you. I just wanted Sammie to check you over."

Riley concentrated on reassembling his handgun that he had cleaned. Cleaning his weapons was the only thing he could do to keep his mind off of things while they waited for Naomi, Raya, and Raven to arrive. He briefly glanced at where Rebecca was sitting on the porch swing. After the confrontation with Teresa he decided to stay as far away from her house as possible. So they were hanging out on the porch of the house that Samantha, Rachel, and the girls were staying at. He placed the handgun on the step he was sitting on and turned to look at her.

"What was the point?" Riley asked. "You knew I wouldn't sit this one out. No matter how injured I am."

"Maybe you need to," Rebecca said quietly.

"Quit trying to protect me," he said abruptly. "Please. I'm not going to stay here when Aurora is being held captive. You know that."

"You can't blame me for trying," she said sternly. "You can barely walk, let alone fight."

"I can aim a gun and shoot. I can also throw knives without any trouble at all."

"Well, if your knives weren't actually magical weapons created by Jenna, then yeah…I guess you could."

Riley sighed and went back to cleaning his second gun. He felt naked without his knives. He didn't like going into a den without them. It was frustrating that Jenna was able to take them away from him so easily. But she had created them, so it would make sense that they would be drawn by her magic. He was hoping that he would find more silver throwing knives in the weaponry, but there were none to be found.

"Don't remind me," he said quietly. "I can use the crossbow though."

Rebecca drew her lips into a tight line, but didn't say anything else. He ignored her obvious disagreement with his decision and concentrated on his cleaning efforts. Rebecca got up and sat next to him on the step. There was silence between them for a while.

When Riley finished cleaning his gun he no longer had anything to do to keep his mind off of things. He looked up at the clear blue sky and tried to notice the beauty of the day. The birds were chirping in a nearby bush and it smelled like spring. It was Aurora's favorite time of year and she wasn't there to enjoy it.

A fresh wave of anger hit him and he involuntarily clenched his fists.

"Riley," Rebecca said as she gently laid a hand on one of his fists. "You know I would never force you to sit this out. But I have to know that you aren't going to get yourself killed to get Aurora back."

"I won't promise that, sis," he said without hesitation. "I'll do whatever it takes to get her back. Even if I die trying."

"Nobody is going to die," Gabriel's voice came from behind them.

Rebecca stood up and gave Gabriel a kiss. She whispered something to him that Riley couldn't hear. She gave Riley a sad look before disappearing into the house. Gabriel stood on the porch for a moment in thought before he sat next to Riley. He had expected the skinwalker to lecture him about going on a mission wounded. He was pleasantly surprised when he didn't say anything.

They sat on the steps in silence. It was interesting how sitting silently with Gabriel was actually comforting. If it were anyone else it would have been awkward or infuriating, but Gabriel always had a calming presence about him. Riley listened to the birds chirp and tried not to think about Aurora's absence too much.

"I would do the same thing you're doing," Gabriel said quietly. "So it would be hypocritical of me to say that you should sit this one out. But that doesn't mean I'm going to let you get

70

yourself killed. We are going to stick to you like glue the entire time."

"You don't have to worry about me, man."

"Like glue, Riley," Gabriel said firmly. "I thought you were dead twice now and it's not going to happen again. Besides, I don't like seeing my wife worried about you."

"I don't think I've heard you talk this much since I woke up," Riley said in an attempt to change the subject.

"None of us are acting like ourselves," he replied grimly. "If it weren't for your visions telling us how she's doing I would've freaked out by now."

Riley knew what he meant. Even though the visions were horrific at least he got to see her.

"I'm barely holding on by a thread, man. Do you have any idea when Naomi is supposed to get here?"

"It shouldn't be long now," Gabriel replied. "Once they get here we'll get in the cars and go."

"Twiddling my thumbs is driving me insane," Riley said through an aggravated sigh.

Gabriel nodded in agreement as he stared at the trees around the community. Riley followed his gaze and noticed something rustle in the bushes. He and Gabriel stood up cautiously as the rustling quieted.

"Was that an animal?" Riley asked him quietly.

"I don't think so," Gabriel replied. "I would've smelled it if it was."

"Is someone watching us?"

Gabriel shed his skin and told Riley to stay there before he bounded into the woods on four legs. Gabriel's tail disappeared into the bushes and Riley hurried into the house. The first person he saw was Marcus and he quickly told him that Gabriel had gone after something in the woods. The skinwalker hurried out the door and sprinted to the trees in his wolf skin. Riley would have followed him, but he couldn't keep up even if he was feeling in top shape.

"What's going on?" Pearl asked.

Riley noticed her sitting in the living room holding baby Leigh.

"I'm not sure," Riley said with a tight shrug. "Gabriel and Marcus are going to check it out."

"I-Is someone after us?" Tanya stammered.

"I don't know for sure, but probably not."

It was a lie, but he didn't want to terrify them.

"I'm headed out there," Jackson's voice came from the kitchen before a gust of air made Riley stumble backwards. He didn't think he'd ever get used to the speed of vampires. Tanya giggled at him when she saw the look on his face.

"What?" Riley asked indignantly.

"Dad a-almost made you f-fall down," Tanya said with a small smile.

"Well, dad needs to watch where he is going when running three hundred miles per hour."

"He's actually faster than that," Pearl said as she fixed Riley with a look. "He could run to the other side of the country within a couple of hours if he pushed himself."

"How do you know that?" Riley asked with wide eyes. "Karven and mom aren't that fast."

"We tested it last night," Pearl said with a shrug. "He ran all the way to Maine and back and he was only gone for about four hours. Karven told him he probably shouldn't do it again though because he was super tired when he got back."

"Why did he do that?" Riley asked incredulously.

"I think he wanted to see if he could find any clues about Aurora," Rebecca said quietly as she walked down the stairs. "I didn't tell you about it because I didn't want you to worry."

"You just didn't want me to get my hopes up," he stated as he folded his arms. "He didn't find anything, did he?"

Rebecca shook her head quietly. Riley was about to ask her another question when they heard footsteps on the porch. He and Rebecca hurried to the door and opened it. Marcus and Jackson stood on either side of a dirty girl with brown hair and wide terrified eyes. Marcus had a firm grip on her upper arm because she looked like she would run if given the chance.

Riley stared at the girl for a moment and gaped. He recognized her as the girl Aurora was supposed to kill for Carvolo.

"This girl was spying on us," Marcus said plainly. "I swear, Carvolo's soldiers just keep getting younger."

"She won't tell us her name," Jackson said sternly. "I'm hoping that she hasn't told Carvolo about you yet. Gabriel's running the perimeter with Veronica to make sure that no one else is out there."

"You're Kate," Riley said as he stared at the girl.

Kate glanced at Riley with fear stricken eyes and shuddered. She quickly looked at the ground.

"Do you know this girl?" Marcus asked in surprise.

"Aurora was supposed to kill her to prove to Carvolo that she was willing to kill for him," Riley explained. "She didn't do it."

"How do you know that?" Kate asked in a small voice.

"Did Carvolo send you here to spy on us or did you run away?" Riley asked her.

"I..." Kate began, but she closed her mouth and refused to say another word.

"We need to get her tracking device out before we interrogate her any further," Jackson said hastily. "I don't want her to lead Carvolo's people here."

"I'll get Sammie," Marcus said as he hurried up the stairs.

"Do you know where your tracking device is, Kate?" Riley asked her. "It'll be less painful if we don't have to go fishing for it."

Kate didn't respond. She stood next to Jackson with the same terrified look on her face. Her refusal to talk indicated that she was more afraid of Carvolo than she was of them. Riley felt bad for her, but they needed answers from her and he was trying not to feel impatient.

"I'm going to find Gabriel and Veronica," Rebecca said. "If there's anymore spies out there they might need all the help they can get."

73

Jackson nodded at her. Riley handed her one of his guns and she hurried out the door. Jackson told Pearl and Tanya to go to their room and the girls hurried out of the living room with baby Leigh. Riley grabbed Kate's arm and escorted her to the living room. He noticed her looking around in awe, as though she had never seen a living room before. Maybe she never had. He gestured for her to sit on the couch and she did without resisting.

"We aren't going to hurt you," Riley said kindly. "We just need to know why you're here."

"I'm not supposed to talk to you," Kate replied timidly.

"If you do talk to us we will do everything we can to help you," Riley said. "By the looks of it you could use some friends."

Samantha came into the living room with a first aid duffle hanging off of her shoulder. Kate eyed the bag nervously and flinched involuntarily. Samantha noticed how scared the girl was and she set the bag down without getting any closer to her. She gave the girl a warm smile.

"Hi, I'm Sammie," she said kindly. "I'm a doctor and I'm here to look you over. Okay?"

Kate didn't respond. She continued staring at the duffle bag like it was a ticking time bomb. Samantha slowly reached out and felt Kate's jaw and neck with gentle fingers. Despite her efforts not to spook her, Kate still flinched as though she was being burned.

"Sometimes I can feel the tracker with a little bit of poking around," Samantha said conversationally. "It seems like with the younger skinwalkers the werewolves have been implanting them in their necks. Unfortunately, I'm not feeling anything."

Kate sat perfectly still as Samantha's hands moved down to her shoulders.

"Do you know where they implanted it?" Samantha asked.

"I..." Kate muttered in a quivering voice. "I don't even know what you are talking about."

74

Samantha glanced at Riley with a concerned eyes. They were going to have to use magic to find the tracker and Rebecca wasn't there to do it. Riley mentally checked himself over and took a deep breath. Using his magic was going to cost him, but the alternative was risking their enemies knowing where they were. Kate was also in danger of being terminated if the werewolves didn't deem her valuable. Considering what Carvolo wanted Aurora to do to her the chances of them wanting her back were slim to none.

"Let me do it," Jackson said.

"You've never done anything like this before," Riley said with a shake of his head. "The only thing you've used your magic for is satiating your hunger or making small things float. Doing something like this without practice first will knock you on your butt."

"It'll knock you on your butt too," Jackson replied firmly. "You don't look like you should use your magic for a while."

"I don't think that you should practice something like this on her," Riley whispered quietly so that only Jackson would hear.

Jackson looked at the girl who sat trembling on the couch with fear-glazed eyes. He reluctantly nodded in agreement, but still gave Riley a small glower. Samantha glanced at them worriedly as she continued examining Kate with her hands.

"I can't find it," Samantha said defeatedly.

"I'll find it," Riley said as he sat on the couch next to Kate. She smelled like body odor and dirt. He wondered when she had showered last. It made him angry and he used that energy to strengthen his pure magic.

"This will hurt a bit, but it'll be quick. I'm just going to bring the tracker to the surface underneath your skin so that Sammie can get it out. You'll be safer with it out of you, okay?"

Kate didn't reply. Riley wasn't sure if she heard him. Her expression reminded him of what Tanya did when she was terrified. The blank stare and expressionless face was hard to look at. Another surge of anger coursed through him and he extended his hand toward Kate's chest. She whimpered as his magic made the tracker move around. He could feel where it was almost instantly and he stopped before he used too much of his energy. He was already gulping for air as it was.

"It's in her upper left arm," Riley said through a gasp.

His abdomen screamed in pain as he struggled to breathe. Jackson grabbed his shoulder and asked him if he was alright. He nodded and laid his head back against the couch. He watched Samantha put a topical numbing agent on the surface of Kate's arm. That was the extent of the numbing they could give her because anything else could trigger the tracker to detonate. No one wanted to tell Kate that because she was already terrified as it was.

It wasn't long before Samantha was holding a small bloody device in her hand. Kate stared at it with a shocked look on her face that hid her pain and terror for a moment. She hadn't been lying when she told them that she didn't know what they were talking about. She must've gotten it when she was too young to remember.

"There," Samantha said as she discarded the broken device in a plastic bag. "You are safe from the werewolves now. The sun is strong today so you should be healed quickly."

Kate didn't say anything as she looked at her arm. Her cheeks were pale underneath the dirt and grime. Riley guessed that she had been following them ever since the attack on their community in Washington. He wondered if they finally found her because she was careless or if she wanted them to catch her.

"Kate," Jackson said in a low voice. "Why were you spying on us?"

"I…" Kate grimaced and took a deep breath. "I'm not supposed to say anything to you. They will kill me."

"Who will?" Jackson asked.

"The others," she whispered. "That were with me."

Samantha glanced at Jackson sharply and he nodded at her. It was her and Rachel's job to protect the children in these situations. She walked briskly from the room and hurried up the stairs. She called for Rachel as she went. Jackson focused his eyes on Kate and she stiffened.

"Why are you here?"

"All I was supposed to do was keep an eye on him," Kate said as she glanced at Riley, who was still sitting next to her on the couch. "I was supposed to report to them so they could tell the leader what's been going on."

"Where are the others right now?"

"They're still in Washington observing the other community. They sent me here on my own."

Jackson and Riley exchanged a glance. It was hard to believe that she would be sent here to spy on Riley on her own, especially when she didn't seem to have any experience. But if she was telling the truth then the Washington community was in danger.

"Why would they do that?" Jackson asked sternly. "You don't seem like you'd do very well on your own."

"I don't know," Kate replied in a quivering voice. "They don't tell me anything."

"We need to warn the Washington community," Riley said breathlessly. "Who knows what the other spies are up to. Roan and Selena can deal with them."

"How do we know that she's telling us the truth?" Jackson asked with a raised eyebrow. "I'm not altogether certain that this whipped-puppy-thing isn't an act."

Riley didn't reply at first. Jackson had more experience interrogating prisoners than he did. But Kate flinched every time Jackson looked at her and Riley couldn't help but think that it wasn't an act. This girl seemed to be genuinely terrified.

"I'm not lying," she whispered hoarsely. "I don't want to die."

Riley glanced at Jackson's hard expression and decided that this had gone far enough. He struggled to stand and ignored the burning in his abdomen. He was exhausted and angry. Watching a teenage girl tremble in fear in front of his vampiric father wasn't helping at all.

77

"She's not lying," Riley whispered to him. "She was hoping that Aurora was there to save her from Carvolo when she found her in the woods that night. I doubt she even knows who I am. You don't, do you?"

It took Kate a moment to realize that Riley had addressed her. She tore her horrified gaze from Jackson and stared at him. She shook her head quickly and looked at the floor.

"See?" Riley said to Jackson. "Why don't you go find Rebecca, Gabriel, and Veronica? I doubt that they have found anyone else, but if they have then we can question them. I think Kate could do with some food and a shower."

Jackson studied Riley for a moment before he gestured for him to follow him into the hallway. Riley sighed and staggered after him. Jackson folded his arms and looked at him reproachfully.

"If you think that I'm going to leave you alone with a possible enemy then you've got another thing coming," Jackson said sternly. "You look like you're about to fall over."

"I'm not defenseless like you think I am."

"Sure you're not," Jackson said sarcastically. "You also didn't inherit your stubbornness from me either."

Riley glowered at him and clenched his fists in frustration.

"Rachel and Sammie have left with the kids by now," Jackson said. "So you and I are it. I'm not leaving you here by yourself."

"Fine," Riley replied. "But Kate is an innocent victim."

"How do you know that?"

"The vision I had with her and Aurora confirms it for me. Plus, not very many people can fake how terrified she is. I think you know that."

Jackson sighed in exasperation and strode over to where Kate sat on the couch. She flinched and shivered violently as Jackson stood over her. Riley didn't know if he was purposely being intimidating or not, but it was upsetting.

78

"If you have any ulterior motives," Jackson said dangerously. "You will regret it. Understood?"

Kate nodded silently and let out a little whimper.

"What have you reported so far?"

"Nothing much," she said in a hushed tone.

"Have you told anyone about me being alive?" Riley asked her. He tried to keep his voice as calm as possible.

"Why?" she asked in confusion. "I noticed that you slept for a few days. Are you supposed to be dead?"

Riley ignored her question and tried not to notice how still Jackson suddenly became.

"What do you know about me?"

"All I've found out is that your name is Riley," she replied shakily. "And you must be a magical being of some kind."

"What have you told your comrades about me?" Riley asked.

"Nothing, besides your location."

The more Kate talked the more she shook. Her voice bobbled and she wrapped her arms around herself.

"How do you keep in contact with them?" Jackson asked her.

"There is a prepaid phone in my pocket."

Jackson held out his hand expectantly and Kate hurriedly pulled out the phone. Jackson grabbed it and crushed it in his hand instantly. Riley noticed a small look of relief pass over Kate's face when Jackson discarded the broken phone in the waste basket.

"What else can you tell us?" Jackson asked as he resumed towering over her.

She flinched as she shook her head.

"I don't know anything...I swear."

Riley put his hand on Jackson's shoulder. There was no way that he could physically make him back off, but he hoped that his touch would make his father calm down a bit. Jackson glanced at him and took a step back from Kate. The girl continued to shiver uncontrollably. Riley didn't know if she was cold or in shock.

79

"How old are you, Kate?" Riley asked her gently.

"I'm not sure," she whispered. "Eleven…twelve maybe."

"Eleven or twelve," Riley said as he looked at Jackson pointedly. He had thought she was older than that. Now he was even more ticked off.

The vampire grimaced slightly and walked out of the room. Riley hoped he felt guilty about how he had questioned the poor girl. It would probably be best if Jackson gave her some space and let Riley deal with her for a bit.

The thing about Jackson was; he'd been extremely protective as a human and as a vampire it just made it worse. But human Jackson would've never interrogated a scared girl this way. Something was off with him and Riley needed to find out what it was. But first he needed to help Kate.

"When was the last time you ate, Kate?" he asked gently.

"I'm not sure," she whimpered.

"I can-"

Riley was interrupted by a rush of air. Jackson was suddenly standing next to him with a paper plate in one hand. It held a sandwich and some fruit. There was a bottle of water in his other hand. Jackson gave the food and water to Riley and disappeared again.

"Here you go," Riley said as he handed Kate the meal that Jackson had, apparently, prepared for her. "Wait here, okay? I'll be right back."

Kate nodded once before devouring the sandwich with an animal-like ferocity. Riley hobbled out of the room and found Jackson staring out the window while he sat at the kitchen table. Riley wasn't sure if he should sit down too. He didn't think he'd get back up if he did.

"What's going on?"

"Rebecca and Gabriel are coming back now," Jackson said as he continued staring out the window. "It doesn't seem like they found any other spies. I contacted Roan and he's on the look out for the others the girl mentioned."

80

"Okay," Riley sighed. "That's good to know, but not what I meant. You were deliberately trying to scare that girl more than she already was. Why?"

Jackson didn't reply, he didn't even twitch. He just stared out the window as though Riley hadn't said anything. Riley stumbled forward and held onto the table for support. He had definitely overdone it with the magic he'd used. He wasn't recovering well like he normally did.

"Dad!" Riley exclaimed to get his attention. Jackson jerked a little and turned to look at him. His eyes widened when he saw Riley leaning most of his weight on the table.

"When was the last time you had any blood?"

"What?" Jackson asked in surprise. Riley didn't miss the bloodlust that flashed in his eyes. "Don't worry about me. You need to lie down before you fall down."

"Jackson Singer, when was the last time you had any blood?" Riley asked him sternly.

"Yesterday."

"Go," Riley said insistently. "Outside. Now. Go find a bunny, or something."

"I'm fine."

"Quit lying and go." Riley would've yelled if he wasn't so weak.

Jackson grabbed Riley so quickly that he didn't have a chance to react. Suddenly, he was sitting in the living room on one of the sofas. His stomach rumbled as it always did after fast transportation with a vampire. He couldn't imagine the pain that throwing up would cause his abdominal wounds and he was relieved when he was able to hold down his lunch.

"I'll go hunting if you promise to stay put," Jackson said in a gravelly voice. "Let yourself recover. You aren't doing anyone any favors by overdoing it."

"You're not doing anyone any favors by starving yourself," Riley mumbled. "Quite the opposite actually."

Jackson's eyes shot toward Kate and he grimaced. It was no secret that vampires were meaner when they were hungry.

"Rebecca and Gabriel are on the porch," he said. "I'll be back by the time Naomi gets here."

Before Riley could reply, Jackson was gone. The door opened soon after and Rebecca appeared with Gabriel close behind her.

"Did she tell you anything?" Gabriel asked as he eyed Kate curiously.

Riley quickly explained everything that Kate had shared with them. Rebecca offered to show Kate to the bathroom so she could get cleaned up. Kate glanced at Riley for a moment and he was surprised to see that she had a calmer look now. Maybe the food and water in her stomach was helping. She sighed nervously and followed Rebecca to the bathroom.

"So what happened out there?" Riley asked Gabriel. "Where's Marcus?"

"Marcus made sure that Sammie and Rachel got the girls out safely," Gabriel replied with a sigh. "Even with the information that Kate gave you there's still a chance that our enemies know more than we think they do. I think it'll be a few days before they come back here."

"Did Jasmine go with them too?"

"No," Gabriel said with a slight grimace. "Teresa doesn't want her to leave with a vampire and a skinwalker that she doesn't know. So Veronica is going to end up staying here with them, I think."

Riley closed his eyes and leaned back into the couch. Demian was going to be alone on his assignment now that Veronica was staying to protect Jasmine. He couldn't help but feel like Teresa was being difficult on purpose, but he knew he was being biased. He didn't know how he would feel about trusting a vampire and skinwalker that he didn't know with his child if he was a parent.

"You look worse than you did before. How is that possible?" Gabriel said as he studied Riley with wide eyes.

"I used my magic to help Sammie get the tracker out of Kate."

"That was stupid, Riley," Gabriel said reproachfully.

82

"I wasn't about to let Jackson do it," Riley said with a half-shrug. It hurt too much to do a full shrug. "Did you know he hasn't had any blood since yesterday?"

Gabriel shook his head in surprise.

"I thought he was on top of that," he murmured.

"Like you said before; none of us are acting like ourselves."

Rebecca came back into the living room with a pillow and a quilt. She handed them to Riley and looked at him with a worried expression.

"You need sleep," she said.

"I'm fine," he said as he tried to hand the bedding back to her.

Rebecca took the pillow and propped it against the arm of the sofa. She made him rest his head on it. He thought about resisting, but he didn't put it past her to use her werewolf strength to force him down. He didn't have the stamina to compete with that. The sofa was too short for his legs and they dangled uncomfortably to the side. He was so exhausted that he didn't care. He was asleep before Rebecca finished throwing the quilt over his aching body.

Chapter 6

Riley woke up to the sound of Naomi's dragon wings. He sat up a little too quickly and instantly regretted it. The pain was excruciating and he lifted his shirt to look at his wounds. They looked redder than they had that morning. Samantha was right; he needed to get them bandaged. He also knew that he was overdoing it, but he couldn't help it. He needed Aurora to be safe no matter how much it hurt to move.

It took him a moment to realize that he didn't have a vision or dream while he had been asleep. It made him feel disoriented. He looked around for the satchel that the wand was in, but couldn't find it anywhere. He pushed down his panic by telling himself that Rebecca had probably put it in the van with the rest of their weapons.

He smoothed down his shirt and took a deep breath. Standing up wasn't going to be fun, but Naomi was there and they had to hit the road. He grabbed the arm of the couch to pull himself up.

The door opened and Rebecca appeared in the doorway.

"You're awake," she said as she eyed him with concern.

"I heard Naomi fly in," Riley mumbled. "Are we ready to go?"

"Yes, but first you need this."

She held a syringe in her hand and Riley looked at it suspiciously.

"If you think that drugging me is the answer just know that I'll never forgive you."

"I'm not trying to drug you, Riley," she said as she rolled her eyes impatiently. "Roan sent some guresh with Naomi. We don't have much, but hopefully it'll be enough to get you better in a day or two."

Riley nodded and she sank the needle in his arm. There wasn't much relief at first, but the pain slowly ebbed away as the magical serum travelled through his bloodstream. Usually the reaction was more immediate, but his injuries were extensive. He wished that they had gurshen on hand, but ever since Sarai died no one had been able to replicate the magical formula correctly without her. It was one secret that they all wished she hadn't taken to her grave. The powerful healing effects of gurshen saved many lives in the past.

"You still look like crap," Rebecca sighed. "I wish I had more to give you."

"It's okay. It's better than nothing."

Rebecca nodded, but she didn't seem convinced.

"Did you put the wand somewhere?"

"It's in the van," she said. "Why? Did you have another vision?"

"No, that's the problem. I was kind of expecting to have one, but I don't think I can if the wand isn't near me."

"Oh, sorry," she said with a furrowed brow. "I wonder if that has any effect on your healing as well."

"It might," he said shakily. "Let's get going."

Rebecca nodded and put his arm over her shoulder. He didn't try to object. He knew he needed help. He hoped that he would be able to walk easier when they got to Montana. The guresh should do it's job by then.

The van was parked outside with the back doors open. A small Buick that Riley hadn't seen before was next to it. Raven, Raya, and Jackson loaded two duffles into the trunk. Apparently they were taking two vehicles, which made sense since they couldn't all fit in the van. Marcus and Gabriel finished loading the back of the van and shut the doors.

Naomi was nowhere in sight. She must've already left for the Nevada den with her team.

The sun was setting in the sky and Riley blinked a few times to get used to the dimming light. It worried him. He'd never had a problem with his vision at dusk before. He needed more sleep and he couldn't wait to get in the van and close his eyes again.

"Did you give it to him?" Gabriel asked Rebecca.

"Yes," she said. "I don't think it's enough."

"I'll be fine after a nap," Riley said gruffly.

"You just had one," Marcus said. "And you still look like death."

"Thanks for that helpful observation, Marcus," Riley said sarcastically.

"Anytime," Marcus replied with a smirk.

"We have a couple of more doses of guresh in the trunk," Raven said as he hurried up to them. "We could give him another one."

"No," Riley said with a shake of his head. "I'll be fine. Let's get going."

Raven nodded and hurried back to the Buick. Jackson was in the driver seat and Raya sat in the back with another duffle back sitting next to her. Raven hopped into the passenger seat and Jackson started the engine.

Rebecca helped Riley get into the passenger seat of the van and he rested his head against the window as soon as the door shut. He barely noticed Marcus put the van into drive before he fell asleep again.

Aurora woke up to footsteps coming toward the prison cell door. Jeremy jerked slightly at the sound and rumbled a low growl in his chest. He must have been asleep too. His warm arm had been around her when she woke up. It was still terribly cold in the room and she was thankful for the werewolf body heat that radiated off of him. No matter how uncomfortable his touch was for her burns. Not that the cold stone floor was doing her raw skin any favors. Her stomach rumbled from intense hunger and she knew that Jeremy was just as hungry, if not more so. There was no use dwelling on her grumbling stomach so she pushed it to the back of her mind.

Jeremy sat up as the door unlocked and slowly opened. Aurora stayed where she was on the floor and tried not to shiver against the sudden chill that assaulted her when Jeremy sat up.

86

She squinted her eyes in the darkness and barely made out the image of Zalina standing in the doorway. Her pink wings extended behind her and her aura suddenly glowed brightly. It was blinding and Aurora quickly covered her eyes.

"Time to go," Zalina said sweetly. "Your father is ready to talk to you now… Both of you actually."

Aurora sat up in time to see Jeremy bolt to his feet threateningly. He took a fighting stance that Gabriel had taught him years ago. The fairy merely laughed in amusement.

"You think that an emaciated werewolf can defeat me?"

Zalina lifted her hand. Pink sparks fizzled on her fingertips. Jeremy glared at her menacingly.

Aurora stood up and folded her arms across her chest defiantly. She wasn't going without a fight and neither was Jeremy. Zalina sighed in frustration and sent a pink ball of energy toward Aurora.

She rolled out of the way and Jeremy rush the fairy in a tackle. Zalina screamed angrily when she hit the floor. Jeremy swung his fist toward her face, but an invisible force threw him off of her before it connected. He hit the wall with a deafening crack.

Aurora bolted to her feet and closed the distance between her and the fairy in two leaps. She aimed a kick at Zalina's face and the fairy went down again. She'd never killed a fairy before, but if she had a silver weapon she could've right then. It wasn't very often that fairies were taken by surprise. Especially powerful ones like Zalina. Fairies were impossible to kill without a silver weapon, but they had the same weak points as a human.

Aurora looked down at Zalina's unconscious form on the stone floor and grabbed her head in both of her hands. She didn't have her supernatural strength, so the task at hand was harder than it normally was. She twisted the fairy's neck and heard the satisfying crack of it breaking. Her arms burned and she winced as she forced herself to stand up straight. The fairy wasn't dead, but she was incapacitated for now.

Jeremy stood up slowly with a tight grimace. His shoulder was out of socket and he quickly fixed it himself with a small grunt of pain. His yellow eyes glowed as he gazed at Aurora standing over Zalina's still form. He was breathing heavily and he looked slightly crazed. It must've been a long time since he'd been in a fight where he felt the need to protect someone else.

Aurora stood still as she waited for his breathing to slow. He blinked a few times and his eyes went back to a soft brown.

"You good, Jeremy?"

It took him a moment, but he nodded.

"We don't have much time," she said in a low voice. "Let's go."

Jeremy hurried over to her and gently grabbed her arm. With how worked up he was she was surprised his touch had been so careful.

"Hop on my back. I'm faster than you are."

"Are you sure?"

Aurora looked at him in concern. He was literally skin and bones. Werewolves needed food to keep up their strength just like any other creature. He looked like he hadn't eaten in a while. She was worried he wouldn't be able to carry her for very long at top speed without collapsing.

"I can make it to the entrance."

"Do you even know where the entrance is?" she asked hesitantly.

"No, but it shouldn't take me long to find it."

Aurora wanted to refuse, but she knew she wasn't fast enough to get out of there without being spotted. Jeremy's speed, if he could manage it, was their only hope. She nodded once and hopped on his back. Jeremy took off so fast that she didn't have time to close her eyes and her stomach flipped from nausea.

It was apparent that Jeremy had never run at supernatural speed before. He smacked into a stone wall and barely prevented himself from falling over. Aurora's body burst into pain and she couldn't hold in an agonized whimper. Luckily, she didn't fall off of his back.

Jeremy swore under his breath and whispered an apology to her. He took off running again and kept better footing this time. Aurora was positive that someone heard them hit the wall. She wasn't surprised to hear yelling echoing through the den prison a few seconds later.

They managed to avoid being spotted, but they knew werewolves were on their trail. Even if they hadn't smelled strongly of den prison and body odor a werewolf's nose would have been able to follow them easily. After a few wrong turns they finally found a large mahogany door. It was a good thing too because Jeremy was winded.

Aurora slid off of his back and he doubled over, gasping.

"Do you think this is it?" she asked quietly.

"I hope so," he replied through a pant.

"You're coming with me," she said insistently.

Jeremy shook his head and stood up straight.

"No," he said firmly. "I said I'd help you escape, but I'm staying."

"I haven't escaped yet," she replied. "Not until the werewolves aren't after me. We still have a long way to go. We don't even know where we are. You aren't staying here."

Cold brown eyes bore into her stubborn green ones.

"Yes, I am. You can make it on your own. I'll hold them off as long as I can."

Aurora took a step toward him and grabbed his arm.

"I'm not leaving without you."

"Don't be stubborn, Aurora," Jeremy growled.

"Don't be stupid, Jeremy," she replied with a glare.

Jeremy was about to argue back when they heard footsteps getting closer to them.

"You need to make a decision now," she said hastily. "I know someone that can help you gain control on the full moon. Are we staying or going?"

Jeremy glared at her angrily and a flash of yellow glowed in his eyes. The anger seemed to give him back some much needed energy that he had lost while running. He gritted his teeth in a snarl and roughly pulled on the door.

"Let's go," he said in a guttural voice.

Jeremy darted out the door with Aurora close behind him. It was just as cold outside as it was in the prison cell and she shivered. Jeremy slammed the door shut and she appreciated the fact that he was there to handle the heavy door. It didn't take long for her to realize that they were in the mountains.

Snow covered the ground and it was so dark that she could barely see. Jeremy grabbed her hand and they began a slow quiet jog down the mountainside as he used his werewolf vision to navigate through the darkness.

They hadn't gone far when they heard the werewolves closing in behind them. Jeremy picked up his speed and Aurora struggled to keep up. His legs were a lot longer than hers and he was a werewolf. When she staggered and almost fell down the steep mountainside, he grabbed her arm and swung her on his back in one quick motion.

It made her arm throb, but she was more worried about the hopeless situation that they were in than her physical discomfort. They were quickly becoming surrounded and Jeremy's heart thudded rapidly beneath her hand. She was sure he could hear her heart beating at a similar pace.

There was no set path down the mountain. If Jeremy was a human they would've stumbled and fallen many times over. Aurora had learned long ago not to waste time wishing for the sun in dangerous situations when she couldn't shed her skin. She still couldn't help but notice Jeremy's struggled breathing and exhaustion as he carried her down the mountain. She felt frustrated and helpless. They would be better off if she could at least see.

Aurora heard someone lurking behind a large rock and she tapped Jeremy's shoulder in warning. She realized she didn't need to do that when he successfully evaded being tackled by the lunging werewolf. As a human he'd always had good reflexes. It was pleasing to see that those reflexes had enhanced as a werewolf. She watched their adversary fall off the mountainside and couldn't help but feel satisfied by his terrified screams. Jeremy didn't skip a beat as he kept up his pace down the steep slope.

They didn't hear their pursuers for a while as they continued their decent. It made them both nervous. The hairs on the back of Aurora's neck tingled as she felt someone watching them. They were most likely surrounded again and Jeremy was slowing down.

He couldn't keep up this pace with Aurora on his back in his weakened state. She thought about just telling him to escape and find her brothers, but she knew that he wouldn't leave her. He had a protective streak a mile wide. He reminded her of Marcus in that way. She didn't want Jeremy to stress anymore than he already was. Suggesting that he leave her and save himself would send him over the edge.

Jeremy was wheezing now and stumbling. Aurora loosened her grip and let herself slide from his back. The moment her feet touched the rocky ground Jeremy bent over to draw oxygen into his lungs.

Aurora glanced around and took in as much of their surroundings as she could in the darkness. From what she could tell they weren't in a good position. They were on a narrow ledge and the drop off was too dark for her to see to the bottom. It gave her an ominous feeling.

They would inevitably be captured unless they came up with a good plan.

"I have an idea," Jeremy panted. "But you're not going to like it."

Aurora raised her eyebrow at him suspiciously. She hoped that he wasn't thinking what she thought he was.

"It'll hurt like hell, but I think we're far enough down the mountain that you'll survive."

Aurora barely refrained from groaning.

"You realize if I break my legs I won't be able to walk until after the sun comes out, right?"

"I'll carry you if I have to," he said through a small gasp. "I don't think we'll get out of here any other way."

"Unless they're crazy enough to follow us."

They heard footsteps getting closer and rumbling growls surrounded them. They were stalking them rather than attacking. The werewolves were taking pleasure in hunting their victims when there was no way out for them. Aurora found it distasteful. She thought only cats played with their prey.

"Are you all in?" Jeremy asked her hesitantly.

Aurora gave him a curt nod and he quickly scooped her up. She wasn't sure where to put her arms that would cause the least amount of damage to his body when they landed. She ended up hugging him under his arms and she closed her eyes.

This is gonna suck.

"Here goes nothing," Jeremy murmured before he jumped off the mountainside.

Aurora counted a full ten seconds before they hit the rocky ground with an agonizing, bone-crushing thud. She flew out of Jeremy's grip and rolled on the rocks until she hit something hard. The impact knocked the breath from her lungs and her ears where ringing. It took her a moment to realize that she had rolled into a tree. Luckily, the ringing in her ears stopped just as quickly as it started.

It was then that she heard Jeremy gasping in the darkness. She managed to stand up with a tight grimace. Her entire body hurt and she didn't know which bones were broken, but she had more than a couple. She staggered forward and was relieved that she was able to stay on her feet.

She found Jeremy a couple of yards away from where she hit the tree. Her vision was fuzzy, so she found him by using her ears. His legs were distorted and bloody. He had managed to sit himself up against a boulder and he seemed to be struggling to breathe.

Aurora stumbled over to him and his brown eyes widened when he saw the condition she was in.

"I'm sorry," he whispered through a pant. "I didn't mean to let go of you. I thought I was a bit more durable than this."

92

"Normally you would be," she grunted. "When was the last time you've had food?"

"What's food?" Jeremy asked sarcastically.

At least his personality was still intact.

Jeremy's legs needed straightening so that he would heal correctly. Werewolves healed almost instantly when they were healthy. Even in Jeremy's condition he would be healed within a few minutes. She didn't want to have to re-break his bones if they healed wrong, so she needed to act quickly. The pain was excruciating as she bent over. She was certain she had a few broken ribs and her left arm was almost impossible to use. It was sheer willpower that made her grab his leg and straighten it.

To Jeremy's credit he didn't scream. He just muttered a string of profanity that Aurora never would've thought to put together. He was more vocal when she straightened the second leg. He was still so quiet that she could barely hear him through the ringing that had started up in her ears again. That didn't mean their enemies hadn't heard him. They needed to get moving soon, or their efforts would be for nothing.

"Well," Jeremy said through gritted teeth. "We can say that we've gone cliff jumping now."

"Was that on your bucket list?" Aurora asked dryly.

"Nope, I hate heights. Even more so now."

Jeremy recovered quicker than Aurora expected. He stood up and pulled his ratted hoodie over his head. He hurriedly wrapped her left arm that hung uselessly at her side. She didn't know how bad the break was, but it would be annoyingly painful until it healed. Jeremy made a sling out of the hoodie and he picked her up again.

"I can walk," she insisted.

She tried to struggle out of his arms, but it hurt too badly with her injured ribs and she sucked in a painful gasp.

"I know that you're hard-core," he said as he navigated down the steep wilderness. "But I'm pretty sure that one of your ankles is busted and you're bleeding from your head. You're probably concussed."

93

"You're wasting a lot of your energy on me." She grunted when he stumbled a little.

"I'm not leaving without you," he replied soothingly.

"I'm pretty sure that's my line," she grumbled in annoyance.

"Yeah, and it's a good one," he said with a hint of a smile. "If we get captured at least we fought our hardest and stayed together."

"I still can't believe you pulled that jump off."

"I didn't," he said darkly. "You got hurt."

"That was inevitable. At least we're not dead yet."

Jeremy grunted, but didn't reply. His pace was slow and he stumbled a lot. Aurora was surprised that he was still able to keep going. Survival instinct was a powerful thing. The terrain began to even out and they were surrounded by trees. The snow was almost gone, leaving mud and dead plants to walk through.

Most people would be making squishing sounds while traveling through mud, but Jeremy's werewolf instincts keep him perfectly silent.

It was Aurora that was having a hard time keeping quiet.

Her breathing was erratic from the pain. She kept hoping she would pass out, but she knew that was wishful thinking. They travelled for a long time. Aurora stared at the sky and hoped for some indication that dawn would break soon. But the crescent moon was bright and the stars were out.

Jeremy paused for a moment and listened. Aurora tried to even out her breathing. It didn't hurt as bad when they were standing still and she was able to stop herself from hyperventilating. Aurora strained to hear anything that would signal danger, but the ringing in her ears hadn't stopped. All she could hear was her own breathing.

"They've caught up to us," Jeremy whispered to her. "Any ideas?"

"Yeah," she panted. "Put me down and get out of here. They want me, not you."

"That's not gonna happen," he replied tersely.

94

"Jeremy," she whispered. "I need you to be safe. Go find my brothers and tell them I'm still alive. Carvolo isn't going to kill me anytime soon, but he might kill you. I can't live with that. I've lost too many people that I care about."

Jeremy fixed her with a heated glare and her heart broke. Tears stung her eyes as his glare bore into her.

"*I just got you back,*" she whispered desperately.

"Aurora," he said gruffly. "I'd much rather face down Carvolo than have to explain to your brothers why I left you here. Don't ask me to leave you again."

Tears spilled from her eyes and he growled at the sight of them.

"Please, Jeremy, don't make me beg."

"You're just going to piss me off if you keep it up," he said angrily.

"You'll travel faster without me," she said through gritted teeth. She was playing with fire, and she knew it. "Leave me here and save yourself."

Jeremy growled furiously and tightened his hold on her. That wasn't what she had in mind and she thought her body would break in half from the bone crushing hold. She knew he didn't mean to cause her more pain, but the beating of his heart told her how furious he was. She was hoping to get him angry enough that he would drop her and take off running.

Which, he did take off running, and she had to endure supernatural speed with broken bones. It was excruciating, but he was running so fast that she couldn't gulp in enough air to scream. She looked into his werewolf eyes and saw something in them that frightened her, and she didn't scare easily.

Insanity had taken over within him.

She could finally see what he meant when he said that he had no control over himself when he shed his skin. They were still weeks away from the next full moon and he looked like he had lost control already. He let rage take over to protect her from their enemies. Perhaps something good would come from his lack of control after all. But that didn't stop her from feeling bad that she was the cause of it. She didn't mean to send him over the edge like that. She hoped they survived long enough for her to apologize to him.

Aurora didn't know how many miles they went, or in which direction they were going. She doubted Jeremy did either since he wasn't exactly himself at the moment. She knew that the werewolves would have no trouble keeping pace with them and eventually Jeremy's stamina would give out. Her mind was racing as she tried to figure a way out of this. The only thing they could do was get Jeremy out, but it was evident that it wasn't going to happen.

She couldn't stop thinking about what Carvolo said to her. He wasn't ever planning on killing her. If she didn't find someway out of this she wouldn't be able to be with Riley again in the afterlife. If there was an afterlife. She hoped there was. She didn't want to imagine a universe were Riley didn't exist somewhere.

Knowing that she would never die was more torturous than anything Carvolo could physically do to her. More painful than broken bones and more isolating than solitary confinement. Jeremy was the only reason she was fighting right now. The only reason she kept going when she wanted to quit.

If Jeremy could survive five years of wanting nothing but to die then she could survive this too. But, if it came down to it, she would sacrifice her life for Jeremy without hesitation. It was more out of selfishness than heroism on her part, but she didn't care. She wanted Jeremy to live a better life than he'd been given and she wanted to be with Riley. If she could make that happen then she would. No matter how much it would hurt Jeremy and her brothers.

Aurora was pulled from her thoughts by Jeremy viciously dropping her to the ground. It had happened so fast that she barely registered the pain before she screamed. The scream was more out of surprise than anything else. Her body was mostly numb now from the adrenaline coursing through her.

It took her a moment to spot where Jeremy went. She watched in shock as he attacked one of their enemies with a ferocity that she'd never seen from a werewolf in human skin before; and she'd seen many horrible things in her life. It was more of an animal mauling than a fight. The enemy werewolf stood no chance while Jeremy tore into him with his teeth and fingernails.

There was so much blood.

The agonizing screams of the dying werewolf quieted and Aurora could hear Jeremy's feral breathing as he mauled a second werewolf that had appeared from the trees. If he kept up this behavior their enemies might think twice about trying to attack him. The only problem was, Aurora wasn't sure if Jeremy knew who was friend or foe at the moment.

He killed the second werewolf as easily as the first one. When he attacked a third werewolf without skipping a beat, Aurora decided she needed to do something before the werewolves decided to shoot him.

Jeremy had been a musician when he was in high school. He'd once told her that if he would have gone on to college he would've been a music major. She had never been much of a singer and she didn't know many songs. But there was a lullaby that her mother used to sing to her when she was a child that she had liked.

She hummed the tune loudly enough that she knew Jeremy would hear it. Even though it hurt she stood up and limped closer to him while she hummed. She knew music would be the most likely thing to calm the rage burning inside of him. Raya's tamer abilities would've been preferable, but hopefully the lullaby would be enough for now. She couldn't remember the words, but the tune was soothing on its own.

She got closer to Jeremy as he continued tearing into the dying werewolf. She knew that she was taking a stupid risk, but this was *Jeremy*. She had failed him before and letting him go on in this blind rage without trying to help would be failing him again.

She continued humming as soothingly as she could. She reached out slowly and touched his shoulder lightly.

Suddenly, she was on the ground with him on top of her. He body slammed her into the mud and she couldn't hum anymore. She couldn't even breathe. She closed her eyes so that she didn't have to stare into his yellow crazed ones anymore. His eyes bothered her more than the blood that cover him.

Even though she thought that her Jeremy would kill her, she was perfectly calm. When she could finally take a breath she hummed quietly again. She could feel him relax slightly. His feral breathing turned into something more human.

Jeremy leaned his bloody forehead against hers and took a few deep breaths. After a few calming minutes of keeping physical contact with her, he shifted and sat in the mud next to her. They didn't move or talk until their breathing was under control again.

"Aurora," Jeremy said breathlessly. "I am very so-"

"Apologizing is only gonna piss me off," she interrupted with a weak smirk. She didn't tease people very often, but she would always make an exception for Jeremy.

She didn't bother opening her eyes. They were surrounded and she didn't want to acknowledge that just yet. Besides, her head was swimming.

"That's not funny," he whispered emotionally. "I could've killed you. I told you that I'm a monster. I am *very sorry*."

She moved her uninjured arm and found his hand. He gripped her fingers tightly and she relaxed slightly at his touch. Physical contact among wolves was a very comforting thing. Solitary confinement made Jeremy starved for it and she insisted on giving it to him any way that she could.

"Monsters don't save their friends like you did today," she whispered.

"I didn't save you. We're surrounded. This was all for nothing."

"Not if you get out of here alive," she said as she squinted her eyes open. He was staring at her face with a tortured look in his eyes.

"I don't deserve to live," Jeremy said incredulously. "How can you not see that after what I just did?"

"It's perfectly normal for a werewolf leader to be protective."

"Not like that," Jeremy said. He was visibly shaking and not because he was cold. "I just killed three werewolves with my bare hands and teeth."

"Maybe so," Aurora said weakly. "But I know someone that can help you get control. Her name is Raya. You don't have to feel like this forever, Jeremy. Just don't let them take you back to that den."

Suddenly, pink light exploded in the darkness. They both shielded their eyes against the magic as an enraged shriek echoed through the night.

Zalina appeared before them and froze them both with her magic. Jeremy growled at her and Aurora noticed the fairy flinch slightly.

Apparently, they succeeded in making her afraid of them.

"I will take great pleasure in torturing and killing both of you," Zalina sneered sadistically.

"Torturing, yes," Carvolo said from behind them. "But we need them both alive, Zalina."

The fairy scoffed incredulously.

"She snapped my neck, Carvolo," Zalina said angrily. "I have no intention of letting her survive the night. The information she has is not worth risking another escape attempt."

"Let's not be hasty, my dear," Carvolo said carefully. "We don't know exactly what she knows."

The fairy stared at the werewolf with hard eyes before turning her attention back to Jeremy.

"Well," Zalina said dangerously. "We don't need *him* alive."

Jeremy screamed as pink light encompassed his body. Aurora tried to protest, but Zalina cut off her oxygen. She tried to struggle, but she felt herself growing weaker by the second.

She couldn't watch Jeremy die. *Not again.*

99

Carvolo stepped forward and put a hand on Zalina's shoulder. Aurora could finally breathe again and the pink light that burst from Jeremy's body subsided along with his screams. He collapsed to the ground in a bloody heap, panting like a marathon runner.

Aurora hoped that none of the blood was his.

"You mustn't kill him," Carvolo said gently. His yellow eyes betrayed the tone of his voice. Aurora learned at a young age to always trust a werewolf's eyes over anything else.

Carvolo was murderously furious with Zalina.

"I've had enough of him," Zalina's shrill voice pierced through the air. "I may have sworn my loyalty to you, Carvolo, but I will not let you stand in the way of my vengeance."

Carvolo nodded once with a small smile on his face.

Suddenly, he growled ferociously and stabbed Zalina in the chest with a silver dagger. The fairy's angry expression fell and was replaced by shock. Then the life left her eyes and her magic visibly vaporized.

Her lifeless body collapsed to the ground at Carvolo's feet and her pink wings slowly disappeared. The surrounding werewolves shifted anxiously at the smell of magical blood.

"Fairies are pointless allies anyway," Carvolo said passively. "Arothor was proof of that."

Aurora stared at her father in complete disbelief. She couldn't help but wonder what he was playing at. He most certainly didn't kill Zalina to protect Jeremy out of the goodness of his heart. He had an ulterior motive and she needed to figure out what it was as quickly as possible.

"Don't look so shocked, Aurora," Carvolo said with a smirk. "You didn't think I'd let her kill your boyfriend, did you? *You just got him back.*"

Aurora and Jeremy glanced at each other in confusion. Carvolo definitely had something up his sleeve and, whatever it was, it wasn't good.

"Of course, your boyfriend did kill three of my followers," Carvolo said thoughtfully. "Even though it was quite entertaining to watch there must be reparation for what was done."

"Carvolo," Aurora said as she stood up slowly. Her determination to hide her pain kept her from wincing despite the shooting pain from her broken ankle. "Take me. Let Jeremy go. Everything that happened was my fault."

"Sure it was," Jeremy said sarcastically as he stood up next to her. She didn't see him roll his eyes, but she knew that he did. "If you want Aurora you gotta go through me."

"Aw! Look at you two! Falling on your swords for each other… How disgustingly romantic!"

Carvolo laughed as his yellow eyes glowered at them.

Suddenly, Aurora felt a surge of strength she hadn't felt in what seemed like a long time. She looked up at the sky and saw that dawn was breaking. She couldn't help but smile as she felt her pain slowly ease away.

Carvolo noticed the sky changing too and he crouched, eager for the impending fight.

Chapter 7

Riley jerked out of his sleep so violently that he hit his head on the door of the van. Marcus involuntarily yanked at the steering wheel and he had to correct himself before going into the other lane. The skinwalker swore under his breath as he got the van under control.

Riley gripped the door handle as he tried to catch his breath. He was so startled by the vision that he hardly felt the pain from his wounds. He noticed that dawn was breaking and he had to fight down the panic.

What he saw was happening in real time. Carvolo was attacking Aurora and Jeremy and there was nothing they could do about it. He didn't even know where they were anymore because they had travelled so far from the Montana den.

"I swear, man," Marcus said in exasperation. "Watching you sleep is like waiting for a bomb to explode. You're quiet one second and then the next it's like you're in a cage fight."

"Riley," Gabriel said quietly. "What did you just see?"

"How far are we from the den?" Riley asked Marcus hurriedly.

"About an hour drive," he replied. "But we were going to stop at a pharmacy first to get-"

"Don't stop," Riley said insistently. "Drive faster."

Riley quickly explained to them what was happening to Aurora and Jeremy. He skipped over the small details and told them only the important things; Aurora and Jeremy's escape, Zalina's death, and Carvolo's preparation to attack them.

"Rebecca," Riley said. "Give me the wand."

"Why?" she asked hesitantly.

"I might be able to get a location on Aurora with it."

"Let me do a location spell. They are outside of the den now so it should work. That way you won't be sleeping when we get there."

102

Riley didn't like it, but he knew that he needed to let Rebecca handle the location spell. He just wanted to see Aurora again and it was killing him that he couldn't.

"Zalina put a protection spell on her," Gabriel said. "I know she's dead, but that doesn't necessarily mean that the protection spell has dropped. Do the location spell on Jeremy. Hopefully they're still together."

Rebecca nodded and whispered the incantation under her breath. Marcus was on his cell phone talking with Jackson who was following closely behind them. Riley felt helpless. He wished that he could teleport anywhere he wanted to go, but he didn't think the wand worked that way.

He looked at the speedometer and saw that they were going as fast as the van would allow. It still wasn't fast enough.

Riley lifted his shirt to examine his wounds. Even with the guresh they were still raw, but the infection seemed to be going away. It didn't hurt as bad, but he still wasn't in fighting shape. He glanced back at Gabriel and noticed him watching him warily.

"Raven gave me this," he said as he handed him a syringe of guresh. "Take it. You need all the help you can get right now."

Riley injected the magical element directly into his abdomen. It took the majority of the pain away and he was able to physically relax for the first time in days. He glanced in the side mirror outside of the van and saw his reflexion. He looked a little better than the last time he saw himself in the mirror. The guresh was working slowly but surly.

"I know where Jeremy is," Rebecca said. "Aurora is still there, but it doesn't look good. Carvolo is having his followers…"

Her voice trailed off and she avoided Riley's stare.

"What?" Riley asked her impatiently.

"He basically handed Jeremy over to his followers. I guess Jeremy killed a few of them and Carvolo is having his minions take it out on him. Aurora has been incapacitated."

"Welhum?" Gabriel asked in a whisper.

103

Rebecca nodded reluctantly. Marcus swore and pushed harder on the gas peddle. The engine whined in protest.

"Take it easy, Marcus," Gabriel said. "We're not going to get there if you kill the engine."

"Shut up, Gabriel," Marcus grumbled as he stomped on the gas peddle even more.

Riley stared at the endless blacktop road. He couldn't shake the feeling that they were going to be too late. He wasn't in control of anything anymore and his wife was in danger. He needed to hit something, but there wasn't anything to punch.

He exhaled in aggravation.

"We'll get there, Riley," Rebecca said soothingly. "It's going to be okay."

Riley knew that she didn't believe that, but he robotically nodded anyway. He wanted to go back to sleep to see if the wand had another vision for him. But with the guresh in his system he wasn't tired at all. He wanted to hold the wand in his hand just to have some kind of reassurance that he was strong enough to save Aurora from whatever was happening to her. But he knew that even the wand wasn't powerful enough to help her now.

Besides, Rebecca had been right when she said that he needed to recover from using it. Killing Arothor, recovering from stab wounds, and all the visions took a lot out of him. His constant sleeping was a sign of that. He would have to rely on his fighting skills and pure magic on this mission.

"How did you deal with this?" Riley asked Marcus. "I literally feel like I'm losing my mind."

Marcus's grip on the steering wheel tightened slightly and his face paled.

"I used to go outside at night after everyone was asleep and punch the crap out of the trees in Jackson's backyard," the skinwalker whispered. "I wouldn't stop until I could see the bone underneath my sliced up knuckles. But I'm not the best example of how to behave in these situations."

"Huh," Riley said humorlessly. "I was just thinking that it would be nice to have something to hit."

104

"You'll have something to hit soon enough," Marcus replied darkly.

Marcus slowed down when they came upon a small town. He had to slow down even more when they went through a school zone.

It was agonizing.

Riley watched as small children with large backpacks hurried toward their school. The sight was so normal that it caught him off guard for a moment. It was hard to remember sometimes that people still lived normal lives in the world, with kids, school, and jobs. No war to fight and no relocating families to keep them safe.

The sight of normalcy didn't last long as they drove further into the town. In front of a small grocery store there was a large group of people standing with cardboard signs. Riley wasn't sure what they were protesting at first. Then he saw a sign with large enough letters for him to read:

Monsters live among us!

They weren't protesting anything. They were trying to create awareness.

Another sign read:

Prayers for London!

"Well," Gabriel said. "That seems to be the appropriate response."

"Carvolo really opened a can of worms with this one," Marcus said in disgust. "I still can't figure out why he let the cameras see him."

"Who knows why he does what he does," Gabriel said darkly. "He's insane."

"I wonder what this will mean for the human population," Rebecca said. "Do you think that we'll see more people trying to be hunters? Usually that's just a family tradition passed down from parents to children. Unless they survived a supernatural attack and decide to become one."

"I think that's a possibility, sis," Riley said. "Unfortunately, this kind of awareness that they're trying to spread will probably get more people killed than it will save."

105

"I agree," Gabriel said. "If people fight back against the supernatural then they're going to die trying."

"Maybe that is Carvolo's plan," Rebecca said angrily. "He's trying to thin out the human population so that they have less people to turn into werewolves."

"The werewolves have changed millions of people in just the past few years," Marcus said. "We gotta find the Ancients Den as soon as possible and end this."

"After we rescue Aurora we'll have time for that," Riley said.

Once they were outside the town limits Marcus hit the gas pedal again. The engine whined, but they ignored it. Riley could feel the van vibrating beneath his seat. He tried not to think about how annoyed Jackson would be if they destroyed his van, but they would do what they had to do.

It wasn't long before they saw the mountain range. Marcus found a deserted parking lot that looked like it hadn't been used all winter. Riley hoped that any human would stay away since he was sure that the mountainside and the woods were crawling with Carvolo's followers.

They got out of the van just as Jackson, Raya, and Raven parked next to them in the Buick. Jackson used his vampire speed to get their gear out. Riley grabbed the bow and arrows instead of the crossbow. Now that he could stand a little straighter he felt like it would be better for Raya to have the crossbow. It was easier to aim and she wasn't as skilled an archer as he was.

Jackson and Raven took a couple guns and plenty of ammo. Rebecca took the second bow and quiver of arrows. Gabriel and Marcus shed their skin and couldn't help but prowl around impatiently as they waited for everyone to get ready. Marcus's brown and gray fur stood up on end in anticipation for bloodshed. Gabriel's black and gray fur was more relaxed, but his eyes blazed with a fire that was rarely ever there.

"I'm going to run ahead to see what is going on," Jackson said. "You guys go at a slower pace."

106

"I think we should split up into two groups," Gabriel said through mind speech. "I doubt Aurora and Jeremy are still in the same place."

"Let me do another location spell on Jeremy first," Rebecca said. "It's better to be sure."

They waited as Rebecca said the incantation. It didn't take her long to open her eyes and, by the look on her face, Riley knew that she didn't have good news. She had moisture in her eyes and her voice quivered a little when she spoke.

"Aurora is not there. Jeremy is still alive, but I'm honestly not sure how."

"We'll split up," Marcus said intently. "Jackson, Raven, Gabriel, and I will go find Aurora. The rest of you go get Jeremy."

"No." Riley clenched his fists to stop his hands from shaking.

"Riley," Jackson said. "We are the fastest ones here. We don't even know where she is yet. You can't come with us."

Riley knew his father was right, but that didn't mean he liked it. He closed his eyes against the pain for a moment and took a deep breath. When he opened them he found that Jackson was watching him in concern.

"Bring her back," Riley said sharply and Jackson nodded.

Raya stared at Riley with soft glowing blue eyes that seemed to see into his very soul. He knew she was trying to calm him, but her powers didn't work on wizards. He clenched his jaw and tried to ignore her gaze. Raya quickly lowered her eyes and turned to give Raven a kiss.

"Be safe," she said to him and he gave her a small smile.

"Always."

Rebecca ran her hand through Gabriel's fur for a moment and whispered something to him. Riley didn't hear Gabriel reply, but that was because he sent a message only to her through mind speech. Rebecca nodded and Gabriel rumbled a growly whine in his chest.

Riley didn't know what they were discussing, but he didn't care. He couldn't help but feel like they all were wasting time.

"We will bring her back, buddy," Jackson said to him reassuringly. "Even if I die trying, okay?"

Riley didn't respond, but he clapped his hand on Jackson's shoulder in appreciation. He didn't want his father to die, but it was a testament to his character that he would put his life on the line for Aurora. There was a time when the two of them hated each other. They had come so far since then. He knew that Aurora's brothers would give anything to save her as well. He knew that he was leaving the mission in capable hands.

Jackson gave Rebecca a swift kiss on the cheek and the four creatures disappeared into the trees. Rebecca, Raya, and Riley stood there for a moment as they watched them go. Rebecca bent down and picked up the bag that contained the syringes full of guresh. Aurora wouldn't be able to use them since Carvolo injected her with welhum, but there was a chance that Jeremy would need them. He probably had the torture element in his system too, but werewolves recovered from that more quickly.

"Let's go," Rebecca said.

The three of them hurried into the dense forest. There was no path, not even a game trail. Rebecca used her magic to clear a small path so that they could easily jog through the woods. It was incredible watching the brush clear in front of them as they made their way toward the mountainside cliffs. Riley tried to find anything that was familiar to him from the vision he had, but he didn't recognize anything. They weren't close enough to the mountain yet.

Rebecca led the way. She knew where Jeremy was so she was the most plausible choice to lead their small posse. Riley was behind her with Raya taking up the end. They kept their eyes peeled for any sign of Carvolo's werewolf followers. Riley wished that he had a werewolf's keen hearing and sense of smell. For now he had to rely on his werewolf comrades to alert him of danger. It was frustrating.

Riley couldn't keep his mind off of Aurora. He hoped that she wasn't in a lot of pain, but welhum wasn't a painless thing. He hoped that her broken bones had a chance to heal themselves before Carvolo injected her with it. But her burns alone were enough to hurt severely with the torturous poison.

Even though he was terrified he was also immensely proud of her. She had successfully beaten down a fairy and escaped her cell. He and Gabriel weren't able to escape the Leaders Den prison, so that alone was impressive. She was also able to calm Jeremy down when he had gone *werewolf psycho* on Carvolo's followers.

Riley didn't tell anyone about Jeremy's psychotic episode. Raya was there now and he felt that it was irrelevant to worry about when she could take care of the problem with her tamer charm.

Riley couldn't shake the feeling that Jeremy was still in love with Aurora. In his visions the werewolf had been a perfect gentleman about her relationship with Riley. But that didn't mean that Jeremy wasn't hiding his feelings. There was no way that after five years of imprisonment that he had any closure with the relationship he had with Aurora. Riley didn't blame him. Aurora was an amazing person, but she was his now and he wasn't going to let her go. Riley didn't think that Jeremy would try to come between them once he knew that Riley was, in fact, alive. It didn't stop him from feeling bad about the whole situation though. If Aurora hadn't thought that Jeremy was dead would they have ever gotten married?

Riley knew that Aurora loved him. She even told him that she never loved Jeremy in the way that she loved him. But the thought that Jeremy had been alive this whole time bothered him. It was hard for Riley not to feel like they had betrayed this poor guy that he had never met. It didn't seem like Jeremy felt the same way in the visions, so that was good. Jeremy seemed like an upstanding guy, but definitely rough around the edges.

109

Watching his entire family get killed by skinwalkers must've been horrible.

Riley accidentally bumped into Rebecca when she suddenly stopped jogging. If she hadn't been a werewolf she would've fallen to the ground. His clumsiness pulled him from his thoughts.

"Jeez," she whispered. "I've never seen you so distracted. Are you okay?"

Riley nodded and mumbled an apology.

"We are surrounded," Rebecca said grimly.

Riley listened closely, but didn't hear anything. He glanced around quickly, but saw nothing but trees and dead plants. Good thing that Rebecca had enhanced senses.

Riley grabbed his bow and fitted an arrow on the string. Rebecca did the same, but Raya walked a few feet away from them. Her crossbow dangled where it was strapped to her hip and she made no move to grab it. Riley took a step toward her, but Rebecca grabbed his arm. He stopped and looked at her questioningly.

"Raya," Rebecca whispered. "What are you doing?"

"Some of them are angry," Raya said in a soothing voice. "Some of them are frightened. But most of them are curious about us."

"The werewolves?"

Raya nodded and glanced over at them. Riley noticed that her werewolf eyes didn't glow yellow like they did when she had the controlling element in her head. There was a light blue glow to them that gave off a hypnotic feel. It did nothing for Riley, but Rebecca gasp when she saw her eyes.

"How do you know what they're feeling?" Riley asked her.

"I'm not sure," Raya replied quietly. "It's just pure instinct. They're all in distress and I *really* want to help them."

"We need to focus on helping Jeremy," Riley reminded her.

Raya nodded and took a step back from the trees she was standing in front of. A deep growl came from behind the tree and Raya froze. Riley and Rebecca pulled back the strings on their bows and waited for the angry werewolf to jump out at Raya.

"Keep coming toward us, Raya," Riley said calmly. "We won't let them hurt you."

Raya nodded and took another step backwards. The growling started up again and Raya stopped moving. Suddenly, a female werewolf darted out from behind the trees and tackled Raya down so fast that Riley didn't have a chance to react. Rebecca had been too slow as well. By the time they realized what had happened, Raya was already on the ground with an angry werewolf straddling her.

"Lower your weapons," Raya said to them from beneath the werewolf. "It's okay. She doesn't want to hurt me."

Riley didn't lower his arrow, but he didn't shoot either. There was something about Raya's tone that told him he needed to listen to her. Raya laid perfectly still with her hands above her head. The werewolf sitting on her just stared at her intently.

"What do you want to do?" Raya asked her calmly. "You're in charge here."

The werewolf stared at her, but didn't say anything.

"I know who you are," Raya said gently. "You're a leader. Aren't you?"

The werewolf's eyes widened for a moment in fear. The fear was quickly replaced by anger and a deep growl rumbled from her chest. It was common for Carvolo to take leaders that he'd turned and force them into submission. Apparently, this was one of those werewolves.

"It's okay," Raya continued in the same soothing tone. "You don't have to do what the leaders say. You can take these followers and go. You don't have to pretend to be something you aren't anymore."

The werewolf stared at her for a moment.

"You're coming with me," the werewolf sneered threateningly. "I have never met someone like you before. You're mine now."

111

"I don't think so," Riley said as he kept his arrow aimed at the werewolf. Rebecca had lowered her bow, but she quickly raised it again. "Get off of her now or I will shoot you."

The werewolf tore her gaze away from Raya and bared her human teeth at Riley. This werewolf didn't seem stable at all. He wasn't sure why Raya had told them not to shoot her. Maybe she wanted to practice her tamer abilities on these crazed werewolves they were facing. But he wasn't about to let this insane werewolf take her.

"Please," Raya said to the werewolf. "He's not lying. You'll die if you don't get off of me. Take the followers and go. They can be yours now."

"You are mine!" the werewolf screamed furiously.

Riley loosened the arrow and it hit the werewolf in the shoulder. She screamed in pain and jumped off of Raya. Before she could barrel toward them Rebecca dropped her with a purple flaming arrow to the heart. Raya jumped to her feet and grabbed her crossbow. Another werewolf jumped out at her and she shot it before it made contact with her. She hurried over to Riley and Rebecca who were fitting new arrows into their strings.

"There's a few more angry ones that might attack," Raya said through a pant. "But I don't think the others will. They're too scared and my presence is making them even more nervous."

"I had no idea that you could sense emotions," Rebecca said as she lit her arrowhead ablaze with her purple flames.

"I didn't know either," Raya replied through gritted teeth. "Until now. Not a lot of good it's doing us though."

"How did you know that she was a leader?" Riley asked as he glanced at the dead werewolf that laid at their feet.

"I don't know. Somehow...I just knew."

"What if they follow us?" Rebecca asked.

Her fingers still held the string of her bow taught.

"They probably will," Raya said. "But I think we should keep walking. If they attack us then we can take them out."

"Sounds like a plan," Riley replied. "We need to get to Jeremy as quickly as possible."

112

Rebecca proceeded through the forest at the same speed as before. She still had her bow drawn with the flaming arrow. Riley tried to match her speed, but he was getting winded. He didn't know how long they had been jogging through the woods. He drew upon his pure magic to help him get through the exhaustion and boost his speed. It would make him tired later, but for now he needed to keep up. If he didn't he'd become a liability.

Suddenly, a large werewolf plowed into Riley, knocking the air out of his lungs. He flew backwards and skidded across the forest floor as though he weighed nothing. Twigs and fallen branches scraped his skin as he slid. When he came to a stop he couldn't take a breath no matter how hard he tried.

The giant werewolf squatted over him with an angry gleam in his yellow eyes. Riley tried to scramble to his feet, but the hostile werewolf grabbed his shoulders in a bruising grip. Pain shot through his side as the werewolf picked him up.

Suddenly, the werewolf's eyes went blank with shock and Riley noticed a silver arrowhead sticking out of his chest. Without another sound, the werewolf dropped Riley and slumped to the ground, motionless.

Riley gasped in air and grimaced when he realized the damage he'd taken. Being tackled by a werewolf wasn't something that a body as fragile as Riley's took very well. He expanded his pure magic to help mask the pain. It wouldn't heal him, but at least he'd be able to stand.

Raya hurried over to him as he struggled to sit up. She put a gentle hand on his shoulder as she rummaged through the small pack of medical supplies that they had. It wasn't much, but she was able to put a bandaid on a cut that he had above his eyebrow so the blood wouldn't drip into his eye.

"I can give you some more guresh," she said as she dug through the bag again.

"No," Riley said as he caught her hand to stop her. "I'll be fine. We need to save the rest for Jeremy. I think he's going to need it more than me."

Raya pursed her lips, but she nodded grimly. She helped him stand up and they saw Rebecca shooting arrow after arrow into the trees. Riley grabbed his bow that had fallen to the ground and gathered up the arrows that spilled from his quiver. Raya rushed to Rebecca's side and aimed her crossbow at crazed werewolves that were coming toward them.

"Craticas razinios," Riley muttered.

A blue flame lit the tip of his arrow and he shot it into the chest of a werewolf that lunged at Raya. The werewolf burst into magical flames and screamed in agony as he was engulfed in the inferno.

"Craticas electios."

He felt the energy leave him as four blue balls of electricity soared toward a group of werewolves that were trying to surround Raya. The werewolves fell to the ground as the electric shock rendered them unconscious. Raya had no trouble finishing them off after that.

Riley looked around quickly for more werewolves that would attack, but didn't see any. He bent over and took a few shallow breaths. He knew that he needed to recover quickly if he was to be of any help later.

"Riley," Rebecca said as she hurried over to him. "Are you alright?"

"I'll live," he said with a tight grimace.

"I heard bones cracking when you got hit," Rebecca said sternly. "Don't lie to me."

"I'm not lying," he said. "I said '*I'll live*', and I will."

Rebecca gave him an incredulous look and he just shrugged in response.

"I think you should stay here," she said as she held out her handgun to him. "You can't fight werewolves with broken bones."

"I don't have broken bones," he said with the same tight grimace.

He didn't take the handgun from her. Even though he couldn't feel it he knew that he had a few cracked ribs. But he couldn't stay put while his sister and Raya went off alone.

114

"Why are you lying to me?" Rebecca asked him sternly. "You and I both know your ribs are cracked."

"My ribs are always cracked," Riley said gruffly. Rebecca shot him a stern look. "I'm not staying here, sis. I'd be werewolf bait. Besides, I need to help save someone. If it can't be Aurora then I'll settle for Jeremy."

"I can stay with him if you want me to," Raya whispered to Rebecca.

Riley rolled his eyes in annoyance.

"No, he's right," Rebecca said with a sigh. "We should all keep moving. Werewolves would come in hoards if we made him stay put. We are pretty close to were they're torturing Jeremy anyway."

"Do you want to do one more location spell before we get there?" Raya asked. "Just to be sure we're headed in the right direction still?"

"No, I think he's still there. If he's not I'll do another spell after we get there."

Raya nodded and helped Riley stand. She put his arm over her shoulder, but he stubbornly pulled away from her.

"I'm okay," he said. "Honestly, I've had worse."

Raya gave him a concerned look, but nodded. Rebecca walked out in front of them, but set a slower pace. It annoyed Riley that he was the reason they had to slow down, but there wasn't much he could do about it. After about a mile he noticed an overpowering smell of death and decay that made his stomach heave.

"What is that?" Raya asked as she wrinkled her nose. "It smells awful."

"It's a dead body," Rebecca said. She suddenly stopped walking and stared at the ground in disbelief. "Or three."

Riley hurried over to her and recognized what she saw immediately. There were three bodies that looked like they had been devoured by a wild beast of some kind. It was too malicious looking to be bear kill. The scene had a ferocious and demented look to it. The dead vegetation was drenched in crimson blood and other pieces that he couldn't recognize.

115

Riley knew that Jeremy did this, but it had been dark in his vision. It looked ten times worse in the daylight. Bugs were greedily buzzing around the bodies.

"I wonder who, or what, did this," Rebecca said in disgust.

Riley kept his mouth shut. He didn't know Jeremy at all, but he did know that the guy had done everything he could to save Aurora. He wasn't about to let these dead bodies taint Jeremy's image in the eyes of Rebecca and Raya. If anyone did find out what happened here it wouldn't be from him.

"This is the most horrible thing I've ever seen," Raya said as she put her hand to her mouth. "And I've seen a lot of crap."

"Let's keep going," Riley said. "We probably shouldn't waste anymore time."

Just as they were about to leave, a dark chuckle came from behind them. The three of them spun around and Rebecca swore under her breath. She was probably cursing herself for not noticing someone sneaking up behind them. Of course, the dead bodies were rather distracting. Riley thought he recognized the chuckling werewolf, but he couldn't place him.

The werewolf was tall, taller than Marcus by far. His broad shoulders were muscular and intimidating. His teeth gleamed in the sunlight as he smiled maliciously at them. His eyes twinkled green with a hint of yellow madness. He held a large silver sword in one hand and a battle axe in the other.

Riley knew that he'd seen the large werewolf before and he was surprised when he couldn't remember where. This particular werewolf was larger than most and not generic at all. He didn't think he could forget someone like that, but apparently he had. Unless his mind was playing tricks on him and he really hadn't seen this creature before.

"Gerard," Rebecca whispered angrily. "I thought you were dead."

"I escaped the Leaders Den before the explosion," Gerard said smoothly. "Carvolo recruited me to help him. Many of the followers in these woods are mine. Including the ones you've killed today. I might spare your life if you promise to replace them, my sweet Rebecca."

Rebecca's werewolf eyes glowed yellow at the intimate way he said her name. It was then that Riley remembered where he'd first seen this werewolf. Painstaking memories flooded through his mind of being tortured at the Leaders Den. He had managed to block out most of the memories after they had been rescued. Gerard had been one of the tormentors that routinely tortured Gabriel. It was unfortunate that he didn't die in the explosion.

"Go," Rebecca whispered to him. "Take Raya and find Jeremy. I'll deal with him."

"Be careful," Riley murmured. She gave him a quick nod without taking her eyes off of Gerard. He nodded at Raya and they hurried off into the trees.

Riley didn't know where they were supposed to go and neither did Raya. He let her take the lead since she had a better sense of smell than he did. He was hoping that she would be able to sniff out where the group of followers that had Jeremy were. There was a strong blood trail that looked like an injured person had been dragged through the forest, probably Jeremy. The blood on the ground would make it easier to find them.

Riley tried not to think about leaving Rebecca behind to fight the giant werewolf by herself. He knew that she could handle it. She was one of the most powerful creatures that he knew. Her werewolf abilities and her witch magic made her stronger than most. He still couldn't help feeling guilty for leaving her to fend for herself though. If anything happened to her he would never forgive himself.

Riley's worry for Rebecca evaporated when they finally came to the end of the blood trail. His stomach clenched at the sight of blood and the awful smell that came from the scene. He had seen some brutal torture before, but nothing could prepare him for this.

Chapter 8

Raya stood frozen next to Riley. He didn't know if it was from shock or fear, or maybe she was trying not to vomit. He would have thrown up himself if he had any food in his stomach. He expanded his pure magic when his ribs began to ache. He was running out of energy and the horrible scene before them wasn't helping at all.

There was a group of ten followers surrounding an extremely bloodied Jeremy. He was chained to a thick tree trunk with silver chains that dug into his flesh. He was slightly suspended in the air with his toes barely touching the ground. His clothes had seen better days and they were so saturated with crimson that Riley couldn't tell what color his shirt was. Jeremy was unsurprisingly unconscious. That meant he was in so much pain that he couldn't stay awake or they had given him a shot of welhum. Riley was willing to bet that it was a combination of the two.

The surrounding werewolves appeared to be taking turns inflicting pain on Jeremy. None of the torturing devices were sanitary, which was probably where the putrid smell was coming from. The werewolves were so engrossed in what they were doing that they didn't noticed Riley and Raya standing merely a few yards behind them.

"They all need to die," Raya whispered dangerously.

Her tone of voice took Riley by complete surprise. The last time he'd heard that tone from her she had Arothor's controlling element in her head. He glanced at her and saw that her eyes were a werewolf yellow instead of the glowing blue she'd had earlier. Her face was heated and her hands were clenched tightly into fists.

"Agreed," Riley said with a nod. "You take five, I'll take five."

Then they attacked. The followers didn't notice them until they were ambushed. Riley stood as far back as he could as he used the rest of his arrows, killing three of the werewolves. Riley tried to pull out his handgun, but he stumbled and lost his footing. Two werewolves advanced on him as he fell to the ground. He wasn't sure what he had tripped over, but it was a critical mistake.

One of the werewolves grabbed his wrist and crushed it with one tight squeeze. Riley's scream was cut off by a choke when the same werewolf grabbed him by the throat. The tight grip instantly cut off the oxygen and blood flow to his brain.

Just before Riley was about to black out he finally got his gun out of the holster and shot the werewolf. He didn't aim. He just pulled the trigger.

The werewolf staggered back with a howl of pain. He didn't think he killed it, but at least he was no longer being choked. He sucked in a breath and his eyes watered from how painful it was. He thought for a moment that the werewolf had crushed something important in his throat, but breathing got easier with each breath he took.

He was just thankful that he still had a windpipe.

Another werewolf grabbed him by the other arm with the same kind of bone crushing grip. Riley screamed loudly as he heard, and felt, his bone snap. The gun fell uselessly from his hand and the werewolf locked eyes with him. She had blood on her clothes and some of it was matted in her hair as well. Her face was hard, but her eyes were empty and forlorn.

Riley had been in enough battles to know the eyes of a killer. This werewolf follower didn't have those eyes. It took Riley by surprise and he forgot the pain he felt for a moment.

"Stop," Raya said calmly, but firmly.

Riley tore his eyes from the werewolf girl and glanced at Raya. Her eyes glowed blue and she was walking toward the werewolf that still had his broken arm in her hand. She looked at Raya and a growl rumbled from her throat. She began shaking and Riley groaned when her quivering hand tighten over his arm.

"Shh," Raya said calmly. "It's okay. You can let him go."

The follower did exactly that. She dropped Riley's arm, not at all gently, and stood up slowly. Riley stayed where he

119

was, but he surveyed as much of the scene as he could with his eyes. Raya had succeeded in taking out six werewolves on her own. Riley wasn't sure how she did it so quickly, but maybe his perception of time was off. That happened sometimes in a battle. Or maybe her werewolf survival instincts kicked in and she was a better fighter than anyone had given her credit for.

Raya walked slowly up to the werewolf that still stood over Riley. The follower visibly relaxed and stopped shaking. She stared at Raya as though she were an angel. Her gaze was almost worshipful. A look of discomfort pass over Raya's face, but she reached out with her hand and touched the werewolf girl's shoulder.

"You can go now," Raya said quietly. "I would suggest you don't return to this place."

The follower didn't say anything, but a small whimper escaped her throat. Suddenly, she was gone. Riley gasped in relief and pain. He couldn't believe that he was stupid enough to let himself trip during a fight. He was usually better than that, but he normally wasn't expanding so much pure magic during a fight. It must've made him physically unsteady.

Raya hurried over to him and knelt down. She anxiously stared at his arms with a horrified look on her face. Riley closed his eyes and tried not to go into shock. They still had to help Jeremy and he needed to get back on his feet. Technically, this was Raya's first mission. Besides escaping the Leaders Den and the battle that took place in their community, she hadn't seen a lot of serious action. He could tell that she was scared and close to losing it.

When he opened his eyes he saw her holding a syringe of guresh over his chest. He instinctively grabbed at her hand to stop her, but he had broken bones in both of his arms. The pain immediately made him lightheaded. He swallowed another scream and just swore instead. Of all the injuries he'd sustained in the past he had never broken an arm. Now both of them were out of commission.

"Don't," he said in a raspy voice. His vocal cords must have taken some damage. "Jeremy needs it."

120

"I know," she said hastily. "I'm sorry. I just…I thought you passed out."

"I didn't pass out. Just give me a second."

Riley closed his eyes again and searched for energy left in him. He couldn't find anything, so using his pure magic to mask his pain was not an option at the moment. Not that he'd be able to use his arms even with his pure magic helping him, but it would've definitely been easier to stand.

Riley decided he needed to buck up and help Jeremy. He owed it to him for helping Aurora. So he opened his eyes and took a shallow breath.

It was incredibly painful, but he managed to sit up. His vision went unfocused and he thought for a moment that he really would pass out. Raya put a hand on his shoulder to steady him and he winced. Being weak in front of her was making him feel uncomfortable. It was probably because he knew that she was scared, or maybe her tamer charm was beginning to rub off on him now that he was injured. He thought it was the former. He didn't feel calm at all.

"So," Riley said hoarsely. His voice was barely above a whisper. "Whatever happened to '*they all need to die*'?"

"What?" she asked almost frantically.

"I was referring to the werewolf you let go."

"Oh…" She blinked a few times in confusion, or shock. "Um, she…something about her just stopped me from killing her. I don't know what it was. We'll probably regret it later."

"I doubt it," Riley said reassuringly. "She's long gone and I don't think we'll see her again."

"Do you want me to help you stand?"

"That would probably be best. Just don't touch my arms or my torso."

"Um…"

Raya looked at him for a few seconds in thought and timidly gripped his shoulders. He nodded, indicating that was okay, and she pulled him up. After another episode of lightheadedness, that would've knocked Riley over if Raya didn't have such a firm grip on him, he was good. Walking was

121

a different story, but he stumbled toward where Jeremy hung by the tree despite the intense agony. They needed to get him down from there before he died. With how much blood was covering the area, assuming it was all his, it was a possibility.

"Raya," Riley said. "I would normally use my magic to get the chains off of him, but that's not a safe option for me right now. We need to see if there's keys, or anything we can pick the locks with."

Raya nodded and started searching the area. Riley tried, but his vision was out of focus. After a few minutes they realized it was pointless trying to go through all the bloodied weapons for a key that probably wasn't even there.

Riley sighed and raised the arm that had the broken wrist. It didn't hurt as badly to move that arm. He used his magic to free Jeremy of the chains and quickly sat down before he fell down.

Jeremy collapsed. He would have hit the ground if Raya hadn't been supernaturally fast. She caught his unconscious form and dragged him to cleaner ground to lay him on. She pulled the guresh out of the bag she had strapped around her and hesitated before injecting him with it.

"Give it to him in the neck," Riley said. "Chest would be better, but under the circumstances…"

Riley didn't have to continue. Raya could see how bad Jeremy's injuries were. His whole torso looked like it had been shredded by a human sized cheese grater. She plunged the needle into the werewolf's neck and quickly pulled out a second dose of guresh.

"This is the last one," she said quietly. "I think you should have it, Riley."

"No, give it to him. He needs it more than I do."

Raya nodded reluctantly and inserted the needle into Jeremy's neck again. She rested his head on her lap, which made Riley nervous. He knew that Raya was a tamer, but she was very anxious. He didn't know if her abilities would work on Jeremy if she was riled up herself. The last thing they needed was for Jeremy to have a moment of insanity when he woke up.

"Raya," Riley said softly. It hurt to talk so he had to keep his voice quiet. Luckily, she was a werewolf and could hear him just fine. "Jeremy has trouble controlling himself when he's under duress. I've seen it in a vision that the wand gave me. He's very dangerous when he loses control. If he wakes up crazed can you handle that?"

Raya took a few deep calming breaths before she looked up at Riley. She had been studying Jeremy's unconscious face while he was talking to her. Riley could see the tension leave her body almost in an instant.

"I got this," she said soothingly. Her eyes were glowing blue again. "He likes music."

"How did you know that?" Riley asked her in awe.

"I'm not sure," she said with a shrug. "I just do. This is very weird. If I wasn't so calm right now I think I'd be freaking out over it. I've never met him before, but I know exactly what to do to help him. With the other werewolves today I just had to give them a small touch. With him it's music."

Silence fell between them for a moment and then Raya started to sing. Riley recognized the song as one he used to listen to when he was in high school. He thought Raya's voice complimented it better than the original artist. She had a beautiful voice. She didn't sound like a professional singer, but it was powerful in it's own way. Even Riley, who wasn't prone to Raya's abilities, felt a bit more relaxed as she sang.

Before she finished the song, Jeremy opened his eyes and growled threateningly. The serenity Riley felt just moments before disappeared. He remembered the dead bodies that Jeremy mutilated the night before and he had to resisted the urge to clench his fists. Raya didn't even flinch as she continued singing. The girl had nerves of steel.

Riley studied Jeremy's body language during the duration of the song. He was stiff and his face looked feral in a way that Riley had never seen on any other werewolf before. His yellow eyes stared up at Raya's blue ones and she smiled softly at him while she sang. Riley couldn't help but think that it was a good thing Jeremy was injured. He had a feeling that they'd both be dead otherwise.

It took Riley by surprise when Jeremy's yellow eyes finally changed to brown. His facial expression shifted from feral to painfully confused. His body was still stiff, but his breathing became more human.

Then he started to hyperventilate.

Raya ran her fingers through Jeremy's bloody hair and continued singing. After a while his breathing slowed and his body seemed to relax slightly. Riley could see the cuts and bruises on his chest begin to heal.

"Who are you?" Jeremy whispered.

His furrowed brow gave away how immensely confused he was. He grabbed Raya's wrist and she stopped running her fingers through his hair. He'd grabbed her in such a quick motion that Riley bolted to his feet despite his injuries. He staggered from the pain, but adrenaline helped him ignore it. If Jeremy was going to hurt her he needed to think of something quickly.

But he didn't hurt her. He just held onto her wrist and stared her dead in the eyes in a challenging way. Raya stopped singing and gave him a small smile.

"It's okay," she said. "We came here to help you. You've been badly injured."

"No kidding," Jeremy grumbled. "Are you a werewolf?"

"Yes," Raya said in a less than soothing tone.

"Great," he said sarcastically.

Jeremy let go of Raya's arm and was suddenly on his feet.

"I'm Jeremy Masters," he said through a grimace. "Thanks for saving me, but why did you?"

Riley opened his mouth to speak, but Raya jumped in so he didn't have to use his voice.

"I'm Raya Adams and he's Riley Hanson. We're members of the rebellion. I think you know about it, anyway, we are here to save you and Aurora Ryder."

124

"Yeah, I kinda got that," Jeremy said, but he paused for a moment. "Wait...Riley Hanson? Aurora told me you were dead."

"I'm not," Riley whispered hoarsely.

"She'll be insanely happy about that, if...we need to go. Carvolo took her."

"We know," Riley whispered as reassuringly as he could. He felt anything but reassured himself, but he wanted to keep Jeremy as calm as possible. "Marcus and Gabriel went after her."

"Do you have a way of contacting them?

"Unfortunately, no," Raya said with a shake of her head.

"That's just fantastic," Jeremy said through a sarcastic sigh.

Riley got the feeling that he used sarcasm as a defense mechanism of some kind. As long as he didn't lose his mind Riley was okay with that.

"We need to get going," Riley rasped. "We have to find Rebecca."

"She's the witch-werewolf-hybrid, right?" Jeremy asked. "Aurora told me a little bit about you guys."

"Yes," Raya said with a nod. "We left her about a mile away to fight off a werewolf that tried to stop us from getting to you."

"We can talk on the way," Riley said as he stumbled forward.

"No offense, man," Jeremy said as he eyed Riley. "But you look like you've seen better days."

"Right back at ya," he replied gruffly. "I dropped a gun in the grass. Do you know how to use guns?"

"Um...it's been five years, but yes."

"I only shot it once so it's good to go," Riley said.

Jeremy picked up the gun and looked it over for a moment. As he got the feel of handling a gun again, Raya put one of Riley's arms over her shoulder. He knew he needed help walking, but he was sure that he was going to pass out if he had to keep his arm there. He gathered up the little energy that he

125

had recovered and used his pure magic to help with the pain. It helped him walk better, so Raya's hands were free to carry Riley's weapons for him.

Raya took point. Riley didn't want her to, but she knew where they were going and he couldn't do it. That left him in the middle and Jeremy at the rear. Normally, Riley would be nervous to have a stranger behind him, but he'd seen Jeremy help Aurora. That made him okay in his book. There was the possibility that he'd lose control, but Raya's abilities really were incredible.

They stumbled along through the forest a little faster than Riley should have. By the time they got to the small clearing where they left Rebecca, Riley was sweating excessively from pain.

It didn't help that his sister was nowhere to be seen. He fought down panic as he search for any clue that could tell him what happened to her.

He didn't have to search long. A furious yell, that sounded like Rebecca, came from the forest. Raya deposited Riley's quiver and bow on the ground and pulled out her handgun. She cocked it and ran toward the sound. Jeremy was about to follow her, but she turned to look at him as she ran.

"Stay with Riley," she said and then she disappeared.

"Okay..." Jeremy said awkwardly. "So what happened to you anyway?"

It took Riley a moment to realize that Jeremy had asked him a question.

"Which time?" Riley asked him humorlessly. "I'm currently suffering from four different incidences."

"That's fun," Jeremy said. Sarcasm again. He reminded Riley of Marcus, but his tone was a lot more dark.

"I got stabbed four times less than a week ago, started having visions that siphons energy out of me, one werewolf broke my ribs, and two more broke both my arms."

"Probably doesn't help that your wife has been missing," Jeremy said solemnly.

"I've had a few visions of you and Aurora," Riley said awkwardly. "I wanted to thank you for helping her like you did."

Jeremy stared at him in confusion as though he thought he'd misheard.

"Um, what?"

"Visions," Riley explained with a shrug. "I saw what Aurora was seeing. I can only do it because I'm a wizard."

Riley's throat was really hurting and he was worried about Rebecca so he didn't bother telling Jeremy about the wand. The poor guy looked like his head was about to explode as it was.

"I didn't do nearly enough," Jeremy said gruffly. "No thanks necessary. I'd do anything for her."

"One good thing has come from this," Riley whispered and resisted the urge to clear his throat. "At least you're free now."

Jeremy scoffed and looked away from him. He shifted slightly as he glared at the trees around them.

"You wouldn't say that if you knew me," Jeremy said with a hint of anger. "I need to be locked up."

"Raya can help you control your wolf. She's pretty amazing."

Jeremy was about to reply when a loud crashing sound came from the forest. Raya flew through the trees and landed a few yards away from them. Rebecca was close to follow and she would've knocked into Riley if she hadn't used her magic to slow her fall.

Jeremy rushed over to were Raya landed and helped her stand up. He took out Riley's gun and cocked it. Rebecca floated to the ground next to Riley in a matter of seconds. She looked battered and extremely angry. A large cut across her cheek was quickly scabbing over.

"Rebecca-"

"Not now, Riley!" she exclaimed furiously. "That sadistic piece of crap is going down!"

Riley gaped at her for a moment. He was fairly certain he'd never seen her this angry.

127

"And here I thought name calling was beneath you," Gerard chuckled as he walked through the trees. "My beautiful flower, why don't you just agree that I have won?"

"If you call me that one more time…"

Rebecca threw a very large purple energy ball at the werewolf. Gerard simply stepped out of the way and the electric ball disappeared. Riley was stunned. He'd never seen one of Rebecca's craticas spells disappear without someone using descenpian.

Gerard chuckled again.

"How many times are you going to try to use your magic against me? I already told you I am immune-"

A loud gun shot echoed through the clearing and blood squirted from Gerard's shirt. The gigantic werewolf immediately dropped to the ground without so much as a gasp. His body twitched slightly and Jeremy shot the dead werewolf a few more times for good measure. The body didn't twitch again after that.

"Where the freak did Sasquatch come from?" Jeremy asked incredulously.

He lowered the gun slowly. He was shaking slightly from pain and malnutrition. Riley was sure that he felt uneasy with strangers after going through that kind of torture; plus he'd just killed someone with a handgun. If that didn't put someone into shock, Riley wasn't sure what would.

Rebecca stared at the extremely bloody Jeremy with wide eyes. She panted slightly from the adrenaline come down and then grimaced when she noticed Riley's condition.

"Seriously!" she exclaimed in exasperation. "You are not leaving my side again. What happened to you?"

"Calm down, sis," Riley replied.

"Riley," Rebecca said darkly. "You do realize that telling someone to calm down only makes things worse, right?"

"What happened?" he asked in a hoarse whisper. "Why was he immune to magic?"

"Why do you sound like that?"

"He got strangled by one of the werewolves," Raya said unhelpfully.

128

Rebecca's eyes flashed yellow for a moment and she took a deep breath. Her fight with Gerard had really ticked her off and Riley's physical condition was only making it worse.

"I'm not exactly sure why he was immune to magic," Rebecca said tightly. "He would've been dead a long time ago if he wasn't. I guess we'll never know."

Raya was about to ask her another question when Jeremy cleared his throat.

"Not to interrupt," Jeremy said. "But shouldn't we get going?"

"Jeremy's right," Riley rasped.

"You should stop talking. It sounds painful."

Riley sighed and blinked a few times to clear his head. Rebecca was right, it did hurt to talk, but talking was the only thing he could do at the moment. Every other part of him was useless. Rebecca picked up Riley's weapons that were on the ground and strapped them to her back. She looked fearsome with two sets of bows and quivers, or maybe it was her angry expression that gave the unsettling effect.

They began their journey back to the parking lot. Riley had to draw upon more of his pure magic to make it through the forest. He was going to crash very soon and it wasn't going to be enjoyable. Jeremy looked like he was in the same situation, but neither of them complained. The girls lead the way and had to slow down a few times to let the guys catch up. It took a couple hours going at the pace they were. By the time they made it to the parking lot the sun was setting.

Riley's heart sank when he noticed no one was waiting for them next to the cars. They should've been back already.

"This day just keeps getting worse," Rebecca said in frustration.

"Where are they?" Raya asked worriedly. "Something must've gone wrong."

"I'm going to go find them," Rebecca said. "Raya, you stay here with them."

Jeremy shook his head quickly.

"I'll come with you," Jeremy said. "I know I don't look it, but I can help."

"No, I'm not leaving Raya and Riley here alone."

Jeremy glanced at them and saw how scared Raya was. His face softened slightly and he gave Rebecca a small nod. Riley had a feeling that he was only agreeing with her because of Raya's emotions. If the situation had been different Jeremy wouldn't have been as easily persuaded to sit out on the action.

"I don't suppose I have a say in any of this?" Riley asked half-heartedly.

"No," Rebecca and Jeremy said in unison.

Riley raised an eyebrow at them. They were both definitely dominate werewolf leaders.

"Well, I'm going to speak my mind anyway," he said with a grimace. "If dad, Marcus, Gabriel, and Raven are down then you're not going to have much of a fighting chance on your own. You are either going to die or get captured."

Raya gasped a little at Riley voicing what they were all thinking. Carvolo must've killed or captured them. If she had been scared before, now she was terrified. Riley felt bad for her, but he didn't know what to do to help her. Jeremy put a hand on her shoulder and quickly let it drop when she looked at his bloodied hand with frightened eyes.

"It'll be okay," Jeremy said to her gently.

Raya looked at his gore covered face and hugged her stomach shakily. Riley knew exactly how she must be feeling. Raven was in danger. Rebecca was trying to tell her to stay put, while a guy who looked like a survivor of a horror movie tried to comfort her. Riley glanced at Rebecca and saw that she was reloading her handgun. She looked him in the eye with determination etched into her features.

"I'm coming back, I promise," she told him calmly.

Riley couldn't help it. He panicked.

There was no way that Rebecca could know this, but those were exactly the last words that Aurora had said to him. He wasn't letting Rebecca go out there alone. It would be over his dead body if she did.

He strode to the van and opened the back doors with his magic. Before he could pass out from magical overuse, or process Rebecca's verbal disagreement of his actions, the wand was in his hand.

The reaction was immediate, like it had been the first time he grabbed the wand when he was dying from the stab wounds caused by Jenna's blades. Blue light erupted around his body and he heard Jeremy string swearwords together in a rather creative way. He wasn't expecting the magical blue light, but it took away his pain and gave him the energy he needed. He took a deep breath for the first time since his ribs got bashed in. His head cleared and his arms were somewhat usable again.

"What the…" Jeremy whispered. "What just happened?"

Riley ignored him and focused on his infuriated werewolf sister.

"Riley," Rebecca said sternly. "What did you just do?"

"You're not going into the woods without me," Riley said in a dangerous tone that he'd never used with her before. "We are staying together. I am *not* going to lose you too."

Maybe it was his tone of voice, or possibly the expression on his face, but Rebecca didn't argue with him any further. Her face softened and she looked at the ground. Riley grabbed a box of protein bars with a bottle of water from the back of the van and tossed them to Jeremy. The werewolf took no time at all opening the package. It must've been a long time since he'd last eaten. He devoured the whole box of protein bars in just a couple of minutes. It was so fast that Riley worried he'd throw it all up if he wasn't careful.

"Raya? Jeremy?" Riley asked. "Are you guys good to go?"

Raya nodded in timid determination and Jeremy mumbled a 'yes' through a mouthful of protein bar.

"This was not what I had in mind," Rebecca said in a defeated voice.

"Gabriel would kill me if I let you go alone," Riley said in a more gentle tone than he'd used with her previously. Maybe it was the initial effects of the wand that made him so rudely adamant before.

Riley grabbed two more handguns and tucked them into his empty holsters and stocked up on more silver bullets. By the time they were ready to go, Jeremy looked a bit more durable and Raya seemed to have some of her courage back. Riley felt tingly all over from the magic the wand gave him. It was a bit uncomfortable, but it was something that he would have to get used to.

Suddenly, a gush of wind knocked into Riley and he stumbled into Raya. He gripped the wand tightly and sent a magical bolt at the person that appeared next to them.

He realized too late that it was Jackson.

The bolt hit the vampire and he fell over with a loud gasp. He stood up just as quickly as he fell. If he were anything other than a vampire he wouldn't have gotten up so quickly.

"Ouch," he whispered tightly.

"Dad!" Riley exclaimed angrily. "Don't do that!"

Rebecca hurried over to Jackson and threw her arms around his neck. He hugged her back, but Riley didn't miss the grim expression that clouded his face.

Something had happened.

Fear gripped Riley when he noticed that the others hadn't arrived with him.

"What happened?" Riley asked. "Did you guys find Aurora?"

"Where's everyone else?" Raya asked timidly.

Jackson released Rebecca and took a small step back.

"In the woods," Jackson said in a small voice. "Not very far in."

Rebecca turned toward the trees, but Jackson grabbed her arm to stop her.

"Something bad happened," he said defeatedly. "We completely failed."

Chapter 9

Despair hit Riley so hard that he almost fell down. He sank into the back of the van and almost dropped the wand. He gripped it tighter in hopes that it would give him a vision of Aurora, or do something to help the situation.

It didn't do anything.

"What do you mean?" Rebecca said in a panic. "Are the guys hurt? Is Gabriel hurt?"

"Marcus and Gabriel are hurt, but they'll be fine."

Jackson didn't sound very reassuring. He glanced at Raya with sorrow clouding his normally bright blue eyes. Grim lines tugged at his mouth as he searched for the words he needed to say.

"No," Raya said firmly.

She took a step back as though she needed to distance herself from Jackson.

"Raya," Jackson said in a gentle voice. There was genuine grief in his eyes. "I'm so sorry. Raven-"

"No," Raya said more aggressively this time.

She staggered backwards and held up a shaky finger as though warning Jackson not to continue. To not say the words that would shatter her already broken world. Her body shook so hard that Riley could almost hear her teeth slamming together.

She looked like she was about to collapse, so Riley hurried over to her. He hugged her tightly as she sobbed into his shirt.

Jeremy was standing close to them with yellow fury burning in his eyes. It was obvious that Raya's grief over Raven's death was making him aggressive. Maybe he was just being protective, but there was enough rage in his expression that it made Riley nervous.

He tightened his fist where he thought the wand still was, but he grabbed nothing but the back of Raya's shirt. It was then that he realized he had left the wand in the van. He had no idea why he was still conscious.

133

Riley watched Jeremy nervously. The werewolf stood perfectly still and blinked a few times. His eyes eventually went back to normal, but he kept clenching and unclenching his fists. Riley turned his attention back to Raya who was still crying uncontrollably. Comforting her was almost distracting enough to keep his mind off of Aurora…almost.

"We need to figure out what to do," Jackson said as sensitively as he could.

Riley knew what Jackson meant. They couldn't drive around with a dead body in the car. They needed to find a way to bury Raven in a way that no one would be able to find the grave. Riley knew exactly how to do that, but for now he just held Raya. She had such a tight grip on him that he was worried she might crack more of his ribs, but he forced himself to ignore the pain.

Riley wasn't sure how long they stood there, but he didn't think he breathed the entire time. When Raya finally let go he took a deep breath and shuddered. He suddenly needed to know what happened. Especially what happened to Aurora. He couldn't believe that she hadn't been rescued. He couldn't help but think if he had gone after her with the wand she would be with them now.

Raven would still be alive.

"What happened?" Riley asked Jackson hoarsely.

Rebecca put an arm around Raya's shoulders before Jackson could speak.

"I'm not exactly sure," Jackson said. "Marcus and I weren't there. Gabriel was with Raven when…when it happened. I came to get you guys. We'll explain everything together."

Jackson beckoned them to follow him and he disappeared into the tree line. Riley stopped by the van and grabbed the wand. When he shut the doors he noticed Jeremy was still standing next to the van. His eyes were yellow again and he blinked a few times before they turned back to brown.

Riley wondered how much effect Raya's tamer abilities had on him before she found out Raven was dead. He didn't know what was going on with Jeremy. He didn't want to ask, but he knew he had to in case he became enraged again.

"Are you in control?" Riley asked him pointedly.

"You would know it if I wasn't," Jeremy replied in a low growl.

"I know you're in control now. I guess I'm just wondering if you can keep it that way. Raya is not in a state of mind to help you out right now."

The werewolf sighed and shook his head dejectedly.

"I don't know," Jeremy said honestly. "With Aurora still gone and Raya's distress…I'm fighting for it pretty hard. Not to mention the fact that I don't know any of you."

"If you so much as look like you might be losing it," Riley said warningly. "Then I will stop you."

Riley held up the wand and Jeremy stared at it. Riley didn't want to threaten him, but he knew what Jeremy was capable of if he lost control. For the first time since they'd rescued him Jeremy seemed to fully relax. It took Riley by surprise.

"Good," Jeremy said with a nod. "That makes me feel a lot better."

Jeremy followed Rebecca and Raya to the tree line, leaving Riley standing next to the van alone for a moment. He took a shaky breath and followed the supernatural group into the woods.

Jackson had been right when he said they weren't far into the woods. Marcus and Gabriel looked awful. Marcus had deep cuts along his arms and legs. His face was bruised and swollen in some places. Even without the bruises he still would've looked grim. There was no hopeful spark in his eyes like there usually was. But when Marcus saw Jeremy his expression brightened a little.

Gabriel's injuries were a lot worse. He had a crooked leg and a few holes in his stomach that were bleed profusely. It didn't look like there was a section of skin on his body that wasn't bruised or bleeding. He seemed to be moments away from passing out. His face was tight with pain, but he sat there in silence. He didn't seem to notice that they had arrived until Rebecca hurried over to him. Gabriel's agonized expression turned to relief when she knelt next to him. She sat him up a little and let him lean against her.

Riley finally spotted Raven's corpse. Someone had covered him with one of the sleeping bags from the van. Raya knelt down next to the body. She was no longer sobbing, but silent tears fell down her face. Jeremy stood apart from the group, maybe a little closer to Raya, but he looked uncomfortable. Riley was content to see that he didn't look enraged anymore. It probably helped him to see a couple of people that he actually knew.

"Jeremy," Marcus said as he stood up. "It's good to see you."

"Good to see you too, Marcus," Jeremy replied with a nod.

Marcus limped up to Jeremy. He ignored Jeremy's bloodied clothes and gave him a quick hug. Jeremy swore quietly as he briefly patted Marcus's back.

"Dude, you know I hate that."

Marcus gave him a small smirk and rested a hand on his shoulder.

"Good to see you haven't changed, Jeremy."

"Is Gabriel okay?" Riley asked Marcus in a whisper.

"He will be," Marcus said. "I think he's a bit better now that he knows you guys are okay. Especially Rebecca."

"I can't believe Gabriel is married," Jeremy said.

"A lot has happened," Marcus replied grimly. "I'm really sorry, Jeremy."

"Don't apologize. It's not your fault," he said with a shake of his head.

"I may not be at fault for a lot of things, but I'm definitely at fault for this."

Jeremy growled in annoyance, but it wasn't aggressive.

"Are you guys going to tell us what happened?" Riley asked impatiently.

"We split up when we first left the parking lot," Jackson began. "Gabriel and Raven went one way. Marcus and I went another. We figured we would cover more distance that way. Even with my speed we didn't want to chance losing her. Marcus and I found Carvolo's trail and we caught up to him pretty quickly, but Aurora wasn't with him."

"She wasn't?" Riley asked. "Where was she then?"

"We didn't know it at the time," Marcus said. "But another leader took her to create a diversion in case we were on their trail."

"We attacked Carvolo, but he had a lot of followers with him," Jackson continued. "Long story short; he ended up escaping after an intense fight. Marcus was injured and I couldn't leave him to follow Carvolo."

Marcus scoffed, which was an odd sound to hear from him. He gave Jackson a nasty glower that was uncharacteristic of him.

"I told Jackson to go anyway, but he ignored me," Marcus said as he folded his arms.

"Carvolo poisoned you with welhum," Jackson argued.

"He's always poisoning someone with welhum," the skinwalker stated firmly. "That doesn't change the fact that he got away."

Now it was Jackson's turn to fold his arms and a flash of bloodlust crossed his eyes.

"We were surrounded by followers. I made a judgment call."

"Yeah," Marcus said sarcastically. "A stupid one."

Jackson held his hands out in exasperation and took a deep breath. Bloodlust flashed in his eyes again before he closed them.

Apparently, he and Marcus weren't very happy with each other at the moment.

"What's done is done." Gabriel's voice gurgled a little as he spoke. "If you two don't knock it off, I'll finish the fight for you. I'm not kidding."

Everyone looked at Gabriel in surprise. His face didn't show any sign that he was angry, but they all knew that he was. He usually didn't threaten people that could wipe the floor with him. It didn't matter anyway because Gabriel's leg was broken. He looked like he'd been stabbed more than a few times and if the bruises were any indication, he'd been severely beaten.

Marcus and Jackson glanced at each other warily, but didn't say anything. Apparently they were taking Gabriel's threat seriously despite how injured he was. Marcus gave Jackson a curt nod and the vampire shrugged in reply.

"Raven and I caught up with a werewolf leader named Tomas," Gabriel spoke softly. "He's one of the old werewolves that was born that way, like Carvolo and Demian. He had so many followers with him I didn't get a chance to count, or even guess, how many opponents Raven and I were facing. I knew we wouldn't survive if we fought them so I tried a diplomatic approach at first. Then Tomas decided to bring Aurora out for us to see her. I knew he was trying to bait me, but when I first saw her I…I lost it. If Raven hadn't pulled me back the fighting would've started a lot sooner."

"What did they do to her?" Riley whispered. He was so terrified that he almost couldn't find his voice.

"I'm not going to tell you," Gabriel replied through gritted teeth.

"Why not?" Riley would've yelled but his throat would allow him to.

"Because if I couldn't handle it you definitely won't be able to," he said grimly.

"Right now I'm imagining the worse possible scenario, Gabriel," Riley said, his voice cracking.

"She's still alive, Riley. At least, she was when I last saw her."

"What happened to Raven?" Rebecca asked in a small voice.

Raya's eyes shot toward Gabriel. They glowed yellow in the darkness as her wolf attempted to ease her pain. Gabriel hesitated for a moment when he glanced at her. Rebecca ran

138

her fingers through Gabriel's dark hair to try to soothe him. He closed his eyes for a moment at her touch and then cleared his throat.

"We were surrounded. So the only option to attempt to get Aurora out of there was to negotiate a trade."

"Seriously?" Marcus asked angrily.

"It's Aurora, Marcus." Gabriel weakly met his brother's eyes. "You didn't see what I saw. You would've done the same thing. Even Raven stepped in and tried to trade himself for her at one point. Two of us for her and they still didn't go for it. I don't know what Carvolo has planned for her, but it's big enough that they wouldn't make the trade.

"When they said no, Raven released his grip on my fur and we both attacked. They were typical followers...not very challenging opponents. There was just a lot of them. We became overrun at one point when I was still in my wolf skin. One of the werewolves stuck a knife in me. It had been dipped in welhum and I couldn't stay in my wolf skin. While I was changing...Raven was stabbed in the heart."

Gabriel paused for a moment and took a deep breath. His whole body was shaking now from pain and exhaustion, both physical and emotional.

"I don't exactly remember everything that happened afterwards. I do remember being stabbed a lot. Somehow I got a hold of a knife and I went completely insane. I don't think the werewolf that killed Raven was expecting me to get back up after being stabbed multiple times. I was just...out of my mind at that point."

Gabriel paused again and turned his head to look at Raya.

"I'm so sorry that I couldn't save him, Raya," he said solemnly. "But rest assured his killer is dead. It wasn't an easy death for him either."

Raya nodded once and looked back at the ground. Her shoulders shook as she began silently crying again. Jeremy, a little cautiously, sat down next to her. Not close enough to touch her, but enough to let her know he was there.

The unstable werewolf earned Riley's respect in that moment.

Gabriel seemed to be getting groggy, but he soldiered on with his story.

"After I calmed down a bit I realized that most of the followers surrounding me were dead. I'm pretty sure I killed them, but it's all a little fuzzy. So I went after Tomas, who still had Aurora. When he realized I was running toward them-"

"You were running?" Rebecca interrupted in concern. "After being stabbed?"

"Sprinting, actually," Gabriel replied gruffly. "I've never had an adrenaline rush like that in my life. I doubt I'll ever have one like it again. Anyway, Tomas saw me coming for him and he took off pretty quickly with Aurora. He was faster than I was, but he didn't have to go far. He had an airplane in a large clearing. I think the werewolves use it to get easy access to the Montana den. By the time I reached the airplane, Tomas was already taking off with Aurora inside."

There was silence for a while as everyone processed what Gabriel told them. Rebecca took off her sweater and took the blood-soaked t-shirt off of Gabriel's stab wounds. She placed the sweater over the wounds and applied pressure. Gabriel didn't flinch, but more color drained from his face. His lips were white and sweat dripped down his forehead.

"So," Jeremy said as he looked at Gabriel. "How did you break your leg?"

"I jumped on the airplane while it was taking off. I couldn't hold on without my supernatural strength and I fell when it went airborne."

"You're lucky you didn't die," Rebecca said in a broken voice. Gabriel gave her hand a weak reassuring squeeze.

"Someone still needs to set his leg," Marcus said. "He wouldn't let me do it."

"That's because you're injured," Gabriel whispered.

Jackson stepped forward and grabbed Gabriel's leg. Rebecca braced Gabriel's shoulders while her father quickly set it. Gabriel groaned, but the sound of bones cracking was louder.

140

"Usually people count to three first." Gabriel panted through gritted teeth.

"That just makes people tense for the pain," Jackson said. "It hurts less when you're relaxed."

"I don't think that applies to him right now," Rebecca mumbled with her face pressed into Gabriel's hair. Riley could see that she was trying to hide her tears.

Shortly after, Jackson left to get medical supplies and more food. Rebecca was busy attending to Gabriel, so that left Riley to magically prepare a grave for Raven. It wasn't something he'd ever done before, but he knew that the wand would know how. He walked around the forest, not very far from the group, to find a place that would be suitable. He was so out of it that he didn't hear Raya come up behind him. She startled him when she made a noise that sounded like a hiccup.

"I think he'd like to be buried here," she whispered as she pointed to a tree. "He always liked the forest and the western larch was his favorite tree. They reminded him of home."

Riley nodded and took a deep breath. He wasn't sure if it would be easy to bury someone beneath a tree. He didn't want to damage the roots, but he was sure that the wand could make it happen. If Raven couldn't have a proper funeral than he should at least be buried in a memorable spot.

Riley held out the wand and let the magic take over. He put his trust in the wand to protect the roots of the tree while creating a suitable grave for Raven. It didn't take long for the hole to appear. Riley noticed Raya watching him with wide eyes. She wasn't crying at the moment, but her face looked like she was in agony. She hugged herself around her stomach and shivered.

"I know it's not the traditional way to prepare a grave," Riley said quietly. "But at least this way the magic will protect him forever. Nothing will ever be able to disturb him."

Raya nodded, though Riley wasn't sure if she heard what he had said. Her eyes were glazed over as she stared at

141

the deep dark hole. She visibly shook herself and stepped closer to him. She reached up and kissed his cheek.

"Thank you," she whispered as a tear dripped from her eye. "I know you're in pain too, but you still comforted me and prepared Raven's grave. You're an amazing person and one of my best friends. I just wanted you to know that."

Raya hurried back through the trees to where everyone else was. As Riley watched her go all of the emotional pain hit him with an intensity that shocked him. He tried to suppress it. He knew that it was stupid to let his pure magic take over, but he couldn't handle it anymore. He wanted to feel nothing for a while...or for forever.

The wand grew hot in his hand as he tried to let his pure magic suppress his pain. The wand was fighting him. It was preventing his pure magic from taking control. He tried to drop it, but he couldn't pry his fingers open. He inhaled and exhaled so fast that he was at risk of hyperventilating. Then he felt a dull ache behind his eyes.

Suppressing your emotions will accomplish nothing...
It's selfish...

Riley gasped as he heard the wand's voice in his head. It wasn't controlling him like it had in the past. At least it wasn't controlling his mind. He still couldn't drop the wand like he wanted to.

It won't bring your friend back.
It won't bring your lover back.

Riley sank to his knees. The voice didn't talk again and the wand instantly cooled. He had full control of his hand, but he kept his hold on the wand. He knew the wand was right. It would only cause more problems if he suppressed his emotions. Aurora needed him to be strong and being strong meant he couldn't give up. Letting his pure magic take over would be a form of defeat.

Besides, Rebecca would never forgive him.

He placed the wand on his lap and buried his face in his hands.

And he let himself feel every painful emotion.

142

Riley moved the wand over Raven's grave. The dirt magically placed itself over the body as though the ground had never been disturbed in the first place. As though there was no grave there at all. It was a good thing the western larch was there. It was the prefect grave marker since they couldn't put a normal one there. He couldn't help but notice Raya's pale face and how hard her body shook from grief.

Jeremy put his hand on her shoulder. She didn't seem scared by his touch this time and he kept it there. Eventually she raised her own hand and held onto his fingers in a death grip.

Jackson, Marcus, and Rebecca stood near the grave with bowed heads and slumped shoulders. Gabriel had fallen asleep when Jackson had given him the pain medication he came back with. They didn't want to wait any longer to put Raven's body to rest, so they decided to let Gabriel sleep through the burial.

They all said a few words except for Jeremy who hadn't known him at all. It was apparent that he was only there to support Raya if she wanted it. She must have really made a huge impact on him. Riley figured he probably wouldn't want to be away from her tamer abilities for a while. There was no way of knowing the full extent of psychological damage that five years of torture and solitary confinement had on Jeremy, but his lack of control was an indication.

Rebecca reverently murmured the protection spell incantation that the fairies had taught her. She held her hand toward the grave and a fluid-like purple mist seeped from her fingertips. It swirled through the air and buried itself into the dirt where Raven's body rested. When the mist disappeared Rebecca lowered her hand slowly. She gave Raya a hug and was the first to leave the gravesite.

Riley stayed for a few minutes longer then decided to follow Rebecca. He was emotionally and physically exhausted.

143

All he could think about was sleep. His stomach growled a reminder that he hadn't eaten in a while and after that all he could think about was food. He was surprised that he even had an appetite after everything that happened.

He got to their campsite that Jackson and Jeremy had set up. There were two tents with a smoldering campfire that held a pot of soup for dinner.

Riley didn't know why they decided to stay there. He was certain that there were followers in the mountains still. He couldn't shake the feeling that they could be attacked at any moment. But everyone was exhausted and Jackson still wanted to find the den and, as he put it, 'blow it sky-high'. No one but Riley seemed to be concerned about the potential threat, especially since all the leaders had escaped. He knew that once he put the wand down he would faint into a coma-like sleep. It was good to know he wouldn't have to worry about their enemies for however long he slept.

Riley grabbed a bowl and ladled soup into it while keeping a firm grip on the wand. He didn't want to sleep until he'd eaten, especially since he might sleep for a long time. Rebecca peeked her head out of the tent door and beckoned for him to come in.

"What's wrong?" he asked after he swallowed. "Is Gabriel okay?"

"He's sleeping, so he's fine for now," she said. "I just think we should talk."

Riley pointed to his bowl of soup and shook his head.

"Rule number one of camping; don't keep food in the tent. The bears might eat us."

He wasn't in the mood for talking anyway.

Rebecca gave him an exasperated look and rolled her eyes. Bears were the least of their worries.

Riley ate the rest of his soup a little slower than when he'd started. He knew what Rebecca wanted to talk about and he didn't think he could handle it. He didn't know how long he'd been gone from the group after Raya left him in the woods. It was long enough that they noticed he was gone.

144

He was sure that someone spotted his private breakdown. The problem with how close knit they were with each other was that it was almost impossible to grieve without an audience. Riley hated it. He wanted to be alone, but Rebecca wasn't going to let that happen. She was probably right though. He shouldn't be alone.

Riley rinsed his bowl and spoon in the bucket of water before following Rebecca into the tent. Gabriel was shirtless with bandages wrapped around his various wounds. He was asleep against the wall of the tent. He laid on top of a sleeping bag with a blanket wrapped around him. It wasn't the warmest way to sleep, but with his broken leg it would be impossible to use the sleeping bag properly. Rebecca sat next to her husband and waited for Riley to kick off his shoes.

"I set up a place for you to sleep," Rebecca said as she gestured to the sleeping bag on the other side of the small tent. It was close quarters, but at least they'd all be somewhat warm.

"Thanks," Riley mumbled.

He crawled into the sleeping bag.

"So," Rebecca said awkwardly. "I think we need to talk."

Riley grabbed the satchel that he kept the wand in.

"No, Riley, don't," she said hastily as he dropped the wand inside it.

Riley closed his eyes in preparation of crashing. He felt the magical connection sever and it was almost like he'd been punched in the stomach. But he was still conscious. Still awake.

He opened his eyes and took a few deep breaths. Rebecca eyed him with a scornful look.

"Darn it," he mumbled tiredly.

"How are you still awake?"

"I don't know," he said with a disheartened shrug. "Maybe I'm getting used to it."

"If you didn't want to talk you could've just said so," Rebecca said quietly.

"I don't want to talk."

Silence fell between them and Rebecca checked to make sure Gabriel was still asleep.

145

"You don't have to talk," she said in a low whisper. "But I need you to listen."

Riley glanced at her and took a deep breath. He didn't want to listen either, but he was pretty sure that wasn't an option.

"I saw what you tried to do. You tried to let your pure magic suppress your emotions again."

Riley didn't respond. He made no indication that she was right or wrong. They both knew what he tried to do. He wasn't going to confirm or deny it. He just waited for her to tell him how stupid he was.

"I'm not sure what prevented you from succeeding, but I'm glad you're still here. That you're still *you*. I don't know what I would do if I lost you like that."

A tear fell down Rebecca's cheek and he had to look away from her. Crying had been contagious lately and he didn't want to deal with that again.

"I know why you tried to do it. So I'm not going to ask you if you're okay because I know you're not. I'm not going to tell you how stupid that was because I'm sure you've already told yourself that anyway.

"But, Riley, Roan told us that most wizards don't come back from losing their control to their pure magic. You've already come back from it once which defied all odds. The fact that you tried to let it take over again…"

She paused to take a shaky breath and he glanced over at her again. She wasn't crying anymore, but she had a broken expression that he'd never seen from her before. It sent chills down his spine. He had to resist the urge to look away when she stared into his eyes.

"You tried to do something that would end up, eventually, killing you. I want you to know; that hurts me."

There was a pause as what she said crashed into Riley like an emotional semi-truck. The pain it caused almost felt physical.

"I don't know what I would say to Aurora if we lost you to your pure magic."

146

Riley couldn't stay silent anymore. He still didn't want to talk, but he thought it was necessary now.

"The wand stopped me and talked me out of it," Riley said quietly. "I wasn't thinking straight. I realized that Aurora needed me to remain myself. I also knew that you would never forgive me. I hoped that you wouldn't find out about it."

Rebecca stared at him with wide eyes for a moment.

"I watched your whole body glow blue for about five minutes. When you started crying I figured what you were trying to do didn't work. I was so upset with you that I almost yelled at you right then and there. But I realized that would've been counter productive. You're lucky I've cooled down a bit."

"I'm really sorry, Rebecca," Riley said sincerely.

"Don't be sorry," she said softly. "Just promise me you won't do anything like that again."

Riley nodded and closed his eyes.

"Promise," he mumbled.

It wasn't long before he fell into a restless sleep.

Aurora couldn't breathe. The claustrophobic situation made her anxious. Usually she was more calm in tight spaces, but there were two people in the small trunk. She had a hood over her head, so she didn't know who it was. It also didn't help that her entire body hurt. To say that she had been brutalized by Tomas would be an understatement. The psychological torment wasn't something she was used to and it was getting to her. They were slowly breaking her.

Watching Raven die had been horrible and seeing Gabriel go completely out of his mind was almost just as bad. She couldn't get the images out of her mind. She also couldn't help but feel guilty about how much Gabriel and Raven begged to take her place. That had been extremely traumatic since she'd never seen Gabriel beg before. When Tomas told Gabriel exactly what he had planned to do with her, Gabriel actually cried… That horrible memory would stick with Aurora forever.

147

Aurora had tried to fight them off. Especially when Carvolo had separated her from Jeremy. She was sure that he was dead now. What the followers were doing to him when she was dragged away… She didn't think anyone could survive that. By the time Tomas had her, there was no fight left in her. When she saw Gabriel, some of the fight came back, but she had been too weak to act on it.

Her heart ached for Gabriel. She was sure that he was dead too. She remembered getting a glimpse of him holding onto the plane as they took off. If he had survived the fall he would've bled to death from his injuries. She was surprised he had the strength to chase the plane down with how badly he was bleeding.

First Riley, then Jeremy, and now Gabriel. If she ever found out that Marcus was dead she would completely lose hope. She would actively try to find a way to die then. She didn't think she could live with knowing how alone she was.

Carvolo was winning.

The car came to a stop and the trunk opened abruptly. Someone yanked the hood off of her head and pulled her out of the trunk by her hair. She flinched, but didn't make a sound. She knew she wouldn't be able to stand and when her feet hit the ground her knees buckled. It took her a moment to realize that Tomas was the one who had her. She panicked again. It wasn't very often that she was terrified, but she was truly alone now.

The werewolf held her up and pulled her close to him. Too close. She could feel his breath on the back of her neck and she shuddered in disgust. His touch made her skin crawl and she felt dirty just by association with this monster. If she didn't have welhum coursing through her veins she would've fought him off.

"Wouldn't want you to fall," Tomas said in a husky voice.

Aurora whimpered. She couldn't help it. It hurt to be forced to stand and Tomas's strong hold on her didn't help.

"What's wrong? Your father wouldn't want to see you in such a cowardly state," he said with mocked concern. "Or

148

maybe he would. Who knows with him? I've known him for so many centuries and I still can't get a read on him most of time. It's infuriating."

Aurora didn't know why he was monologuing, but it was somehow terrifying. His mouth crept closer to her ear with each word he spoke and she shuddered at the stench of his breath. He was a very disgusting individual.

"Get the witch out of the trunk," a voice said.

Aurora tried to find who it was in the dark, but she couldn't see much. A terrible screech came from the witch as one of the werewolves pulled her out of the trunk that Aurora had occupied with her.

Aurora gasped when she realized who it was.

"Jenna," Aurora whispered angrily.

She had killed Riley and she had been in the trunk right next to her. Hot fury coursed through her and all she wanted in that moment was to get her hands on the witch.

If some of the fighting fire came back to Aurora, it was quickly doused when Tomas threw her to the ground with his werewolf strength. She didn't even try to move when Tomas squatted down next to her.

"I wouldn't talk again if I were you," he sneered.

"Tomas," Carvolo said warningly.

"You gave her to me," Tomas said with a smirky tone. "Did you not?"

"That was temporary," Carvolo replied. "Don't do that again."

"Or what?" Tomas countered with a deadly grin.

Carvolo's sadistic laugh echoed through the night.

"I think we both know what will happen, Tomas."

"I'm not that easy to kill, Carvolo," Tomas said in a low dangerous voice.

Tomas grabbed Aurora around the waist and made her stand up again. She was instantly lightheaded from the pain and exertion. She couldn't pull away from him if she tried.

"Let's not be uncivilized," Carvolo said assertively. "We need to make a deal with the witch. I was hoping you and I

149

would be on the same side. My daughter can be negotiated later."

"I'm no ones property," Aurora whispered defiantly.

Carvolo laughed.

"Spoken like a true Ryder," he said sarcastically. "You never cease to make me proud."

Aurora didn't understand that at all since Ryder was their mother's surname. As far as she knew Carvolo didn't have one of those.

"What do you want with me!" Jenna screamed angrily.

"Is the magical suppressant wearing off yet, witch?" Carvolo asked. "We created it especially for magical beings. It takes away their magic for a few hours. I'm hoping you have it back to place a stronger protection spell on Aurora."

"Why would I help you?" Jenna said fiercely. "You kidnapped me."

"If you do then I will forgive you for killing my chosen one," Carvolo said. "All my fairy allies are gone, so I need a replacement. I believe you will do."

"Huh," Jenna said thoughtfully. "What if I refuse?"

"Then I have no problem killing you where you stand."

Jenna laughed hysterically and Carvolo watched her with hungry eyes.

"You've convinced me," she said happily. "It also helps that I despise Aurora. If any of her little friends are trying to find her I would love to put a stop to it."

"They won't be able to once we get her to the Ancients Den," Carvolo said. "I would also like to put the protective responsibilities of our ancient ones on your shoulders. If you would be willing to accept?"

"Wow, Carvolo," Aurora said through a pained grunt. "You're desperate."

Carvolo spared her a quick glance, but otherwise ignored her comment.

"That is actually a very interesting proposition," Jenna said.

150

"You're the most powerful magical being of your kind," Carvolo said. "The Ancients Den is still protected by Arothor's spells, but it'd be convenient if you would be the keeper."

"Of course," Jenna said with a grin. "I will be your ally, but I will not be a prisoner. I get to do as I please."

Carvolo's smile was all teeth as he took a step closer to Jenna.

"I wouldn't have it any other way," Carvolo said. "Shall we make this official then?"

Jenna grinned and muttered a complicated incantation. She and Carvolo shook hands and a black mist swirled around their arms.

"If you betray me or I you," Jenna said quietly. "We both die."

"Sounds fair," Carvolo said with a smirk.

Then they kissed. Aurora's stomach twisted as she resisted the urge to gag. She didn't know if it was from the grotesque scene or the trauma she'd been through that made her nauseous.

"I believe the rebel fairies have been tracking Aurora somehow. They seem to be on our trail since we've captured her. I need you to put a stop to that."

"Anything for you, my dear," Jenna said happily.

Jenna muttered a very long and harsh sounding incantation. The air around them became dense with black magic.

Aurora coughed as black smoke engulfed her.

Chapter 10

Riley came out of the vision slowly. The last few bits were blurred and hard to remember. He sat up with a small gasp. He was sweating and his heart felt like it was going to beat out of his chest. It caused a dull ache that got more painful by the second.

He took a few deep breaths and glanced around him. It was dark in the tent and Rebecca was gone. He looked over at Gabriel and saw that he was awake. He was pale and completely motionless. If it weren't for the way his eyes shifted he would've looked like he was dead.

Which wasn't comforting at all.

"What did you see?' Gabriel asked hesitantly.

"Nothing good," Riley said as he rubbed his eyes with shaking hands. "Jenna is working for Carvolo now. She put a spell on Aurora. I don't think that I'll be having visions of her anymore."

Gabriel swore.

"They're taking her to the Ancients Den."

Gabriel swore again and tried to sit up, but laid back down when red circles appeared on his bandages. Riley didn't know why he thought sitting up would help the situation.

"Don't move, man," Riley said in a hollow tone. "The last thing we need is for you to bleed to death."

"We have to do something," Gabriel croaked quietly.

Riley didn't reply. He felt the same way, but he didn't know what they could do. Demian had been searching for the Ancients Den for centuries and they still didn't know where it was. They had vampires that could run faster than any other creature on the planet and they still weren't fast enough to find it. Arothor had warded the Ancients Den with protective spells centuries ago that can't be broken. Riley didn't want to believe that Aurora was lost to them forever, but he couldn't help but feel hopeless.

Suddenly, a loud explosion sounded in the mountains that shook the ground slightly. Riley instinctively grabbed the wand and scrambled out of his sleeping bag. Gabriel held out his hand and weakly grabbed Riley's upper arm.

"It's okay," he muttered. "Jackson went to destroy the den about an hour ago. Rebecca went with him."

"Where's everyone else?"

"Still sleeping, I think."

"Why are you awake?" Riley asked him. "You shouldn't be."

Gabriel looked horrible. Riley hadn't realized before how close to death Gabriel had been, and still was. He had been so concerned about Raven's death and Aurora that he barely notice that his best friend had almost died. He just hadn't realize before how severe Gabriel's injuries were. He thought it wasn't possible for him to feel any worse. He'd been wrong.

"You woke me up," he replied. "Sounded like you were having a nightmare."

"That's nothing new," Riley said gruffly. "Sorry."

Riley watched Gabriel closely for a few seconds. He had seen Gabriel injured so many times in the Leaders Den that he knew exactly what the skinwalker needed without having to ask. He placed the wand down and opened the tent door. Without having to crawl outside he grabbed a bottle of water and new bandages that were placed next to the tent. It was nice that Jackson kept the supplies within easy reach.

He helped Gabriel drink the water and was in the process of changing his bandages when Rebecca zipped the door open.

"Everything okay?"

"How'd the bombing go?" Riley asked.

He wasn't ready to talk about the vision he had and her question would have sparked that conversation.

"It was completely vacant, but they won't be able to come back to it anymore now."

She helped Riley finish bandaging Gabriel's stab wounds. Luckily, they weren't infected, but they weren't healing either. They looked deeper and the bleeding wasn't slowing down like it should. It looked worse than before.

"Is there a chance that they used begraw on you?" Riley asked grimly.

"I don't know," Gabriel mumbled.

Rebecca put her hands over Gabriel's bandaged wounds.

"Incantartus infecto," she muttered over and over again.

Small droplets of yellow liquid rose from the bandages. Gabriel exhaled as though he'd been holding his breath.

"Well, maybe that was most of the problem," Rebecca said guiltily. "Sorry, I should've tried this before."

"Don't apologize," Gabriel said as he grabbed her hand. "I'll be fine."

She bent over and kissed him. Riley left the tent to avoid telling Rebecca about Aurora. He figured Gabriel would tell her anyway. He found Raya sitting next to the smolders of the campfire. She looked tired and completely listless.

"Couldn't sleep, huh?" Riley asked as he sat across from her.

"I don't think I'll ever sleep again," she whispered without taking her eyes off of the glowing embers.

"I wish I had that option," Riley mumbled mostly to himself.

Dawn was breaking, which meant they had to get going. Now that the den was destroyed the werewolves might come back. Their enemies never took it lightly when a den was destroyed. Riley grabbed the bucket of water and poured it on the smoldering embers. Smoke erupted from the ground and Raya stood up quickly with her hand over her nose.

"Sorry," Riley said to her. "I guess I should've warned you."

"It's okay," she said stiffly. "I'll help you get things to the van."

Raya bent over to pick up a bag and Riley stuffed the dishes in a storage box. He realized then how difficult it was to do the mundane tasks. His injuries from the day before made it

154

hard to open and close his hands. He gritted his teeth and tucked the wand in his belt. Until he could get some guresh he needed to be very careful.

Jeremy emerged from the other tent with Marcus close behind him. The skinwalker looked tired and he still limped horribly. Someone had bandaged the cuts on his arms and his face was still pale. Apparently he didn't have any begraw in his system because he was up and about.

Jeremy didn't look as pale or sickly as he had the day before. Food and proper rest had helped him a lot. Riley assumed that it didn't have anything to do with Raya's tamer abilities because she didn't seem to be using them at the moment. Just by observation, Riley had found that she couldn't calm those around her if she wasn't calm herself. With Raven's death he didn't think she would be calm again for a while.

"Riley," Jackson's voice came from the woods.

Suddenly, the vampire was standing next to him.

"I think we should talk," his father said to him in a solemn voice.

Riley's stomach flipped. Rebecca must've told him what he had tried to do the night before. He was seriously regretting his moment of insanity. All he wanted to do was help take down camp and move on to the next mission. At least that way he'd be physically and mentally preoccupied. Talking wasn't going to help anything, but he followed Jackson into the trees anyway.

"Rebecca told me you're having a hard time," Jackson said when they were out of earshot of the others. "And that you almost did something stupid."

Riley didn't say anything. He had hoped that Rebecca wouldn't tell anyone, but Jackson was their father. He would've found out eventually anyway.

"Yeah, it was stupid."

Without warning, Jackson hugged him. Riley didn't know what to do with his arms because he couldn't move them. It seemed like he'd lost all of his strength. He couldn't think. He couldn't even breathe.

155

"I'm so sorry," Jackson said in a broken voice. "I'm so sorry I couldn't get her back to you."

Riley was finally able to move his arms and he hugged his father back.

"It's not your fault," he whispered.

"We are going to get her back," Jackson said firmly. "She's strong and smart. She'll hold out until we can find her."

A lump formed in Riley's throat. He didn't know if it was possible to get her back anymore. But at the same time he couldn't just resign her to her fate. The werewolves that had her were sadistically barbaric. It made him physically ill to imagine what she was going through. Unfortunately, it wasn't hard to imagine what they were doing to her either. He had to stop thinking about it, or it would destroy him. At the same time, if he did stop thinking about her he felt like he would lose her forever.

He gripped the back of Jackson's shirt and didn't let go for a long time. It was easier to hide from the others how scared he was, but Jackson was a different situation entirely. He proved once again that he was an amazing father. Besides the speed and the strength being a vampire gave him, intuition was his superpower.

Riley didn't say anything after he broke off the hug. He didn't need to. He was sure that Jackson knew what he was thinking. That he wasn't as optimistic that they'd find her as he used to be. Carvolo had won. Riley couldn't shake the feeling that he would never see Aurora again now that the ancients had her. The best thing he could do now was go on missions until they won the war. If he couldn't get Aurora back then he was determined to finish what she had worked her whole life to accomplish. He wasn't going to let this destroy him. He was going to fight because he knew that's what she would want him to do.

The trip back to the Washington community was a long one. The first thing they did was find a full service truck stop.

156

Riley managed to disable all the cameras with the wand so that no one would be able to record them. They were mostly worried about someone seeing Jeremy, who looked and smelled like he'd survived a nuclear bombing. After showers and clean clothes they felt a little more comfortable in their travels. It was still a tiresome trip that was endured mostly in silence.

Gabriel still wasn't back to normal by the time they got back. Rebecca was worried, but Gabriel had assured her that he was fine. It was hard to be convinced of that when every bump in the road made him moan in pain. His leg still wasn't healed so Jackson and Marcus ended up carrying him into Demian and Veronica's house. Marcus's limp was gone and he had taken off the bandages a few hours ago. All that was left of his wounds were faint scars that were rapidly clearing up.

The teams that went after the other two dens were back before them. They heard on the road that they had an easy time for the most part. Naomi could've taken the entire Southern California den down by herself without her team's help. Karven's team had a bloody fight in Nevada, but at least they didn't have any casualties.

Selena and Roan had repaired the entire community over the past few days. There was no longer evidence that they had blown up the community when the enemy invaded. It was amazing how the fairies were able to utilize their magic in that way. Riley wondered if the wand was able to do that, but he knew it wasn't pertinent to the tasks at hand. Winning the war was more important than things he could repair or create.

The living room was crowded with people. Karven and Naomi were sitting in the arm chairs. Roy was there too. Riley hadn't seen him since before the attack on their community. He was sitting in his wheelchair next to Naomi. He had a lot more color in his face than he had before. Riley took a moment to feel relieved that his friend seemed to be getting better. Not very many humans survived being crushed by a large chunk of concrete like he did.

Samantha and Rachel were there, which surprised Riley. He hadn't expected to see them until they were sure the enemy wasn't spying on them anymore. Roan and Selena must've taken care of the spies and replaced the protective spells on their communities. Pearl and Tanya were nowhere in sight and neither where the babies. The girls were probably babysitting in one of the bedrooms while the meeting was in session.

Veronica was there with Teresa and Jasmine. Riley couldn't help but wonder if Teresa was officially moving to their community now that the threats had subsided. He never had to actively avoid seeing people in the community before. Even when Sarai was alive they didn't avoid interacting with each other no matter how unpleasant it was. It would be interesting to see how the situation with Teresa and Jasmine played out. Riley couldn't shake the feeling that it wasn't going to end well. At least it would make it easier for him to avoid home and concentrate on missions. He wasn't intending on being stationary for very long.

When Teresa saw him, she stood up from her seat and grabbed Jasmine's arm. The young girl stood up with a look of annoyance on her face. The werewolf led her daughter out of the house without saying a single word to anyone.

Jasmine gave Riley a small smile before she was rushed out the door. Riley would've returned the smile if the circumstances were different. He didn't miss the hostile glare that Teresa threw at him before she shut the front door. He winced in spite of himself. He didn't want her attitude toward him to bother him, but apparently it did.

Jeremy came into the house shortly after Teresa closed the door. Samantha stood up from the couch and hurried toward him with a small smile on her face.

"Hey, Sammie," Jeremy said with a grin.

She threw her arms around his neck and he sighed lightly.

"I know you hate it, but I couldn't resist," she said as she let him go. "It's very good to see you."

"After five years in a den prison hugs aren't so bad," he replied with a smirk, but Samantha's smile fell.

"Don't let him fool you," Marcus said. "That's not what he said when I hugged him. He still hates it."

Samantha laughed and kissed Marcus in greeting. Leave it to Marcus to make any situation seem lighthearted. It was a nice talent to have, but Riley had to work hard not to find it annoying at the moment. He wanted to get the meeting over with so that he could know what to do next.

"How are the babies?" Marcus asked her.

Riley noticed Jeremy's eyes widen. Marcus must not have told him about Leigh and Elizabeth.

"They're a handful," Samantha replied. "I haven't slept for days."

"Do you have kids?" Jeremy asked in confusion.

"Yeah," Samantha said with a smile. "We'll tell you about them later. You should probably meet Demian."

Riley left the three of them and went to sit next to Veronica. She looked at him in concern, but he ignored it. He sat forward with his elbows resting on his knees. He hoped that she wouldn't ask him if he was okay. She knew he wasn't and he didn't want to have to lie to her or tell her how he felt. He wouldn't have sat next to her if there was another option, but all the other sitting spaces were filled in the living room.

But she didn't say anything. She timidly touched his back with the tip of her fingers. When he didn't jerk away she slowly made circular motions on his back. He didn't know why he found it comforting. Nothing should have been comforting to him, but he felt himself relax a bit as she rubbed his back. She didn't stop even when Demian stood in front of the room to begin the meeting.

"I think it's best to keep this short," Demian said reverently. "We'll have a short memorial service for Raven in the meeting room at the warehouse tomorrow afternoon. We will make further plans to find the Ancients Den to liberate Aurora as soon as possible. If anyone has any ideas that can help further this process along…please, don't hesitate to share."

There was a suffocating quietness in the room that made Riley tense again. It didn't help that everyone was shooting quick glances in his direction. He didn't know what they were watching for. Maybe they expected him to snap. Veronica rubbed his back a bit more aggressively to get rid of his tension knots. He thought about asking her to stop, but he realized that her touch was the only thing keeping him grounded at the moment.

Riley glanced at Demian when he didn't continue talking. He didn't think he'd ever seen the werewolf look so forlorn before. Not even he could hide how distraught he was about Aurora and Raven. He bowed his head and took a deep breath.

"We have a new member…" Demian began, but he shook his head. "No, that's not right…he's not a new member. Jeremy Masters has been rescued and is taking his former position in the rebellion. Of course, if that's what he wants?"

Jeremy glanced awkwardly at everyone in the room and nodded. It wasn't surprising since he didn't have anywhere else to go. As long as Raya's tamer abilities kept him calm he should be fine. Riley was actually surprised that Raya wasn't in the room with them. Even though she wasn't a part of the council she had been a major player in their mission. Maybe she needed time to herself.

Demian concluded the meeting and everyone filed out of the living room. Riley stood up to leave and realized for the first time how much pain he was in. He had left the wand in the van so that was probably why. In order to keep the pain away he needed the wand close to him. He mentally kicked himself for leaving it in the van.

"You two," Samantha said as she pointed a finger at Riley and then at Jeremy. "Follow me."

"Why?" Riley asked. He tried to keep the annoyance out of his tone, but he wasn't successful.

"Don't ask stupid questions, Riley," she said with a stern look. "You both look like you've been run over by a steam engine."

"I'm fine," Jeremy said with a wave of his hand. "I'm pretty sure I've had more food in the past day than I've had all month."

"That's precisely why you need a checkup."

Jeremy swore under his breath and rolled his eyes.

"Curse all you want," Samantha said as she placed her hands on her hips. "But you're not getting out of this."

"I think Gabriel needs your attention more than we do," Riley replied.

"Tracen's got him covered."

Samantha walked out of the living room, expecting them to follow her. Riley sighed and grimaced when she turned to look at them sternly. She went into the guest bedroom, but didn't shut the door.

"I'd forgotten how persistent she is," Jeremy mumbled and Riley nodded. When things became medical Samantha didn't mess around.

The room no longer had a full size bed in it. It had been replaced by a hospital bed and medical equipment lined the walls of the room. There was even a stretcher that hadn't been in the community before. It was good that they finally had one. A few weeks ago, Tracen had to use plywood to carry Aurora after she was burned by the magical explosion that almost leveled their community. That painful memory didn't help Riley's mood at all.

"Do you know where your tracker is?" Samantha asked.

She motioned for Jeremy to sit on the hospital bed.

"I'm pretty sure it fell out when Carvolo's followers tried to kill me slowly," Jeremy said gruffly.

"Where did it used to be?"

"In my arm," Jeremy replied. "At least that's where I remember them putting it."

"Rebecca already searched him," Riley said. "He doesn't have one."

Samantha nodded and checked Jeremy's neck and jaw with her fingers.

"What are you doing?" Jeremy asked with a low growl.

"Sometimes when a werewolf is starved they develop tumor-like bumps on their necks."

"Seriously?" Jeremy asked with a raised eyebrow. "Why is that?"

"I have no idea, but you seem to be in the clear. Just keep eating, but don't over do it. If you eat too much at one time it can cause problems. And, this is probably most important, keep hydrated."

Jeremy nodded patiently even though his body language was exuding impatience.

"Make sure that you take a few days to just rest," Samantha continued. "Even though you're a werewolf you still need to realize that you aren't invincible. What happened to your legs?"

"Huh?"

"You're legs? You're walking abnormally."

Jeremy's face hardened at Samantha's question and he blew out a harsh exhale.

"He and Aurora jumped off a cliff and he broke both of them," Riley said pointedly. He doubted Jeremy had any intention of telling Samantha what happened, so he decided to cut to the chase.

Samantha and Jeremy stared at him for a moment.

"How did you know about that?" Jeremy asked incredulously.

"I told you I had visions of you guys."

"Oh, yeah," Jeremy said with a shrug. "That wasn't exactly my best idea."

"And then he ran on them right afterwards while carrying Aurora," Riley continued. "They probably didn't heal correctly even though Aurora straightened them."

"Okay…you're really freaking me out, man," Jeremy said with wide eyes.

"Why on earth would you do that?" Samantha asked in a hushed whisper.

"We were surrounded and I didn't see another option," Jeremy said solemnly. "I don't know if Aurora noticed, but we were being hunted by that fairy. I didn't catch her name."

"Zalina," Riley said helpfully.

162

"Yeah, she was onto us. I knew that she wasn't going to take prisoners after Aurora broke her neck. The only option was to get out of there ASAP and Aurora wasn't going to be fast enough. That's why I ended up carrying her."

"Well," Samantha said. "I won't look at your legs now, but if you don't start walking normally we might have to re-break them. It might just be that they need rest too. I'll give it until tomorrow."

"Am I dismissed, doc?" Jeremy asked in a sarcastic tone.

"Not yet. I think I'm going to need your help with Riley."

"Come again?" Riley asked in confusion.

"Rebecca told me you had a broken arm and wrist," Samantha explained. "Your arm looks crooked from where I'm standing. If it needs re-broken then Jeremy will have to do it for me. The sun is down and I don't want to have to hit you with a hammer or something."

Riley looked down at his arm. He knew she was right. He'd noticed on the road how crooked it was, but he just didn't care. It was probably an indication that he wasn't in a healthy frame of mind.

He sighed and mentally cursed himself for following Samantha into her torture room.

"You do know that I've never done anything like that before, right?" Jeremy said bluntly.

"Oh, it'll be fine," Samantha said as though they were discussing the weather. "I'll talk you through it."

Riley looked at the door and seriously thought about escaping. Samantha motioned for him to sit on the hospital bed and he reluctantly obeyed her. He took off his shirt as she requested and the horrified gasp in the room came from Jeremy.

"What the hell happened to you?"

Riley looked down at the stab wounds that still weren't healed all the way. They looked worse than they had before. Even with the guresh he'd taken it still wasn't healing right.

Probably because he hadn't taken the time to rest. Not that he had any plans to do that anytime soon.

"Riley," Samantha said in a soft whisper. "I shouldn't have let you go. They gave you guresh, right?"

Riley nodded. She motioned for him to lay down flat on his back and he did with a tight grimace. She poked and prodded his abdomen as he tried not to moan in pain. When he couldn't take it anymore he batted her hand away and tried to sit up. Samantha ended up helping him and he sat on the bed, panting.

"They should be healed by now. What exactly happened to you on the mission?"

Riley told her about all the injuries that he sustained and how the wand helped him deal with the pain. She studied his arm and his wrist with severe scrutiny.

"I don't think the wand heals you at all," she said grimly. "Your stab wounds are worse and your broken bones are still broken from what I can tell. It just prevents you from dying. I assume you don't feel pain when you're holding it?"

"Nope," Riley whispered with an agonized grunt as she poked his abdomen again. "Why do you keep doing that?'

"I need to find out if you have any internal damage."

"I don't think I do. If the wand didn't take care of the internal damage than I'm sure the guresh did."

"Your arm needs set," Samantha said as she gripped his arm gently. "After I set it I'll give you some more guresh. Hopefully Roan and Selena will figure out how to replicate Sarai's gurshen and we'll be able to heal you more efficiently."

"You don't think the guresh will do the trick?" Riley asked tiredly.

"Not if you don't stay in bed."

"I'm not staying in bed."

"Actually, you have no choice," the doctor said sternly. "As a council we've decided that you will stay in bed until you're completely healed."

"How do you guys make these decisions without me?" Riley asked her incredulously. "Do you have secret meetings or something?"

"Group texting."

Riley rolled his eyes. He didn't have time to rest. He needed to go on a mission as soon as possible. Lying in bed would do nothing but drive him crazy. He was about to get up and walk out of the room when Samantha laid a hand on his shoulder.

"I was serious, Riley. No one is going to let you leave this house if you try."

She quickly set the broken bone in his arm and he yelled in shock. Jeremy winced in empathy.

She said that she didn't need to set his wrist and he praised the heavens for that.

"Now, you've got a decision to make; you can either stay here or go home. But either way you will be in bed. And don't try to escape because I'm faster than you are and I'll sedate you. I've done it before so don't test me."

"I'm pretty sure I would hate you forever if you drugged me," Riley said, half-jokingly.

"Where have I heard that before?" Samantha asked as she glanced knowingly at Jeremy.

"Hey, I had very good reason to not be sedated in that situation," Jeremy said as he raised his hands submissively. "Gabriel was gone, Aurora was fighting werewolves by herself, and Marcus was unconscious. I had to help."

"You had a broken arm and a bone sticking out of your leg," Samantha said incredulously.

"So what?" Jeremy retorted snottily. "I thought we were all dead anyway."

Samantha sighed and turned her attention back to Riley.

"You two will get along famously."

She studied his neck and winced. She gently touched his throat with the tips of her fingers.

"What happened here?"

"A werewolf tried to strangle me."

165

"Well, I don't feel any extensive damage," she said as she kept poking his bruised neck. "Try to stay hydrated and don't talk unless it's necessary."

"Sure thing, doc. Can I go home now?"

"After I splint your arm I'll have Jackson come get you. You shouldn't be walking unless it's absolutely necessary."

Riley sighed in defeat and let Samantha fix him up. He didn't relish the thought of having to stay in bed and he kept on thinking of ways to get out of it.

As though she could read his mind, Samantha sank a needle into his arm before he could protest. He was asleep within seconds.

Chapter 11

Riley stared at the chessboard and pretended that he actually wanted to play. Tanya sat on the end of his bed and stared at the game board with a studious expression. The two of them had been spending a lot of time together playing chess the past two weeks.

The healing process had been slow. He still wasn't cleared by Samantha to get out of bed, much to his chagrin. Even with guresh and rest the stab wounds were being stubborn. Samantha thought it was because he overdid it, and he thought it was because the blades had magically slowed the healing process. He hadn't told her that because he didn't want her to freak out over his injuries anymore than she already did. Even the wand that sat on his bedside table hadn't been able to speed up the healing.

Pearl came into the room with Jasmine close behind her. Riley couldn't help but stiffen. Pearl knew that Jasmine wasn't allowed around him. Unsurprisingly, the girls didn't care. Even when he tried to send them away, to honor Teresa's wishes, the girls just laughed at him as though he was joking.

"Pearl… Jasmine…" Riley said warningly.

"Oh, come on," Jasmine said with a giggle. "Are you going to tell me that you never disobeyed your mother when you were a kid?"

He definitely was not, so he closed his mouth and looked back at the chess game.

"That's what I thought," Jasmine said with a smirk.

"Well," Riley said nonchalantly. "If your mom tears my throat out for hanging out with you it'll be you fault."

"She won't do that," Pearl said darkly. "He's bluffing."

"Nope," Riley said with a shake of his head. "I'm not bluffing."

"Checkmate," Tanya said without a stutter.

Riley gave her a small smile. She had slowly been getting better with her speech. The fact that she could put two syllables together without a problem made him happy. If only for a moment.

"Why a-are you s-smiling?" Tanya asked. "I won."

"Because I'm not a sore loser," Riley replied with a smirk. He didn't want to compliment her on her speech in front of others. He'd noticed that she got embarrassed by that in the past.

"Did Tanya tell you that we shed our skin for the first time yesterday?" Pearl asked him with a hint of excitement in her voice. She usually didn't get excited about anything.

"What?" Riley asked incredulously. "No. When where you planning on telling me?"

"I d-don't know," Tanya said in a small voice.

"She's scared about it," Pearl said evenly.

"No, I'm n-not," she said as she folded her arms.

"So, what do you girls look like in your wolf skin?" Riley asked in an attempt to change the subject. They would argue back and forth for a long time if he let them.

"I am a gray wolf and Tanya is a red wolf."

"I got to see it," Jasmine said happily. "It was so cool."

The girls talked a while longer about how exciting it was to see Pearl and Tanya in their wolf skin. Jasmine came up with different games they could play in the yard that day.

As if on cue, Rachel poked her head in the room and told the girls it was time to play outside. The girls said goodbye to Riley and hurried out of the room. Rachel stepped in and closed the door behind her.

"How are you feeling today?" she asked warily.

"Ready to take on the world if anyone would let me," Riley said in a hopeful tone.

"I don't think Sammie will go for that," Rachel said. "You still look pale."

"Lack of sunlight will do that to a person," he replied with a smirk.

"Riley," Rachel said, ignoring his ridiculous claim that the lack of sunlight was the problem. "I think you need to talk to someone."

"What do you mean? You just extracted three hyper girls out of my room."

"I mean a therapist," she said hesitantly. "You seem to be in a black depression. I'm not sure how to pull you out of it."

"Like I said-"

"If you say it's lack of sunlight again I might smack you."

"Whoa," Riley said as he raised his hands in surrender. "Would you really smack a guy suffering from depression?"

He was trying to be funny, but Rachel didn't find it very amusing.

"I am very worried about you," Rachel said quietly. "So is your dad."

"Does saying that out loud help anyone feel better?"

Rachel sighed, but didn't say anything else on the subject.

"Jeremy is here," she said as she opened the door. "He came to speak with you. I"ll send him up. We will be revisiting the conversation about you seeing a therapist."

Riley opened his mouth to argue, but Rachel was already gone. He sighed and leaned angrily back into his pillows. He briefly wondered how long it would take them to realize that he'd left if he escaped through the window. Too bad he wasn't as fast as a vampire.

There was a knock on his door before it opened.

Jeremy looked a lot better than he had the last time Riley saw him. He had gained a lot of muscle in the past couple weeks. If it wasn't for his curly hair and facial features Riley wouldn't have recognized him. Jeremy glanced around uncomfortably for a moment before Riley beckoned him into the room.

"Hey," Riley said. He tried not to grumble, but he wasn't sure if he pulled it off.

"Sorry to come over unannounced like this," Jeremy mumbled as he grabbed a chair.

"Don't worry about it."

"You play chess?" he asked as he nodded toward the chessboard that Tanya forgot to put away.

"My sister, Tanya, does. She ropes me into it."

"Dude, how many sisters do you have?" Jeremy asked with a raised eyebrow.

"Two half sisters, two adopted sisters, one step sister, and one sister-in-law."

Jeremy stared at him for a moment and blinked his eyes a few times. It made Riley uneasy. He had noticed in the past that Jeremy blinked a lot when he was trying to remain in control of his wolf. His eyes didn't turn werewolf yellow, so that was a good sign.

"Sorry," Jeremy said as he shook his head. "I didn't come here to talk about your family. I was going to ask you for a favor."

"I'm not sure I can do much with Dr. Sammie hanging over me, but I'll do my best."

"The full moon is next week," the werewolf said grimly. "To be honest...I'm terrified."

Riley didn't say anything, but he nodded in understanding.

"You saw in your vision what I did to those three werewolves I attacked," Jeremy said in a tight whisper. "I just don't know why you haven't told anybody about it."

"I didn't think it was important," Riley said with a shrug.

Jeremy stared at him incredulously.

"Don't you have a high IQ?" Jeremy asked sarcastically. "Why would you think something so stupid?"

"Hey," Riley said as he sat up a little straighter. "You tried to save my wife. I'm not going to gossip about you when it's not something we need to worry about."

Jeremy stared at him for a few seconds before glancing at the floor. His shoulders were tense and his hands were fisted in his lap. He took a shuddering breath before replying.

"I almost killed her, man," Jeremy said gruffly. "I'm not sure how I stopped myself. I am not a stable werewolf. I have to fight for control constantly...every second of the freaking day. It's completely terrifying when I shed my skin."

170

Riley studied Jeremy for a moment in thought. Even though he looked a lot healthier he still looked just as haggard as the day they rescued him. He wasn't calm and he looked completely exhausted. Not physically, but emotionally.

Apparently he wasn't acclimating well to being around other people.

"Aren't Raya's tamer abilities helping?" Riley asked in concern.

Jeremy chuckled humorlessly.

"No," he said with a shake of his head. "I'm pretty sure that girl hates me."

Riley was genuinely shocked by that.

"Did you do something to her?" he asked hesitantly. He couldn't see Jeremy hurting Raya on purpose, but there was always a possibility that he lost control and took it out on her.

"No…well, I don't know," Jeremy said with a shrug. "She avoids me all the time. It doesn't really matter anyway. I don't think she calms me like she does everyone else. She's tried it a few times and it backfired."

"How so?" Riley asked.

"Whenever she uses her tamer abilities around me I get this intense need to protect her. I've never felt like that before, not even when Aurora and I were escaping the Montana den. I wasn't expecting that and neither was she. Demian had to get involved before I hurt someone."

"What did Demian do?"

"He shot me with a tranquilizer dart. I've gotten a bit better at controlling that protective urge in the past few days, but I think I completely freaked her out. Not to mention the poor kids that were around us at the time."

Riley took a deep breath to try to relax. He didn't know why Jeremy's revelation was scaring him. He'd been with them for two weeks without any major incident, but they hadn't experienced him during a full moon yet.

"I told Demian that I want to be chained up this full moon," Jeremy said as he looked at the floor. "He said that he didn't think that was a good idea. He thinks my problems stem

171

from being locked up for so long and that restraining me isn't going to help. I've been trying to convince him that he's wrong but he won't listen to me."

"Well," Riley said with thoughtful consideration. "Demian is a pretty stubborn guy, but he's also very old. He's seen a lot of things that most of us will probably never see. Maybe he knows something you don't. Maybe he's dealt with werewolves like you before."

Jeremy sighed and shook his head in frustration.

"Raya's abilities don't help me like it does other werewolves. I freaked out and tore three werewolves to pieces with my bare hands without even a second thought. I am afraid that I'm going to kill someone, or at least seriously maim."

"Okay, then Demian will chain you up," Riley said nonchalantly. "If you keep insisting he can't stop you from doing it."

"That's actually why I'm here, man. I need you to help me with this. I've never been chained up during the full moon before. I was hoping that you'd be willing to guard me with your wand. The fairies already said no."

"You asked Roan if he'd guard you during the full moon?" Riley asked with a smirk.

"Yeah," Jeremy said with a small grin. "He got pretty upset that I would ask him to do such a menial task. It's funny how ticked off fairies get... So, will you at least think about it?"

"No need," Riley said with a nod. "I have no problem doing that if it'll make you feel more at ease."

"Thanks, man," Jeremy said quietly.

"I can try to talk to Raya too. Make sure she's alright."

"No, it's okay. I can figure it out," he replied quickly. "She's my responsibility."

He said it in such a determined tone it almost sounded like a warning, so Riley let it drop.

Jeremy got up to leave, but he stopped at the door. He hesitated before turning back around.

"Do you mind if I ask you a personal question?"

Riley couldn't help but feel the sudden slight tension in the air. Despite being uncomfortably vulnerable, he nodded cautiously.

"How did you two meet?" he asked quietly. There was no doubt who he was asking about. Saying Aurora's name out loud had been painful for everyone lately.

"High school," Riley replied and Jeremy smirked.

"What?"

"That's where I met her too," he said with a shrug. "I was a jerk though. Which I'm sure you weren't."

"No," Riley said as he shook his head. "But she was a jerk."

"Really?" Jeremy asked with a surprised look on his face. "That doesn't sound like her."

"I think she lost herself when she lost you."

It should've been an awkward conversation. If they were both humans it would've been, but there was something about the way Jeremy held himself while he talked. He seemed concerned and curious instead of jealous or sad. It had surprised Riley at first that Jeremy had taken their marriage as well as he did. But he wasn't surprised anymore. Jeremy was a good man who deserved a lot more than what life had dealt him.

"I'm glad she found you," Jeremy said sincerely. "I'm sorry I couldn't do more to save her."

"She's still out there somewhere," Riley replied quietly.

Jeremy nodded and then left.

Riley felt the wave of despair that usually came after talking about Aurora. He rubbed his eyes hastily and shuddered. He had to figure out a way to convince Samantha to let him out of bed. The two weeks of bedrest had sent him to a dark place.

He looked at the wand, but knew that it couldn't help him heal faster. If anything it would cause more damage because he felt like he could do anything with it in his hand. He leaned back on his pillows and closed his eyes. He heard the girls playing in the backyard and let the sound of their laughter distract him.

Riley felt restless the next morning, so he got out of the bed to take a shower. He ignored Samantha's instructions to keep the wounds dry. His arms had healed quickly, as well as the other bruises and scrapes that he received. It concerned him that the knife wounds still weren't healed when all his other injuries were.

There wasn't much he could do about it.

After his shower he examined his wounds in the mirror. They were no longer infected and they looked like they were scabbed over nicely. He didn't think he needed to rest anymore, but everyone had been serious about him staying in bed. Every time he tried to sneak out of his room, even to eat breakfast at the kitchen table, he got a stern talking to from someone. Mostly Rachel, but it was even more annoying when Jackson did it. It made him feel like he was five years old, but at least their hearts were in the right place. Even if he didn't appreciate it.

He wrapped a towel around his waist when he realized he forgot to grab clean clothes from his closet. When he opened the door he found Rebecca waiting for him in the hallway. She was leaning against the wall with her arms folded. He grimaced and rolled his eyes.

"What was that look for?" she asked in confusion.

"I assume you're here to rip me a new one for taking a shower."

"Even though mom wanted me too that is not why I'm here," she said with an aggravated sigh. "I need to talk to you, but I think you should get dressed first."

Riley saw her eyes widen when she noticed his healing wounds.

"Those look a lot better," she said in a relieved tone.

Riley snorted grumpily and hurried to his room. Rebecca followed him so he went into his walk-in closet to get dressed. She scowled at him when he emerged wearing denim jeans and a red t-shirt that said 'Rebel' in black letters across the front.

"Really?" she said, clearly unimpressed.

174

"I'm making a statement," he replied with a shrug. "I'm *done* with bedrest. Sammie will have to sedate me if she disagrees."

"Did you really put that much thought into it?" Rebecca asked incredulously.

"No, I just picked up the first shirt I saw," Riley said with a smirk.

"Well, if you aren't going to get back in bed we might as well go outside and-"

Riley was already out of the bedroom before she finished her sentence. He knew he had to leave quickly to have the slightest chance of avoiding the vampires in the house. Not that his attempts at escape had been successful in the past. He wasn't optimistic that he'd avoid them.

As expected, Jackson appeared at the bottom of the stairs before he made it to the living room. He stood there with his arms folded and a stern expression on his face. His dark hair was disheveled from his vampire speed and it only made him look angrier. If Riley wasn't so annoyed he might have responded a bit more cautiously.

"I'm starting to feel like a freaking prisoner," Riley said furiously. "I'm perfectly fine. I'm just going outside."

Jackson didn't say anything, but he didn't move either. Rebecca went down the stairs and looked at their father.

"Dad," she said. "I think he's fine. I saw his wounds and they're scabbed over."

"Sammie said that you could do damage internally," Jackson said sternly. "I shouldn't have let you go on the mission in your condition."

Riley snorted in aggravation.

"You're still feeling guilty about that?" he asked incredulously. "It's been two weeks."

"I'm your father, buddy," Jackson said. "I should've stopped you from going."

Riley was about to lose it and he did his best to keep his tone respectful. He wasn't sure if he pulled it off or not.

"For the last time; it wasn't your choice. I wasn't about to stand on the sidelines while everyone else went to rescue Aurora. Can we let it go, please?"

"Sure, just go back to bed," Jackson said.

All the strength left Riley at once when he thought about all the hours of bedrest that he'd gone through. He'd rather be stabbed by Jenna's knives or have his arms broken again than to go back to bed. He slumped against the railing and took a deep breath to calm himself.

"I can't mentally handle it anymore," Riley whispered.

Rebecca and Jackson watched him in concern for a moment before Rebecca turned her attention back to Jackson.

"Dad," Rebecca said and Jackson turned to her with a dark expression. "I won't let him overdo it. We're just going to talk outside."

"Fine," Jackson said grumpily. "But Sammie needs to check you out before you're officially in the all clear. Don't try to do anything or I'll haul your butt back to bed. You know I will."

Riley rolled his eyes, but nodded. He really hated being treated like a child, but with how terrible of a patient he had been he knew he deserved it. Bedrest wasn't for the faint of heart.

Jackson stepped aside and let him leave the house. The first thing Riley did was take a deep breath. It was finally summer time and it inevitably made him think of Aurora. He was glad that Rebecca needed to talk to him so he didn't dwell on his feelings.

They walked to their tree stump in silence. When Riley was about to sit down on the grass something furry caught his eye. A small gray wolf jumped on Rebecca and she fell on the ground with a laugh.

Pearl wagged her tail and licked Rebecca's face.

"Pearl!" Rebecca wailed. "That's disgusting!"

A red wolf ran up to Riley and pawed his leg gently. Tanya was a bit smaller than Pearl was in her wolf skin, but her fur was thicker. The red and orange colors of her pelt glistened in the sunlight. Excluding Aurora's white wolf, she was the most beautiful wolf he'd ever seen. Riley rubbed her head with his fingers and she leaned into his leg.

"What are you two doing out here?" Riley asked. "Mom told me you were supposed to be catching up on school today."

"They can't answer you," Rebecca replied. "Gabriel says it'll be a couple years before they can use mind speech."

"That's good to know," Riley said as he smirked at Pearl.

Most wolves couldn't glower very well, but Pearl managed a good one. She even growled, which sounded more cute than menacing. Riley chuckled when she tried to nip at his arm. Tanya tackled her sister to the ground which resulted in a game of chase. Riley watched the young wolves play for a bit before he sat down next to Rebecca.

"That's so cool," Rebecca said. "They seem happy."

"Yeah," Riley replied with a smile.

"I'm glad mom and dad get to raise them together. It's kind of like a second chance for them."

Riley nodded in agreement, but didn't reply. He didn't want things to get too emotional. He just wanted to enjoy being outside for as long as Jackson would let him. Rebecca scooted closer to him and took a deep breath. She seemed nervous and Riley thought about asking her what was wrong, but he decided to let her tell him without any prompting.

"So," she began hesitantly. "I've been talking to Roan about the last vision you had of Aurora."

When she paused, Riley raised an eyebrow at her. He didn't know what she was waiting for, but he was trying not to be impatient with her hesitancy.

"Specifically about your mom, well, Jenna. Calling her 'your mom' seems wrong...sorry."

"What did you guys talk about?"

"Carvolo asked her to be the keeper of the Ancients Den, right? I asked Roan what that meant and he gave me a pretty thorough lesson on how powerful protection spells work. If you want something to remain hidden a magical being has to be it's keeper. Arothor was the first keeper since he put the protective spell on the den in the first place. After he died, Roan assumes that Zalina took his place as keeper. When Carvolo killed her they needed to find another magical being powerful enough to hold the protective spells in place. The keeper is the only one that knows where the Ancients Den is. Jenna is now the only person on Earth that knows where we can find it."

"So if we find Jenna, we find Aurora," Riley said with a nod. "We already knew that."

"Yeah," Rebecca agreed. "But there's a catch. If we did find Jenna she would die before she would be able to betray Carvolo. She wouldn't be able to tell us where the den is because of the spell that bound them together."

Riley nodded in understanding. He frequently saw Carvolo and Jenna kissing in his nightmares while the black magic engulfed them and Aurora. Riley wasn't sure why their magically binding kiss freaked him out so much, but it did.

"Did Roan have anything to say about that?"

"He said it's a spell that is only breakable by the death of that magical being," Rebecca replied. "Unless the wand can do it."

"Can it?" Riley asked with a raised eyebrow.

"Roan doesn't know. He wanted me to ask you if he could study it for a while to see if he can get a better idea of what it is capable of. We don't want to confront Jenna if the wand isn't going to be able to help us."

"What if we just killed Jenna? Wouldn't the protective spells deteriorate eventually?"

Riley was surprised for a moment that he could talk about killing his mother was such nonchalance. He knew he should've been worried about that, but he didn't give it a second thought.

"No," Rebecca said firmly. "We can't let that happen. If the keeper dies and isn't replaced the protection spell will increase in strength over time until eventually no one will be able find, or leave, the Ancients Den. Aurora would be stuck there forever."

They fell into a thoughtful silence. There had to be something that they were missing. Riley kept hoping that the solution to the problem would present itself if he kept thinking. But he thought of nothing else for the past two weeks and he still had nothing to go on. They sat there for a while watching Pearl and Tanya play in the yard.

"What would happen," Riley said thoughtfully. "If we let Carvolo know that I'm still alive?"

"He'd come for you," Rebecca said in confusion. "We already know that."

"Exactly, and since he's in the Ancients Den that would mean he'd send Jenna after me. Maybe that's how we get Aurora back."

"That's too risky, Riley," she said with a shake of her head. "Dad wouldn't let you do it and Demian would never go for it."

"I'm not talking about trading me for her. I'm just-"

"Don't lie." His sister glowered at him. "That's exactly what you're saying and I'm not falling for it. Aurora would despise us if we let you do that."

Riley slumped back against the tree stump in defeat. He didn't know what else to do and it was killing him. He just wanted to go on a mission to get his mind off of things. Violence always seemed to distract him and saving people gave him a purpose. If he couldn't save Aurora he needed to be protecting humans from the werewolves. He didn't want to stay in the community any longer.

"Roan can study the wand," Riley said quietly. "But I'm not going to wait around for his results. Is there a mission that Demian needs me to go on?"

Rebecca gave him a worried look and he sighed.

"I'm fine," he said. It was a lie so he rephrased it. "I'm physically fine."

"Marcus, Gabriel, and I are leaving to rescue some people that were kidnapped by werewolves in Portland."

"Perfect. I'm coming."

"Riley…"

"I can't do this anymore, sis," he said in a defeated whisper. "I need to be doing something."

179

"I know," she said as she rested her head on his shoulder. The gentle touch soothed both of them. "Marcus, Gabriel, and I feel the same way. We've all been going stir crazy too. But you aren't as durable as we are. Even with the wand. I don't think you realize how close you came to dying, Riley. It was very scary."

"I do realize," he told her reassuringly. "I know I've been a horrible patient about it, but it's challenging staying in bed when all I want to do is find Aurora."

"Do you think dad will let you go? Your wounds bothered him the most. He almost broke the dining room table when he heard the wand wasn't actually helping you heal."

Riley vaguely remembered that. He had been doped up on pain killers that Samantha had given him at the time. Jackson couldn't get control of his magic for a few minutes and he'd turned the dining room into a whirlwind of silver magic. It was then that they figured out that Jackson's aura was silver.

"He'll be fine," Riley said. "He'll probably insist on coming with us, but I'm okay with that as long as he quits babying me."

Riley sat up straighter when he noticed Jackson walking toward them from the other side of the yard. Pearl and Tanya noticed him too and they both jumped on him without warning.

Jackson fell back on the grass with a chuckle and let them wrestle with him. Riley was grateful that the girls didn't try to tackle him. He didn't think his skin would hold up well to their sharp claws and pointy teeth. Watching Jackson play with them took Riley's mind off of things and he was able to relax.

Pearl was definitely the more aggressive of the twins. She snarled ferociously and clawed at Jackson. Tanya was a bit more playful and pranced around with her tail wagging.

Jackson grabbed Pearl around her middle and pinned her to the ground so she couldn't gash him with her paws. She grumbled a small growl and Jackson chuckled.

"Just try to get out of that, missy," Jackson teased.

Tanya took the opportunity to jump on Jackson's back and sank her teeth into the back of his shirt. Riley heard fabric tear and Tanya quickly jumped off of him. Jackson let go of Pearl and she bolted a few feet away from him and crouched down. She looked like she was preparing to pounce in a few seconds.

"Darn it, Tanya," Jackson grumbled. "This was my favorite shirt."

Tanya whimpered and sat down on the grass. A huge chunk had been ripped off of the back of Jackson's shirt and she eyed it apologetically. Jackson laughed and grabbed Tanya and wrestled her to the ground. She yipped happily and leapt away when he let go of her. Pearl finally pounced and landed on Jackson's chest. She made a few more holes in his shirt with her claws.

"Time to call it quits before I lose all my clothes," Jackson said with a laugh.

The girls yipped happily and ran off into the trees. Jackson stood up and brushed himself off before walking toward them again.

"Never thought I'd see you playing with the wolves," Rebecca teased.

"Whatever you do, don't pick a fight with them," Jackson said with a smirk. "If I wasn't a vampire I'd probably be dead, or at least severely injured. They don't pull their punches at all."

"How often do they stay in their wolf skin?" Riley asked.

"Since they first changed; probably about half the time," Jackson replied. "It's a good thing that they've almost finished up their school year because it's been practically impossible to get them to concentrate."

"They're just excited about it," Rebecca said with a small smile.

Riley didn't miss the envy in her tone. Being a werewolf was tough and being a skinwalker was a lot easier. Riley was happy with just the way he was, but he wouldn't hesitate letting Carvolo turn him into a werewolf if it meant he could save Aurora. He didn't know if it would come to that, but if it did he was prepared to do it. He knew he couldn't let anyone else know that though. Especially Jackson.

"You're going to need more shirts if this becomes a daily ritual," Riley said lightheartedly.

Jackson smiled in amusement, but it faded quickly.

"I overheard what you guys were talking about."

"What you mean to say is; you were eavesdropping," Rebecca said knowingly.

"Um…yes," Jackson said with a nod. "Anyway, I'm not going to be able to go with you on this mission, so I don't think-"

"You do realize I'm an adult, right?" Riley said in annoyance. It was impossible for him not to be defensive at this point. "I'm not going to stay here because you can't go on the mission with me. I'm a fully trained soldier and I can handle myself."

Jackson took a deep breath and closed his eyes. Riley was pushing him over the edge, but he didn't care. He trusted Jackson enough not to give into his bloodlust. He was impeccably good at maintaining his control.

"That's not what I was going to say, buddy. I don't think that you should go on a mission without the wand."

Riley blew out a small breath of relief. At least Jackson was finally being reasonable.

"I can protect myself without the wand. I don't feel like I should use it unless I absolutely have to. It takes a lot out of me."

Jackson thought about that for a moment before nodding.

"Fine, but you're not going unless Sammie gives you the all clear. She'll be here in about ten minutes."

"I can just go to her house," Riley replied. "I'm sure she's busy with the babies."

Jackson shook his head and opened his mouth to argue, but Rebecca beat him too it.

"No, Riley," Rebecca said. "Until she checks you out you shouldn't be walking around too much."

Riley had to swallow his retort. He felt fine and they knew it. They just couldn't help but be overprotective because that's the type of people they were, so he let it drop. The three of them sat in silence while they waited for Samantha to show up.

Riley hoped that she cleared him. It would make things easier because he was going no matter what Samantha said. He'd had enough of bedrest. He knew Rachel had been right when she said that he needed therapy, so this mission was his therapy. It was probably unhealthy, but it was the only thing that could help him. Saving people was all he could do to stop himself from plummeting into darkness.

Chapter 12

Riley crouched next to Gabriel in the dark alleyway. So far, Portland was not his favorite place to visit. Only because it was crawling with werewolves. Most of them were followers, but he assumed that there were a few leaders as well.

People with signs spreading awareness of the monsters in their midsts crowded the sidewalks on almost every block. Riley wasn't exactly sure what the crowd's plans were since most people knew what happened in London. It wasn't hard to notice what was happening in other cities as well.

People were disappearing left and right. The police departments had a lot of rebel shapeshifters that had taken the places of police officers that had been changed or killed by the werewolves. The rebellion was running out of shapeshifters though and they were spread very thin. It was dangerous for the rebels outside of the communities. But if they didn't do something to try to save all the humans they could while they figured out a way to find the Ancients Den…then they would lose what remained of humanity.

Riley had hoped that after he killed Arothor the werewolves would have to regroup and slow down a little, but the opposite seemed to be happening. Without the fairies to help keep the natural order of things the world was crumbling. Humanity was now aware of the dangers they faced. That was a sign that the situation had become more desperate. More hopeless. Other countries and continents were worse off than America was.

"Are you ready?" Gabriel asked him in a hushed whisper.

"Yeah," Riley replied.

Marcus and Rebecca had already made it into the building that held the human hostages that the werewolves were saving for the full moon. They got separated when a hidden bomb went off and a wall crumbled between them. They weren't sure if Marcus and Rebecca were hit with the debris and there was no way to find out until Riley magically removed the chunks of concrete.

"I'm surprised no one has come to investigate the explosion," Gabriel said.

Riley was too busy concentrating to care. It was hard work moving the debris and he started to sweat from the exertion of his pure magic.

"Dude," Gabriel said urgently. "You're bleeding."

"That's what happens when you get hit by a chunk of concrete," Riley said through a wince. "At least it didn't crush me."

Gabriel dusted off the first aid duffle bag that had landed a few feet away. Riley ignored him as he continued clearing the debris. There was no sign of Marcus or Rebecca. He really hoped they had gotten to a safe place. They had come too far on this mission for them to fail now.

It had taken them four days of investigative work to locate the missing civilians. The werewolves had done a better job than usual covering their tracks. He hoped that Marcus and Rebecca just went forward with their plans to free them when they got separated.

Riley moved the last of the debris and stumbled backwards shakily. If Gabriel hadn't grabbed him he would've fallen over. The skinwalker held a needle and syringe in his hand and Riley shook his head vigorously.

"No, save the guresh."

"This is hemioc," Gabriel said as he inserted the needle into Riley's wrist and pushed down the plunger. Riley couldn't help but sigh in relief when the magical adrenaline hit his veins. "Thanks."

"I'm going to patch you up before we go."

"Why? It's not that bad."

"It's precisely that attitude that got you two weeks of bedrest," Gabriel said in a low voice. "Don't make me regret bringing you with us."

Riley rolled his eyes and let Gabriel put a telfa pad over his wound. Even though it was dark he could tell that he would have an impressive bruise on his hip. He pulled his gun out of it's holster and let Gabriel take the lead. He didn't miss the limp Gabriel had as they entered the destroyed warehouse. It wasn't good that they were both injured before the fighting had even begun. He hoped that Marcus and Rebecca were in better shape than they were.

"The whole place is rubble," Gabriel whispered. "I'm not sure where to go."

"Craticas luminias," Riley muttered.

A blue ball of light engulfed the warehouse. Riley gasped as he had to expand his pure magic. Black spots formed in his vision and he blinked furiously to stay conscious. He usually left the luminias spells to Rebecca because it was dangerous for him without the wand. He was surprised he didn't immediately black out.

"Are you good, Riley?"

He couldn't talk yet, so he just nodded. He stumbled after Gabriel and the blue ball of light followed them through the warehouse. There was still no sign of Marcus and Rebecca, so they followed the easiest path in hopes that they were going in the right direction. The warehouse wasn't very big and it was disconcerting how quiet it was.

Riley studied the ground to see if anyone was trapped under the debris. Frustratingly, he didn't see anything but dust. His chest tightened with worry. He didn't like not knowing what happened to Marcus and Rebecca. Gabriel picked up his pace and Riley had to struggle to keep up with him.

"I think there's a basement," Gabriel said. "They must've-"

Gabriel was cut off by an animal-like growl that suddenly echoed through the warehouse. It was immediately followed by terrified shrieks. Riley followed Gabriel toward the source of the sounds and searched frantically for a stairway. The shrieking subsided, but the growling didn't. It sounded like it was getting closer and Riley gripped his gun tightly in his hand.

Suddenly, Gabriel tapped his shoulder twice and Riley darted to the left without hesitating.

186

A huge grizzly bear emerged from underneath the rubble that Riley had been standing on just seconds before. Gabriel was still too close and he had to roll out of the way. Riley aim his gun at the animal, but didn't fire a shot. He knew that his handgun would do nothing but make the bear angry.

The bear roared as it struggled to get free of the rubble. It shook dust off of it's massively bulky fur and grunted aggressively.

Riley didn't have time to wonder what a bear was doing loose in the middle of Portland before it charged him.

He darted behind a chunk of concrete, but it didn't prevent the bear from jumping on top of him. Riley rolled onto his stomach to protect the most vulnerable parts of his body. He covered the back of his head with his hands and wished he hadn't dropped his gun. He waited for the crazed bear to maul him, but nothing happened at first.

The bear stood over him and roared loudly. Then it slowly sank it's claws into the flesh just above Riley's hip. He winced at the pain, but was determined to keep quiet and as still as possible. Playing dead was the only thing he could think to do in this situation. The bear used it's paw to force him to roll onto his back. He tried to resist, but the more he did the deeper it's claws sank into his skin.

Saliva dripped on Riley's face from the bear's muzzle. It didn't stink as badly as Riley thought it should. Bears generally had a very strong odor. He smelled minty toothpaste when the bear's breath hit his face. That's when Riley knew that this wasn't a real bear. It was a shapeshifter.

The shapeshifter bear growled and batted Riley's chest with it's paw. Panic and adrenaline coursed through him when the strong paw prevented him from taking a breath. Riley took inventory of how strong his pure magic was before deciding that the shapeshifter would kill him if he didn't do something quickly.

"Craticas winidio," Riley barely whispered.

The bear was pushed off of him by a strong gust of magical wind. Riley sat up in time to see the bear crash into a cracked beam. The shapeshifter shed it's bear skin before it hit

187

the ground. It quickly changed into a cougar and snarled with it's long fangs.

Riley glared at the shapeshifter and raised his hands with another craticas spell on the tip of his tongue. He knew using more of his magic would make him pass out. He had already extended his pure magic too far tonight, but he didn't know what else to do.

"I wouldn't do that if I were you, wizard," a voice behind him said casually.

Riley turned sharply and saw a beautiful woman holding Gabriel at knife point. She was dressed in tight black clothes with a leather jacket covering her top. She had silver knives strapped to her belt and black boots that looked like something a character in a spy movie would wear. Riley spotted an empty holster strapped to her underneath her jacket and he briefly wondered where her gun was.

Gabriel seemed to be unharmed besides a bruise that was rapidly appearing on his left temple. Riley discovered that the woman was a werewolf when her eyes flashed a glowing yellow in the receding light. The blue ball of light was growing dim and Riley couldn't use his magic to fix it while the werewolf held Gabriel at knifepoint.

She held Gabriel's wrists in a tight grip behind his back. She lifted his arms up slightly to put pressure on his joints and flashed her werewolf eyes at Riley. Even though there was a knife at his neck, Gabriel looked completely serene. His calmness usually rubbed off on Riley, but he was still shaking from being attacked by a bear. He didn't think he'd be able to act calm again anytime soon.

"Make one wrong move and I'll open his throat," she said threateningly. "Skinwalkers don't have much chance of survival if they bleed out."

As if to prove her point she pressed the knife against Gabriel's skin and a trail of blood dripped from a small wound. Gabriel's breath quickened, but his calm expression didn't change. Riley quickly lowered his hands and held them in front of him in submission.

"That's better." She smiled cruelly. "The rebellion must've found another wizard. Unless the rumors of Riley Hanson's death have been greatly exaggerated. I'm betting on the latter."

The cougar purred happily and Riley couldn't help but notice that it was creeping closer to him. With it's shoulders hunched, it stalked him like a predator. It made the hairs on the back of Riley's neck tingle and he had to resist the urge to back away from the animal.

He suddenly felt sorry for the wild rabbits that were unlucky enough to serve as vampire meals in the community's woods.

"Maybe Carvolo will give us a handsome reward for finding you," the werewolf said with a sneer. "Or, better yet, maybe I'll turn you and keep you for myself."

"You couldn't handle me, lady," Riley said with a sneer of his own.

"Don't be so sure," she said as she tightened her grip on Gabriel. The knife bit into his skin again and he winced this time.

"I'll do whatever you want. Just drop the knife."

Gabriel gave him a stern look, but Riley was too preoccupied with the cougar that was standing right behind him to care.

"That's an interesting offer, but I think I like my knife right where it is. Take him down, Sterling."

The cougar jumped on Riley. He fell as the giant cat sank it's claws into his back. He covered the back of his head with his hands and blood filled his mouth when his face hit the floor. The instinct to protect his head from the long fangs was stronger than his need to brace for the fall. He just hoped that he didn't break any teeth.

The cougar grabbed the back of his shirt with it's fangs and growled fiercely. It sent chills down Riley's spine. He knew that this was a shapeshifter, but he couldn't help but think about all the survival guides he'd read in high school. He didn't think that the cougar would kill him, but his body didn't believe his brain's logic. He was shaking and sweating from terror.

Riley didn't know how long they sat there, but the cougar didn't move. Riley never stopped shaking. It was hard to breathe with the heavy animal sitting on his back and he was pretty sure that he passed out at least once.

Then, as if the cougar had been waiting for something, it removed it's claws from Riley's back. It dragged him by the shirt through the debris. Riley wasn't against following it if the cougar gave him a chance to walk, but it never did. When they went down the stairs Riley had to brace himself with his hands and knees on the steps so that he wouldn't get injured while the cougar dragged him.

By the time they made it to the basement Riley's shirt was torn completely off of his body. His hands were scraped raw and his knees were bruised. He stayed down on all fours on the concrete floor and glanced at the cougar that held his torn shirt in it's strong jaws.

"There are a million easier ways that you could've gotten me down here, you freak," Riley mumbled defiantly through his bloody mouth. Blood was streaming out of his nose as well.

The cougar growled and dropped the shredded shirt. It charged him and head butted him in the side with such force that Riley lost his breath. He fell and didn't move as the cougar stood over him possessively. Riley wished he hadn't lost his handgun. He would've been able to kill the shapeshifter easily from this position if he still had it.

"Sterling," the werewolf girl said from somewhere in the dark basement. "Come guard the skinwalker."

The cougar scratched Riley's shoulder with it's sharp claws before obeying the werewolf. Riley sat up slowly and ignored his discomfort. He wasn't severely injured, but he had a few cuts and bruises. There wasn't much light in the basement, but he spotted Gabriel sitting in a chair. He was tied with ropes, which was interesting since the enemy werewolves usually used silver chains or handcuffs.

190

The werewolf grabbed Riley by the back of the neck and forced him to his feet. His knees wobbled, but he refused to stagger in front of the woman. She shoved him against the concrete wall and cuffed his wrists to silver chains above his head. He thought it was interesting that she saved the silver chains for him instead of for Gabriel. He could already tell that Gabriel was working to free himself from the ropes. He knew Gabriel well enough that he recognized what he was doing by just one glance. Their enemies wouldn't be able to see that the skinwalker was doing anything but calmly awaiting his fate.

"Comfortable?" the werewolf asked sarcastically.

Riley had to resist the urge to spit blood in her face. He didn't know how short her temper was yet, and he didn't want to risk getting himself killed just to show defiance. So he spit the blood on the floor before answering her.

"Yep," he replied lightheartedly. "My feet are on the ground, so I'm good."

"Oh," she said with a seductive smile. "This is gonna be fun. I'm definitely keeping you. Carvolo can find another chosen one."

"So you're defying your leader's wishes," Riley said with a tsk tsk. "You little rebel."

"Carvolo is not my leader," she said slyly. "Technically, he's my cousin. Sterling and I are mercenaries. I've been separate from the werewolves for a long time. I only do odd jobs that the werewolf leaders are willing to pay me for."

"Sounds like a promising career," Riley said, hoping to get her monologuing.

She must've known what he was doing because she menacingly leaned in close to his face. She was tall for a woman, almost as tall as him and he was six foot. Her long blond hair was pulled into a high ponytail. The lean muscles of her body matched the physique of someone who spent their days at the gym. But she was a werewolf, so she came by the muscles naturally.

She grabbed one of Riley's belt loops and pulled him away from the wall so she could frisk him for weapons. When she got to his feet she removed his socks and boots. That's where she found his silver ankle knife that Jackson had given him before they left. She pulled it from the small sheath and examined it.

"Cute throwing knife," she said as she tossed the blade into the air and caught it. The action was so casual that it was apparent she was an experienced knife thrower. "I think it'll go nicely with my ever growing collection."

She pointed the tip of the knife at Riley's chest and he stepped back until he hit the wall again. She followed him and lightly traced the cold silver blade over his bare chest. He blatantly ignored her and glanced at Gabriel. Riley hoped that he'd made some progress getting out of the ropes that bound him. Since Gabriel was being discreet it was taking a while.

The cougar stood in front of Gabriel at eye level. Riley couldn't see if they were staring each other down, but it wouldn't surprise him if they were. Gabriel hated most shapeshifters. Even the ones that they recruited for the rebellion he barely tolerated, except for a select few. Once Gabriel was free he and the shapeshifter would go at it and it wasn't going to be pretty.

"I see you don't scare easily," the werewolf said in amusement. "Most of the people I interrogate would be begging for mercy at this point."

She pressed the blade gently into his skin and Riley felt the familiar sting of it piercing through. A trickle of blood fell down his chest and he sighed into the pain.

"Well, you know," Riley said casually. "I've gone a few rounds with sadistic psychopaths like you before."

"I can see that."

She lowered the blade down to his abdomen where the scabbed over stab wounds were still healing. She spotted the telfa pad and tore it from the scrape that Gabriel had patched up. It was still bleeding a little.

"You must be one tough little boy to have survived these stab wounds. Most wizards would've been dead."

"I'm not like most wizards."

192

"That's good to know," she said with a smile. "So, don't you think I should ask you a few questions before we get too carried away?"

"It's been tried before. You won't get much out of me."

"We'll see about that," she said with a pleasant smile. "I have this extraordinary truth serum that one of my magical friends helped me invent. The ancients would do anything to get their hands on it. Once I inject it into your bloodstream you will tell me anything just to make the pain stop."

"Sounds exciting," Riley said as enthusiastically as he could. "I bet you feel really successful when your victims scream and beg."

The werewolf smiled widely. Riley was having a hard time getting a read on this one. Out of all the people who've tortured him she seemed to be the most experienced. The others either got offended easily or were too robotic in their jobs to care. Then there were those who were afraid to cause pain or were reluctant in some way. This woman didn't fit into either category. She was her own type of psychopath.

"Since you're not a *normal* wizard," she said lightly. "I can only assume that you can use your magic without tiring, or at least, without tiring as much as a *normal* wizard would. So to protect everyone here I'm going to give you a little something before we begin."

She rolled a tray table on wheels closer to her. There were knives, saws, and countless needles filled with different colored liquids. She grabbed a syringe filled with a brown liquid and advanced on Riley. He stiffened and clenched his sore hands. She inserted the needle into his abdomen and he hissed in pain. He could feel the poison spread through his body and he started to convulse. He moaned through the pain until it eventually subsided.

When it was over he couldn't feel his magic. He had to resist the urge to panic at the lose of it. He took a deep breath and gave his torturer a small chuckle.

"Is that all you got?"

"That was only the first round," she said with a smirk. "I can tell you'll be hard to break. You remind me of that other skinwalker that came here with you. Tall, blond, and seriously hot."

Riley glanced over at Gabriel and their eyes met. She had Marcus and Rebecca, as well as the human hostages they were supposed to be rescuing. They had expected a lot of untrained followers. Instead they got an extremely old werewolf leader and her pet shapeshifter.

"I still haven't broken him yet," she said with a calloused grin. "Of course, I haven't checked on him since you guys came in. He's been screaming for so long that I don't think he can physically scream anymore. I can ease his pain if you just tell me what I want to know. Since he's too stupid to cooperate I'm sure he would appreciate you alleviating his agony."

"What did you do to him?" Gabriel's voice was only a whisper, but the werewolf turned to him sharply.

"Sterling," she said patiently. "Please gag him. I will tolerate no further interruptions."

The shapeshifter shed it's cougar skin and took the shape of a monkey. Riley thought it was odd that the shapeshifter didn't change to human form to do a human task. The monkey grabbed a dirty cloth off of the floor with it's hands and hopped toward Gabriel.

Suddenly, the skinwalker pulled his hands free of the rope and punched the monkey in the face. The monkey shrieked and fell to the ground. Before it could recover Gabriel grabbed the monkey and threw it into the wall. The shapeshifter changed back into a cougar in midair and roared angrily.

Gabriel broke into a limped run and the cougar took chase. Riley could do nothing but watch helplessly as the cougar chased his friend down the dark hallway. He didn't hear Gabriel scream so he assumed that the cougar hadn't caught him...yet.

"Well," the werewolf said as she turned her attention back to Riley. "That was unexpected."

"Really?" Riley asked with a raised eyebrow. "Why else would you tie him with ropes if you didn't want him to escape?"

The werewolf smiled that same wide smile and her eyes glowed in the darkness.

"You are insightful."

"Not really," Riley said nonchalantly. "I just pay attention. You said you were torturing Marcus. What did you do? Give him your truth serum and leave him to suffer in hopes that he'll eventually tell you what you want to know? You're wasting your time. Marcus is a diehard who will never break."

"You seem to be unbothered by the suffering of your friend," she said as she sorted through her torture equipment. "How very insensitive of you."

"You couldn't be more wrong. When I get loose you're a dead girl."

The werewolf smiled at his threat.

"Awe, but if you killed me you wouldn't know which serum is the antidote for your friend's pain. It would be cruel to leave him to suffer for the rest of his life...which would be short with the kind of agony he is in. He would eventually find a way to kill himself to end it, or his body would shut down. Either way, without my antidote he will die."

Riley clenched his teeth when she picked up another torture serum off of her tray. He didn't know if she was lying or not. but he really hoped that she was.

"So," he said as he looked her in the eye. "Your plan is to hold the humans down here hostage until the full moon for the werewolves. They'll pay you and you'll go on your merry little way with your pet shifter."

"Sterling is not a pet," she said with a smirk. "He is my follower. That is what happens when you change a shapeshifter into a werewolf. He can't stay in human skin for more than a few hours at a time and he changes into a werewolf on the full moon. Interesting though that he doesn't have the werewolf eyes or the extraordinary strength."

"So he *is* a pet," Riley said with a nod. "I guess you're in the right line of work. You like to inflict pain."

195

"You make the unsafe assumption that I'm the one who changed him," she replied with a shrug. "I actually rescued him from his first leader and he's been my partner ever since. Just as you can rescue yourself and your friend from severe pain if you answer my questions."

"It's funny…you keep telling me I need to answer your questions, but you haven't asked me a single one."

The werewolf paused for a moment and then laughed.

"I suppose you're right," she said through her chuckling. "I've never interrogated someone like you before. You're quite easy to talk to. Of course, that's all part of your plan to stall me. Under very different circumstances I'm sure we'd be friends. Maybe even a little more than that."

Riley snorted.

"Not on your life, sweetheart," he replied darkly.

She moved so fast that Riley didn't have time to blink before her face was merely a half an inch from his. His breath quickened in surprise and she smiled slightly. She inhaled deeply and closed her yellow glowing eyes for a moment. Riley wished he could back away from her, but there was no give to the concrete wall behind him.

"Wizard blood has an exquisite smell," she said dreamily. "Maybe I won't change you this full moon. It could be fun to just keep you as you are."

Her face moved closer and she pressed her forehead against his. Riley closed his eyes and did his best not to tremble. He'd never had his personal space invaded like this while being interrogated before. To say it was disconcerting would've been an understatement.

"Now tell me," she said in a soothing tone. "Where is your wand?"

"It's in a safe place," Riley whispered.

He knew that he had just confirmed her suspicion about the wand's existence, but he didn't really care about that.

"Where is that safe place?"

"On an island in the Caribbean," Riley said impassively.

Her forehead was still pressed against his as though she was trying to telepathically read his mind. He was thankful that werewolves didn't have that ability.

"Lying doesn't become you," she said with a small chuckle. "I'll give you one more chance to answer."

She took a step away from him and grabbed a syringe off of her tray.

"Where is that safe place?"

"On top of Mount Everest. Let me tell ya, it sucked getting it up there."

"I knew you'd be a challenge for me," she said nonchalantly.

Riley felt the needle pierce his abdomen and the pain came quicker than it did during the first round. It felt like fire was spreading through his veins. He gripped the chains tightly in his hands and concentrated on breathing. It hurt, badly, but it was nothing compared to the pain he'd received in the past from torture incantations. He didn't even scream.

"Should we increase the intensity?" the werewolf whispered. Her face was only a half an inch away from his again. "Or you can tell me where the wand is hidden. If you do I promise I'll make the pain stop for you and your friend."

The burning increased unexpectedly and Riley groaned. He tried to speak, but all he could manage was a small grunt.

"Take your time," she said in a mockingly polite tone. She sounded almost motherly. "Once you find your voice again you can tell me. I'm a patient woman."

The werewolf took a few steps away from him and he was finally able to relax into the pain. Having her so close made him tense, which was probably the whole point.

"Why do you want the wand?" Riley asked in a shaky whisper. "What good could it do you?"

"You aren't in a position to ask questions," she said as she picked up another syringe. She got up close and personal with him again. Her nose touched his and he couldn't help but shudder.

"Maybe you need another dose. Unless you have something to tell me?"

"I actually didn't want to say anything," Riley said through a gasp. "But since you insist; you're breath smells horrible."

The werewolf chuckled.

"You think you're pretty funny, don't you?"

"I think I'm hilarious," he said as he mustered up a smirk.

The pain wasn't subsiding and it was zapping his energy. The silver cuffs were cutting into his wrists as it became harder to hold himself upright. He leaned his head against his raised arm since his neck wasn't able to hold it up anymore.

The werewolf grabbed his dark hair that was matted from sweat and jerked his head upward. A fiery needle sank into his neck and he screamed.

Chapter 13

Riley couldn't remember what he was supposed to tell the blurry figure in front of him. All he could think about was how much unrelenting pain he was in. He convulsed uncontrollably and it felt like every cell in his body was taking turns exploding. His vision suddenly went black and he couldn't remember where he was. He couldn't even remember who he was.

He would do anything to make it stop.

A needle poked into his left forearm and his vision came back almost immediately. His clustered thoughts began to make more sense and he finally remembered what was going on. His screaming stopped, but he was still in tremendous pain.

"This is a little different than a traditional interrogation, Riley," the sadistic blond said casually. "There's degrees of pain. I just gave you the highest dosage of the most potent serum that I have. I gave you a small amount of revive, that's what I call the antidote, to take some of the edge off. I assume you can understand me now?"

Riley didn't answer her. He just panted in pain and hoped that he wouldn't throw up.

"What I just gave you…what you just experienced…is happening to your friend right now. You said his name was Marcus, right?"

Riley opened his eyes and met her icy blue ones. She was standing so close that her body touched his slightly.

Riley thought better about hoping against the vomiting. Now was the perfect time for it. Unfortunately, all he felt now was dizziness along with the intense agony.

"You understand what he's going through," she said in a falsely sympathetic voice. "You're the only one that can save him from it and yourself. Now just tell me where you've hidden the wand."

Riley wasn't sure how she expected him to answer her. He was pretty sure that the screaming had destroyed his vocal cords. But he gave it a try anyway.

"I took it-" Riley whispered hoarsely, He tried to clear his throat but it didn't help. "I took it to a beach."

"To a beach?" the werewolf asked when he stopped to take a painful gasp. "What beach?"

"In Florida," he replied. "I gave it to a manatee. He's keeping it safe for me."

She stared into his eyes in confusion for a moment. She brushed his cheek gently with the tips of her fingers. He was too weak to try to resist her touch. The feel of her fingers on his skin only made the burning pain worse.

"You know," she said gently. "I think we might be getting somewhere. That wasn't nearly as clever as your other lies."

"Whatever," he whispered. "I had you going until I mentioned the manatee."

She stuck another needle into his abdomen and the pain increased a few notches. He resumed screaming until his voice gave out. Then he threw up. The blond werewolf must've been expecting it because she held out a bucket for him before it happened. When he was finished being sick he broke out in a cold sweat and he shook violently.

"I'm going to leave you here to think it over," she said. "I'll be back in about an hour. I don't think you're going to like what I have planned next, so I suggest you try to come to your senses."

She turned to walk away, but then looked back at him.

"Rest assured, I will be checking in with your comrades," she said with a smirk. "I'm sure that Sterling has reunited the escaped skinwalker with your other companions."

Riley didn't have the energy to watch her leave. The pain was so intense his vision was blurred again. He thought he would be relieved to have her gone, but he found that her presence had been distracting from the pain. Now he had nothing to focus on. No one to give a snotty retort too. Fierce agony was the only thing left.

If the whole community wasn't at stake he would've told her where the wand was after the mindless pain he went through. He couldn't imagine how Marcus was coping. He

200

probably wasn't. That amount of pain was just too much for a body to take.

Riley closed his eyes and wished that he would pass out, but he didn't think it would happen. Time seemed to stand still. Seconds felt like minutes and minutes felt like hours.

When the werewolf came back he was positive that she had been gone for more than one hour. But the pain confused his thought processes so he didn't really know how long she'd been gone. Not that her return was something that he'd been looking forward to. He clenched his fists when she got closer to him. She pressed two fingers to his carotid artery and grinned happily.

"Erratic and dangerously fast," she said conversationally. "You have a high threshold for pain, but a pulse never lies."

Riley avoided looking at her and rested his head against his arm. His hands and arms had gone numb a long time ago which only added to his discomfort.

"Are you ready to tell me where the wand is? Marcus would really appreciate it. He couldn't tell me because he says he doesn't know where it is. Neither do your other companions. So you'd really be helping him out if you told me."

Riley perked up a bit when she told him that. Little did she know that she just gave him the courage he needed to stay strong. All three of them knew that Roan was studying the wand. If Marcus was willing to suffer this kind of pain, and if Rebecca and Gabriel were willing to let him do it, then Riley had no problem being uncooperative. If he did end up telling her where it was, Marcus would never let him forget it. That's assuming she didn't kill them after she got what she wanted.

Riley mumbled something unintelligible and the werewolf invaded his personal space again.

"I didn't catch that," she said softly.

"I'm gonna kill you," he whispered shakily.

The werewolf bristled at the ominous threat, but she quickly covered up her reaction.

"Oh, no more jokes?" she asked in amusement. "Now we're getting somewhere. Where is the wand?"

"I don't know where it is either," he replied in a raspy voice.

"You're lying," she whispered dangerously. "I'm going to change my tactics if you don't answer me. What happens next will be a bit more-"

She stopped in mid-sentence and gritted her teeth in a nasty snarl. Riley had yet to see her lose her temper and it surprised him that she suddenly seemed angry. Maybe it was annoyance? He was in so much pain he didn't try to figure it out.

"Friends of yours, I assume?" she asked menacingly.

Riley tried to hide his confusion from her. He hadn't heard anything, but he also didn't have werewolf hearing. She quickly picked up one of the torture serums and Riley tensed involuntarily. She injected him in the arm and he screamed hoarsely as more fire spread through his veins.

He didn't know how it was possible that he was still conscious.

There was a loud blast as another explosion rocked the floor above them. Terrified screams came from the hallway that Gabriel had been chased down. The shapeshifter, in grizzly bear form, charged past them and up the stairs.

The werewolf grabbed Riley's chin forcefully and made him look at her. She leaned in close to his face and her lips lightly touched his. Riley took in a sharp breath as her kiss became more aggressive. Her lips felt like fire and the burning was unbearable. The pain from her kiss almost sent him into another screaming fit. The closest thing he could compare it to was Sarai's kiss of death. But even this was more painful. He almost lost his mind to the agony.

"Who are they?" she whispered. "How did they find us?"

"I-I...don't know," Riley managed to whisper as he hyperventilated. "I don't know."

She grabbed another needle and stabbed it into his neck. The extraordinary pain came instantly and nothing else mattered except for the fire in his blood. He couldn't do anything

202

but scream. He could only think about how much he wanted the pain to stop.

His torturer backed away from him without him noticing and ran up the stairs.

"Riley? Riley? Can you hear me?"

He wasn't screaming anymore so he could hear whoever was speaking to him. Her voice sounded familiar but his brain wasn't able to figure out who it was. His eyes were closed since it took too much energy to keep them open. The pain was so severe that he could barely comprehend anything else. Even responding to the person in front of him was impossible.

Someone put a gentle hand on his cheek and he cried out in pain. The hand was so hot that it felt like his skin was sizzling.

Whoever it was quickly removed their hand.

"I'm sorry, Ry. I didn't know that would make it worse."

"Don't touch him," another familiar voice echoed in the basement. It was a deep and gravelly male's voice. "The stuff she gave him can make the skin very sensitive. If you have to touch him, don't do it lightly. The firmer the touch the less painful it is."

"We need to do something. He can't go on like this."

Riley struggled to open his eyes. When they fluttered open he saw Naomi looking at him with intense concern. Even through his blurred vision he recognized her by her black hair with red and blue lowlights. She had changed her hairstyle since the last time he saw her. Her forehead was creased with fury and her lips were drawn into a tight line. Her fiery red dragon eyes were hard to see in the dim lighting.

"Hey, Ry," she said to him soothingly. Her gentle tone didn't match the furious look on her face. "We're gonna get you down once we find the key. I tried to melt the chains, but sometimes silver is too much even for me to handle."

203

A light came on and Riley blinked a few times against the brightness. His head throbbed and he groaned. The urge to vomit hit him, but he managed to fight it. He really didn't want to throw up all over Naomi. He had a feeling he'd never live something like that down.

He finally noticed that Raya and Jeremy were there. Raya was rummaging through the contents of a small bag and Jeremy had the blond werewolf torturer slung over his shoulder with a silver knife in her spine. She hung limply and her arms swung loosely whenever Jeremy moved. The sight gave Riley a spark of relief.

Jeremy dropped the werewolf to the floor without trying to be gentle and hurried over to the tray of torturous syringes. He sorted through them carefully as he studied each one. After a few minutes of examining them he swore in frustration.

"What's going on, Jeremy?" Naomi asked without taking her eyes off of Riley's face.

"It's not here," he replied tersely.

He stalked over to the blond werewolf and roughly pulled the knife from her spine. He grabbed her by her leather jacket and threw her against the wall with his forearm at her throat. She sneered at him angrily with her glowing yellow eyes. She tried to fight him off, but apparently Jeremy was a lot stronger. Or at least angrier. His whole body shook with rage as his yellow werewolf eyes pierced into the female werewolf's. Her efforts to free herself from Jeremy went unnoticed by him.

"Where is the revive, Hanna," he demanded in a soft growl.

"Jeremy," she said through a strangled gasp. "Looks like you escaped after all. You always told me you never would. Is the monster still raging inside of you? It certainly looks like it."

Jeremy pulled her from the wall and slammed her back into it with a loud crack.

"Where is it?" he yelled loudly.

"Why would I bring it all with me?" she asked with a menacing laugh. "I wasn't supposed to interrogate anyone on this assignment. Riley and Marcus were just bonuses. I already used what little I had during the interrogation."

"Marcus?" Naomi whispered urgently. "He's been tortured too?"

The blond werewolf, Hanna, laughed cruelly. Jeremy threw her to the ground and inserted the knife back into her spine. She didn't make another sound. He stood over her paralyzed body and shook with pent up fury. It was obvious that he was fighting every instinct he had to kill Hanna.

Jeremy blinked a few times until his werewolf eyes turned back to a soft human brown.

"I found a key," Raya said timidly. "Hopefully it's the right one."

Jeremy spared her a glance before studying Riley's condition for a moment.

"Before we get him down we need to relieve his symptoms somehow," Jeremy said gruffly.

"Without the, what did you call it...revive? Um, how will we be able to help him?" Raya asked quietly. "Is there an antidote of some kind or adrenaline we can give him?"

"Revive is what Hanna calls the antidote," Jeremy explained. "It will take the symptoms away almost immediately depending on how much she gave him. By the looks of it she gave him everything she had. Without the antidote it'll take a few days before he doesn't feel pain and it'll be a week before he's back to normal. I don't know if anything else can help. But I do know that if we move him too much in this state he could have a seizure."

Naomi finally looked away from Riley and stared at the formidable werewolf.

"How do you know all of this, Jeremy?" Naomi asked skeptically.

"The werewolf leaders used to hire her to interrogate me," Jeremy said gruffly.

Raya glared sharply at Hanna's still form and snarled in her throat. It took her a moment to stop staring at the paralyzed werewolf with murder in her eyes. Jeremy seemed startled by

205

Raya's reaction for a moment, but he covered up his emotions quickly.

"Do you think hemioc would help?" Raya asked Jeremy in a calmer tone. She rummaged through the contents of their first aid duffle. "There's guresh in here as well, but Riley's not exactly wounded so I don't know if it'll help him the same way."

"Hemioc would be better," Jeremy said with a nod. "It'll give him a boost, but I don't think it'll take the pain away. We'll be lucky if he doesn't start spasming-"

Riley couldn't keep up with the conversation. He was hearing everything they said, but he couldn't comprehend any of it anymore. A fresh wave of torturous pain seeped through his body and his mind went blank with agony.

It wasn't until Raya started toward him with a needle in her hand that he freaked out. He wasn't in his right mind and he couldn't think clearly. She was his friend and only trying to help him, but he still didn't want her anywhere near him with that needle. His fists clenched and he mumbled something incoherent through a tight moan.

"I think he tried to say something," Raya said with wide eyes.

"Riley?" Naomi said gently. "Can you say that again?"

"Please…no…" he breathed through a small whimper. "No…no…please."

Naomi looked at him in confusion. Raya stood a few feet away with the needle in her hand with the same expression. Jeremy only nodded in understanding and took the syringe from Raya. He hid it from Riley's sight quickly.

"He doesn't want to be stabbed with a needle again," Jeremy explained. "And I don't blame him."

A spark of relief went through Riley. At least Jeremy understood. The relief was soon replaced by more pain and he went mindless again.

"Well, what are we supposed to do?" Naomi asked in frustration. "Even if he could swallow it in his current condition I don't think that the hemioc will work as well when it's not inserted directly into the bloodstream."

206

"Distract him," Jeremy said grimly.

Naomi sighed and kicked a stool toward Riley. She stood on it so that her face was almost level with his. His head still rested on his arm and he stared at her with wild eyes. He was breathing fast and he moaned as a fresh wave of fierce pain coursed through his body.

Naomi took his face in her hands with a firm grip that wasn't too tight. He winced in anticipation for more pain. But instead of more heat her hands felt cool on his face. It made him shiver more intensely.

"Look at me, Riley," she said calmly. His blue eyes found her red ones and she held his gaze. "It's going to be okay. Just concentrate on me and listen to my voice. I'm not going to let anyone hurt you."

A needle sank into his neck. He tried to jerk away, but Naomi held him still.

"Shh," she said soothingly. "It's okay. It's just hemioc. We're trying to get you back on your feet so we can go help the others."

Riley vaguely remembered that there were other people that needed saving, but it was a fleeting thought through the fierce pain. Another needle entered his neck and he tried to jerk away again.

Suddenly, some of the pain subsided. He took a ragged breath and his eyes softened a little. Naomi ran her fingers through his hair to try to get him to relax a bit more.

She told him a story about when she blew fire at a castle in the medieval times because the lord that lived there was imprisoning innocent serfs. She could talk until the cows came home, and it had been a while since their last conversation. So she unloaded on him with the heroic tale while Jeremy continued injecting him with the magical adrenaline.

Riley didn't know how much hemioc Jeremy gave him, but it gave him a spark of energy. He was able to think a little more clearly. The horrific pain was still there, but it was a bit more manageable. He was now aware of his numb arms and hands and how sore his legs were. He squirmed a little to try to find a more comfortable position.

"Are you ever going to tell me who does your hair?" Riley asked when he could finally use his voice again. He sounded like someone who'd smoked two packs a day for fifty years.

Naomi grinned flirtatiously.

"Nope," she said as she tossed her hair off her shoulder. "Drake would disown me if I ever told anyone that he's my stylist."

"Shucks," Riley rasped. "So I can't ask him to do mine?"

Naomi gaped at him incredulously.

"What on earth would you do to your hair? You're super attractive just the way you are."

"I was thinking of going with lime green."

Naomi laughed and glanced over at Jeremy who was holding another syringe of hemioc in his fingers. He was staring at the two of them as though they'd lost their minds.

"I think he's had enough of that stuff," she told him. "Do you think we could get him down now?"

"Does he always talk nonsense after being tortured?" Jeremy asked with wide eyes. "Or was one of those syringes filled with something a little more fun?"

Naomi smirked and jumped off of the stool.

"No, he just uses humor to deflect from how infuriated he is," Naomi explained.

"Please," Riley rasped tiredly. He quickly realized that their banter was wearing him out instead of making him feel better. "Get me down."

Raya hurried forward with a sliver key in her hand and gave it to Jeremy. The werewolf unclasped the silver cuffs from Riley's bloodied wrists. He barely managed to stay on his feet before Jeremy wrapped an arm around his waist to steady him.

Naomi and Raya dragged Hanna to the silver chains and cuffed her before pulling the silver knife out of her spine that paralyzed her. She immediately pulled angrily against the chains and screamed at them furiously.

Riley had been trying the whole time to get that kind of angry reaction from her. Apparently being chained helplessly to a wall did the trick.

"What are you going to do, Jeremy?" Hanna hissed at him angrily. "You gonna take your revenge and give me a taste of my own medicine? Bring it on!"

Jeremy stared at her for a moment in thought. Riley would've been perfectly fine with giving Hanna a dose of the torture serum that was still coursing through his veins. He couldn't even stand on his own. The pain was so extraordinary that he had to focus on his breathing so he wouldn't hyperventilate.

Jeremy proved to be the better man when he shook his head.

"Nope," he said nonchalantly. "I may be a monster, but I'm not a sadistic psychopath like you are."

Naomi and Raya picked up their supplies and led the way down the hallway. Jeremy and Riley took up the rear. They ignored Hanna's furious cursing as they left her chained to the wall. The further they went down the hallway the darker it got. Naomi manipulated her flames in the palm of her hand to light the way for them. The orange flame brought with it a comforting heat. It was then that Riley realized how cold he was.

After a few minutes of walking they heard a loud gasp and a few terrified shrieks.

They'd come across the human captives. There were fifteen of them locked in a large silver cage. All of them were horrified and a few looked sick or injured. Raya ruffled through Hanna's bag to look for another key. She pulled out an old looking key, but it didn't fit the lock.

Naomi held her flamed hand to the bars and the fire wrapped around the front of the cage. Riley expected the heat to increase, but it didn't. The people in the cage huddled together in fear, but Naomi left the flames on the metal until it melted a large hole. The fire retreated back to her hand until she held the ball of flame like she had before.

"You guys can come out now," Naomi said to the terrified captives. "I promise you won't get burned from the melted metal. My fires cool off instantly if I want them to."

"What kind of freaks are you?" A big man who stood in front of the others glared at them angrily.

"The kind that just saved your lives," Naomi said sweetly. "You're welcome."

It didn't look like any of the captives were too injured to walk. Even if they were Riley doubted they would appreciate being stabbed with injections of guresh. None of the captives moved, so Naomi and Raya walked on. Jeremy and Riley stumbled after them with an awkward gait.

"If you need a break let me know," Jeremy said as he half dragged Riley along.

"No," Riley gasped. "Just find them."

Jeremy nodded and he picked up the pace to catch up to Naomi and Raya. Riley expected to find another cage, but instead they found a steel door. The key Raya found fit the lock and Naomi pushed open the heavy door. Inside the room were two small prison cells. Marcus and Rebecca shared one and Gabriel was chained up in the other.

Marcus looked terrible. Rebecca had a tight grip on his torso with his head in her lap and his legs twitched every few seconds. It looked like he was having a seizure, but Riley knew it was probably just pain that caused the reaction. Rebecca was keeping him still so that he wouldn't hurt himself more.

Gabriel was calmly examining his chains with a furious tick in his jaw. He was probably trying to avoid looking at his brother's agony by mapping an escape plan in his head. He had a large scratch that ran from his right shoulder to his left hip, presumably from the cougar shapeshifter. It was deep and bleeding, but he didn't seem to be losing too much blood.

It took Rebecca and Gabriel a moment to notice them standing in the doorway. Relief washed over their expressions when they saw them. Naomi kicked in the door to Gabriel's cell and Raya hurried in to see if she could unchain him.

Jeremy propped Riley up against the wall and hurried over to Marcus and Rebecca's cell. Rebecca's ankle was chained to the concrete floor and Naomi tried to use her flames to free her, but it didn't work. Jeremy grabbed the key that he'd used to free Riley and took the cuff off of her ankle.

Rebecca hurried out of the cell to get out of Naomi and Jeremy's way as they worked to get Marcus stable. She seemed to panic a little bit when she saw Riley. He was still in so much pain that he could barely speak. Rebecca rushed over to him and knelt down in front of him.

"I heard you screaming," she whispered desperately. "Somehow she took my magic away and I couldn't stop her."

She didn't touch him, which he appreciated. She must've figured out how much it hurt to be touched while trying to help Marcus. He took in a sharp breath to try to keep calm as he shook from the agonizing fire that seared his veins.

"Not. Your. Fault," he managed to whisper. "Marcus?"

"He's not good," she said quietly. "He screamed for so long and then he just stopped. He hasn't made a sound since, but he kept twitching and jerking. I had to hold him still because I was worried that he was seizing and I didn't want him to hurt himself."

Gabriel and Raya hurried over to them anxiously. Rebecca stood up and hugged Gabriel tightly. He kissed her on the top of the head and held her. She was shaking uncontrollably, which was abnormal for a werewolf. Her fists clutched at Gabriel's torn shirt in a compulsive way. She buried her face in his chest and inhaled and exhaled as though she were practicing yoga.

"Is she okay?" Riley mouthed to Gabriel.

He shook his head once in reply and Riley gritted his teeth in pain and anger. Hanna must've given Rebecca some of the serum so she couldn't use her magic. At least she didn't have the mindless pain that Marcus was going through.

Jeremy came out of the cell with Marcus slung over his shoulders in a fireman's carry. The skinwalker looked like he was unconscious, but Riley knew that he wasn't. Jeremy didn't

211

wait for anyone to follow him before he walked out the door with Marcus.

"We've got to go," Naomi said. "Raya, can you help Riley?"

Raya nodded and she helped Riley stagger to his feet. Naomi lit the hallway with her fireball and they made their way slowly through the darkness.

"Did anyone kill the shapeshifter?" Gabriel asked quietly. "Because if not we need to rectify that."

"I'm not sure if I killed him," Naomi said. "But I sure did deep fry him. He didn't get up afterwards and I didn't have time to check if he was dead. It's kinda hard to concentrate when you hear your friend screaming."

"What about the blond werewolf?" Gabriel asked.

"She's chained to the wall just up ahead," Jeremy replied.

He was carrying Marcus as though he weighed no more than a feather. Riley was sure that Marcus despised every second of being carried. He was an alpha wolf and they tended to hate looking weak. Especially in front of other dominant creatures like Jeremy, even if they were close friends.

"I'll deal with her when we get you guys out of here," Naomi said darkly. "Then I'll meet you at the motel."

"What do you plan on doing to her?" Raya asked uncertainly.

"I'm going to contact Demian and Jackson before we make that decision," Naomi replied. "I don't know if we should be taking prisoners."

"She shouldn't be allowed to live," Jeremy said sternly. "If she ever escapes then she'll torture again. We need to make sure we destroy her serums too."

"I already did," Raya said. "After you looked through all of them and said the antidote wasn't there I got rid of them."

"That's good to know," Jeremy said in his gravelly voice.

When they made it to the open room that Riley was tortured in they found Hanna pulling against the chains furiously. Riley shuddered at the sight of her and Raya's grip

212

around his waist tightened so he wouldn't collapse. Seeing Hanna caused panic to grip him and he started to hyperventilate. He didn't like the fact that he was scared of her, so he mentally blamed it on the severe pain that he was in.

"Raya, Jeremy," Naomi said angrily as she watched Riley's reaction to seeing Hanna. "Get Riley out of here. I'm just going to deal with her now."

Riley had never seen Naomi like that before. Not even when they thought Rebecca had betrayed them. He'd fought battles with her and he'd seen her cry when Roy got hurt in the explosion weeks ago. Even then she had never been this furious.

Naomi was going to kill Hanna for not only hurting Riley and Marcus, but for the psychological damage she caused them. Riley knew he shouldn't want her to, but he didn't care. Naomi was protecting them in her violent dragon way.

Gabriel and Rebecca took point so that Jeremy wouldn't have to fight off potential enemies with Marcus on his shoulders. They walked up the stairs slowly in case the shapeshifter was still alive. The smell of scorched flesh and fur burned Riley's nose and he had to resist the urge to gag. If he threw up he would rather it not be all over Raya.

It didn't take them long to realize that the shapeshifter's dead body was decomposing at the top of the stairs. They hurried past it and made their way through the debris.

The second explosion had done a very small amount of damage. Naomi must've absorbed it. That was lucky because the warehouse looked like it would collapse if it took much more damage.

There was no sign of the human captives, so they assumed that they had escaped. Which could mean that Naomi didn't have much time before the police arrived. Riley wasn't too worried about it though. Naomi could handle the human police if she had to.

It took them a while to trudge through the mounds of concrete and other debris. When they finally made it outside Riley gulped in the fresh air as though he'd been submerged in

213

water. He hadn't realized before how hard his lungs had been working in the warehouse. The quality of air was a vast change.

Their compact car had five small seats. With Riley's and Marcus's condition it was even harder to find room since all they wanted to do was lie down. Riley rested his head against the backseat window and Marcus did the same on the other side of the car. Rebecca was sandwiched between them in the middle seat. Riley could feel her shaking next to him and it made his skin feel raw.

Jeremy elected to stay behind with Naomi so that they didn't have to try to squeeze him in too. To everyone's surprise it was Raya that vehemently protested his suggestion.

"You're not leaving me alone with four injured people," she said vexingly. "Just get in the passenger seat and I'll sit on your lap."

"That'll be fun to explain to the police if we get pulled over," Jeremy said sarcastically as he folded his arms across his chest. "A driver with a torn up chest and three torture victims in the backseat. Should make for a good headline I suppose."

"Just get in, Jeremy," Gabriel said as he sat in the driver seat. "I can avoid the police."

"Should you even be driving?" Rebecca mumbled in exhaustion.

"I'm fine, honey," Gabriel told her reassuringly. Then turned his attention back to Jeremy. "Get in. We need to leave."

Jeremy sighed and squeezed into the passenger seat. His knees hit the dash because the seat had to be moved forward in order for Marcus to fit in the back. Raya sat on his lap and closed the door without any further protest from Jeremy. Gabriel put the car in drive and they headed for the motel.

Chapter 14

The burning liquid that came out of Riley's mouth was nasty. Rebecca held his head as he spit the bile into the toilet since he'd lost the ability to hold up his own head properly. It had been two days of pure misery. The pain was subsiding slowly, but he literally hadn't slept for almost three days.

There was a point when he couldn't take it anymore. He'd asked Gabriel to knock him out just so he could take a mental break from it all. Gabriel probably would've done it if Jeremy hadn't stopped him. The torture element specifically kept the victims awake to prolong the discomfort and exhaustion. Any attempt to knock Riley out would've been useless.

The second day of his recovery had been spent throwing up, so he past the time lounging on the bathroom floor. Rebecca had insisted on keeping him company even though he told her she didn't have to multiple times.

Marcus was a lot better off now than Riley was. The sun was helping his body sweat out the torture element quickly. Riley couldn't be more envious. Marcus had a fever, but at least he wasn't constantly vomiting. Rebecca was slowing getting her magic back. She had tried incantartus infecto to help the detox process along, but she didn't have enough power yet. Riley still couldn't feel his pure magic at all and it scared him. He tried not to entertain the thought that it was gone permanently because he knew that it wasn't. It was still terrifying to be without it for so long.

While they were stuck in the motel room, Naomi and Jeremy went werewolf hunting. Most of the leaders in Portland were now dead and their followers were starting to leave the city in small hoards. It was easier than expected since Naomi was able to use her fire. It was very nice having her help. It was not surprising to look back on the historical legends of dragons and see how much people feared them. If they had more

215

dragons in the rebellion they probably would've won the war already.

Riley retched again and more foul tasting bile spewed from his mouth. He coughed and gagged for a moment before slumping back down to the floor. His whole body shook from pain and exhaustion. Rebecca sat next to him and gave him a sympathetic look.

"Well," he said through a gasp. "That was awful."

"You look miserable," Rebecca replied sadly. "I wish there was something I could do."

"I wouldn't mind throwing up this crap if it helped take the pain away, but it doesn't."

"You seem to be more lucid than you were yesterday," Rebecca said encouragingly.

She threw a blanket over his shivering form and lifted his head to place a pillow under it.

"You should try to sleep."

Riley grunted and closed his eyes.

"I've been trying for two days, sis,"

"I know, but maybe you've thrown up enough of that crap that you might be able to now."

Riley didn't want to think about throwing up anymore so he quickly changed the subject.

"Have you guys figured out what to do about Jeremy?" Riley asked in a whisper. "For the full moon."

"We aren't going to make it back to the community in time for the full moon," Rebecca said worriedly. "I think Jeremy is scared out of his mind. He hasn't really talked to anyone since we got here. Not even to Gabriel."

"Why did he come anyway?"

"Raya said that Demian ordered him to," Rebecca said tersely. "I think he wanted Jeremy to have something to do to keep his mind off of things. I don't think he expected it to be this bad."

Riley snorted and gave his sister an incredulous look.

"Of course he knew it was bad. He sent Naomi and a berserker werewolf."

Demian had told them before they left that he believed Jeremy was a berserker. A very rare type of werewolf that was stronger and more violent than what was normal. In ancient times they were used as the protectors of their packs. Especially over the tamers. But abuse and imprisonment turned them into uncontrollable rage monsters. It would explain Jeremy's behaviors.

They weren't sure how Jeremy felt about Demian's assessment since he refused to talk about it.

"And a tamer," Rebecca said thoughtfully. "Yeah, you're right...Demian knew we were in trouble."

"I told him I'd help him out this full moon," Riley said regretfully. "But my pure magic is MIA and the wand is in Washington."

"We can only hope that my magic is strong enough to contain him if he freaks out. Besides, Raya is here too."

"Raya's abilities don't help him."

Rebecca nodded in agreement, but there was a slight smirk on her face.

"I think that's because he likes her."

"Seriously?" Riley asked in surprise.

"Well, I don't know for sure if he does, but she definitely doesn't feel comfortable around him either. That's what she told me anyway."

Riley had to take a moment to process what Rebecca just said. The pain was starting to come back with a vengeance and he had to take a few deep breaths. Rebecca scooted closer to him and ran her fingers through his hair to massage his scalp. It helped a little.

"Why?" he whispered. "Raya has no reason to be scared of him. Berserkers exist to protect tamers."

"I don't think she's scared of him. She just doesn't feel comfortable around him."

"What's the difference?"

"I can't really explain it," Rebecca said with a shrug. "I guess it's a girl thing."

Riley closed his eyes and grimaced. The conversation was no longer distracting him from the pain. There were times now that he got short breaks from the burning agony, but it wasn't often. Jeremy said it would last for a few days, but he wouldn't be back to normal for about a week. So Riley wasn't sure how long the pain would last. He wondered how often Hanna tortured Jeremy. For him to know as much as he did about the recovery process Riley could only imagine that it was too many times.

"I think we should get you to bed," Rebecca said. "You're uncomfortable enough without laying on the hard tile floor all day.'"

Riley sat up as quickly as he could and threw up again. Rebecca had to grab him to keep him from falling over.

"Or not," she said tightly.

Riley opened his eyes blearily. It took him a moment to realize that he'd been asleep. Pacing footsteps in the motel room woke him. He wondered how long he slept. He felt groggy and dehydrated, but no pain. He gasped in relief when he realized that the burning agony was gone, but he didn't expect it to last. His energy was completely nonexistent. It was a struggle to sit up in bed. He had muscle aches, as though he had a fever, but he didn't feel hot. He shivered a little when the blanket dropped from his shoulders.

It was Jeremy that was pacing the floor. A quick look around told him that they were the only ones in the room. Jeremy seemed agitated and his yellow eyes flashed in the dimly lit room. Riley was about to lay back down since he didn't want to freak him out, but Jeremy's eyes met his almost instantly.

Terrifying rage burned in Jeremy's eyes. Riley wasn't sure what set the werewolf off, but he knew that he was in extreme danger. He didn't dare move as Jeremy breathed in ragged breaths. Riley searched within himself for a spark of his

218

pure magic, but he found nothing. His only possible defense against the feral werewolf was still gone. He had no idea what the others were thinking. They had left him defenseless against a mentally damaged berserker werewolf so close to the full moon.

To Riley's surprise, Jeremy's breathing gradually slowed and his eyes stopped glowing. He took a shaky breath before sitting on a chair next to a small table. He looked at Riley in concern for a moment then stared at the floor. Riley didn't say anything and the atmosphere became awkwardly tense.

"I'm sorry, man," Jeremy said with a shake of his head. "I think I was having some kind of panic attack. I didn't mean to wake you...or scare you."

"You get panic attacks?" Riley asked.

"Sometimes. Usually right before the full moon."

"Which is tomorrow?" Riley had a hard time keeping track of days lately.

Jeremy nodded, but didn't look up from the floor.

"Where is everyone else?" Riley asked.

"Raya went to get you some ice."

"Ice? Why?"

Jeremy grunted incredulously, but still wouldn't look at him.

"Dude, you have like a one hundred and six degree fever. I'm surprised you're awake."

"I'm not taking another ice bath," Riley said with a grimace. "That's not happening."

Jeremy tore his eyes from the floor and looked at him questioningly.

"Last time I had a fever like this Sammie had Marcus dunk me in an ice bath."

"I don't think she's planning on giving you an ice bath," Jeremy said in amusement. "Although, I would pay to see something like that."

"Where's everyone else?"

"They left," Jeremy said in a dark tone that wasn't directed at Riley. "Demian said they were needed somewhere in

219

California. I'm not sure on the specifics. Rebecca tried to wake you before they left, but you were dead to the world. The four of them are flying there right now. I guess we'll be driving the car back to Washington the day after the full moon."

There was silence between them for a moment while Riley processed what Jeremy had just told him.

"What the crap was Demian thinking?" Riley asked incredulously.

"Is it just me or does he seem to be a little, um... Is insane the right word?"

"Yes," Riley said severely. "Is this some crazy scheme to get you to face the full moon on your own with no chains?"

"Probably," Jeremy replied. "So I'm going to take off after Raya gets back. With any luck I'll find some vast forest that I can wait out the full moon in."

"I don't know if that's a good idea either, Jeremy," he said with a shake of his head.

"It's the only option at this point. Demian didn't believe me when I told him that Raya doesn't have the same effect on me. I've seen the way the other werewolves, and even some of the skinwalkers, look at her. It's almost like they don't feel anything but peace and calm when she's around them. I don't feel that at all. When I woke up after you guys rescued me and she was singing...I was so scared that I was going to hurt her that I stopped her from touching me. It doesn't help that I think she hates me either."

"Why do you think she hates you?"

"It's just the vibe I get from her," Jeremy said with a shrug. "Maybe I'm reading her wrong, but I've had a lot of girls in the past hate me. So I know what to look for."

"I'm still not following-" Riley began, but Jeremy kept talking.

"She's overly nice one second and then the next she's not. It's super confusing. The other day we were casually talking about something random. Then, all of a sudden, she got angry because I told her what kind of music I used to like. Who gets angry about music anyway? And whenever I give her a

220

compliment she glares at me and stalks away as fast as she can."

"I think you've been in seclusion for too long," Riley said in a small whisper. "That's not the behavior of a girl that hates you."

Jeremy went unnaturally still and stared at him for a moment.

"What do you think it is then?"

"Maybe she knows you like her," Riley said with a shrug. "Raven just died so she's not sure how to deal with that."

"I never said I liked her," Jeremy said as he gave Riley an exasperated look. "She's seventeen years old."

Really?

Riley had thought she was sixteen. She must've had a birthday recently. Either way it didn't matter. Jeremy was twenty-five years old, but he didn't look a day over seventeen himself. His body would forever be frozen in that youthful look.

"In the supernatural world age doesn't matter. And you don't have to say that you like her in order for it to be true. Maybe that's why you don't feel calm around her like everyone else does. You see her as a person, not as a tamer."

"You aren't calm around her either," Jeremy said pointedly.

"I'm a wizard," Riley said. "For some reason it doesn't effect me the same way. I had a panic attack with her around once too. I think she finds people that aren't effected by her abilities less intimidating. Give her time. She'll come around."

"I'm still leaving," Jeremy said as he firmly changed the subject. "I'm not going to be anywhere near you guys tomorrow."

The door opened and Raya marched into the room. She had a bag of ice dangling heavily from her clenched fist. She stared at Jeremy with an intense glower that Riley had never seen from her before. Even when she had Arothor's controlling element in her head she'd never given anyone that look before.

For a tamer she sure seemed to be upset a lot on this mission.

"You aren't going anywhere, Jeremy," she said in a low growl. "You're way too hard on yourself and that's why…maybe that's why I get mad at you."

Jeremy stared at her with wide eyes for a split second.

"Oh, so you were listening to our conversation," Jeremy said sarcastically. "That's just…great."

"Here, Riley," Raya said a little too forcefully. She shoved the big bag of ice into his weak arms. "Hug this before your fever burns holes through your organs."

"Wow…that was graphic," Riley said through a shiver.

Raya ignored him and turned her attention back to Jeremy.

"You aren't going anywhere," she said again vehemently. "It's unsafe."

"No, me staying here is unsafe," Jeremy said tersely. "Trust me."

Raya sighed and placed her hands on her hips in frustration.

"That's not true. Give yourself a chance. The full moon is a lot different when you aren't trapped."

Jeremy growled menacingly as his eyes changed to show the unstable wolf within him.

"You have no idea what you're talking about," Jeremy said slowly.

"Don't I?" Raya asked assertively. She ignored his ragingly aggressive behavior like a pro.

"No," Jeremy said in such a feral voice that Riley involuntarily gripped the ice bag in anticipation. Jeremy was holding onto his control by a thread. "You don't. I killed-"

Jeremy stopped talking for a moment and took a deep breath. His glowing eyes dimmed and he looked down at the floor. He shook his head and then looked at Raya with pain clouding his brown eyes.

"I killed my best friend on the full moon," he murmured sadly. "His name was John Terrance and I'd known him since kindergarten. Carvolo threw him in the cell with me and I had absolutely no control. Ever since then the werewolves couldn't

222

keep anyone in my cell during the full moon…unless they wanted the prisoner dead. I've killed more people than John. People that I hardly knew.

"I mutilated three werewolves with my bare hands. I almost killed Aurora too. I still don't know how I stopped myself. That happened three weeks *before* the full moon. Riley saw it all in a vision, but for some reason he didn't want to tell anyone."

Raya and Jeremy stared at Riley who was shivering uncontrollably with the ice bag. Even though he felt cold, heat rose in his cheeks.

"Don't look at me," he said through chattering teeth. "Pretend I'm not here."

"Those mutilated bodies we came across; you knew what happened and you didn't say anything?" Raya asked incredulously.

"I plead the fifth."

Raya stared at him incredulously for a few seconds before turning back to face Jeremy. He stood up from the chair with his fists clenched. He took a breath as though he was trying to calm himself.

"I have absolutely no control on the full moon. I have to fight to keep myself from tearing things apart every day. You think that it has to do with being locked up, but it doesn't. I haven't been locked up for almost a month now and nothing has changed."

There was silence for a few minutes after Jeremy finished. When it was apparent that he was getting antsy and that he might bolt for the door, Raya grabbed one of his clenched fists. Jeremy's breath caught in surprise by her touch, but he didn't pull his hand away.

"Maybe I don't understand everything that you've gone through," she said in a small whisper. "But I do understand what it feels like to fight for control and to feel trapped. I had a controlling element in my head for months. I almost killed Chase, one of my best friends, because of it and I hurt a lot of other people. As a tamer my instinct is to help werewolves.

223

Carvolo tried to force me to go against my most basic nature and it messed with my head. Just like he's messed with yours for almost five years."

Jeremy stared at her as she spoke. His hands were no longer clenched into fists and he let her thread her fingers with his.

"I know you think that you don't deserve to be free and it terrifies you that you are," Raya said soothingly. "I wish I could help you with that, but we both know why I can't. The person you're in love with shouldn't keep you calm all of the time. I don't think that's how love works."

Raya paused and looked Jeremy in the eye. Riley stared at them awkwardly. His body shivered, but he barely felt the cold anymore. These two needed to talk in private and he was intruding. But they were so engrossed in their conversation that they didn't seem to care that he was there.

"I don't hate you...quite the opposite, actually. I'm sorry that I let it come off that way, but I feel guilty about my feelings because Raven just died. I'm having a hard time dealing with that."

"Raven would want you to be happy, Raya," Riley blurted out before he could stop himself.

Raya dropped Jeremy's hand and turned to look at him. She had tears glistening in her eyes, but she blinked them away quickly.

"I thought you pled the fifth," she said with a small glare.

Riley tried to grin, but he couldn't manage it. He was so tired that he was surprised he was still sitting up. The uncertain atmosphere in the room wasn't helping anyone else feel better either.

"Demian told me to stop you when you tried to leave," Raya said quietly. "He said that I needed to help you get through the full moon. That it would be easier for you if you weren't chained up. I didn't tell him that I don't effect you the same way as everyone else, but I should have."

"He wouldn't listen anyway," Jeremy said tightly. "I already told him that your tamer charms don't work on me."

"Yeah, well, forcing you to stay here against your will is still imprisonment. So I won't try to stop you if you really want to leave," Raya said meekly. "But the full moon still terrifies me as much as it does you. I don't want to do it alone, but if you leave I'll understand. Just make sure you come back because I don't think I can lose you too."

Jeremy growled softly, but sat back down on the chair. Riley was impressed with Raya's manipulation technique. Even if she was sincere with what she said it came off in a way that Jeremy would feel like he needed to stay to help her. Maybe that was the key. Maybe if he felt needed by her during the full moon he would be able to cope better.

The only problem was Riley. He would be in danger the entire time with no way to protect himself.

"I'll stay under one condition," Jeremy said quietly. "Riley has to have weapons and he's got to promise that he'll kill me if he needs to."

"Dude," Riley said as he exhaled. "I doubt I can even squeeze a trigger right now. Besides, I'm not promising that."

"Then I've got to leave," Jeremy said firmly. "I'm sorry, Raya. I just don't trust myself."

Suddenly, there was a knock at the door and everyone stiffened. Raya started for the door, but Jeremy quickly grabbed her arm to stop her. He went to the eyehole and peeked through. He relaxed a little, but sighed in exasperation.

"Perfect," he muttered sarcastically.

Jeremy pulled open the door and Jackson stood in the hallway. Without waiting for an invitation Jackson walked into the room. He noticed Riley on the bed and his expression darkened.

"How long have you been like this, buddy?" the vampire asked gruffly.

"Trust me, this is nothing compared to yesterday," Riley replied weakly.

Raya took the melting ice from him and stored it in the mini freezer. Riley laid down and covered himself with the cold and moist blanket. The ice bag seemed to have a slow leak, but the dampness didn't bother him.

"You're sure the person who did this is dead?" Jackson asked.

"Naomi killed her," Raya replied from the kitchenette. "He was in a lot of pain for a little over two days, but he's still very sick. I had to get him ice to reduce his temperature."

Riley ignored them as they discussed his condition. Marcus had, apparently, made a full recovery or else Gabriel wouldn't have let him go to California. At least Riley *assumed* he was fully recovered. Marcus could be very persuasive with his alpha wolf tendencies.

Riley's phone vibrated on the nightstand and he grabbed it feebly. It was a text from Demian and he stared at it for a moment trying to get his eyes to focus properly.

I bet you thought I was deserting you this full moon, so I'm sure you're pleasantly surprised. Get some rest, recover, and stop worrying. Jeremy will be fine.

Demian ended the text message with a yellow emoticon face that was winking. Riley stared at it for a moment before he grunted in annoyance.

"When did Demian develop a sense of humor?"

Jackson took the phone from him and chuckled after he read the message.

"I would've come when we realized you guys needed help, but Zach and I were working on finding Jenna. Demian convinced me to wait until we got somewhere."

"What?" Riley asked anxiously. "Did you find her?"

"I'll tell you all about it after you sleep," Jackson replied.

"No, tell me now," Riley said as he struggled to sit up again. "Did you find her?"

Jackson put a hand on his shoulder and tried to push him back down on the bed. Riley shook him off and Jackson gave up trying to force him to rest since he didn't want to use his supernatural strength to do it.

"No, we haven't found her," Jackson replied solemnly. "But we know where she's been and where we think she's headed. We aren't exactly sure on the last part, but Zach is still looking into it."

"Do you think Jenna knows that Riley is alive?" Raya asked worriedly. "If she does she could be coming for him."

Jackson blew out a breath and nodded in agreement.

"That's what we are trying to figure out. Until we find out what her motives are we aren't going to find her. Unless she comes back to the community for some reason."

"I could drop hints for her," Riley said quietly. "If she comes to me then we could get her to tell us where the Ancients Den is."

"But only if the wand can break the binding spell she put between herself and Carvolo," Jeremy reminded him.

Riley nodded. Roan was looking into that, but they hadn't heard if he'd gotten anywhere with it. He hoped that the brown fairy found good news. The only way to get Aurora back was using Jenna to find the Ancients Den. He had been reluctant to cling to that hope, but he did so anyway. It was the only thing he had left.

"Get some rest, buddy," Jackson said as he patted his shoulder. "The full moon is going to be a long night and we need you on your feet. I'm going to keep watch outside. I spotted a few werewolves on my way here, so I'm going to make sure they stay away."

Raya nodded to Jackson and he left the room.

Jeremy sighed in frustration and his whole body tensed as he stared at the wall. Riley had a funny feeling that the werewolf was contemplating punching a hole through it. Raya noticed Jeremy's demeanor and started humming a popular song from the nineties. Jeremy didn't relax, but he stopped staring at the wall so intently.

"I haven't heard that song since I was a kid," Jeremy said in his gravelly voice. "It was one of my mom's favorites."

"She liked boy bands?" Raya asked in slight amusement.

She handed Riley a blue electrolyte sports drink. He took it from her gratefully and took a small swig.

227

"I don't know. She just liked that song," Jeremy replied nonchalantly.

"I'm pretty sure I have yet to find a song that you don't know," Raya said with a smile.

"Try anything from the past five years and I won't know it."

Raya's smile fell from her face and she wrapped her arms around herself with a wince.

"Sorry," Jeremy mumbled unconvincingly.

Riley finished the entire bottle of sports drink and had to fight down nausea. He hoped that he didn't throw up again because his esophagus was raw enough. Besides, he knew his body needed the electrolytes.

"Do you want another one, Riley?" Raya asked when she took the empty bottle from him.

"Better not," Riley muttered.

Raya nodded in understanding and told him to let her know if he needed anything else. Riley laid down again with a small sigh. He didn't fall asleep, but he was so exhausted that he couldn't move. The discomfort that his muscle aches brought was multiplied when a fresh wave of pain burned through his veins. It wasn't as painful as it had been the past couple of days, but it was disheartening to know that the torture element wasn't completely out of his system yet. He rested his head against the pillow as comfortably as he could and settled in for a sleepless night.

"Are you going to sleep at all?" Raya asked Jeremy in a quiet whisper that Riley could barely hear.

"Probably not," Jeremy replied gruffly.

"You should try. It might help if you're well rested tomorrow."

There was silence between them for a while. Riley could hear the crickets chirping in the hedge under the motel window.

"What do you think the chances are that Jackson will let me leave?"

"Probably not very high," Raya said honestly. "But I can try to talk to him if he doesn't let you."

228

"I can handle him," Jeremy said tightly. "I'll see you after the full moon."

Jeremy walked to the door, but Raya followed him and grabbed his arm with a gentle touch.

"Jeremy, wait," Raya said in a panicked voice. "Is there nothing I can do to get you to stay?"

Jeremy hesitated at the door and turned to look at her. She tried to hide how terrified she was to be alone on the full moon, but her body trembled slightly. Jeremy's demeanor softened a little and he let go of the doorknob. He swore quietly and closed the distance between them. He took her gently into his arms and hugged her. She stiffened a little at first, but relaxed into him with a small sigh.

Riley watched them from the bed and didn't dare move.

They hugged for a while until Raya finally pulled away from him. She wiped her eyes with her fingers and looked down at the floor.

"I'm sorry," Jeremy said sincerely. "I just don't know what to do. I couldn't live with myself if I hurt you."

"I'm a werewolf, Jeremy," she replied quietly. "I'm tougher than I look. Besides, Jackson will be there and he's a wizard-vampire-hybrid."

"Still, I don't-" Jeremy began.

Raya interrupted him when she reached up and took his face in her hands. She pulled him toward her and gently met his lips with hers. Jeremy didn't hesitate as he kissed her back. With a sharp inhale he eagerly pulled her closer to him. He kissed her as though he'd been waiting his whole life for this moment. When their lips parted they hugged again.

"You may not trust yourself," Raya whispered to him breathlessly. "But I do trust you and I need you."

Jeremy sighed shakily and nodded.

"I'm not gonna be able to sleep tonight," he said grimly. "So you take the bed and I'll keep watch with Jackson."

Raya gave him a worried look. She kept perfectly still as though she was afraid he'd disappear if she moved.

229

"I promise I'll be here when you wake up," he told her reassuringly. "I'm not going anywhere."

Raya nodded quietly and went to the second twin bed that was on the other side of the motel room. Riley quickly closed his eyes so that she wouldn't realize that he had been awake the whole time. He doubted that she'd want anyone to know that she kissed Jeremy.

Chapter 15

Riley took a deep breath as he stared at the darkening sky. The full moon was just minutes away and he didn't have his magic back yet. He was still feeling sick, but his temperature was down significantly from what it had been the day before. He didn't like the situation, but it was nice that Jackson was there in case Jeremy couldn't handle the full moon.

"You feeling okay, buddy?"

"Not really," he replied tiredly. "I'm not sure it was a good idea for me to leave the motel room."

"Probably not, but you were a sitting duck in there," his father said gruffly. "This town still has quite a few werewolves prowling around and all of them will be looking for someone to change."

"Jeremy didn't feel comfortable changing in the motel anyway," Riley said as he tried to ignore his shivering. "That's my point; I shouldn't be anywhere near him."

There was rustling in the bushes next to them and Raya appeared from the shadows of the forest.

"Everything will be fine," Raya said as she approached their camping spot.

"Where is Jeremy anyway?" Riley asked as he pulled his blanket tighter around his shoulders.

"He's waiting behind those trees," Raya replied as she gestured to a cluster of trees a few yards away. "I just wanted to make sure that you guys have everything you need."

"Riley's got bullets and I got my fangs," Jackson said with a smirk. "I think we'll be fine."

Raya nodded and took a shaky breath. Riley could see that she was nervous and he didn't blame her. Raya had unpleasant experiences on the full moons that she endured with their enemies. Ever since she was rescued she had their community werewolf pack that helped her through the full moon. Now she was expected to help a berserker werewolf when she still wasn't comfortable doing it alone.

231

"You got this, Raya," Riley told her reassuringly. "Jeremy will be fine and so will you."

Raya nodded again and closed her eyes. When she opened them they glowed blue in the receding light.

"Jeremy and I will probably spend most of the night behind those trees," Raya told them in the soothing tone she took on whenever her eyes went blue. "If you need anything-"

"We'll be fine," Jackson said with a nod. "Just concentrate on getting through the night."

"Okay," she said. "See you when this is over."

She hurried away from the campsite as the light of the full moon flooded the ground. It wasn't long before they heard the sounds of werewolves changing. It didn't sound pleasant. One of them made rough growling noises. Riley was willing to bet it was Jeremy.

"Do you want to talk about it?" Jackson asked him out of the blue. "About what happened to you?"

"Not really," Riley said half-heartedly. "It's over and done with. Naomi took care of Hanna, so there's really not much to do about it anymore."

"You know…" Jackson said with a sigh. "I've seen a lot of crap as a hunter. I've done a lot of bad things as a hunter too. I've seen a lot of torture. It makes me sick that you've endured it as often as you have. Rebecca included. At least she can heal quickly if it happens to her, but you've endured it more than she has."

"I'm okay. It's not bothering me."

"Riley," Jackson said gently. "Did you even notice that your nineteenth birthday was a few days ago?"

Riley was stunned for a moment. He hadn't been keeping track of the dates. All the days seemed to mesh together since Aurora was taken. Not that he cared. Birthdays were irrelevant. So was his age.

"What's your point?" he whispered dejectedly.

"I think you've got more stress than you can handle," Jackson said. "And it worries me that you won't talk about it. I know you've talked to Rebecca a couple of times about Aurora,

232

but I've never once heard you say anything about the times you've been held captive and tortured."

Riley sucked in a breath as the memories assaulted him for a moment. Nausea hit him for a split second, but it vanished just as quickly as it came. Unfortunately the slight panic he felt didn't go away.

This was why he never talked about it. He didn't want to relive the hell he'd been through in the past.

"There's nothing to say," Riley replied with a shrug. "No point in dwelling on things that can't be changed."

Jackson stare bore into him and Riley knew that his father wasn't buying it.

"You have nightmares all the time."

"Those only got bad after Dur Den Thome," Riley explained almost defensively.

"So you're telling me that your nightmares only have to do with what happened to the fairies? That the horrible things that have happened to you don't bother you in the slightest?"

Riley didn't know what to say to that, so he kept his mouth shut as he stared at the ground. The truth was; it did bother him. All the things he'd been through and everything he'd seen was taking a toll on him. He did have nightmares about the things that he'd survived, but most of the time he had nightmares about people he couldn't save.

"I'm worried about you, buddy," Jackson whispered with a concerned tone.

"You want to know what my nightmares are about?"

Riley looked up to meet Jackson's eyes. The eyes that stared back at him reminded him of the ones he saw in the mirror everyday. Tired, blue eyes that had seen too many horrible things. There was no doubt where he inherited his eyes from.

"I see my family and friends die. I don't know why, but the things I've already been through don't bother me as much as the things that I can't control. I'm terrified of losing the people I love. That's what my nightmares are about. Watching Luca and Mystie die is what started it all. Nothing more."

233

Jackson took a second to process that and then nodded in understanding.

"So, you're saying that you aren't bothered by what happened to you in the basement of that warehouse?" Jackson asked in mild disbelief.

"Sure, it bothers me," Riley said with a shrug. "Pain sucks and being tortured is terrifying, but that's all it is…pain… of which I have a very high threshold for. I promise you; I'm okay. If that ever changes you'll be the first to know."

"Alright," Jackson said with a nod. "But what about Aurora?"

Moisture filled his eyes and Riley had to blink a few times to clear them. The empty feeling in his chest seemed to grow every time he thought about his wife.

"My nightmares are all about her lately," he replied shakily.

"It's getting to you, isn't it?" Jackson said knowingly.

Riley sighed, but didn't reply.

The growling and howls coming from the trees around them became more intense. It made Riley anxious, but Jackson seemed perfectly calm. No werewolves came toward their camp, so Riley was able to relax after a while.

"Rachel wants you to see a therapist."

Riley shot Jackson a cold look and he raised his hands defensively.

"Hey, don't shoot the messenger. I'm just telling you what she wants. I never said I agreed with her."

Riley snorted in disbelief and looked up at the full moon that lighted the night sky. It would've been a beautiful night if the woods weren't full of psychotic monsters that wanted to bite him.

"Seeing a therapist might be beneficial," Jackson pointed out diplomatically. "But it's completely up to you."

"I wonder what the therapist would think about my wife's werewolf father kidnapping her. And how all my family members are different species of supernaturals," Riley said nonchalantly. "I wonder which psych ward they'd lock me up in."

"One with padded walls and straight jackets, no doubt," Jackson said with a chuckle. "Rachel found a skinwalker that's been working with Tanya and Pearl. She's pretty amazing."

"I think I'll pass," Riley said. "Talking about my problems doesn't solve anything. It doesn't make me feel any better either."

"It may not make you feel better," Jackson said with a thoughtful nod. "But sometimes talking helps you feel like you're not alone."

Riley looked at the ground as tears filled his eyes again, but he refused to let himself cry. He promised himself he was done with that weeks ago.

Jackson reached over to him and rested his hand on his shoulder.

"You're not alone in this, buddy."

Riley nodded and sighed tiredly.

"Thanks, dad. That means a lot."

Jackson gave his shoulder a small squeeze before he let his hand drop. They sat there in silence for a few minutes before they heard rustling in the trees where Raya and Jeremy were supposed to be. A low growl emitted from the darkness and Jackson stood up slowly.

A giant werewolf emerged from the shadows of the moonlit trees. Riley had never seen a white werewolf before. The color of his coarse fur reminded him a little of Aurora's fur when she was in her wolf skin. Most werewolves looked mangy, but there was something terrifyingly beautiful about him. Riley would have stared at his fur longer if he hadn't noticed the bared fangs that glistened in the moonlight.

Jeremy didn't seem happy to see them. Riley wondered what had happened to Raya. They hadn't heard sounds of a fight. They had been so engrossed in their conversation that they didn't think anything was going wrong. But Jeremy's demeanor indicated otherwise.

"We've got problems," a voice said in Riley's head.

It took him a moment to realize that Jeremy was using mind speech. It was then that he noticed that there was no blood on Jeremy's fangs or his fur. He let out a sigh of relief, but it was a short lived feeling.

"What problems?" Jackson asked in concern.

"Werewolves are after me," Raya said timidly.

She appeared behind the white werewolf. She was significantly smaller than Jeremy in her werewolf skin. Her dark brown fur blended with the trees a lot better than Jeremy's did, but Riley didn't think that would be a problem. It was only fair that their enemies could see Jeremy coming, even then they wouldn't have much of a fighting chance.

Riley stood up with his gun in his hand and Jeremy growled at him threateningly.

"Probably not a good idea, Riley," Raya told him warningly. "He's still getting used to this whole thing. Just stay where you are. He's actually doing surprisingly well."

"I don't know about that," Jeremy said furiously through mind speech.

"Quit being hard on yourself," Raya replied sternly.

"Why are there werewolves after you, Raya?" Jackson asked, getting straight to the point.

"They're just drawn to my tamer abilities. Jeremy has already chased away three of them."

"Wait," Riley said incredulously. "You chased away three werewolves and there was no bloodshed? So much for you being a berserker werewolf."

Jeremy growled aggressively and bared his fangs.

"I've never thought I could do something like this, Riley," Jeremy said warningly. "So don't push it."

Suddenly, a tan werewolf jumped at Riley from the shadows of the forest. Jackson moved him out of the way so quickly that his head spun. Nausea overcame him and he vomited in the bushes. When he was through being sick, he glanced up to see Jeremy in a ferocious fight with the werewolf that tried to attack him.

It was brutal. Riley had never seen a werewolf fight the way Jeremy did. His opponent was so outmatched that Riley almost felt sorry for it. Even when the werewolf was down

236

Jeremy didn't stop attacking. It wasn't until Raya pressed her nose against his back leg that he finally stopped.

Jeremy was panting and his yellow eyes rolled wildly. Blood coated his white fur and saliva dripped down his muzzle. To Riley's surprise, Jeremy walked away from the dead werewolf and stood in front of him protectively. Riley didn't move and he tried to avoid eye contact with the massive werewolf. He wasn't sure what was going on and he didn't want to ask in case Jeremy wasn't all there. He breathed a sigh of relief when Raya prowled over and laid down next to Jeremy.

"We think the werewolves want you," Raya explained to Riley. "Jackson is checking the woods. Jeremy and I will protect you if anything tries to get at you."

"I thought they were coming for you?" Riley said in confusion.

"After that werewolf tried to attack you I don't think I'm the only one they want. Most of them seem out of control."

"It's probably the first or second full moon for a lot of them," Jeremy said angrily.

"I've gotta say," Riley said to the white werewolf that was crouched next to him. "You're doing a lot better than I expected."

"I'm surprised too," Jeremy told him.

"I told you," Raya said brightly. "It's different when you're free."

"It's still hard."

Raya whined in agreement and silence fell between them. The werewolves that prowled the woods howled in the distance. A shiver ran down Riley's spine. He couldn't tell if it was from nerves or the cold. He had lost his blanket when Jackson had moved him away from the attacking werewolf. Raya shifted closer to him so that they were touching. Her fur was coarse, but warm. After a while Riley was comfortable enough to fall asleep.

He wasn't asleep for long when he woke up to Jackson talking to the two werewolves.

"I think we're in the clear," his father said. "Most of the followers are outside of the city limits. I don't think that they'll bother us anymore though."

"Why do you think that?" Riley mumbled.

"I politely asked them to leave us alone," Jackson said with a smirk.

"Really?" Raya asked incredulously.

"No, I killed them until they got smart and ran away."

Jeremy let out a snort that was followed by a low growl. Raya put her paw next to his, but he didn't seem to relax. No one asked him what was wrong. They knew if Jeremy sensed danger he would let them know by attacking the threat without warning.

"Have you heard anything from Rebecca?" Riley asked.

Jackson didn't take his eyes off of Jeremy while he answered Riley. It looked like there was some kind of silent stand off between them. There was tension in the atmosphere, but Riley was too tired to worry about them attacking each other. Jackson was professional enough to avoid Jeremy's fangs and claws if he lost control anyway.

"Gabriel texted me a while ago and said that it's crazy there. Naomi is helping them corner the werewolves away from the humans with a fire barrier."

"So they're okay then?"

"Sounds like it," Jackson replied with a nod.

Riley nodded and closed his eyes again. The ground was hard and uncomfortable, but he was so exhausted that it didn't stop him from falling asleep.

"Are you sure you don't want me to ride back with you?" Jackson asked as he shut the trunk of the car.

"No," Riley said. "You need to get back home and help Zach find Jenna."

The vampire stared at him for a moment. Bloodlust flashed across his eyes even though he just drank three squirrels. It had nothing to do with hunger. He was worried.

"It's tough for me to leave you in this condition, buddy."

"All I need is rest," Riley said as he tried not to roll his eyes. "I don't need you in the car with me in order to do that."

Jackson sighed, but nodded. He turned to Raya, who was standing next to the passenger side door, and gave her an urgent look.

"Don't let him overdo it," the vampire told her sternly.

"I don't need a babysitter," Riley said in exasperation.

Jackson stared at him incredulously for a moment. Riley couldn't stop himself from rolling his eyes this time.

"Your past behavior, while recovering from injuries, proves otherwise."

"I'm not injured. I'm just a little under the weather."

"Is your magic back yet?" Jackson asked him with a raised eyebrow.

Riley didn't reply. He glanced up at the sky to avoid meeting his dad's vampire eyes instead.

"That's what I thought," Jackson said gruffly. He turned back to Raya. "Make sure he does nothing but rest the entire time."

"Sure thing," she said with a small nod.

With one last goodbye, Jackson ran off in a blur. Riley blew out a sigh of relief and slumped against the car. He felt like he could relax a bit without Jackson's constant parental concern. He loved his dad, but sometimes it was too much.

"You guys ready to get out of this crappy town?"

Jeremy's voice echoed from the stairway that he was hurrying down. He had a stony look on his face. He had been extremely cranky all morning no matter how much Raya tried to calm him down. Jackson had made it a point to avoid the berserker because he seemed to agitate him even more.

"Yeah," Raya said timidly. "Would you like me to drive?"

"No," Jeremy said stiffly. He cleared his throat and looked at the ground for a moment. "I mean…I think it might be best if I drive."

"Okay," Raya replied with an understanding nod. "Just let me know if you want me to take a turn."

"I can also-"

"No, Riley," Raya and Jeremy interrupted him in unison.

"Just sleep it off, man," Jeremy told him.

Riley rolled his eyes and climbed into the backseat of the car. It was cramped, but he managed to sprawl out over the seat. He tucked a sweater under his head and closed his eyes. The muscle aches had come back and he was out of pain killers. The only way he could ignore the discomfort was by thinking about Aurora, but that was even more painful.

He didn't know if she was still alive. Carvolo had said that he was going to keep her that way, but he hardly ever told the truth. He had to fight down panic as he thought about what could be happening to her. There was nothing that he could do, but rest in the backseat of a stupid car. He couldn't even clean a weapon because they were all in the trunk. It was going to be a miserable trip.

"Do you need anything before we go, Riley?"

Riley opened his eyes and saw Raya glancing at him from the passenger's seat. He shook his head and Jeremy put the car in drive.

No one talked as they drove through the city to get to the interstate.

"This is a four hour trip," Raya said pointedly. "Can we please not let it be four hours of silence?"

"I'm not very good company right now," Jeremy replied curtly.

Riley kept his eyes closed and pretended to be asleep. He didn't want to talk to anyone. Especially since all that was on his mind was Aurora, and he didn't want to talk about her. The more he talked about her the more screwed he felt the whole situation was. He had to try to remain hopeful or else he would lose it.

240

"Just because you're grumpy doesn't mean we can't talk," Raya replied. "Unless you're mad at me for something."

"I'm not mad," Jeremy grumbled in a husky voice.

"Care to tell me why you're upset then? I thought last night went pretty well...all things considered."

"Well, I don't," he replied angrily. "I mauled a werewolf and I don't know how you were able to stop me."

"I think it was the mind speech," Raya said thoughtfully. "I've never sang through mind speech before. It was soothing for me too."

"I still don't know why you think music helps calm me down," Jeremy said in annoyance.

"Um...past experiences proves that it does."

"Then why did I mindlessly kill that thing last night?" Jeremy asked sarcastically.

"You didn't mindlessly kill," she said in a soothing voice. "That werewolf tried to attack Riley. You were protecting him."

Jeremy didn't reply and there was silence for a few minutes.

"What's really going on, Jeremy?"

"I don't like killing like that," he said gruffly. "No matter if that monster deserved to die or not. I don't like losing control."

"It'll just take time," Raya said. "I think I can help you if you let me. It's supposed to get easier."

"That's what everyone keeps telling me," Jeremy said with sarcasm dripping from each word.

"I still think you're too hard on yourself," Raya said with a shake of her head.

"You don't know everything that I've done. You wouldn't say that if you did."

There was silence between them for a few seconds before Raya sighed in aggravation.

"Are you ever going to stop feeling sorry for yourself?" Raya asked forcefully. "Or do you just hate yourself? I honestly can't tell."

Riley's eyes flew open as the atmosphere in the car swiftly changed. Jeremy was gripping the steering wheel with white knuckles, but he didn't say anything for a moment.

"I'm not feeling sorry for myself and I don't hate myself. I'm a dangerous monster, Raya," Jeremy said in a surprisingly calm tone. "I need to be locked up. I don't know how to make you understand that."

Raya didn't respond for a while, but the tension in the car was so thick that Riley had a hard time concentrating on anything else. He wasn't sure why their conversation was making him anxious.

He really wished he could give them some privacy.

"I'm sorry that I sounded harsh," Raya said apologetically. "But I've seen a lot of crap in my life too. Demian says that is why I'm a tamer. For me, being a werewolf is supposed to be a positive release from my human life and it hasn't been. It's been terrible…until I met you. I don't know what it is about you, but being around you makes me feel happier. I guess it's killing me that you don't feel the same way."

"I do feel happier when I'm around you," he replied softly. "But I don't trust myself and that's why I'm so guarded."

"Don't you think that time could help with that?"

"I don't know," he said grimly. "Maybe."

They drove in silence for a while. Riley closed his eyes again when the tension disappeared. He was quickly torn from his thoughts when Jeremy spoke again.

"Just so you know, Raya, physical touch isn't my thing. I don't hug very many people and I definitely don't kiss just anyone. I really care about you and that's why I have to be careful. I wouldn't be able to live with myself if I hurt you. Don't let last night fool you; if it wasn't just you and me there it would've been different in a very bloody way."

"Riley was there."

"Riley isn't a werewolf," Jeremy explained. "And there's something non-threatening about him. It's possible for me to keep control around him, but Jackson was a different story. It was all I could do to keep myself from attacking him."

242

"Don't let Riley hear you say that you think he's non-threatening," Raya said with a smirk in her voice.

"Heard it," Riley said as he opened his eyes. "And I'll never forgive him."

There was a stunned silence in the front of the car that quickly turned awkward. Riley had to resist the urge to laugh. At least listening to their conversation had been distracting for a while.

"Seriously," Jeremy said indignantly. "It's not nice to pretend to be asleep, man."

Raya glanced back at him with an awkward expression drawn on her face.

"You saw us kiss the other night too, didn't you?"

"Um, I plead the fifth."

"I hate you," she stated with a smirk.

"I've heard that before," he replied nonchalantly.

Raya turned in her seat and faced the windshield.

"How are you feeling?" she asked. "Are you hungry?"

"Sure," Riley mumbled.

Food had been hard for him to keep down since his experience with Hanna. He wasn't too excited about the prospect of trying to eat, but he didn't want Raya to start mothering him. He had noticed she did that occasionally to people that where hurt or in distress. She was their community's mother hen, but Riley wasn't brave enough to tease her about it.

Jeremy pulled up to a fast food restaurant off of the interstate. They had been driving for about two hours, so they decided to stretch their legs. It took some convincing, but Raya finally let Riley get out of the car too. Apparently, Jackson had engaged the child's lock on the back doors and she had to open the door for him.

"Next time I see him I'm gonna whip his vampire butt," Riley said as he disengaged the child's lock.

"Serves you right for eavesdropping on private conversations," Jeremy said with a smirk.

"Hey, it's not my fault you guys assumed I was asleep."

243

"Uh-huh," Raya said with her arms folded. "By the way if you tell anyone about this-"

"Tell anyone about what?" Riley interrupted in mocked confusion. "I have no idea what you're talking about."

Raya stared at him incredulously.

"I think he's feeling better," Jeremy said with a roll of his eyes. "Maybe we should make him walk the rest of the way home."

"I bet you would love that," Riley said as he raised an eyebrow at Raya.

She punched him in the arm. Even though she did it in jest Riley knew that he'd have a bruise.

They went into the restaurant and ordered some food. It didn't take them long to eat and they hurried out the door. It was a nice break from the car, but they needed to get back to the community as soon as possible.

Riley was about to open the car door when Jeremy suddenly collapsed to the ground. Riley glanced down and saw a throwing knife in the werewolf's back. He knelt down and immediately grabbed the handle. It burned his skin like a hot flame, but he didn't let go.

"Raya! Get in the car!" Riley exclaimed as he pulled on the hot knife.

It was a struggle, but he finally yanked it out of Jeremy's spine. He didn't take the time to look at his burned hand. He had a feeling that Raya was in danger. He stood up quickly and saw her struggling to get the passenger door open. It wouldn't budge despite her werewolf strength.

Jeremy stood up with a feral growl coming from his throat. His yellow eyes flashed angrily as he looked down at the bloody knife that Riley dropped.

Slowly, the knife began to spin. It steadily got faster as it rose in the air.

"We need to get out of here," Riley said tersely.

He knew what was coming next. He searched desperately within himself for his pure magic. It wasn't there and he couldn't help but panic. He couldn't go up against something like this without his magic.

"Should we run to the woods?" Raya asked urgently.

Suddenly, four knives soared through the air from the trees next to the parking lot and surrounded Raya. She let out a terrified gasp as they halted in midair around her torso. She stood perfectly still as the knives twisted in the air impatiently, hungry for blood. Her breathing was short and rapid as the scorching hot knives greedily surrounded her.

Jeremy growled angrily. He was silenced when the spinning knife buried itself into his spine again. Riley searched frantically for the sixth knife, but couldn't find it anywhere. Suddenly, he felt a burning sting slice across his upper arm. The sixth knife soared toward his face and he flinched. It stopped merely an inch from his nose and he resisted the urge to close his eyes. He watched as the deadly knife spun in the air in front of his face. He took a deep breath to steady himself. He didn't dare move because he was sure the knife would kill him if he did.

Then the knife lowered itself and floated closer to his neck. The hot blade touched his skin and he winced as the sharp edge bit into him. Warm blood trailed down his neck and he tried not to flinch again. It took him a moment for his vision to focus. When it did he finally saw the person that he'd been wanting to find.

He was beginning to rethink that strategy.

"I heard that you've been looking for me, Ry," she said in a snarky tone. "I wonder where you got that bright idea from. Especially since our last meeting didn't bode well for you."

Chapter 16

"I have to admit," Jenna said as she sauntered closer to Raya. "I was surprised when I heard that you were alive, Ry. I was certain that you were bleeding out when I saw you last."

Riley didn't reply. He was too busy watching the knives that were circling Raya. He had to get her out of this.

"Um, hello," Jenna said in a voice that reminded Riley of Lucy Bremmer. "I'm talking to you, Ry. Eyes on me."

"Please," Riley said calmly. "Jenna, let her go. It's me you want."

"Since when did you start calling me 'Jenna'?" She placed her hands on her hips and shook her head in disappointment. "How very disrespectful."

Jenna flicked her fingers and one of the knives sliced Raya's torso. She screamed in shock, but didn't move from where she stood. Riley thought he heard Jeremy growl from where he was paralyzed on the ground, but he wasn't certain.

"Okay, mom," Riley said hurriedly. "I'll call you whatever you want me to. Please, just don't hurt her."

"Ugh, how nauseating," Jenna said as she rolled her eyes. "Your wife has been gone for… What? A month or so? You've already replaced her with a younger girl. You remind me of Bill Hanson. Like father, like son."

If he wanted to tick her off he would've addressed the fact that they both knew Bill Hanson wasn't his father. Or that he and Raya were just friends. But he kept his mouth shut and tried to give Raya an encouraging look. Her face was stricken with fear and she seemed to be struggling to catch her breath.

"Okay," Riley said as he took a breath to calm himself. "What do you want?"

"I'm so glad you asked."

Jenna flicked her fingers. The knife that was embedded in Jeremy's spine twisted out of his back. Jeremy growled and jumped to his feet. The knife flew straight at his chest and

246

stopped an inch from his heart. Jeremy didn't even flinch. He glanced at Raya then stared coldly at Jenna.

"I want you," Jenna said with a smirk at Jeremy. "A berserker werewolf. I haven't seen one of your kind for centuries."

"So," Riley said in confusion. "You're here for Jeremy? Why?"

"I'm not sure why Carvolo wants him, but he does," she cackled. "As for you, Ry... You and I will have some fun before this is over."

"You aren't going to kill me," Riley said confidently. "I'm pretty sure you would die if you did, right?"

Jenna glared at him furiously.

"Seems like you and your friends have been spying on me."

"No," Riley said with a shake of his head.

"Don't lie to me," she said with a snarl that would make a werewolf proud. "You won't like it when I'm angry."

"Don't get mad at me because you were stupid enough to make a deal with Carvolo."

Jenna sneered at him and flicked her fingers again. Another knife sliced through Raya's skin and she let out a panicked yelp. Jeremy growled and Riley had to put a hand on his arm so he wouldn't walk into Jenna's knife that was still pointed at his heart.

"Stop it," Riley said sternly. "If you hurt her again you'll get nothing from me. Let her go."

"I don't want anything from you."

"Yes, you do. Let her go," Riley said through gritted teeth. "I will cooperate and you'll be able to hand me over to Carvolo."

"The problem is; I'm not supposed to take you to Carvolo without the wand. So where is it?"

Jenna eyed Jeremy hungrily throughout the entire conversation. Jeremy didn't even seem to notice since he'd been preoccupied with watching Raya, but it made Riley uneasy to have his mother eyeballing his friend.

247

"It's in the-"

"No, Riley," Raya said in a quivering voice. "Don't tell her anything."

Jenna snapped her fingers and Raya began to choke.

"You're gonna wanna leave her alone right now," Jeremy whispered dangerously.

"Oh, so you do speak?" Jenna asked with a smirk. "What are you going to do about it, berserker?"

"Let her breathe," Riley ordered calmly. "Now."

Jenna continued smirking as Raya's face turned a light shade of blue.

"If you want the wand then let her go, right now!" Riley yelled at her.

Jenna laughed hysterically as she flicked her fingers again. Raya choked in air as she tried to remain as still as possible with the four knives surrounding her. They were still spinning like tops in the air. Two of them were red with her blood.

"Get the knives away from her and I'll tell you where the wand is."

"Tell me first and then I'll let your girlfriend go."

"That's not going to happen, mom," Riley said. "I don't trust you to keep your word."

Suddenly, the knife pulled away from Riley's neck and buried itself into his left shoulder. He screamed as the burning blade seared through him and pulled out of his shoulder quickly. He was surprised to see that there was minimal blood. The heat had cauterized the wound.

"If you think hurting me is the answer then you're sorely mistaken," Riley said through a grimace. "I'm not telling you a single thing until you let her go. You still have a knife on me and Jeremy. You don't need her too."

"Ugh, you're no fun, Ry," Jenna said with a pout. "Fine, we'll play it your way. But I'm locking her in the car so she can't try anything."

"Fair enough."

248

Jenna flicked her fingers and the four throwing knives surrounding Raya flew to their owner. The door to the car magically opened and Raya was pushed inside by an invisible force. The door closed automatically and she immediately tried to open it again. She pounded on the window once in frustration and looked at Jeremy with wide eyes.

Jenna chuckled as she watched the werewolf girl struggle.

"Now," Jenna said happily. "Are you going to keep your part of the deal? Or do I have to hurt you some more?"

"You said that Carvolo wants me?" Jeremy said in his gravelly voice. "Why is that?"

"I don't know and don't care. The wand, Riley. Now."

"It's in the trunk," Riley said as he gestured to the back of the car. "Feel free to grab it."

Jenna stared at him for a moment with a stern look on her face. The knives surrounding her flew toward Jeremy and stopped just before stabbing him. Riley exhaled shakily and swallowed. He wasn't in as much control as he hoped to be in this situation.

"I'm your mother, you stupid wizard," Jenna said in a dangerous voice. "I know when you're lying to me. Where is the wand?"

Riley searched for his pure magic again. He was surprised when he felt a spark of magic within him. It wasn't much. Not nearly enough to get them out of this situation, but maybe he could buy them some time.

The last time he tried to use descenpian against the knives things went badly. He didn't want history to repeat itself, so he decided to go a different route. He quickly drew his gun from the back of his jeans and aimed it at Jenna's head. The witch cackled with laughter.

"Get the knives away from us," Riley said sternly. "Or you're dead."

"You can't kill me, Ry," she said through her laughter. "You don't have the guts."

"You have no idea what I'm capable of, Jenna. Do it now."

"If you shoot me my darlings will kill you and the berserker."

"I highly doubt that," he said confidently. "I remember you telling me that you lost their loyalty when you lost your magic. I bet they'll fall to the ground the second your body does."

"If you kill me you'll never see Aurora again."

"If Carvolo gets his hands on the wand I'll still never see her again," Riley said nonchalantly. "You always said that men are dogs. What makes you think that I care more for her than I do for myself?"

Jenna glared at him for a moment. Jeremy jerked his head toward Riley and stared at him. Riley was concentrating so hard on his performance that he barely noticed the werewolf's confused expression.

"You wouldn't dare kill me," Jenna said happily. "But this is so interesting. You're a better actor than I ever gave you credit for. No wonder you hid who you really were from me for so long."

"Craticas razinios!" Riley exclaimed as he pointed his fingers at the knives that surrounded Jeremy.

The blue flames engulfed the knives and Jeremy gasped as the fire singed his skin. The werewolf quickly jumped out of the way of the flames. Riley was surprised that the knives didn't follow him. Before he could see where Jeremy went he was blinded by searing pain in his chest. He glanced down and saw the scorching hot knife sticking out of him.

Riley dropped the gun and used his hand to grab the burning knife handle. It took him a few tries, but he finally pulled it out of his shoulder. He muttered the craticas spell for fire again and the knife in his hand burst into flames. He let it fall to the ground as the blue fire engulfed the silver blade.

Riley could barely stay upright. He leaned heavily against the car door and tried to pry it open. Jenna's spell prevented anything from getting in or out. He noticed Raya frantically trying to open the door for him and Jeremy.

Jenna shrieked angrily as the blue flames burned through her throwing knives. There was the popping sound of a gunshot and Riley collapsed to the ground. He barely felt the bullet enter his leg, but he couldn't stay upright anymore. Jenna aimed his gun that he'd dropped at his chest. He refused to panic despite the murderous glint in his sadistic mother's eyes. He mustered up the last of his pure magic and spoke in a shaky voice.

"Descenpian."

Black spots scattered his vision as the last of his energy left him. Raya pushed the door open for him and pulled him into the backseat with her werewolf strength. Jeremy was already in the driver's seat and he put the car in gear. The back window spiderwebbed from a bullet that came through and lodged itself into the radio. Jeremy swore furiously as he hit the gas pedal. Luckily the bullet didn't damage the engine.

Riley could hear Jenna's shrill screams as they drove out of the parking lot. Luckily, no other cars were around, but Riley was sure that people had seen their confrontation. Their enemies really didn't care about the humans knowing about them anymore.

They drove for about ten minutes before Raya insisted that she look at Riley's wounds. She rolled up his pants and looked at his calf muscle. The bullet went straight through it. At least Riley didn't have to worry about digging a bullet out and it was lucky that it didn't damage his fibula. Raya disinfected the hole with peroxide and wrapped it.

The injuries that Riley was most worried about were his two stab wounds. It had taken him too long to recover from the last ones he'd had from Jenna's knives. Luckily, these weren't as life threatening. She definitely hadn't been trying to kill him like she had last time they'd met.

Jeremy got on the phone and called Jackson. Riley grimaced when Raya insisted that he take off his shirt so that she could see his stab wounds. His adrenaline was subsiding and his injuries where starting to really hurt. He glanced at her cuts that she had sustained and was relieved to see that they were mostly healed. He had been worried that the enchanted knives would have done more serious damage to the werewolves. He was glad that they didn't.

He let Raya tend to his wounds as he rested his head against the seat and closed his eyes.

"Jenna wanted the wand?" Demian asked in an even tone.

If Riley didn't know him so well he would've missed the underlying confusion in his voice.

"Yeah," Riley said with a nod. "Carvolo must've been looking for the wand when he thought I was dead. Now that he knows I'm alive I'm sure that he wants both me and the wand."

"That still doesn't make sense considering that the wand is useless without you," Samantha said. "Right?"

"Who knows why he wants what he wants," Jackson said quietly. "The real problem is; he knows Riley is alive."

"I don't care so much about that," Riley said. Jackson stood up and started pacing Demian and Veronica's living room. "We need to find out how Jenna got her information. She knew that Jackson and Zach have been looking into her whereabouts. She didn't specifically mention their names, but she knew we were spying on her."

"Are you sure you're not reading into that, buddy?" Jackson asked him.

"I don't think so," Riley said with a shake of his head. "There's something about the way she said it. I could be reading into it, I guess, but I think it's something that we should consider."

"I agree," Demian said with a nod. "It's better to be safe than sorry. I will look into it. If anyone in our community is a double agent of Carvolo's we will soon know."

"Can I go now?" Riley asked when Samantha finished wrapping his stab wounds. Raya had done a hasty job of it in the car, but Samantha wanted to stitch him up.

Riley didn't want to be rude, but he needed a break. He still wasn't feeling completely back to normal despite the fact that his pure magic was back. He just wanted to be alone for a while.

Demian nodded and Riley left the house. He was glad that no one followed him. He wandered around the community while lost in thought in the summer evening.

Before he realized where he was going he found himself on Gabriel and Rebecca's porch. Since Aurora was abducted he'd never had the nerve to come here. His hands shook and his breathing picked up. He turned around to leave and was startled to see Veronica standing a few feet behind him.

Veronica hadn't been there for the meeting and Riley didn't blame her. If it wasn't necessary for him to have been there he would have skipped it too. Any news regarding their evil mother was hard for both of them to handle. She looked pale even though her skin was slightly tanned.

"I'm sorry," Veronica said. "I saw you leave the house, but you look like you want to be alone."

"No, it's fine," Riley said with a shrug. "Are you okay?"

Veronica sighed angrily and shook her head in disgust.

"You're the one that was attacked by her...again."

Riley walked off of the porch and gave his sister a hug. She gripped his shirt tightly and let out a small sob.

"I'm so *sick* of her hurting you. If I see her again I'll kill her."

Veronica was significantly shorter than him, but he bent down to kiss her on the top of her head anyway.

"We need her alive, Veronica."

"Once we don't," she said stiffly. "She's a goner."

They broke off the hug when Roan suddenly appeared next to them. His brown wings stretched out behind him and his aura dimly lit the darkness around them. He held the wand out to Riley without any kind of verbal greeting.

253

"Did you find anything?" Riley asked as he took the wand.

"I have found that it's more capable than any of us imagined," the fairy whispered.

"Are you being cryptic for a reason?" Riley asked with a raised eyebrow.

Roan ignored Riley's dry humor and continued.

"I believe the wand will be able to break any spell or curse that you want it to. It is worth a try using it against Jenina."

Riley nodded and the fairy gave him a grim look.

"What's wrong?" Riley asked skeptically. The fairies weren't generally so expressive with their body language. Something wasn't right.

"Selena and I are leaving," he replied sadly. "The protection spells that have been placed on the communities are permanent. So you need not worry."

"You're leaving?" Veronica asked incredulously.

"We have recently been made aware that the werewolves are hunting the remaining fairies and killing them. We are almost extinct as it is, so we are going to create another Dur Den Thome. Our species needs to be saved immediately."

Riley nodded in understanding, but Veronica's fists clenched in frustration.

"Good luck, Roan," Riley said as he held out his hand. "It's been good knowing you."

"Likewise, Riley Hanson," Roan said as he shook his hand. "Perhaps our paths will cross again in the future."

Riley gave him a small smile and the fairy disappeared. Veronica sighed and folded her arms across her chest.

"It'll be okay, Veronica," Riley said diplomatically. "They're doing the right thing. The werewolves need to be stopped from eliminating their species."

"I know," she said through clenched teeth. "I just wish he would've given us some warning first. Demian had no idea about this."

"Fairies don't work that way," Riley said with a shrug. "They have their own agendas most of the time. They only do things if it pleases them."

"Thank heavens witches and wizards aren't all like that."

Riley shrugged again and glanced at Gabriel and Rebecca's house. He felt his heart rate pick up and he let out a shaky breath. He had no idea why he came to the house. Nothing but pain was to be found here. He had one day with his wife...one...it hadn't been nearly enough. He always imagined that he'd spend multiple lifetimes married to Aurora and it all had been taken from them.

"Do you want to talk about it?" Veronica asked hesitantly. "Or I could let you be alone for a while."

"I think being alone is a bad idea for me," Riley explained grimly. "For some reason I was stupid enough to try to go in there."

He gestured to the house. Veronica's expression somehow became more forlorn. She grabbed his hand and reached up to kiss his cheek.

"You never know," she whispered. "It might be therapeutic to go in there."

Riley highly doubted that, but he nodded unconvincingly. They walked away from the house and slowly meandered onto the dirt road. They didn't say much to each other, but it was nice to be able to just spend time together. Riley didn't know how the future would turn out for the two of them. For now, it was nice to just be siblings.

"How are Teresa and Jasmine adjusting to the community?" Riley asked.

He already knew that Jasmine was adjusting well, but he didn't want Veronica to know that she secretly hung out with him.

"Jasmine is doing great," Veronica said as she gave him a knowing look. "But you already knew that."

"How would I know that?" he asked with a small smirk.

"Anyway," she continued. "As for Teresa...I can't really get a read on her anymore. I think she's unhappy though."

255

That didn't surprise Riley. Teresa didn't seem like a person who was happy on a good day. It worried him that Veronica couldn't get a read on her follower though. Leaders were supposed to know what was going on with their followers. He gave his sister a worried look and she reciprocated it.

"What's wrong?" she asked in concern.

"Why can't you get a read on her anymore?"

"She's closed off," Veronica said. "I decided it was best to give her some space. It's awkward enough with our family history. I didn't want to make it worse by forcing her to do anything."

"She's a follower," Riley said incredulously. "She needs that from you. She needs to feel like she's got a purpose or she will find someone else that will give her one."

"I know," Veronica said indignantly. "Raising Jasmine is her purpose right now. Why are you all of a sudden worried about her?"

"I don't trust her," Riley said reluctantly.

"That's only because you know that she doesn't like you," she replied.

"That's not the reason," Riley said with a shake of his head. "I don't trust her because she almost attacked me. I saw it in her eyes. She even told me that she wants me dead."

"She's not a spy for Carvolo, Riley," she replied sternly. "I would know it if she was."

"What if Carvolo commanded her to lie to you? You wouldn't be able to tell if she's lying to you then."

Veronica didn't say anything as they walked up the stairs of the Singers porch. Before they reached the door she grabbed his hand again.

"I'll look into it," she said tersely. "I'll keep an eye on her."

"Be careful," Riley whispered to her.

She nodded and gave him a tight hug before she hurried down the steps and into the night. Riley sighed and opened the front door to find Pearl and Tanya doing the last of their schoolwork for the semester in the living room.

"You know," Pearl said evenly when she looked up at him. "You should probably stop playing with knives. They're bad for your health."

"I'll keep that in mind," Riley said with a smirk.

"H-how did you g-get hurt?" Tanya asked.

"I came face to face with an old enemy today. She likes to use knives."

"Ouch," Pearl said with a deadpan expression. "I'm glad you're okay."

Riley gave each of them a kiss on the forehead before he went upstairs to his room. He collapsed onto his bed without changing his clothes. He hadn't realized until then how exhausted he was. The fight with Jenna had taken a lot out of him, both physically and emotionally. He was surprised that he was holding it together as well as he was.

It was moments like this that he missed Aurora the most. She was the most comforting thing he had in his life and now she was gone. It had been hard seeing the visions the wand gave him, but at least with them he knew how she was doing. That he could see her. In a way, it felt like he'd been there with her. Now she was completely alone.

He needed to use the wand to break the binding spell Jenna put between her and Carvolo. He figured that she would come to him since he knew that someone in their community was a spy. He knew who it was too, even if Veronica wouldn't admit it. He didn't know how he knew, but he had learned a long time ago to trust his gut feeling.

Riley almost put the wand in it's accustomed place on his bedside table, but quickly thought better of it. He had a strong feeling that he needed to keep it close all night, so he tucked it next to him. He didn't think that anyone would try to break into his room to steal it, but he'd rather be paranoid than sorry.

He was about to close his eyes when the door to his room creaked open.

Rebecca stood in the doorway sheepishly.

257

"Hey," he mumbled through a yawn. "Glad to see you made it back."

"Yeah, you too," she said with a nod. "I know you probably want to go to bed, but I had to see you. I heard about what happened."

"I'm hoping to draw Jenna out," Riley said. "Roan thinks the wand will break the binding spell between her and Carvolo."

"I also heard that Roan and Selena are gone."

Riley didn't reply. Even though it was bad timing he understood why the fairies left. Their priority needed to be preventing their species from becoming extinct. The werewolves had destroyed too many things and the fairies didn't need to be one of them.

"How do you think Jenna will come to you with the protection spell in place?" Rebecca asked tentatively.

"There's a spy," Riley said. "She'll tell Jenna where I am."

"How do you know that?"

"I just do."

Riley glanced down at the wand and could feel it grow hot next to him. He didn't know if it was giving him some type of seer power, but it had definitely communicated something to him regarding Teresa.

Rebecca sighed and sat on his bed. She glanced at the wand and a satisfied look crossed her face. She gave him a quick nod and smiled slightly.

"What?" Riley asked in confusion.

"I'm just glad that the wand is on our side. The spy is Teresa, right?"

Riley didn't confirm or deny it, but the look he gave his sister said it all.

"What do you think her plans are?"

Riley thought about it for a moment before he answered.

"Well, so far she's told Jenna that we've been spying on her. I'm not sure what she's got planned next. I'm hoping that she'll tell Jenna where the community is, which will shatter the protection spell. The only problem is-"

"You can't tell anyone what's going on because it'll tip Teresa off," Rebecca finished for him. "Which puts everyone else in danger."

"I'm mostly worried about Pearl, Tanya, and the babies. Roy too since he's defenseless right now."

"Do you think we should tell mom and dad?" Rebecca asked.

"I've been thinking about it and I'm leaning towards doing that, but I'm not sure," Riley said as he rubbed his eyes tiredly.

"Does the wand have any advice?"

Riley chuckled humorlessly.

"That's not how it works."

Rebecca nodded in understanding. There was a knock on the door and Gabriel quickly opened it. The skinwalker looked tired, but he had a determined glint in his eye. Riley assumed that he had heard most of their conversation, which wasn't surprising. He strode over to the bed and sat on a chair.

"Do you think Teresa suspects that you know?" Gabriel asked, getting straight to the point.

"I'm not sure," Riley said with a shrug. "Things won't go smoothly if she does."

"Well," the skinwalker said with a sigh. "I don't think it's wise to keep your parents and Marcus and Sammie in the dark. They have children to protect."

"I agree," Riley said with a nod.

"I'll head over there," Rebecca said. "I promised to help Sara out with the babies so that Marcus and Sammie could take a break for the night."

"I think it's weird that Sara is still around," Riley said with a grunt.

"Don't we all?" Gabriel said grimly. "But I suppose she's coming around. She's not so traitorous since Luke died. He was the alpha in their pecking order, so Sara's been lost without him."

259

Riley suddenly felt a pang of guilt for his opinion about Sara, but he didn't dwell on it. She could've chosen not to follow her brother even if he was her alpha.

"Well, I better go."

Rebecca gave Riley a light punch on the arm and kissed Gabriel before leaving the room. Gabriel stayed where he was and they sat in silence for a while. There was something oddly comforting about the stillness in the room. It would've been peaceful if the situation was different.

"How are you holding up, man?" Riley asked.

"You haven't had any more vision of Aurora, have you?"

"You'd be the first to know if I did."

Gabriel nodded and looked at the floor. Riley's chest tightened in grief. He couldn't help but think that time was swiftly running out. He hoped that Teresa acted soon.

Chapter 17

Riley had a hard time remaining still as he watched Teresa and Jasmine sit on a blanket in Demian and Veronica's front yard. They were merely reading a book together, but he couldn't stop clenching and unclenching his fists nervously. The fact that the young girl was being raised by a traitor was a hard pill for him to swallow. It was aggravating that he couldn't do anything about it.

Pearl and Tanya had been running around in their wolf skin all morning. Despite telling Jackson and Rachel about Teresa being a spy they were still in the community. Riley didn't know why they weren't taking him seriously. It only made his nervousness worse.

Tanya stalked over to him and laid her furry red head on his knee. She breathed a sigh through her nose and closed her eyes. As if on cue, Pearl jumped him from behind. He rolled out of the way and grabbed her around the neck. She was a lot stronger than he was, but she let him take her down. She was getting better at play fighting without seriously injuring anyone. But Riley would still have some bruises.

"I can't play right now, little sis," Riley said as he patted her between the ears.

Pearl huffed and shed her wolf skin. Tanya followed suit.

"You never play anymore," Pearl said roughly.

Tanya looked at him and nodded her head in agreement with her sister.

"I know," he replied. "I'm sorry.

Riley studied their sad faces and suddenly had an idea. "Would you two be willing to help me out?"

Both girls nodded eagerly.

"Could you ask Jasmine to play with you today?"

Tanya nodded, but Pearl looked at him questioningly. The skinwalker girl was too insightful for her own good. She couldn't know about Teresa, so Riley quickly thought of an excuse he could give her.

261

"I just need to talk to Teresa for a while," he lied.

Pearl knew he was lying, but she didn't call him on it. Which was unusual. His nervous demeanor probably gave away how crucial the situation was. So all she did was nod with a furrowed brow.

"Later," she whispered to him. "You're gonna tell me what is going on."

"Make sure you girls stay close to home," Riley replied, ignoring her comment.

They hurried over to Demian and Veronica's house to invite Jasmine to play. The human girl happily accepted the invitation and they ran off together.

Teresa immediately stood up and took out her cell phone. Riley wished he knew for sure who she was calling, but he thought he had a pretty good idea who it was.

"I saw what you did there," Jackson said as he walked up to him. Riley was finally getting used to him appearing out of nowhere.

"She's a spy, dad," Riley replied without taking his eyes off of Teresa. "Pearl and Tanya are not safe here. You need to have them go with Sammie, the babies, and Roy. They're leaving in an hour."

"You still haven't explained why you think-"

"I don't think, I know," Riley interrupted him tersely.

"Buddy," his father said as he put a hand on his shoulder. "Do you have seer powers now?"

"No, I don't," Riley said as he turned to face him. "The wand does. Please, dad, get the girls out of here."

"What about Jasmine?"

"She should probably be taken away from Teresa as soon as possible."

"Riley," Jackson said with an unconvinced expression.

"If you don't believe me then listen to the conversation she's having. I guarantee you she's talking to Jenna or Carvolo."

Silence fell between them as Jackson's brow furrowed in concentration. Riley had no idea that the vampire could listen to a phone conversation from this far away. Apparently his wizard-vampire-hybrid status gave him extraordinary powers even by vampire standards. They stood there in silence until Teresa hung up the phone. Jackson's eyes flashed with a bloodlust that Riley had never seen from him before. He had to resist the urge to take a step away from him.

"What did you hear?"

"Jenna is coming," Jackson replied gruffly. "I'm not sure when, but soon."

"Did you hear any more details?"

Jackson shook his head as the bloodlust deepened in his eyes. He bared his fangs as he stared at Teresa like a starving man stares at a steak. He looked like he was about to go after her. A low growl erupted in his chest that made the hairs on Riley's neck tingle.

He put a hand on Jackson's arm to keep him grounded. Luckily he was able to snap out of hit quickly.

"I need a blood bag before I get my hands on that woman and drain her dry."

"We need to tell the council about this without raising suspicion. We want Jenna to come to us. That's going to be how we find the Ancients Den."

Jackson nodded and took out his cell phone.

"So, I'm going too?"

Riley glanced at Jasmine and saw a puzzled look on her face. He had been helping Pearl and Tanya pack a small suitcase with clothing and toiletries. Jasmine fit the skinwalker girls' clothes so they didn't have to raise suspicion by packing her own clothes in front of Teresa.

"Yeah," Riley said with a nod. "Your mom asked Rachel to take you."

"She never said anything to me," Jasmine whispered dejectedly.

"It's a recent decision," he replied.

"I'll need my inhaler," Jasmine said worriedly. "It's on my dresser."

Riley froze for a moment. He had no idea that Jasmine had asthma. He took out his phone and texted Jackson so that he would snatch it from her room. He didn't think that Teresa would notice an inhaler missing.

It didn't take them long to finish packing. Riley knew that he looked tense. The girls had been unusually quiet, especially Pearl. They knew that something was going on, but they were smart enough not to ask questions. The one that Riley felt horrible for was Jasmine.

There was a chance that the girl would never see her mother again. Teresa was working for Carvolo and couldn't be trusted. She had chosen her werewolf leader a long time ago and she had been playing them ever since. She hadn't raised any suspicion until Riley came into her life. Her hatred for him had given her away along with the wand's subtle seer power. There was no way that they would allow Jasmine to be with her mother alone ever again.

They were basically kidnapping Jasmine. It gave Riley a sick feeling, but he knew that it had to be done. Teresa thought that she was going to spend the night with Pearl and Tanya at the Singers house. That way the girls would be long gone before the fighting started. It was the only way to keep her out of danger since Teresa obviously cared more about her leader's interests than her own daughter's safety. It sickened him even more that Jasmine had been in danger this whole time and no one knew it until now.

The council had decided to allow Teresa to continue with her plan without raising any suspicion. They weren't exactly sure when Jenna was coming to the community, but Riley had a feeling it would be very soon. Everyone that needed to know about it was prepared. Now what they needed to do was get the children out of the community.

"Where are we going exactly?" Jasmine asked.

"There's a community in Colorado that Rachel is supposed to visit," Riley said convincingly. "She thought it would be fun for you girls to go on a road trip."

"Sammie and the babies are coming too," Pearl stated. "And Roy."

She gave Riley an intense look. She knew something was up.

"It'll be fun," Riley said as enthusiastically as he could.

The door opened and Rachel told the girls it was time to go. Pearl grabbed the small suitcase off of the bed and the three girls left the room. Riley didn't miss the concerned look Pearl gave him before she disappeared down the hallway.

"You be careful," Rachel told him.

Riley nodded as he hugged her. He knew that she didn't like the plan that the council came up with. She held him for a moment before kissing his cheek. Then she disappeared.

He took a shaky breath before hurrying into his bedroom. The wand was still tucked safely in his belt, but he needed additional weapons. The wand took a toll on his body, so he would only use it when he absolutely had to.

He strapped his quiver and bow to his back along with his gun holster. Rebecca, Gabriel, and Marcus appeared at his door with their weapons. They were going to stay with him until Jenna came. They didn't know what to expect, so they prepared for every possible contingency.

"Dad eavesdropped on another phone call," Rebecca informed him. "Jenna will be coming tonight. We aren't sure what time exactly."

"I thought dad left?" Riley said urgently. "The kids need the extra protection."

"Don't worry," Gabriel replied. "He's gone now. Karven is on his way to meet them as well."

"Veronica and Demian are staying at the warehouse," Marcus said. "Most of the skinwalker kids are gone now too, but we still have Zach, Chase, and Celeste."

"When did they all leave?" Riley asked in confusion.

"Demian sent a lot of the kids to different communities while we were in Portland," Gabriel explained. "It's too unsafe here for most of them now. But Naomi, Jeremy, and Raya decided to stay too."

"Hopefully we'll be enough," Riley said grimly. "Hopefully Jenna doesn't bring an army with her."

"Drake is on his way," Rebecca told him. "But he's still five hours out."

Riley had the feeling that Jenna would invade their community before then. He didn't think that the twelve people they had were going to be enough against her. He wasn't sure why he thought that, but it made him edgy. At least the girls were safely with their three vampire bodyguards.

"Well," Gabriel said with a sigh. "All we have to do now is wait."

There was a knock at the front door. Riley's breath caught and he had to take a moment to calm himself. He knew who it was, but he didn't know why she was there. He grabbed his gun from it's holster before cracking the door open. Gabriel, Rebecca, and Marcus had left to help patrol their borderers.

"Where is my daughter?" Teresa snarled at him.

"She's asleep," Riley lied convincingly.

It was very easy for him to lie to protect the ones he cared about.

"I thought you wouldn't be here," Teresa said sternly. "Jazzy won't be around you."

"I'm leaving right now," Riley replied. "I just had to get my weapons from my room."

"Why? There is trouble?"

Riley shook his head and shrugged.

"No trouble. They just need cleaning."

Teresa's eyes glowed yellow in the porch light. She growled and sprinted away unexpectedly. Riley cursed under his breath and took out his cell phone. He sent out a mass text to warn the others that Teresa was on to them. He relied on the wand to tell him which direction Teresa was going as he tried to follow her, but it was impossible for him to keep up with her supernatural speed.

It wasn't long before Veronica caught up with him. She was dressed mostly in black and she had two gun holsters strapped to her. Along with two knives sheathed to her hips. She had a solemn look on her face as she eyed him carefully.

"Do you know where Teresa went?"

"I think she's close," Riley explained. "She stopped running. She either met up with Jenna or she's trying to catch us off guard."

"You were right," Veronica said sadly. "You were right about everything."

Riley looked at her in concern.

"Jenna brought a small army of werewolves to the community. Everyone else is busy dealing with them."

"How outnumbered are we?" Riley asked grimly.

"I didn't have time to count before I came to find you. Naomi is using fire to even things out."

They proceeded cautiously into the woods. It was dark, but warm. The summer night air would've felt soothing on any other night, but after five minutes of navigating through the thick trees Riley was sweating profusely.

He had a gut wrenching feeling that things weren't going to go their way tonight. The fact that the wand had been giving him seer powers made him feel uneasy. He knew that something bad was going to happen, but he didn't know what to do to prevent it.

Veronica took point since Riley couldn't see much in the darkness. He didn't dare create light because he didn't want to give themselves away. If they could catch Teresa off guard the situation might be more in their favor. But the darkness around them made Riley nervous. It was tempting to create light anyway because of how still everything was. There wasn't even the usual sound of crickets.

He could tell that his sister felt the same nervousness. Her shoulders were stiff and her hand gripped her gun a little too tightly. Riley held his bow out in front of him and fitted an arrow on the string. He knew that they would be attacked soon. He just didn't know if it would be Jenna or Teresa. It was going to be hard for them to take out either one. Riley set his emotions aside and tried to clear his head of any thought other than surviving.

Suddenly, a throwing knife flew passed his ear. He was too slow to move out of it's way and he felt it slice through his ear lobe. The other five knives soared at him. He instinctively dropped his bow and raised his hands. They stopped right in front of him and circled him menacingly. He was about to throw his magical flames at them when he heard Jenna's cackling laugh.

"My darlings are now immune to your craticas spells, Ry."

Riley and Veronica watched as their mother emerged from the dark trees. The knives continued circling Riley, but he was sure they would cut him if he tried to move. Veronica flinched at the sound of Jenna's voice. She didn't have any knives surrounding her, but that didn't surprise Riley. He was sure Jenna thought Veronica would be on her side. She had no idea how wrong she was.

"Mom," Veronica said hoarsely. "Get the knives away from him. Please."

"If I do that, Veronica, he will take that wand he's got and kill me. You wouldn't want that, would you?"

"Of course not," Veronica replied. "He's not going to kill you. We want to help you."

Jenna cackled maniacally. She flicked her fingers and a silvery ball of light appeared. It became so bright that Riley had to blink a few times for his eyes to adjust. The knives inched closer to him. They didn't stop until the hot silver blades were touching him.

"I don't believe that," she replied with a cackle. "He'd kill me if he could. The only thing keeping him from doing it right now is the fact that he needs me to get to his precious Aurora."

Veronica sighed in frustration and held one hand up while she holstered her gun. She put both hands out in front of her with a pleading look and Jenna sneered at her. Riley wasn't sure what Veronica was doing, but he didn't think it would work. Jenna was psychotic. Reasoning with her was a mistake.

"Don't you want to be free, mom?"

Jenna scoffed at her in disbelief.

"Veronica, you of all people should know that there's no such thing as freedom."

"What if we offered a way out?" Veronica asked warily as she took a cautious step towards her. "What if we helped you get away from Carvolo."

"The only way that can happen is if Carvolo dies betraying me," she said with a smirk.

"Well, Riley can-"

"No, Veronica," Riley said warningly.

One of the knives sliced into his arm and he gasped. The other knives spun in the air close enough to drill holes in his shirt.

"My darlings don't want you to talk, Ry," Jenna said nonchalantly. "You made them angry the last time they saw you."

Riley took a shaky breath and stared at Jenna. He found it interesting that she spoke of her knives the same way he did the wand. He briefly wondered how many magical objects there were in the world that had similar characteristics.

He tried to ignore the blades burning his skin as Jenna studied him for any sign of weakness.

"Mom, this is ridiculous," Veronica said diplomatically. "I know that you love us. We're your children."

"It is true. I do love you, Veronica. Unfortunately, I think we both know how I feel about your sorry excuse for a sibling."

Veronica glanced at Riley and their eyes met for a moment. He saw a flash of anger cross his sister's face and she blinked a few times to maintain control. If he wasn't surrounded by knives she probably would've attacked Jenna with all her werewolf strength.

"Besides," the witch continued lazily. "I couldn't help but feel betrayed when you decided to take in Bill's mistress and their homely little-"

"Don't say anything against Jasmine," Veronica said sternly. "She is completely innocent and has nothing to do with any of this."

One of the knives buried itself into Riley's shoulder. The other knives sliced through his shirt simultaneously, causing multiple bloody cuts on his torso. He grabbed the knife that was sticking out of his shoulder and pulled it out as quickly as he could. It all happened so fast that he almost didn't hear Veronica scream.

"Leave him alone!"

"Oh, calm down, Veronica," Jenna said with a nonchalant wave of her hand. "I didn't hurt him that bad. Look, he's not even crying."

"What do you want, Jenna?" Riley asked angrily.

He was either too furious or in too much shock to feel the pain.

"Where is that berserker friend of yours?" she asked lightly. "The one with the delicious blond curly hair, soft brown eyes, and that deep husky voice that melts my black heart."

Riley shivered in disgust at Jenna's description of Jeremy. He really didn't like her objectifying Jeremy, he'd been through enough crap in his life as it was.

"Safe from you," he said stiffly.

"I highly doubt that," Jenna said with a chuckle. "Right about now my little army of werewolves should be looting through your homes. I'm sure it didn't take much to kill your friends. Of course they better not have killed my berserker. Carvolo would have my hyde."

Riley snorted, but didn't say anything. Jenna was severely misinformed if she thought her army could take them down that quickly.

270

"I'm also supposed to kidnap a set of infant twins," Jenna said dryly. "I'm not exactly sure why Carvolo wants them. Something about them being his grandchildren."

Veronica was about to take a step toward Jenna, but she thought better of it. Riley clenched his fists and took a few calming breaths. Apparently Teresa told Carvolo about Leigh and Elizabeth. He was relieved that they got them out, and that they had three vampire bodyguards for protection.

"You can forget about the babies," Riley said. "As for Jeremy, I think you've bitten off a little more than you can chew. He would wipe the floor with you."

"I thought I told you not to talk," Jenna said angrily.

The knives bit into his skin again and he grimaced. He had blood dripping from various wounds. He wasn't sure how much more of this he could take. He was mostly worried about the blood loss, but so far it wasn't too bad. Veronica seemed to be more effected by the knives than he was though. Which could prove to be problematic if her werewolf instincts took over.

"If you're going to kill us then just get on with it," Veronica snarled.

"Unfortunately, I can't kill the wizard. And I don't want to kill you Veronica. You're my daughter."

"What are we doing here then?" Riley asked in frustration

"Luckily, Ry," Jenna said with a grin. "You brought the wand to me. Which means that I will be able to take you to Carvolo now. But first, Veronica, I need you to lure my handsome berserker here."

"That's not going to happen," she replied tersely.

"I guess your brother will be stabbed a few more times," the witch's eyes twinkled in the silvery light. "What a shame."

Veronica took a shaky breath and grimaced. She grabbed her cell phone as she shook her head dejectedly.

"Don't, Veronica," Riley said sternly.

She ignored him and called Jeremy. Riley grimaced as he listened to his sister tell Jeremy that they needed his help. The temptation to grab his wand was unbearable, but he knew that the knives would stab him if he did. He had to figure something out, but he couldn't come up with anything. Being around Jenna messed with his emotions so much that he couldn't function normally.

Veronica was still talking on the phone when she suddenly dropped it. Riley watched her for a moment in confusion. She had a blank look on her face before she staggered. She gasped a short intake of air and fell to the ground.

Teresa stood over her in the shadows of the trees. She held a large syringe in her hand and a bloodied knife in the other. Veronica laid at her feet with blood pouring out of a wound in her back.

It wasn't healing.

Riley's breath quickened and panic coursed through him. He rushed to Veronica's side without thinking about the knives. Luckily, they didn't follow him.

Jenna shrieked angrily. The knives surrounded her protectively as Teresa pulled out a gun. She aimed it at Riley who was now holding Veronica in his arms. He glared at the werewolf to hold back the tears that threatened to fall from his eyes.

"You took Jazzy," Teresa murmured angrily. "I don't care what Carvolo says. You. Done."

Before she could pull the trigger all six of Jenna's knives entered her chest simultaneously. She immediately dropped the gun and took a few steps backwards. She collapsed to the ground, but the knives didn't remove themselves like Riley expected them to. He glanced at Jenna in shock.

"No one tries to kill my children but me," she shrieked angrily. "And I've always hated her."

In one swift motion, Riley had the wand in his hand. A silver mist burst from the tip of the wand. It wrapped itself around Riley and Veronica in a protective barrier. He cursed himself for not keeping the magical shield in place during their confrontation with Jenna. Veronica wouldn't be hurt now if he'd been able to do so.

Riley aimed the wand at Jenna and she smirked at him as the knives raced toward him. They hit the invisible shield that surrounded him and they all shattered into tiny pieces of sharp silver.

Jenna shrieked and collapsed to her knees. She wrapped her arms around herself as though she were in pain. The silver shards of her knives littered the ground around him and Veronica. Riley was relieved to see that they were truly destroyed and would never hurt anyone ever again.

Riley used the wand to immobilize Jenna. He knew that her magic wasn't strong enough to break the hold the wand had on her. So he ignored her and concentrated on examining his sister.

Veronica was unresponsive and her breathing was shallow. She wasn't healing from the stab wound and she was bleeding profusely. He recognized the symptoms and his mouth went dry. He cradled her to his chest tightly and waited for Jeremy to find them.

Chapter 18

Riley heard Jeremy cursing in the darkness. He quickly used the wand to create a blue ball of light so that he could see the werewolf. Riley wasn't surprised to see that he looked awful. He was covered in tons of blood and dirt. His curly hair was matted and his clothing was torn. Despite his appearance he didn't seem to be injured at all.

"What happened, man?" Jeremy asked in shock.

"We need to get Veronica to Demian. Now."

Jeremy nodded in understanding. He bent down to pick up Veronica, but Riley stopped him.

"You don't want to touch her," Riley explained. "You'd get a nasty shock. The wand put a powerful shield around us. I'll carry her."

"So…I have to escort your psycho mom?"

"Sorry," Riley replied with a shrug. He could allow Jeremy to touch Veronica if he wanted to, but he needed to be the one to carry her. If she was going to die in the next few minutes it would be in his arms, not Jeremy's.

Jeremy sighed and rolled his eyes. Riley pointed the wand at Jeremy and the silvery protective barrier encompassed him and Jenna as well. Once Jeremy and Jenna were shielded, the werewolf grabbed Jenna by the arm and yanked her to her feet. He gave her a shove and ordered her to walk.

"Is she going to be okay?" Jeremy asked as he eyed Veronica's limp petite body in Riley's arms.

"I don't know," Riley said gruffly. "She's been injected with an old werewolf disease. Normally she would be fine after given the cure, but she's been wounded. It's going to cause problems. She's still breathing for now, but that could change at any second."

"Demian is at the warehouse," Jeremy replied. "Let's get her there."

Jenna mumbled something under her breath and Riley used the wand to silence her. If she couldn't speak she couldn't use her magic. At least that's what he hoped. Without her knives she didn't seem like such a dangerous threat anymore.

They hiked through the woods until they came to the training fields. The warehouse was close by and it wasn't long before they were running through the front doors. They hurried to the medical room.

Everyone was in there except for Naomi and Marcus. Gabriel was helping Demian bandage up Chase who had a large cut across his chest. Raya, Celeste, and Żach looked a little worse for wear, but Chase had the worst injuries. Gabriel had cuts all over him, but his face was composed. Too composed. It was then that Riley noticed that Rebecca also wasn't there.

Demian glanced at Riley and his eyes instantly glowed yellow. A deep feral growl vibrated through the old leader's chest. Veronica seemed to grow heavier in Riley's arms under the werewolf's gaze.

Suddenly, Demian was standing in front of them. He extended his hand to touch Veronica before Riley could warn him. A blue electrical current hit him and he flew backwards.

Riley grimaced as he watched Demian slowly stand up. The enraged werewolf glance at Jenna and growled again furiously. The witch stared at Demian in shock. She still couldn't speak or defend herself from the angry werewolf. Riley was inclined to watch her struggle in terror, but he knew that he needed to calm Demian down before the situation got out of hand.

"She didn't do this," Riley said in a raspy voice. "Teresa did."

"And she's dead," Jeremy said helpfully. "Well, at least she looked dead."

Riley spotted a stretcher next to the wall and he hurried over to it. He laid Veronica down and tucked the wand in his belt. The protective barrier around them broke the second he lost contact with her. Riley nodded at Demian to let him know that it was safe to touch her now. The werewolf hurried over to examine his wife.

"Where's Rebecca?" Riley asked shakily.

Gabriel didn't respond as he finished wrapping Chase's wound. Jeremy didn't respond either as he hurriedly escorted Jenna to a chair at the other end of the room. Zach and Celeste studied the floor as though there was something interesting beneath their feet. Raya's face paled as she glanced away from Riley.

Something bad happened to Rebecca too.

"Gabriel," Riley said sternly. "Where is Rebecca?"

Terror gripped him when Gabriel didn't answer right away. His carefully composed expression deteriorated and he ran a hand through his hair.

"Gabriel-"

"She's in there," Gabriel said softly.

He pointed to a door at the other end of the room. Riley hurried toward it, but Gabriel put a hand on his arm. Riley shook him off and tried to open the door, but Gabriel put his arm out to stop him.

"She's not dead," Gabriel's voice shook when he spoke. "But she's sick. Like Veronica."

"Like Aurora was," Riley said grimly. "And we sent all the vampires away. With no way to contact them. How could we be so stupid?"

Gabriel didn't respond. He just stared at the ground as he tried to regain his calm composure.

"Where's Naomi and Marcus?"

"They're burning bodies," Raya replied. "There's a lot of them, so we didn't count how many."

Demian strolled past Riley and grabbed a few syringes of healing elements off of the lab table. They didn't have very many elements left. Selena and Roan weren't able to make enough before they had to leave. Demian had been working on making more before they found out Teresa was Carvolo's spy.

They all watched quietly as Demian mixed different magical liquids in a vial. Riley recognized what he was doing. He was creating a mild suppressant for the werewolf disease. With Veronica's injury it was probably necessary for her. He

276

didn't know if Rebecca had been injured. It didn't look like Demian was going to have enough of the liquid for both of them, so he hoped she wasn't.

It was then that it hit him. His sisters were going to die if they didn't get in contact with the vampires. If Rebecca wasn't injured she had a few weeks, but Veronica didn't. He took a breath to calm himself as he watched Demian work.

"Demian," Gabriel said cautiously. "We should get Veronica on a bed."

Demian didn't reply, so Gabriel picked up Veronica with gentle arms. The fact that Demian let Gabriel even touch her was a statement of how much he trusted the skinwalker. Werewolves were very protective over the people that they claimed as theirs, especially when they're injured.

Demian had wrapped a bandage around Veronica's wound, but there was still blood all over the white gurney. Riley opened the door for Gabriel and followed him inside. There were three beds in the room. Riley was willing to guess that it was Jeremy, Chase, and Zach's room.

Rebecca was unconscious on one of the beds. She had an IV placed in her arm, but Riley knew that it wouldn't do much to help her. It was probably there to make her feel more comfortable when she did wake up. Riley was relieved to see that she wasn't wounded. Just sick. He could live with that for now.

Riley helped Gabriel get an IV ready for Veronica. After it was in place Demian strode through the door with a look etched into his features that Riley had never seen before. He backed away from the bed from sheer instinct. He noticed that Gabriel did the same. The werewolf was giving off some pretty scary vibes.

They watch Demian insert the needle into Veronica's heart. When he depressed the plunger Veronica gasped, but she didn't open her eyes. Demian studied her face for a moment and checked her eyes with a flashlight. The werewolf exhaled in aggravation and set the flashlight down on the end table.

"Do we know when Jackson is supposed to contact us?" he asked through a growl.

"In a few days," Gabriel said grimly.

"Veronica doesn't have that long. I'm going to go find them."

"No, Demian, let Drake and Joey do that. You need to stay here with her."

Demian growled and rounded on Gabriel. The skinwalker stood his ground as the werewolf advanced on him. Riley grabbed the wand as he stared at the enraged werewolf. He had never seen Demian like this before. He was becoming unhinged. Riley didn't think that was possible. Demian always seemed to be in control.

"*You need to calm down*," Gabriel said in a fearlessly commanding tone.

Gabriel may be the youngest of his skinwalker siblings, but that didn't make him any less dominate as a wolf. Even a werewolf leader like Demian had to take notice when Gabriel used such a commanding voice.

Their eyes remained locked for a long time. Finally, Gabriel stepped away from Demian and stood next to Rebecca's bed. Demian took a few breaths and turned to face Riley.

"I need to know what happened," he whispered roughly.

Riley briefly told them about their encounter with Jenna and how Teresa had attacked Veronica from behind. Demian's angry expression didn't change while he listened, but at least he wasn't growling anymore.

"The dragons are looking for the vampires, Demian," Gabriel said softly. "They'll find them. Veronica is going to be just fine."

Demian nodded, but Riley wasn't sure if the werewolf believed it. Riley didn't know if he did either. They couldn't lose Veronica, especially now. He looked at Rebecca's still figure lying on the bed and he felt tears burn his eyes. It was then that he became uncontrollably furious. There was only one person that he could confront that was responsible for this.

Riley gripped the wand tightly in his hand and walked briskly from the room.

He hardly noticed the other people in the medical room as he made his way toward Jenna. She was sitting in a chair with her hands tied behind her back. He assumed that Jeremy took her magic from her with the elements the fairies had left for them. She hadn't made an attempt to escape and the wand's magical hold on her had diminished a while ago.

Riley barely heard the shocked gasps from the people in the room when he grabbed Jenna by the collar of her shirt. He threw her into the wall as hard as he could. He held her there as she gasped for breath. He assumed that he'd knocked the wind out of her, but he didn't care.

"If either of them dies from this," he told her menacingly. "I swear I will kill you. Aurora is the only reason you aren't dead right now."

Jenna groaned for a moment and then she chuckled.

"There it is," she said through a crazed smile. "I was wondering what it would take to break you. You've lost your mind and gone dark side. Like mother, like son."

Riley gritted his teeth and tightening his hold on Jenna. It took him a moment to realize that Raya was standing next to him. She put a gentle hand on his arm that held Jenna against the wall. Her tamer abilities didn't work on him, but her calm touch gave him something else to concentrate on. He was still angry. He was still hurt. He still held a lot of hate for the woman that smiled cruelly at him. But Raya's simple touch gave him the tools he needed to refocus his brain. He still didn't move away from Jenna, but at least he was breathing normally again.

"I know you're hurting, Riley," Raya whispered to him. "And she's caused a lot of that pain. But you have to remember that she's your mother. You will never come back from this."

Raya stopped talking when Riley met her eyes with his. They were glowing blue. For the first time he really wished that her abilities worked on him. He wished he could feel calm. He didn't want to feel like this, but unfortunately he did. He tore his gaze from Raya and glared back at his mother who was still sneering at him.

"I'm not going to let you hurt yourself by hurting her," Raya continued softly. "Let her go, Riley."

When Riley didn't budge she put her other hand on his shoulder. She gently massaged the knots in his muscles that shook violently from the rage coursing through him.

"It's going to be okay," she said reassuringly. "Let her go."

Riley took another deep breath and lowered his arm from Jenna's chest. The witch's eyes hardened into a glare. He forced himself to take a step back. Raya still had a hold of his arm and he was grateful for it. She was literally the only thing keeping him from doing something that he would regret later.

"You brought the disease here," Riley said angrily as he pointed a trembling finger at Jenna. "You were supposed to give it to Jeremy and Rebecca so you could deliver them to Carvolo safely. But Teresa ruined that plan by trying to kill Veronica with it."

"You're delusional if you think I'm going to tell you anything," Jenna said happily. "But you shouldn't want me to. If I did betray Carvolo's trust I would die and we all know what happens if I die."

"What would happen?" Jeremy asked sarcastically. "Because, honestly, I don't see the downside."

Jenna cackled at Jeremy, but didn't answer him.

"Aurora would be locked in the Ancients Den forever," Riley explained gruffly. "Unless they find another keeper, but if they did we'd have a lesser chance of finding it."

"You have no chance of finding it," Jenna said with a maniacal chuckle. "You're never going to see Aurora again. Unless you let me take you in."

"It's a tempting offer, Jenna," Riley said forcefully. "But I have a better way."

"Ry, I thought we were past the '*Jenna*' thing. I'm your mother. Calling me anything but '*mom*' is disrespectful."

280

Something snapped in Riley's brain and anger surged through him again. He would've lunged at her, but Raya kept a firm grip on his arm. He knew it took her werewolf strength to keep him still. If he tried any harder to get at Jenna he'd probably dislocated his shoulder.

Jeremy took a step between them. He growled angrily at Jenna and she flinched in horror. She began to shake a little as the berserker werewolf inched closer to her in a stalking manner.

"I would be very careful what you say," Jeremy whispered dangerously. "I haven't known Riley for very long, but I've never seen him this pissed off. He's not a person that you want to have angry with you."

Jenna sank back into the chair. She avoided Jeremy's intimidating stare by looking at the floor.

Riley relaxed a little. There was something comforting about having Jeremy stand up for him. Somehow it made him feel safe in this horrible situation. It was odd, but he decided that he'd just go with it for now.

"Why does Carvolo want me too?" Jeremy asked when he turned to look at Riley. "I have no idea what he could possibly want from me."

"Maybe he wants to create love triangle drama."

Marcus and Naomi were standing in the doorway. Marcus was covered in blood and ashes while Naomi looked like she had just gotten ready for a punk rock concert. Not a single red and black hair was out of place. Her dark eye makeup wasn't even smeared. She was dressed in black skinny jeans and a brick red jacket. Apparently she fought in her dragon skin the entire time without getting a single scratch.

"What's that supposed to mean, Marcus?" Jeremy asked incredulously.

"Well, Riley's married to Aurora and you used to date her," the skinwalker said with a shrug. "Maybe he wants to put the three of you in a room together just to see what happens."

281

Riley and Jeremy stared at Marcus in horror. He couldn't have made the situation more awkward if he had walked into the room naked. Naomi patted Marcus's shoulder reproachfully.

"Smooth, Marcus," she said sarcastically. "That really lightened the mood."

"Why would you-" Riley began, but Jeremy interrupted him.

"That's just...wrong."

"I'm not saying it's not weird or...*wrong*," Marcus replied calmly. "But it makes sense to me. Carvolo would definitely do something like that. Why do you think he put Jeremy in the cell with her in the first place? It's psychological torment. I wouldn't put it past him."

Riley was no longer relaxed after hearing that and all the anger surged back into him. He suddenly felt like they were wasting precious time.

"That's besides the point," Riley said angrily. "I need to find out where the Ancients Den is. In order for me to do that Jenna and I need to be alone for a while."

"Not happening," Jeremy said with a shake of his head.

"He's right, Riley," Raya said gently. "You shouldn't have to do this alone."

Jenna laughed, but cut it short when Jeremy growled at her again with his yellow eyes drilling into her.

"I can't even imagine what you're going through right now," Marcus said as he glared at Jenna.

"We can leave though," Chase said. "Demian wants us to get some rest anyways."

Riley glanced over at Chase, Celeste, and Zach. They did look exhausted. Zach was already leaning against the wall with droopy eyes. They were all injured and they looked like they could use a good night's sleep. Riley would've probably felt the same way if he had the time to feel anything else put panic and anger. He knew that he was still bleeding from his knife wounds, but no one had seemed to notice them yet. He had a feeling the wand was the only thing keeping him upright.

Marcus nodded at them and the three skinwalkers disappeared through one of the doors. Riley gripped the wand tightly in his hand. He wasn't sure how to do what needed to be done, but the wand always knew. It vibrated in his hand and he pointed it at Jenna.

The witch's eyes grew wide with fear. A blue mist erupted from the tip of the wand and wrapped itself around her. She gasped and her eyes rolled to the back of her head. A black mist came out of her body and evaporated when it met the blue magic that came from the wand. Jenna gasped and writhed as the black magic from the spell seeped out of her body. When there was no more black magic left, the blue magic disappeared.

"It's done," Riley whispered as he stared at the wand. "The spell between her and Carvolo is broken."

Jenna looked at the wand with fear in her eyes.

"You've lost the advantage, Jenna," Riley said fiercely. "Tell me where the Ancients Den is."

"Why would I do that?" Jenna asked him angrily. "You'd kill me if I did."

Looking into her sadistic eyes made Riley lose every ounce of self-control that he had. He needed to find his wife and he no longer cared how he did it.

"Don't think I won't resort to hurting you to get Aurora back," he replied menacingly. "Where. Is. It?"

Jenna glared back at him for a moment and she laughed. Riley raised the wand and pointed it at her again with a torture incantation on the tip of his tongue. Raya gently touched his arm again and Marcus moved in front of him.

"No, Riley," Marcus whispered. "I know the desperation you're feeling, but-"

"Get out of the way," Riley said through gritted teeth,

"This isn't something you have to do, Riley," Naomi said soothingly. "There's got to be another way."

"Get out of the way, Marcus," he said again sternly.

Marcus didn't move and Riley would've punched him if Raya didn't have a tight hold on his arm. Gabriel came into the

283

room at that moment and his face paled when he figured out what was going on.

"Riley, this isn't you, man," Gabriel said cautiously. "You don't want to do this."

Riley glanced at the man that knew him better than he knew himself. He didn't think he'd ever find another best friend quite like Gabriel even if he lived ten thousand lifetimes.

But Gabriel was wrong this time.

"That's the thing, Gabriel," Riley whispered furiously. "I *do* want to. I've wanted to do this for a *very* long time."

There was silence in the room for a moment before Jenna started cackling with sadistic glee. Jeremy growled and flashed his yellow berserker eyes at her again. She stopped laughing instantly.

"You say that now, but I don't believe you," Gabriel replied calmly. "It would destroy you tomorrow and I care too much about you to let that happen."

Riley didn't move or say anything. He continued glaring at Marcus who still stood in front of him to protect his insane mother. All those childhood years of neglect and abuse flooded his memories for a moment. Now this monster was the only one who could save Aurora. He didn't think there was going to be another way for this to end. He had to interrogate her.

"I think we could all use a ten minute break," Naomi said. "Jeremy and I will watch over the psycho witch. The three of you take Riley out to get some air."

Raya nodded and Gabriel mumbled that he agreed. Marcus put a hand on Riley's shoulder and tried to steer him away.

"No," Riley said firmly.

"Aurora wouldn't want you to do this," Marcus said forcefully. "If you don't come willingly I'll knock you out. Don't test me."

It wasn't an empty threat, but they both knew that Marcus couldn't actually knock him out now that he had the wand.

Riley shook Raya and Marcus off of him and marched out of the room. He knew that they were following him, but he didn't slow down. He went outside and took a deep breath of the night air. He wasn't surprised when it didn't help him. He had never felt like that before in his life. It was like all of his humanity had been siphoned out of him when he saw his sick sisters on those beds. He had lost too much already and he couldn't take it anymore.

His hands started shaking and he looked down at the wand. He briefly wondered if the wand was controlling his emotions somehow. That would explain why he was so angry, but he knew it wasn't the wand. He couldn't blame this on anyone but himself. If his friends hadn't been there to stop him he didn't know what he would've done. Or how far he would have gone.

He tucked the wand into his belt and took a shaky breath. He found a place to sit and ran his hands through his hair. It was all starting to hit him now. He had been prepared to torture someone to get information. He was still prepared to do it if he needed to, but the realization of it scared him. He barely recognized himself at the moment.

Marcus and Raya stopped at the front door of the warehouse, but Gabriel continued walking toward him. Riley avoided looking at him when he sat down next to him. They sat in silence for a few minutes.

"I can't believe I'm willing to do something like that," Riley finally whispered. "I can't believe that I'm perfectly fine with hurting someone. I've been tortured so many times and I couldn't imagine wishing that upon my worst enemy, until tonight."

Gabriel glanced at him and then nodded in agreement.

"Desperation makes people do crazy things sometimes," Gabriel said. "But there's got to be another way."

"There isn't," Riley said defeatedly. "She won't give up the Ancients Den if I don't force it out of her."

"How often does that actually work?"

Gabriel had a point. Most people would take their secrets to the grave if they could. Jackson used to have success with torture when he was merely a hunter. But Riley wasn't Jackson, and Jenna wasn't a random monster.

He wasn't thinking straight and he doubted Gabriel was either. He felt like he was missing something. He grabbed the wand from his belt and stared at it. He didn't know if the wand could provide any answers, but he hoped it would.

"Could the wand give you the ability to read her mind?" Gabriel asked gently.

"Probably," Riley said with a shrug. "But I don't want to do that. I can't...I can't go there."

The idea of being sucked into Jenna's mind made him nauseous. He knew he wouldn't be able to handle what he'd see there. It would damage him beyond repair.

"Okay, that's understandable," Gabriel said with a nod.

Riley suddenly had an idea. It was a crazy idea, but he had a feeling that it would work. He stood up quickly and hurried toward the warehouse.

"Riley, where are you going?" Gabriel asked as he stood up.

"I know what I have to do," he replied vaguely.

Marcus and Raya looked at him warily as he walked past them through the warehouse door. He found Jenna sitting in the same chair with a permanent sneer plastered to her face. Jeremy and Naomi were talking quietly in the corner. They stopped their conversation and stared at him in surprise for a moment.

"That wasn't ten minutes, Ry," Naomi said in annoyance.

Riley ignored her and stood in front of Jenna.

"If the wand can break the spell," Riley said to her. "How much are you willing to bet that it can make me the new keeper?"

Jenna's face paled, but she didn't reply.

"Riley," Gabriel said as he came up behind him. "Are you sure you want to do that?"

"Sounds risky, man," Marcus remarked.

Riley didn't acknowledge them. He was too busy concentrating. He pointed the wand at Jenna with a steady hand. She glared at him with such intense hatred that Riley couldn't help but flinch. Despite everything she was still his mother and the look on her face broke his spirit a little more.

Riley suddenly felt the wand take over. He muttered complicated incantations that he'd never heard of before. The wand was using him as a vessel and he had absolutely no control of what he was doing or saying. It didn't take long for Jenna to start screaming. The magical force he felt coming from the wand was so powerful that he could barely comprehend what was going on around him.

Gabriel tried to grab him, but an invisible force stopped his hand in midair. Suddenly, Riley was no longer standing in the medical room.

Riley was standing in a large room that had a medieval castle feel to it. There was a large stone fireplace with a mantle. Stained glass windows with elegant designs glittered in the sunlight from outside. He wasn't sure where he was or what time period he was in. He remembered it being night time when he was in the warehouse. The last thing he remembered was the wand helping him take Jenna's place as keeper of the Ancients Den.

It was then that he realized he was having another vision. But it wasn't happening in real time and he wasn't seeing the future. He was seeing something that already happened in the past. He had a feeling that he was seeing his first glimpse of what the Ancients Den looked like on the inside.

He turned around and saw that in the middle of the room was a large rectangular stone table. He didn't see anyone at first, but then two large oak doors opened at the end of the room. Ten werewolves entered the huge room from a long dark hallway. Riley recognized Lekiah and Avestan. He assumed that the rest were also ancient ones.

He gasped when he saw Carvolo walk into the room behind the group with Aurora by his side. She had silver chains around her wrists and ankles. She looked starved, weak and she had been beaten severely. If Carvolo didn't have a tight grip on her arm she wouldn't have been standing.

Riley suddenly had a very hard time remaining calm.

He had to resist the urge to run to her by reminding himself that this was a vision. It was all in his head. It was really hard knowing that all this had already happened and there was no way to prevent Aurora's suffering. The anger and guilt he felt for not being able to stop this made him physically sick.

Jenna appeared behind Carvolo with an infuriating smirk on her face. She sauntered into the room as though she owned the place. Riley didn't miss the annoyed glances from some of the ancient ones.

"It's been a while since I've been here," Jenna said in amusement. "It's still as creepy as ever."

"Carvolo," Avestan said sternly. "Why did you kill Zalina? And why would you bring Jenina here?"

"I had my reasons, father," Carvolo said nonchalantly. "Besides, Jenina can't betray us. If she does then she's a dead witch."

"True story," Jenna said with a feral smile. "You have my full cooperation."

Riley ignored the conversation as he stared at Aurora. He took a deep shaky breath and had to turn away from her before he lost his mind. He couldn't look at her anymore knowing that he couldn't help her. She looked like she was moments from death and he couldn't bear it. He studied the room for clues. Anything that could give away the Ancients Den location.

He walked around as he searched and finally noticed something on the mantle. It was a rolled up scroll. He reached out and was surprised that he could touch it. He picked it up and unrolled it. Relief surged through him when he realized it was a map.

Suddenly, the medieval room dissolved and he was standing in the medical room again. Jenna was unconscious on the floor and everyone else in the room was gaping at him in awe.

Riley looked at his hand and was surprised to see that he was no longer holding the wand. It had transformed itself into the map.

Chapter 19

"What the-" Jeremy was flabbergasted. "What just happened?"

"Um," Raya said timidly. "Riley, can you hear me?"

Riley looked up from the map in his hand and stared at her. Gabriel tried to grab his arm again and he seemed surprised that he was able to touch him now.

"Where did the wand go?" Marcus asked hesitantly. "And where did the scroll come from?"

"The wand is the scroll," Riley explained. "And the scroll is a map."

"A map?" Gabriel asked with a raised eyebrow. "To where?"

For the first time in a long time Riley smiled a true smile. Gabriel stared at him in confusion.

"To the Ancients Den."

A stunned silence fell in the room. It was so quiet that Riley could hear Jenna panting on the floor. They all turned to look at her as her eyes fluttered open. Riley wasn't sure what the wand did to her. All he knew was that he was the keeper now. Hopefully the ancients where none the wiser about it.

Jenna slowly stood up and tried to move her hands. She realized that they were still tied behind her back and she looked at them with wide eyes. She struggled against the ropes binding her hands for a moment before she started hyperventilating. She let out a choked sob and looked up at Riley with tears running down her face.

"You did this to me!" she screamed at him furiously. "You took it!"

It took Riley a moment to realize what she was so upset about. The wand didn't just make him the new keeper of the Ancients Den. It had taken Jenna's magic from her.

This time she will never get it back...

The wand's voice couldn't have said anything more reassuring to him in that moment.

"Look at me, you stupid wizard!" Jenna shrieked with pure loathing contorting her face. "Look what you have done!"

Riley advanced on Jenna so quickly that she flinched. His face was inches away from hers as he gave her a smile. She glared back at him in disgust.

"Good," he said softly. "You will never hurt anyone else ever again. I'll rest easier every night knowing that. Have a nice life, Jenna."

Somehow she slipped her hands from the ropes binding them behind her back. She raised her hand to slap him, but he was too quick. He grabbed her wrist and roughly shoved her hand away. Without a second glance at her, Riley left the room. He decided that he'd let his friends figure out what to do with her. There was no way he could deal with that emotional crossroad. He needed to talk to Demian anyway.

He found Demian sitting in a chair next to Veronica's bed. He looked like he had calmed down a little bit. His eyes widened when he saw what Riley held in his hand.

"Where did you get that, Riley?" Demian asked in disbelief.

"The wand gave me a vision of the Ancients Den," Riley explained. "Then when I came back to the present the wand had transformed itself into the map."

Riley unrolled the scroll and handed it to Demian.

"I'm leaving," Riley told him. "Take a picture of the map and send reinforcements as soon as you can."

Demian took out his cell phone and snapped a few pictures of the map. The map transformed back into the wand after Demian had the information he needed.

"That's incredible," the werewolf murmured. "But this isn't a good idea, Riley."

"I know how to get there," Riley said assertively. "You're not going to be able to stop me."

"You'd be going in without any help," Demian said quietly. "I can't leave Veronica or Rebecca right now. The dragons just barely located the vampires and our recruits aren't prepared to move yet. Please, just wait."

"I'm done waiting," Riley said with a shake of his head. He glanced at his sisters and sighed in frustration. "Please, take care of them."

Demian glanced at Rebecca and Veronica and nodded solemnly.

"You know I will."

"I'm going to get Aurora back," Riley said confidently. "Everything is going to be fine. Just make sure that my sisters are alive when all this is over."

"Once Karven gets here I will administer the antidote." Demian put a hand on Riley's shoulder and looked him in the eye. "You are an incredible young man, Riley. I know you can end this. Just don't kill yourself doing it."

Riley nodded and left the room. He found Naomi waiting for him in the hallway. She had a stern look on her face. He didn't know if she was going to be up to the task he was going to ask of her. All he knew was that she was his only mode of transportation. She placed her hand on his arm before he could speak.

"Marcus and Jeremy are coming with us too," she said solemnly. "We aren't going to let you do this by yourself."

Riley was speechless for a moment. He didn't know if that was a good idea, but Marcus and Jeremy were both stubborn alpha wolves. There wasn't going to be a way for him to talk them out of it, so he decided he wouldn't even try. They didn't have time for that.

Gabriel strode over to them and hugged Riley. It took him by surprise since Gabriel didn't hug very often. Or ever.

"You be careful," the skinwalker said gruffly. "Once Rebecca is better I'll be right there. Okay?"

"Just take care of her," Riley said as he clapped his hand on Gabriel's back. "Don't worry about us. Everything is going to be fine."

Gabriel sighed grimly and then smirked.

"Don't let Marcus do anything stupid…or Jeremy. They're both basically insane."

Riley gave him a small smile and nodded.

"I think that's exactly what we're going to need on this mission," Naomi said with a flirtatious smirk.

Gabriel handed Riley a syringe of guresh. Riley looked at it with wide eyes. He had thought that Demian used the rest of the healing elements to help Veronica. Apparently Gabriel had grabbed one for him.

Riley looked down at his knife wounds for the first time that night. He was covered in his own blood and Veronica's. He hadn't realized how much of it he had lost until now. The wand must've been keeping him going, but that didn't mean he didn't need medical attention.

"You're going to need that before Naomi takes you anywhere," Gabriel said.

"There's no more left," Riley said. "Is there?"

Gabriel shook his head in response.

"Don't get yourself killed, alright? Demian and I will work on getting some more made while we wait for the vampires. But that's not going to do you any good before we get there with reinforcements."

"Don't worry," Riley said in a harsh whisper. "I'm going to get her back."

Gabriel nodded solemnly as emotion clouded his eyes. He blinked it away quickly.

Riley injected the guresh into his abdomen. He refused to say goodbye, so he gave Gabriel's shoulder one last squeeze before he left the warehouse with Naomi.

Marcus was standing in the training field waiting for them. He had a duffle bag in his hand that Riley assumed was supplies for the trip. He had changed his clothes and looked a lot cleaner than he had before.

Jeremy had changed his clothes too. Raya was standing next to him with her arms folded and a strained look on her face. Riley couldn't tell if she was angry or worried…or both. Jeremy put his arm around her waist and she turned to face him.

"You better come back," she told him sternly. "I'm going to be really ticked off if you don't."

293

Jeremy smirked slightly before kissing her.

"That goes for the rest of you too," she said as she looked at Riley, Marcus, and Naomi.

"Jeremy, what have you done?" Marcus asked with a raised eyebrow. "It looks like you're rubbing off on our tamer."

Naomi laughed, but all Riley could muster was a small smile. Raya's eyes flashed yellow for a moment as she stared at Marcus.

"I'm not kidding," she said to him. "Please be careful."

"You have nothing to worry about, Raya," Marcus said confidently. "The four of us are the supernatural version of a Navy SEAL team."

"Um, really?" Jeremy asked sarcastically.

"Dude, I'm trying to make your girlfriend feel better. I'm doing your job here."

Naomi interrupted the ridiculous banter by shedding her human skin. Her blood red dragon scales glimmered in the moonlight. Marcus tossed Riley a clean shirt and he quickly stripped off his ripped and bloody one. Raya gasped when she saw his wounds.

"I can patch you up before you leave."

"No," Riley said to her. "I'll be fine."

She walked up to him until she stood directly in front of him.

"I can't lose Jeremy," she whispered to him. "Or you. Please, come back."

"I promise I'll do everything I can," he said as reassuringly as he could.

She nodded with a small frown. That was all he could promise and she seemed to accept that.

He quickly strapped on his gun holsters. He gave Raya his quiver of arrows and bow because he didn't think there would be room to bring them too. He had a feeling that their weapons would be taken from them at some point anyway. He knew it was unrealistic to think that they'd be successful in getting Aurora back by themselves. He just hoped that they'd be able to hold the werewolves off until their reinforcements arrived.

"How am I supposed to know where to go?" Naomi asked through mind speech.

"Brace yourself."

Riley put his hand on Naomi's forehead. Her scales where rough against his skin, but he lightly pressed his palm into them. He closed his eyes and expanded his pure magic. He concentrated on relaying the information that he needed to give her. The magic poured out of him in a rush. It felt like the wind had been knocked out of him.

Naomi snorted and smoke blew out of her nostrils. She tried to move her head away from his hand, but an invisible force kept them connected. Riley wasn't sure how long they stood there. When they finally broke apart he staggered backwards. Marcus grabbed his shoulders to keep him steady.

"What the heck was that?" Naomi exclaimed. Riley winced at the loud voice in his head. "That hurt. Like really bad!"

"Sorry," Riley managed to gasp. "I think there's a reason wizards usually aren't keepers."

His knees were shaky and all he wanted to do was sit down. He was happy to see that Jeremy had finished strapping the saddle on Naomi's back.

"What just happened?" Marcus asked in confusion.

"I assume you know how to get there now?"

Naomi tossed her head in what looked like a nod.

"Who would've thought the Ancients Den would be located in Canada. Of all places…"

Riley wasn't sure how the magic around the Ancients Den worked, but he had a feeling that the location had changed multiple times over the centuries. It just happened to be in Canada right now. Which was convenient for them since it would only take a few days for them to fly there.

"Really?" Marcus asked in disbelief. "That's irritating."

"Yeah, it's practically in our backyard," Jeremy said darkly. "Where in Canada?"

"Somewhere in Ontario I think," Riley said as he rubbed his head. "I'm not sure exactly where. All I know is how to get there. You guys probably won't be able to see the den until I use the wand to open the door."

"That's crazy," Raya whispered.

Naomi suggested that they get going. Raya gave Riley a gentle hug so that she wouldn't disturb his wounds. She whispered to him to be careful and he promised her again that he would. Being careful didn't mean that nothing bad would happen, but he didn't tell her that.

Marcus was the first to jump on the saddle. Riley used his magic to float himself onto the dragon's back. He was surprised that he still had some energy left after he was situated. He should've been exhausted.

Jeremy gave Raya one last kiss before jumping onto the saddle behind Riley. It was going to be an uncomfortably crowded journey, but Riley was glad they had volunteered to come. It was good to know that his friends had his back. Especially since Aurora's life hung in the balance.

"Jeez," Naomi said as her sides heaved. "You guys better pray that we don't fall out of the sky."

"Is that your nice way of saying that we should eat less, Naomi?" Marcus asked in a high pitched voice.

Naomi chuckled and spread her wings. Soon they were flying into the starry night.

"I feel like we need to make some sort of plan," Jeremy said tersely.

They were sitting around a camp fire that Naomi created. They had travelled for a day and a half before she insisted that she needed a rest. No one blamed her. Between the three of them she had been carrying over five hundred pounds.

"Does he not know that we usually like to go in without a plan?" Marcus asked Riley. "Because plans always end up going wrong."

"It's true," Riley said with a shrug.

"You guys are ridiculous," Jeremy snarled.

"The only plan I can come up with is…not dying," Riley said uncertainly. "I only know where the den is. Besides the one room that I saw in the vision I have no idea what it looks like on the inside."

"You said you saw ten ancient ones, right?"

"Jeremy, I can only assume they were ancient ones," Riley replied patiently. "There could be a lot more. Like I said; we are going in blind with absolutely no concrete information."

"I don't like this," Jeremy said with a shake of his head.

"Join the club," Marcus replied. "Let's just agree that Aurora is the mission. Getting her out is our main goal…and survival."

"Once we have Aurora," Riley said. "We'll gather as much information as we can while we are there. Demian is sending reinforcements. So we'll try to take them out after they get there."

Jeremy sighed and grimaced. Riley completely understood how he was feeling. He didn't like going in without more information, but he couldn't stand not knowing how Aurora was coping. He couldn't live with himself anymore if he didn't at least try to free her.

"Are you boys done arguing yet?" Naomi mumbled.

She had been trying to get some sleep. They should have been trying to do the same, but Jeremy needed to be put at ease. He had been on the verge of losing his control. Riley assumed it was because of the uncertainty that laid before them. It didn't help that they were all exhausted from their travels.

"Sorry, Naomi," Jeremy said in a strained voice. "I'll shut up now. You guys go to bed and I'll take first watch."

"No, I'll do it," Marcus said in his no-nonsense-big-brother-tone. "You need to sleep. You'll feel better if you're well rested."

Jeremy grumbled a string of swearwords before reluctantly nodding. He situated himself on the ground next to the fire. He closed his eyes, but he still didn't look relaxed. Riley had a feeling he wouldn't be sleeping anyway.

"How are you holding up?"

Marcus glanced at him for a moment before looking back at the campfire.

"Carvolo knows about my girls and he's after them, so... fantastic."

Riley could tell that Marcus was very stressed out. He told him while they were traveling what Jenna had said about kidnapping his daughters. The fact that Marcus couldn't be there to protect them was weighing on him. Even with vampire bodyguards it was still scary.

"They're safe," Riley said reassuringly.

"We don't even know where they are," Marcus said gruffly. "So we don't know that for sure."

"The vampires are with them."

"They were until the dragons found them," he replied. "Now Karven is helping Veronica and Rebecca. We have no idea if the werewolves followed the dragons to them or not. They're gigantic creatures with wings and it's hard not to notice them when you know what to look for."

Riley grew still. He hadn't thought about that before. It gave him an anxious feeling in the pit of his stomach. He hadn't expected to get much sleep that night, but now he knew he wouldn't get any.

Marcus had a very good point. If Carvolo was having the dragons followed then there was a possibility that they knew where their family was. They still had Jackson, Rachel, and Samantha to protect them, but that didn't mean they were perfectly safe. No matter how powerful they were; two vampires and a skinwalker could be beaten by hoards of werewolves. Especially when trying to protect five young girls.

Riley rubbed his hands over his face and sighed.

"Sorry, man," Marcus whispered. "I didn't mean to make things worse. I'm sure they're okay."

"Everything is going to turn out fine," Riley said grimly. "It has to."

Marcus nodded as they stared into the fire in silence.

Naomi landed a mile away from where the Ancients Den was located. They had a feeling that a flying dragon with three supernatural creatures on her back would alert the ancient ones that something was up.

"Naomi should lead the way, I think," Riley said after they got the saddle off of Naomi's back and stashed it behind some bushes. She quickly shed her dragon skin and stood in front of the three men. The difference in their height compared to hers was drastic. If a human saw them they would have no idea that this small woman could transform into a giant dragon.

"Age and beauty before annoyingly moronic," she said flirtatiously. "I agree."

It had been a long couple of days.

"That's coming from a girl who-"

Riley nudged Marcus in the ribs to shut him up. He and Naomi where close friends and they had been going at each other nonstop for almost two days. It was exhausting.

"Okay," Marcus said with a roll of his eyes. "I'll just leave it at this; we have no idea how old you actually are. There's a possibility that I'm older than you."

"I highly doubt it."

"Wait," Jeremy said in confusion. "You don't know how old you are, Naomi?"

"I'm so old I lost count centuries ago."

"Okay, fine," Marcus said with a shrug. "So you're older than me."

Riley gritted his teeth and tried not to clench his fists. He couldn't take the bantering anymore. He knew that it was just the way they coped with stressful situations. He was usually the same way, but the result of this mission would determine whether his wife lived or died.

"You're uncharacteristically quiet, Ry," Naomi said as they hiked through the dense trees.

He flinched when she called him '*Ry*'. Not very many people called him that, but Jenna was one of them. Maybe Aurora wasn't the only thing that was bothering him after all.

"That's probably typical for someone who wanted to torture his psychotic mother."

Naomi sighed and linked her arm in his.

"You don't have to worry about her ever again," his friend said soothingly. "You won't ever have to see her again either. Gabriel told me that he would make sure Roan took care of her."

"Do I even want to know what that means?" Riley asked in a shaky whisper.

He had been okay with killing Jenna a few days ago. She had been an evil witch that threatened the safety of everyone he knew and loved. Now she was nothing but a human girl with severe psychological issues. It seemed like it would be murder to hand her over for execution. Thinking about it made his stomach hurt.

"Roan can keep her incarcerated in a place that she can never escape," Naomi explained. "I don't know if that makes you feel better or worse."

"Better," he said stiffly. "Thanks."

They continued trudging through the thick bushes and trees. The sun was setting, leaving pinks and oranges streaked across the sky. It was beautiful, but unfortunate at the same time. Marcus wouldn't have his strength when they entered the Ancients Den. At least they had Naomi and Jeremy with them.

"How are we going to know when we get there?" Jeremy asked.

Riley gripped the wand in his hand and closed his eyes for a moment. They were close and he knew exactly what to look for. In about a mile they would be at the entrance. He took a deep breath and continued following Naomi.

Suddenly, the wand grew hot in his hand and he was forced to stop. He couldn't move for a moment while the wand relayed some scary information to him. He was close enough to Aurora now that he knew exactly what was happening to her at that moment. She was in a dark room and she was extremely weak and in pain. His heart thudded rapidly in his chest. He needed to get to her, but he also knew that they had been located by the enemy. They were being surrounded.

He began to shake and he couldn't catch his breath.

"Riley?" Marcus whispered in concern.

"We are going to be overrun," Riley said as he exhaled forcefully. "Naomi, you have to get airborne. Now!"

An arrow raced toward them and hit Naomi in the shoulder. She grunted angrily as she yanked it out. She transformed into her dragon skin and blew flames in the direction of their attackers.

Marcus and Riley hopped on Naomi's back with Jeremy right behind them as arrows soared past him. Naomi took off before Jeremy could reach them and he had to leap. Riley quickly grabbed his arm and caught him in midair. He winced when he felt the strain on his shoulder, it felt like Jeremy weighed a ton. There was no way that he was going to be able to hold onto him for very long.

He felt himself slipping and Marcus grabbed his waist to keep him on Naomi's back.

"Let go!" Jeremy yelled over the sound of the wings. "I'll be fine!"

Riley didn't let go even when Jeremy tried to slip out of his grip. He used magic to get him onto the dragon's back safely. Riley could feel the sharp scales digging into his skin, but tried to ignore it. He wasn't going to be able to stay on much longer without doing damage to himself.

He used the wand to stop the flow of the speeding arrows. Some of them were magically enhanced with deep red flames. Riley's heart quickened when he realized what that meant. If the ancients had another magical being that they didn't know about it could mean that this whole thing had been a trap.

Riley quickly shook the thought from his head. If it was a trap then so be it. He would do whatever he needed to do to get Aurora back. Even if it's just to see her for one last time.

He quickly scanned the treetops to see if he could spot their enemies. It didn't surprise him that they were well hidden. Naomi's breathing was labored as she hovered in the air. Her wings flapped weakly and they dipped lower to the ground with every movement.

"Naomi's not doing so well," Marcus said gruffly. "We need to land."

Naomi's sides heaved as she struggled for breath.

"I think the arrow I was hit with was magically enhanced in some way, but I'll be fine."

They all knew she wasn't fine, so they ignored her.

"We need to lighten the load," Jeremy said as he shifted behind Riley. "That way she won't have to land."

Marcus shook his head sternly.

"He's right, Marcus," Riley said. "You and Naomi should stay in the air to create a diversion. Jeremy and I will use that to get inside the den."

Marcus and Naomi were both silent for a moment. The sound of her dragon wings cut through the violent tension that surrounded them. Marcus glanced at Riley over his shoulder.

"Are you certain that this will work?"

"Honestly?" Riley shook his head dejectedly. "I don't know."

Marcus looked at them for another moment before reluctantly nodding his head. With a quick goodbye, Riley and Jeremy launched themselves off of Naomi's back. Riley had a firm grip around Jeremy's waist as they fell toward the ground. The wand slowed their fall, but wasn't able to help them avoid the scrapes from the dense trees. When they hit the ground they took off at a quiet run toward the den entrance.

Riley was surprised to find that no one tried to stop them. It made him wary and more than a little suspicious. Even with Naomi and Marcus as a diversion there still should've been at least a few werewolves after them once they hit the ground. By Jeremy's aggravated body language Riley knew he was thinking the same thing.

"When do you think the ambush will come?" Jeremy asked in a gravelly tone.

"Probably after I open the den door with the wand."

Jeremy nodded absently as they trudged through the trees and roots that tried to trip them. Riley could see the den entrance even though Jeremy couldn't yet. He scanned the area and wasn't surprised to find that they had a clear path to it.

"I think you should wait here," Riley whispered. "Both of us don't need to get taken today."

"They want me too," Jeremy said with a shake of his head. "I'm curious as to why."

"Well..."

"Yeah, I know," he said grimly. "This idea sucks."

"I just want to see her, man." Riley whispered.

"We're going to make sure that happens," Jeremy replied firmly.

Riley knew he should feel guilty for dragging Jeremy into this, but he didn't. At least the werewolf knew what he was getting himself into. Riley had no expectations that once they were taken they'd ever see the light of day again. But he would do whatever he could to save Aurora and finally end this war.

The entrance was hidden in the rock of the mountainside. They didn't have to climb very far to get to it. Riley was actually surprised by how easy it was to reach it. When he found the door he tried to pull on the handle. He knew before he tried that it wouldn't work, but he yanked on it anyway. When it didn't budge he took the wand out of his belt.

The wand glowed blue and flew out of Riley's hand. It buried itself into the stone and blue light erupted from the door.

Riley and Jeremy took a step back as the light cut though the darkness. When the light finally dimmed the door slowly opened. The wand fell to the floor inside the den entrance. Riley hurried forward to pick it up.

As he bent down, a hand grabbed him by the shoulder and threw him inside the den. He landed on the cold hard floor and saw a dark figure pick up the wand. Jeremy was thrown inside the den too and landed a few feet from Riley. A loud snarl escaped his throat and his yellow eyes pierced through the darkness.

"I'm glad to see you finally made it, Riley," a low voice rumbled from the shadows of the dimly lit hallway. "Welcome to the Ancients Den."

Chapter 20

Riley could make out Carvolo's triumphant sneer in the dim light. His yellow eyes flashed as he picked up the wand. It took a moment for Riley to register what had just happened. The tie that Riley and the wand had was completely severed, leaving an empty hole in his pure magic. He had to stifle a gasp as he watched Carvolo study the intricate designs that covered the wand.

"You've brought me my berserker," Carvolo said as he casually tucked the wand into his sleeve. "You practically gift wrapped him and handed him over."

"Don't talk about me like I'm not here," Jeremy whispered in a low and dangerous voice.

Carvolo chuckled in amusement.

"I'm glad to see that you haven't changed, Jeremy Masters."

"So this was your plan?" Riley asked. "Send Jenna to give me the location of the Ancients Den and then just wait for us to come? How predictable."

"And yet, you fell for it. Didn't you?"

Riley smirked with arrogant amusement.

"Of course," Carvolo explained. "I still thought you were dead when I killed Zalina and had Jenina take over her duties. When I found out that you were alive I knew that you had the wand. It was the only thing that could've saved your life from those injuries. So it wasn't that hard to figure out. That's when I decided to use Jenina to get you here. She didn't know the extent of the wand's power which made it easy to fool her into confronting you."

Riley had to suppress a chuckle as he listen to Carvolo monologue.

"And you didn't think that we'd figure out that you had a plan? You did everything but lay out the breadcrumbs for us to find the place."

"And yet...you still fell for it."

Riley gave Carvolo that arrogant smirk again.

Carvolo ignored the smirk and turned his attention to Jeremy.

"I'm glad that you came," he said. "I have to admit I wasn't sure you would."

"Why do you want me too?" Jeremy asked gruffly.

"Do you have any idea how rare your kind is?" Carvolo asked in a reverent tone. "I couldn't pass up getting you back. All that uncontrollable rage makes you indestructible among our kind. You are literally a killing machine. I was shocked when you didn't kill those followers that I ordered to torture you. I was hoping to unleash you on unsuspecting mothers and their daughters. For old time's sake."

A tremor of pent up emotion ran through Jeremy and he shivered slightly. Riley could've swore he saw tears in Jeremy's eyes as he took a shaky breath.

Carvolo just laughed at him.

"You're never going to get me to kill for you," Jeremy whispered. "Never again."

Carvolo grinned and squatted down to meet Jeremy's eyes.

"We will see about that."

Suddenly, a blood red ball of light appeared in the darkness of the hallway. The immediate brightness blinded Riley for a moment. Jeremy snarled and jumped to his feet aggressively. Carvolo didn't move as he stared at Jeremy in amusement.

When Riley was able to see again, a beautiful woman with long brown hair walked toward them. She was medium height with a medium build. Something about the way she carried herself demanded the attention of all those around her. Her blue eyes had a yellowish glow to them. Riley couldn't help but stare at her. She was beautiful, but that wasn't the reason he couldn't take his eyes off of her. He could sense powerful magic, so powerful that he had a feeling it would've rivaled Arothor's.

"Are you going to introduce me to the chosen one, dear Carvolo?" the woman asked in a sweet voice.

"Riley Hanson," Carvolo sneered. "This is Arodia, the daughter of Arothor."

Riley was speechless. He couldn't ignore the terror coursing through him like he usually did. If Arothor's daughter was a witch-werewolf-hybrid then they were in more trouble than he originally thought.

"I assume he brought us my father's wand," Arodia said with a smile. "I very much would love to see it."

Carvolo took the wand out of his sleeve and handed it to her. Once the wand touched her fingers there was a shift of magic in the room. Riley suddenly felt drained of his pure magic and extremely exhausted. He could feel the wand trying to reach out to him. The need to get the wand away from her was overwhelming.

"I have been waiting many centuries for this moment," she said as she caressed the designs on the wand with a gentle finger. "My father's most powerful creation and his most cherished descendant are now at my disposal."

"Are you an ancient one?" Riley asked gruffly.

"No," she said in amusement. "I am far younger than even Carvolo. But that doesn't make me less powerful than they are. They have kept me secret for so many centuries because I am the only one that can control the chosen one with the wand."

It took Riley a second to process what Arodia just said.

"Wait," he said with a shake of his head. "I thought the legend said that anyone could control me with the wand. Supposedly."

Arodia chuckled sweetly and lowered her gaze to Riley who was still sitting on the cold floor.

"Rumors; spread to confuse and torment," she said slyly. "Shall I demonstrate?"

She pointed the wand at Riley and he stiffened. A voice in his head told him to stand. It didn't sound, or feel, like the wand making a command. It was something different. It was more sinister and more compelling. The need to do what the

307

voice wanted surpassed everything else he wanted and needed. He could feel all his strength and independence slowly slipping away.

Which was why he planted his butt firmly to the stone floor and didn't move. He was not going to lose himself like this.

Arodia looked at him in confusion for a moment and sent another command at him. This one was stronger, but Riley held himself as still as possible as he closed his eyes. Beads of sweat dripped down his face and he tried to keep his breathing normal. He kept his mind focused on how close he was to seeing Aurora and pictured her face.

"You are a stubborn one," Arodia said nonchalantly. "Never mind, Carvolo. We will work on the control later. For now we are needed in the great hall. The ancients are anxious to meet our guests."

"I'm pretty sure the word you're looking for is *prisoners*," Jeremy said in a way that sounded like a threat.

Arodia's eyes flashed yellow as she threw a silver knife at Jeremy. It all happened so fast, but Riley was expecting it. With speed and strength that he didn't know he possessed, he jumped to his feet and threw out his hands.

"Potego!"

The blade stopped just short of piercing Jeremy's heart. Like always, Jeremy didn't even flinch. He was shaking with anger and his eyes glowed werewolf yellow with a sick glint of insanity. His breathing was erratic as he struggled to regain control. Riley couldn't help but wince. He needed Jeremy to remain calm and he wasn't anymore.

"Now, Arodia," Carvolo said warningly. "Didn't we talk about this? I want the berserker alive."

"For what, Carvolo?" she asked haughtily. "Your plaything? Sometimes I think you're more cat than wolf."

"Let's not be insulting, my dear," Carvolo said sweetly, but his eyes were now yellow too. Riley had to fight down the panic when he realized he was surrounded by enraged werewolves that were holding onto their control by a thread.

"If he speaks to me again I will kill him," Arodia said softly. "Berserker werewolves are a blight to our species and I have no tolerance for them."

Carvolo gave her a curt nod and went to grab Riley by the arm. Jeremy growled threateningly at Carvolo before he touched Riley. Carvolo hesitated slightly, but still grabbed Riley roughly by the upper arm. Before anyone could try to kill Jeremy again, Riley stepped in front of him despite Carvolo's iron grip.

"Jeremy," Riley said as he met his eyes. "Are you good?"

Jeremy blinked a few times, but his breathing still sounded feral and shook with uncontrollable rage.

"Come on, man," Riley said as he took another step toward him, surprisingly Carvolo released him. Jeremy's growl deepened, but Riley didn't back down. "We have to go with them or they'll kill you. I promised I'd do everything I could to stop that from happening."

He didn't want to say Raya's name out loud in front of Carvolo and Arodia, but Jeremy would know who Riley made the promise to. Some of the anger in Jeremy's eyes cleared as he continued blinking. He stopped shaking and took a more human sounding breath.

"Impressive," Carvolo said in amusement. "Too bad though. I was hoping that I'd have to take care of the berserker in a more forceful way. I guess we'll have time for that later."

Jeremy kept his eyes on Riley. He gave him a quick nod and they followed Arodia down the hall. Her red ball of light floated in front of her. Riley thought it was odd that there were no lights or torches to light the way. In all the other dens he'd been in they had at least a little bit of light, but it was pitch dark here.

Riley recognized the huge double doors that led to the great hall from the vision he had. Arodia opened the doors with her magic and continued walking to the large table in the middle of the room. This room was lit with chandeliers and a red flamed fire that burned in the fireplace.

Every chair in the room was filled with werewolves. Riley wasn't sure if all of them were ancients but he counted twenty of them. Lekiah and Avestan sat next to each other. They both looked proudly at Carvolo as he escorted Riley into the great hall. No one touched Jeremy, but he followed them reluctantly.

"Has the chosen one had his magic suppressed yet?"

One of the werewolves stood when he spoke. He had a shadow of a beard and his dark hair hung to his shoulders. He wasn't extremely tall, but his arms were lanky. He waved his long fingers around when he spoke.

"He will not overpower me," Arodia said with a smile. "I didn't see the need."

"I suggest you do it now," another werewolf said. Riley wasn't sure which one it was because they didn't stand, but it sounded like a female voice.

"You guys are actually scared of me," Riley said with a grin. "How funny is that?"

Carvolo whacked him on the back of the head. It hurt, but Riley ignored it. The standing werewolf took a slow step around the table. He stalked menacingly up to him with a predatory look in his eyes. Riley was sure that it was meant to intimidate him, but it did nothing but tick him off.

Suddenly, the ancient werewolf stabbed a needle into Riley's neck. He refused to show weakness in front of these formidable creatures, so he kept his composure. He clenched his fists as the pure magic within him faded.

"What is your plan from here, Carvolo?" the werewolf asked as he continued to stare at Riley as though he were a steak. Riley met his eyes and glared at him. He knew it was stupid to challenge the werewolf in anyway, but he was on the verge of exploding. He was so angry that he could hardly breathe. These were the creatures that were holding and torturing Aurora. He wanted them all dead.

"My daughter will help us break him," Carvolo said in a business-like tone. "He will be ready for the change by the full moon and he will easily bend to our will."

Riley gritted his teeth and took a deep breath through the nose. He didn't want Aurora brought into this at all. He would lose every ounce of control and he was hanging on by a thread as it was.

"I was under the impression Arodia would be able to control him without difficulty," Avestan said as he stood. "Is there an issue?"

Arodia stepped forward and aimed the wand at Riley.

"Tell us the rebellion's plans," she whispered the command, but it sounded like screaming in Riley's head. He closed his eyes as the urge to talk assaulted him. He clenched his mouth shut and tried to breathe. His head pounded and he began to shake.

He wasn't sure how long he fought the compulsion. It was all he could do to remain upright by the time Arodia gave up trying to control him. He took shallow breaths and glared at her defiantly.

"Our faith in the daughter of Arothor has been misplaced."

Riley looked at the ancient werewolf that took his magic and gave him an arrogant smirk. If he wasn't struggling to breathe he would have given him a snarky comment.

"Don't be hasty to pass judgement, Edward," Arodia said calmly. "He needs to be broken before he will comply. He has obviously been trained by the fairies. Something that we weren't expecting."

Riley risked glancing at Jeremy. He still wasn't sure why Carvolo wanted him here. He was surprised that they hadn't thrown them in the dungeon yet. It was even more astounding that their enemies hadn't taken their weapons. It made him wonder if the ancients wanted them to make a move. Most of them seemed to be bored with the whole scenario.

Lekiah stood up and made her way toward Riley. He had a momentary flashback to when she interrogated him in Fairbanks and he stiffened a little as she came closer. She tilted her head to the side and took a deep breath. She smelled him in a manner than was more wolf-like than human.

"I'd forgotten how delicious you smell, Riley Hanson," she said quietly. "Wizard blood is so rare to find these days. It's a shame that you will no longer be one after the full moon."

"Are you offering to let me go?" Riley asked sarcastically. "Because that would be awesome."

Lekiah smirked and turned toward Carvolo.

"My son, I think it's time you take him to your precious Aurora. It seems he is getting bored with this charade, as am I."

Carvolo nodded and grabbed Riley's arm in a firm grip. He closed his eyes to compose himself. The temptation to grab his gun and start firing at the ancient ones was overwhelming. But he knew that he wouldn't get far with Arodia trying to control him with the wand. Jeremy seemed to be contemplating the same thing since he had to fold his arms to stop himself from fidgeting.

"Carvolo," Avestan said. "Relieve them of their weapons first."

A look of disappointment flashed across the ancient werewolf's eyes for a moment. It was then that Riley knew for sure that they had passed some kind of test. It was all a mind game. It was all about control. They wanted them to attack so Arodia could sweep in with the wand while his mind was preoccupied.

He was suddenly concerned about seeing Aurora. He knew she wasn't in good shape and that might weaken his resolve. That's what the ancients wanted. That was what Carvolo had planned. He didn't know what he was going to do, but he knew that he couldn't let Arodia control him. They could lose the war if he let her.

He was glad that Jeremy was there. Carvolo's plan was to make the situation more awkward, but he trusted Jeremy with Aurora's life. The werewolves didn't realize that. They were expecting jealousy to rule their emotions and cause Riley to give in easily to Arodia's control. Little did they know that Jeremy's presence was going to hinder their plans.

Carvolo and Arodia cuffed silver chains around their wrists and ankles after they disarmed them. They began their

312

long journey to the dungeon with Carvolo leading the way and Arodia following close behind. Jeremy and Riley walked side by side. Dimly lit lanterns appeared as they walked through what seemed to be a tunnel. It was dark, cold, and damp.

Riley could feel magic in the air and wasn't surprised to see that the lanterns were floating on their own accord. With nothing tethering them they followed them down the tunnel. The glow had a reddish tint to it. It wasn't hard to figure out that Arodia had created them.

"How are you holding up?"

"Not good, man," Jeremy whispered. "It was all I could do not to attack those psychos."

"I know what you mean."

"No talking," Carvolo growled at them.

Riley's anger spiked at the sound of Carvolo's voice. He knew he couldn't let himself lose control, so he did what he always did in situations like this.

"Why not?" he asked sarcastically. "Are you afraid that we might say something mean about you?"

"No, Riley Hanson," Carvolo said in annoyance. "I just don't want to hear your crap."

"So that's a *yes* then," Riley whispered to Jeremy. "I think he's just too sensitive."

Carvolo growled ferociously, but Riley didn't flinch. He just gave the angry werewolf a triumphant smile. Carvolo was so easy to tick off and it definitely made him feel better to see their enemy flustered.

"We'll see who the sensitive one is once we get to Aurora's cell," the sadistic werewolf said angrily.

They stopped abruptly and Carvolo sank a needle into Jeremy's neck. He shuttered, but didn't make a noise or otherwise react. When Carvolo yanked the needle away, Jeremy staggered slightly.

"Just a little bit of welhum to keep you civil," Carvolo said with a sneer. "The last time you and Aurora were in a cell together you attacked my fairy. Let's just say I've learned my lesson."

Jeremy glared at him, but kept his composure. Arodia's strong fingers grabbed the back of Riley's neck in a painful grip. Her lips brushed his ear as she inhaled. An uncomfortable shiver ran down Riley's spine.

"I'll be back for you," she breathed into his ear. "You'll bend to my will eventually."

Carvolo pressed his hand against the stone wall and it cracked open. The crack slid sideways to reveal a barred prison door. The lighting was so dim that Riley couldn't see into the cell, but the odor coming from the tiny room was overwhelming. Carvolo turned to Riley and smiled at him viciously.

"Don't feel badly if she rejects you. First loves are hard to get over."

Riley's jaw clenched as he glanced at Jeremy, who just rolled his eyes in annoyance. Apparently Marcus had been right about the love triangle thing. It was just so stupid.

"You don't know what you're talking about, Carvolo," Riley whispered softly.

He knew he shouldn't give Carvolo the satisfaction of replying, but he was so angry he couldn't stop himself.

"Keep in mind that she did love you once," Carvolo said with mocked sincerity.

Riley knew that Carvolo was trying to get him to lose control of himself. So he took a deep calming breath through the nose. With Arodia right there ready to use the wand against him he needed to be calm. No matter what Carvolo put Aurora through he couldn't have a break down. He couldn't let the emotional abuse get to him.

"You aren't going to live much longer," Riley whispered dangerously. "You're a dead werewolf walking."

"Tough talk from a guy who is now incarcerated."

Riley chuckled at that. He couldn't help it.

"I've been incarcerated before," he replied with smirk. "It didn't stick the first time. What makes you think it'll stick now?"

Without another word, Carvolo threw him into the dark cell and he hit the ground hard. The stone floor was cold and bloodstained. The smell of decay and unwashed bodies burn his nose, but Riley barely registered it. He couldn't see and he didn't think his eyes would adjust to the pitch black darkness. He felt Jeremy land on the ground next to him and heard the sound of something small and metal hit the floor. The door closed with a loud clank.

"Oh no, Aurora," Jeremy whispered in horror.

Riley couldn't see her, but Jeremy's tone almost caused him to panic. He blinked furiously to try to get his eyes to adjust. Suddenly, a dark red ball of light appeared in the room. Riley had to close his eyes against the intense brightness for a moment.

When Riley could see again he understood why Arodia gave them the light. She wanted him to see Aurora. To see what they had done to her.

She was asleep, or unconscious, as she sat in the corner of the cell. Her head drooped to the side in an uncomfortable position. She looked like she hadn't eaten much since they took her. She was so thin Riley could see her bones protruding through her torn and bloodstained clothes. She was wearing the same outfit she wore the last time Riley saw her.

Riley took a step toward her, but Jeremy grabbed his arm. He didn't know why Jeremy tried to stop him from getting to her. He was about to throw Jeremy off of him when he held out the key that Carvolo had left them. Riley took it and quickly unlocked the cuffs from his wrists and ankles. He practically threw the key at Jeremy as he hurried over to Aurora.

He squatted down in front of her and gently grabbed her wrist to feel her pulse. It was slow, but steady. Her skin felt too warm under his hand as he touched her forehead. She had a fever, but he couldn't tell how high it was. Her breathing was shallow and ragged, as though she was in pain even when she was unconscious. He gently moved her matted hair out of her face with trembling fingers. There was so much dirt and blood in her hair that he couldn't make out the blond color that he loved so much.

"Aurora, sweetie," he whispered gently. "Can you hear me?"

Suddenly, Aurora's eyes flew open and her green irises glared back at him. Her eyes were bloodshot and furious. She exploded to her feet without warning. Riley barely had time to stand up before she attacked him with strength that he didn't know she possessed in her condition.

She slapped his face so hard that his head snapped back. He tried to step away from her so that she wouldn't damage herself further, but she grabbed his jacket and pulled him in. She brought her knee up and nailed him in the stomach. He was surprise by how much it hurt. The blow left him coughing and struggling to stay on his feet.

"Leave me alone," she rasped angrily.

She raised her hand to hit him again, but Jeremy grabbed her around the waist.

"Aurora, stop," he said in a husky voice.

"Let me go," she exclaimed as she tried to pry his hands off of her.

"I will," he told her reassuringly. "Just relax, okay?"

She didn't relax. She kicked and struggled. She hit Jeremy in the face with her elbow and blood squirted from his nose, but he didn't even flinch. He kept his grip around her waist as she tried to fight him off.

"Aurora," Riley said in a broken voice. "I know you're not going to believe this, but it's me. I swear…it's me."

"I've heard that before," she said defeatedly. She stopped trying to fight off Jeremy as the exhaustion overpowered her adrenaline. "Why don't you just leave me alone?"

Riley didn't reply because he couldn't. Emotion trapped the words in his throat and he had to blink back tears. She looked so helpless and so scared. He wondered how many times Carvolo sent shapeshifters to torment her. He was glad when Jeremy was finally able to let her go. He didn't think that touching her was going to help her remain calm.

"We are going to back away from you, okay?" Riley said when he could finally speak again. "No one is going to touch you. But, I swear, it's us. Jeremy survived. I survived."

316

Aurora's eyes clouded over as though she were in a daze. Riley stopped trying to explain things to her when he noticed her reaction. Talking wasn't helping either. She backed into the corner and sank back down to the cold floor. Riley and Jeremy made sure to give her as much space as possible. The cell was very small, but they managed to sit on the ground without crowding her too much.

She wouldn't look at them. She drew her knees to her chest and wrapped her arms around her legs. She looked so tired, both physically and mentally. She needed rest, but Riley knew that she wouldn't let herself fall asleep thinking that they were her enemies. He glanced at Jeremy who was staring at her with concern etched into his features.

Jeremy sighed and scooted toward her. Aurora stiffened, but didn't look at him. Riley grabbed his arm and shook his head sharply. The last thing Aurora needed was for Jeremy to get closer.

"Trust me on this," Jeremy said through a soft growl. "I can get her to snap out of it."

Riley reluctantly let go of Jeremy's arm and he scooted toward her until their legs practically touched. Aurora seemed to be holding her breath as she huddled back into the corner as much as she could.

"Get away from me," she whispered in a trembling voice.

Riley had never seen her so scared before. Anger surged through him and he suddenly had the urge to punch something. He could tell that Jeremy felt the same when a deep growl erupted from his chest. His eyes flashed yellow and he closed them for a moment.

"Aurora," Jeremy said in a soft voice that didn't match his temper. "I'm not wearing any cologne this time. No one is trying to trick you."

She tightened her grip around her legs and looked away from him in disbelief.

"I know the kind of mind games that Carvolo likes to play," he continued. "I know you feel like you can't trust anyone or anything. You feel like you can't trust yourself either. But I

317

remember you told me once that the one thing you could always trust was your nose."

Aurora closed her eyes and took a shaky breath.

"What is your nose telling you?" Jeremy asked her gently.

It took a few minutes, but Aurora finally opened her eyes and stared at Jeremy.

"I want to believe that it's you," she whispered shakily. "You smell like a werewolf."

"Yeah," Jeremy said with a nod.

"But they've tried to trick me before and you're still bleeding," she said with a shake of her head.

"Carvolo gave me welhum before he threw us in here."

Aurora blinked a few times and let out a small sob. A single tear fell down her cheek.

"Then why are you here with a shifter?" she asked Jeremy.

"I'm not dead, Aurora," Riley said breathlessly. "It's me."

She wiped the tear from her cheek and nodded slowly. Jeremy moved out of the way so Riley could get closer to her. She didn't relax, but she didn't shrink away either. He didn't think she believed that it was really him yet, so he didn't touch her.

"How?"

Riley told her everything. She stared at him with empty eyes the whole time. It broke his soul to see her like this. He didn't know everything that happened to her, but he was going to make sure that no one else touched her ever again.

When he was finished talking he slowly reached out his hand and set it on top of her knee. She didn't flinch or try to pull away from him. Instead she placed her hand on top of his and let out a small gasp.

"I never thought I'd see you again."

"I'm here," he whispered. "I'm here, Aurora."

Aurora threw her arms around his neck and he pulled her onto his lap. He kissed her softly and felt her tremble in his arms. He'd been so afraid that he'd never be able to do this

318

again. For the first time in so long he felt peace. Not even the damp den prison could stop the warmth that kissing her gave him. He buried his face into her neck and took a deep breath. Not even weeks of imprisonment could take away her lavender scent that always calmed him.

He finally found her.

Chapter 21

Riley opened his eyes when Aurora stirred in his arms. She had fallen asleep shortly after she realized that he wasn't a shapeshifter. It looked as though Jeremy had fallen asleep too, but it was possible that he was just trying to give them some privacy. Riley hoped that Jeremy didn't feel like he was intruding because he was glad that he was there. If it weren't for Jeremy he wasn't sure if he would've been able to convince Aurora to believe him.

"I think this is going to bruise," Aurora whispered as she gently brushed her fingers across his cheek. Her fingers felt so good on his skin that he barely heard what she had said.

"That's because my wife is a martial arts goddess."

Riley meant it as a compliment, but her eyes drooped as though she were ashamed.

"I'm so sorry I didn't believe you," she said sadly. "I can't believe I hurt you."

"Hey," he said softly. "Don't take that on. You did everything exactly right. I don't think I've ever been so proud in my life."

Aurora took a shaky breath and shook her head slightly.

"No, it's not okay, Riley. I would've tried to killed you if I had a weapon. I just...I couldn't let them hurt me again."

Riley kissed her forehead and pulled her closer to him.

"I'm serious, Aurora. Don't feel guilty for fighting back. You wouldn't be you if you hadn't."

Aurora's lips pressed into a tight line as tears filled her eyes. Her fingers tightened around the front of his shirt as though she was afraid he'd disappear.

"They've been trying to make me forget who I am ever since they brought me here," she whispered. "I thought you were gone and I thought Jeremy was gone. And Raven-"

Riley's arms tightened around her when she let out a small sob. He expected her to continue sobbing, but she didn't.

320

"In case you're wondering," he said quietly. "Gabriel did survive falling from that plane."

Aurora pulled away from him and studied his face. A tear fell down her check and he wiped it away with his thumb.

"Really?"

The hesitant hope in her eyes threatened to overwhelm him. She really had thought that Gabriel was dead.

"Yeah," he nodded. "He's fine."

"I've never felt so alone in my life. The things they did to me… I've never been good at dealing with Carvolo's mind games."

Riley tried not to clench his fists. He didn't know if he could hear this without losing it. He knew that he needed to know what they did to her, but he didn't know if he could handle it. It must've been bad to break her like this. She was the strongest woman that he'd ever met, and he knew that if she needed to talk he had to be there for her.

"We can talk about it if you want," he whispered.

"Later," she said with a small shake of her head. He didn't miss the pain that flashed across her face when she said it.

"You aren't alone, Aurora," he said as he kissed her forehead. "You never were. I know it felt like it, but we never stopped trying to find you…I never stopped."

She nodded and buried her face into his chest.

"I know you probably can't say much here," she said quietly. "But please tell me you have some sort of plan."

"Apparently they don't make plans," Jeremy interjected with a snort.

"That's true," Riley said with a smirk.

Aurora turned her head to look at Jeremy. His nose had stopped bleeding, but he seemed tired. Riley didn't know when the welhum would wear off. Jeremy wasn't injured so that was one good thing they had going for them.

"Who put Marcus in charge?" Aurora asked incredulously and Jeremy chuckled.

"Demian is going to send reinforcements as soon as possible," Riley whispered so quietly that he doubted even Jeremy could hear him.

"Seriously?" she whispered back with wide eyes. "You two came alone?"

"Well," he said into her ear. "Marcus and Naomi came too. Our plan was just to get to you and we'd figure the other stuff out later."

Aurora nodded in understanding, but Riley could tell that she was worried. That wasn't going to change anytime soon.

"Also, I lost the wand."

"You…what?"

Jeremy told her about Arodia taking the wand and she shivered. It took Riley a moment to realize that she had no idea that Rebecca had given him the wand in the first place. Luckily Aurora didn't ask any questions about it, she just took the partial information in stride.

"That woman is crazy," Aurora said through chattering teeth. "We need to figure out how to get the wand back."

Suddenly, a flash of red light burst into the room. Arodia appeared with the wand in her hand. She was wearing red traditional fairy robes which took Riley by surprise. He had no idea that other magical beings could wear them. He assumed that they wouldn't be allowed to. But she stood there in the attire as though she wore it everyday.

She flicked the wand through the air theatrically and sneered at Aurora.

"It's not polite to call someone names, Aurora Ryder."

The three of them stood up slowly. Riley would much rather Aurora stay down, but he knew that she wouldn't. She didn't want to appear weaker than she already did. He moved in front of her so that she was tucked safely behind him. He had made a vow not to let anyone else touch her and he would keep it even if it killed him.

Arodia pointed the wand at Riley and he was forced to take a step toward her. There was no voice in his head and he didn't feel the need to obey her. But he wasn't in control of himself. He barely heard Aurora say his name as he took another step toward Arodia. He felt more like a robot with every step he took.

"You see, Riley Hanson," Arodia said when he stood directly in front of her. "I never *really* tried to control you. As you see, I can make you do anything I want with ease. You are my puppet for as long as I am holding your wand."

Riley glared at her angrily. It was the only thing he could do to stop himself from panicking. She had complete control over him. She didn't even have to verbally order him to do it. All she had to do was think about what she wanted and he did it. No training from Roan could've prepared him for this and it was terrifying.

"I could make you kill the berserker for me," she said with a sneer. "Then I could have you kill your lover. Unless you have a better offer for me than what the ancients have given me."

Suddenly, Riley felt his body turn around to face them. Jeremy was standing in front of Aurora as she gripped his arm tightly. Riley tried to breathe, to calm himself so he could fight this compulsion. It was nothing like he'd ever experienced before. So he decided to do what he aways did when he was terrified. Ask questions.

"How long have the ancients kept you prisoner here?" Riley asked Arodia quietly.

"Centuries," she said in a husky voice. "Which is why I didn't tell them that your wand destroyed the protection spells around this place when it opened the door."

"Wait, what?" Riley asked in confusion.

"You didn't feel the magic evaporate around this place when it happened?" she asked him incredulously. "It almost knocked me over."

That was the best news Riley had heard all day.

"Your dragon friend is planning on infiltrating the den soon. But she has no help aside from the skinwalker that came with you."

"Why are you telling me this?" Riley asked grimly. Her willingness to cough up information couldn't be a good sign.

"Because I expect that you're going to need the information," she whispered into his ear. Her lips brushed across his jaw and he tried not to shiver in disgust. "Lekiah was right. You do smell good."

Riley's eyes never left Aurora's as Arodia invaded his personal space. Jeremy looked like he was seconds away from attacking the witch-werewolf-hybrid and Riley really hoped that he didn't. Aurora's grip on his arm seemed to be the only thing stopping him from lunging forward.

"Kiss me," she whispered as she stepped in front of him.

It felt like he got stabbed in the gut as he resisted the compulsion. He kept his focus on Aurora. He didn't let his eyes leave hers. She gave him an encouraging look that gave him the strength he needed. It was so painful his eyes started to water, but he refused to blink.

"Well, it looks like you are stronger than I gave you credit for. Maybe you can be of use after all."

Arodia grabbed a fistful of his shirt and used her werewolf strength to pull him even closer to her. He successfully broke the compulsion, but it left him so exhausted he could barely stand. He still found the strength to grab her wrist and push her hand away. She chuckled humorously.

"If I give you the wand you must promise me that you will finish off the ancient ones. So I can live the rest of my existence without constantly looking over my shoulder."

Riley gave her a sharp glare.

"Who says that you won't have to look over your shoulder?" Riley asked her menacingly. "I think I've proven to be more formidable than you thought I'd be."

She chuckled and leaned in closer to him.

"Just because I have a hard time controlling you doesn't mean you're formidable," she said slyly. "You're just stubborn."

"That is an understatement," Riley said with a glower. "But you should know that if I ever see you again I will end you."

"Understood," she replied with a smile. "Just one last thing; are you sure you won't kill the berserker for me?"

Jeremy growled threateningly. Arodia glared at him and bared her human teeth.

"I think Jeremy just answered that question," Riley said as he folded his arms across his chest. "You better get out of here before he decides to kill you."

"Word of warning," Arodia said tersely. "He will kill everyone in his path because he is an uncontrolled monster."

"You know nothing about him," Riley told her defensively.

"I know his kind," she replied. "I've killed his kind before."

"Sounds like you're the real monster then."

Arodia sneered at him and stepped so close that they were practically hugging. Apparently she had no idea what personal space was.

"Not even tamers can help berserkers."

"That's because they don't need tamers to help them," Riley told her. "They are their protectors."

Aurora stared at Riley with wide eyes. Her hand rubbed up and down Jeremy's arm as she tried to calm him. She had no idea that Jeremy was a berserker or what that even meant. No one really did until Demian had explained it to them.

"You are naive," Arodia said with a shake of her head. "Tamers are worthless creatures and berserkers are mindless monsters."

Riley couldn't help but chuckle at the ridiculousness of that statement.

"I don't think I'm the naive one here. You have been locked away for centuries. You don't understand how the real world works."

Arodia sneered at him and shoved him away. She turned to face Jeremy.

"I will let you live today because you will help kill the ancient ones. But the next time I see you I won't let you walk away."

Jeremy snarled at her, but Aurora's hands on his arm stopped him from attacking. Arodia dropped the wand on the ground and disappeared as quickly as she came. Once she was gone her magic left the room, leaving them in complete darkness.

Riley dropped to his knees and felt around for the wand. He didn't have his magic back yet and he needed it to create light so they could see. His fingers found it and all of his pure magic came rushing back to him. He sighed as he felt the power flow through him and a ball of blue light erupted from the tip of the wand.

Riley immediately got to work creating a protection spell for the cell. He wasn't as good at it as Rebecca was, even with the wand. But at least they would have some privacy to talk for as long as they stayed in there. After the magical blue mist sank into the walls of the cell he tucked the wand in his belt and sat down.

He knew his body had been taxed over the edge. He could see his hands shaking and his heart thudded rabidly in his chest. The wand was blocking him from feeling any discomfort, but he needed to be careful. Resisting Arodia's compulsion had taken a great toll.

Jeremy and Aurora both sat back down too. Aurora looked like she was going to collapse soon anyway. Riley scooted over to her and let her lean on him.

"That was incredible," she whispered to him in a tired voice.

"We can talk now without anyone being able to eavesdrop."

Jeremy wasted no time in getting to the point.

"So that socially awkward psycho says Naomi and Marcus are planning on breaking into the den," Jeremy said skeptically. "And the impenetrable protection spell that was put into place by Arothor was somehow broken. Do we trust her to give us accurate information?"

"Absolutely not," Riley said with a shake of his head. "Which is why I think we should disregard everything she said. Let's assume that Naomi and Marcus can't get in unless I open the door for them."

"Keep in mind," Aurora said. "She did give you back the wand, Riley."

"Yeah, but like you said; she's crazy."

Aurora nodded tiredly and snuggled in closer to him.

"Jeremy, you have better eyesight than I do. Do you remember how to get to the entrance?"

Jeremy took a deep breath and nodded.

"Are you ready to get out of this cell, Aurora?" Riley asked her as he rubbed his hand up and down her arm.

Aurora nodded, but she seemed wary of the idea. Riley didn't blame her, and he doubted that she was going to be able to walk very far. He wished he could do something about it, but they didn't have any magical elements. He could only hope that Gabriel was on his way with some by now.

Riley took the wand from his belt. A silvery mist came from the tip and wrapped itself around the three of them. Jeremy stared at the wand incredulously.

"I don't think I'll ever get used to that."

Riley pointed the wand at the door and it exploded. He grimaced when the noise echoed through the dungeon. He wasn't expecting that to happen, but the wand was unpredictable at times.

"I'll carry her, you make sure no one tries to stop us."

Jeremy nodded and cautiously peeked his head out the door. Riley lifted Aurora in his arms and he was amazed by how light she was. He had to push the thought to the back of his mind. If they were going to make it through the day he couldn't think about how hungry she must be.

"I can walk, Riley," she whispered weakly.

He smiled at her and gave her a lingering kiss.

"I know, but I'm not going to let you."

Aurora sighed and rested her head on his shoulder. He hurried after Jeremy into the dark tunnel. The magical blue ball of light followed them, but it didn't give off as much light as Arodia's lanterns had. Luckily, Jeremy's werewolf vision didn't seem to be bothered by it.

It didn't take long for them to run into a few werewolf guards. Riley wasn't sure if they were leaders or followers, but they gave them no trouble at all. Even without a weapon Jeremy was able to kill them with his bare hands.

It wasn't easy to watch. Aurora buried her face into Riley's shoulder and took a shaky breath, but it didn't bother Riley at all. This was one of the reasons Jeremy was there. He would make sure they got Aurora out no matter what.

After the werewolves were dead Jeremy turned to look at them. His eyes were yellow and wild, but he was breathing normally. He blinked once and his eyes stopped glowing.

"I'm good," he said before Riley could ask. "Let's go."

Riley carefully moved around the bloody mess as he followed Jeremy down the tunnel. Nothing was familiar to him, but he was sure that Jeremy's werewolf senses would get them through the unfamiliar den.

They walked for a long time. It was slightly surprising that no other werewolf tried to attack them. Riley wasn't sure why that was and it made him nervous. He kept glancing behind him to make sure that they weren't being followed even though he knew Jeremy would tell him if they were.

"Okay," Jeremy whispered as he touched the side of the tunnel. "It's here."

"Really?" Riley asked incredulously.

It didn't look like how he remembered it, but the door had been open at the time.

"Yeah," the werewolf nodded. "I know it doesn't seem like it, but I'm sure of it."

Riley nodded and put Aurora in Jeremy's arms. He pulled out the wand and pointed it at the entrance. The wand flew from his hand like it did the first time. It buried itself into the door and blue light blinded them. The door broke open and fresh air hit them. It felt amazing.

Jeremy gave Aurora back to Riley and glanced outside. Riley didn't hear or see anything that would indicate that they were in immediate danger, but that didn't mean they weren't. Jeremy cautiously stepped out into the cool morning air and

Riley followed. It was still dark out, but the sun was beginning to peek out over the mountains.

Aurora shuddered as the light began to chase the darkness away. That was a cause for concern since the sun was supposed to energize her. She seemed to slump into him even more and her breathing became labored. Her fingers dug into his neck as pain rippled through her.

"Aurora," he whispered into her ear. "Talk to me. What's going on?"

"I'm fine," she breathed out the two words like it took too much energy to talk. It only made it more obvious that she was lying.

"I know you're not," he responded quickly.

"The sun makes me feel…everything…more profoundly."

It was hard to watch her struggle to explain. She needed food and a lot of rest. If they could find Naomi's saddle they'd be able to get her some, but there was no guarantee that it was still where they left it. It also didn't help that Riley couldn't see Naomi or Marcus in the sky. He could hear werewolves in the bushes now so they'd obviously been spotted.

Jeremy grabbed a thick branch that was attached to a tree standing a few feet away from them. He tore it off without so much as grunting. If killing the werewolf guards in the dungeon didn't prove that the welhum was out of his system then that certainly did. He wielded the branch in front of him like a large club and waited.

"You think they're stupid enough to attack us?" Riley asked as he adjusted Aurora in his arms.

"You might want to set her down," Jeremy replied gruffly.

Riley made sure the wand's protective barrier around Aurora was still strong before he set her down next to the tree. He kissed her forehead and tried not to let his concern for her distract him from the battle that was coming. She was barely lucid as he laid her down and he wanted nothing more than to lay down next to her. He smoothed a chunk of dirty hair out of her face before standing up.

The werewolves came so fast that Riley barely had time to think, let alone say an incantation. Jeremy barreled through their enemies while swinging the branch. The makeshift weapon didn't last very long. It broke in half after hitting three werewolves. So Jeremy went back to using his hands to kill.

Riley used the wand to fight without getting too far away from Aurora. Even if she was magically protected he didn't want to take a risk with her life. She seemed to be seconds from passing out and he knew that she was fighting it hard. She kept blinking her eyes open and breathing in harsh rasps.

The magical barrier around Jeremy faded and he began sustaining injuries. Riley tried to fix it, but they were overrun and he didn't have the time. Jeremy was bleeding from various wounds, but it didn't seem to phase him. He threw two werewolves into the trees at the same time while a third jumped on his back.

Riley used his magic to throw the werewolf off before it could stab Jeremy in the heart. No matter how many they killed it seemed like twice as many kept coming. Even with the wand they weren't equipped to fight off those numbers alone. Jeremy was running out of energy which caused him to become feral. Which was not a good thing since he could decide to attack Riley or Aurora if he didn't recognize who is friends were.

Riley breathed out a sigh of relief when he heard the sound of dragon wings. He glanced at the sky and saw Drake's blue scales gleaming in the morning light. He descended toward them and three figures jumped off of his back as he blew flames at their attackers.

When he landed Gabriel tossed a knife to Riley. He caught it by the handle and immediately threw it at a werewolf that was too close to Aurora. Rebecca and Raya landed a few yards away from each other and helped Jeremy fend off a hoard of werewolves that surrounded him.

"I'm so glad you made it," Riley told Gabriel.

"I'm glad you're still alive," his friend said with a smirk.

"Did you have any doubt that I would be?" Riley asked incredulously as he waved the wand at a werewolf that tried to jump him.

"I don't know how to answer that without getting into trouble," Gabriel replied good-naturedly and Riley chuckled.

It didn't take long for the werewolves to retreat after their reinforcements arrived. It helped that Naomi and Marcus were spotted flying toward them from the east. Riley wasn't sure what they were doing coming from that way.

Naomi and Drake both landed and Marcus slid off of Naomi's scaly back. His clothes were torn and bloody, but his scrapes healed quickly in the sunlight. Naomi shed her dragon skin, but Drake stayed the way he was.

"What happened to you guys?" Riley asked.

"We got sent on a wild goose chase," Naomi said bitterly. "I'm sorry we're late."

Riley waved off her apology and knelt down next to Aurora. She was unconscious and her breathing was shallow. Everyone stared at her for a moment in shock. Marcus's expression showed more than just shock or concern. He looked murderously furious. He knelt down next to his sister and put a hand on her forehead.

"Gabriel," Riley said gruffly. "Please tell me you brought some guresh."

Gabriel shook his head dejectedly as he pulled a duffle bag off of Drake's saddle.

"No guresh. We didn't have time to finish making it. Demian should be on his way with some by now, but he's at least a day out. I do have hemioc."

Gabriel took the syringe and stuck the needle in Aurora's chest. She immediately gasped and tried to sit up. Riley held her down by her shoulders and Marcus kept her head still with his hands. Riley was surprised that he was strong enough to hold her shoulders down with the sun out.

"You need food, sis," Gabriel said in a soft voice.

"Gabriel, Marcus" she mumbled. "You have no idea how good it is to see you."

331

Marcus's face softened a little when she said his name, but he still looked like he was close to losing it. Rebecca hurried over with a granola bar that she was quickly unwrapping. Aurora took no time at all in devouring it. Raya handed her a bottle of water and she chugged it down so quickly Riley was surprised she didn't choke.

Riley touched her forearm and frowned. Her fever seemed worse than it had before and she was shaking. He wasn't sure if the hemioc was doing much for her besides giving her the energy to stay awake. He knew from experience that they couldn't give her too much food and water at one time. So the granola bar and bottle of water would have to do for now.

"What's the plan, guys?" Naomi asked.

"I'm going to hunt down Carvolo," Marcus said. He didn't even try to hide the anger in his voice. He practically shook with it. Seeing Aurora in this condition was having a nasty effect on him.

"I agree," Gabriel said harshly.

"He's in the den," Riley explained. "Along with the ancients. I think we should be able to take them out with the wand and Raya."

"Me?" Raya said incredulously. Jeremy was standing next to her, but he wasn't touching her like he normally did.

"Yeah," Riley said with a nod. "Your tamer abilities. I have a strong feeling that we are going to need them."

He wasn't sure how he knew that, but the wand grew warm in his hand.

"She's not going in there without me," Jeremy said with a snarl. He was still struggling to get himself under control after their battle. He had blood dripping from his clothes and his fists were clenched at his sides.

"I wasn't expecting her to," Riley explained to Jeremy since he obviously needed the reassurance. "She shouldn't go in there without you. It wouldn't be safe."

"Drake and I will stay out here," Naomi said. "We'll make sure nothing gets in or out."

332

Marcus and Riley both nodded at the dragons in agreement.

"I'm going with you," Aurora whispered to Riley.

"Aurora-"

"No, Riley," she interrupted him desperately. "I'm not missing this. I *can't* miss this."

Everyone stared at her for a moment. Even with the hemioc she looked like she would pass out at any moment. Riley absolutely didn't agree with her. He didn't want her anywhere near the ancients and Carvolo. After what they did to her he wanted to hide her in their bedroom and never let anything happen to her again. That's what he wanted, but he knew that wasn't what she needed. She'd been fighting this war her whole life. It would destroy her if she didn't see it through to the end.

Riley nodded reluctantly and Gabriel gave her another dose of hemioc since she was going to need it. She grimaced as the magical adrenaline coursed through her veins.

"Do you have any information that you can give us?" Marcus asked Aurora gently.

"There's twenty ancient ones," she said hoarsely. "They all possess a type of power that is rare or unheard of in werewolves. They're all very dangerous and hard to kill. Even with Riley's wand it's going to be nearly impossible. Most of the older leaders, like Carvolo and Tomas, are here as well. I'm not sure how many..."

She stopped talking and swallowed. She visibly shivered as she thought of the werewolf leaders. Riley grabbed her hand and rubbed his thumb over her knuckles. Marcus pressed his forehead against hers like he'd done countless times throughout their lives. He made a comforting noise in his throat that sounded like a whine. Aurora gradually stopped shivering and once she was calm again Marcus moved his forehead away from her. He kept his hand on her head as though he knew she needed that contact from him.

"We could wait for reinforcements," Raya said in a quiet voice.

"They're not gonna make it in time," Gabriel said. "Our best option is to confront them when they least expect it."

"Are there anymore hybrids that you know of, Aurora?" Riley asked.

"There's one more besides Arodia," she replied. "I'm not exactly sure who, but I know it's a male."

Riley grimaced. He knew that witch-werewolf-hybrids were powerful enough, but he had a feeling that a wizard-werewolf-hybrid would be much more powerful. His pure magic would make him difficult to defeat in battle.

"We can do this," Marcus said encouragingly. "I know we can. There's a reason that we are all here together. We are the best people for this job and we are going to get it done."

Everyone stared at Marcus where he was sitting next to Aurora. Any anxiety among the group disappeared and was replaced with a quiet determination. They all nodded in agreement and began making preparations to enter the den.

Rebecca stepped over to Riley and he stood up and hugged her tightly. He was so happy to see that she was better. Seeing her sick had done a number on him.

"You have no idea how good it is to see you," he told her.

"I heard about everything that happened with Jenna," she said hesitantly. "I can't even imagine."

Riley glanced at Aurora where she sat under the tree helping Marcus and Raya do a weapons check.

"I'm okay now."

"No matter what happens," Rebecca said quietly. "At least you found her."

"Yeah, at least there's that."

Chapter 22

The tunnels in the den were eerily quiet. Riley had expected to be attacked by the leaders, but the halls remained empty. He kept a firm grip around Aurora's waist as they followed with the group. Even though she could walk without help he wanted her close. He needed her close.

He and Rebecca created balls of blue and purple light that flooded through the dark tunnels. Jeremy led the way again with Raya right beside him. Rebecca, Gabriel, and Marcus took up the middle while Riley and Aurora brought up the rear. Seven against more than twenty super-powered werewolves. If Riley was being honest he didn't like those odds.

They made it to the double doors that led to the great hall. Riley wasn't sure if they should open the doors, but Jeremy had never been one to wait around for anything.

He pushed the heavy doors open with a loud bang. Then he stormed right into the large room with Raya tucked next to his side as if he owned the place. They all hurried in after them. The great hall was crowded with the ancients and the leaders. Riley's heart sank when he saw that there was a lot more than just twenty enemies to face. He didn't even waste the mental energy to count them all.

The large table that had been in there earlier was gone. A bright yellow fire burned in the fireplace and Riley was willing to bet the male hybrid Aurora told them about made the magical fire.

The werewolves stood perfectly still as they entered the room with their weapons drawn. No one seemed surprised to see them burst into the room. They were so outnumbered that it seemed almost hilarious that they would attempt something so stupid. A few of the ancient ones smiled at them in a way that felt like pity.

"Welcome, rebels," Lekiah said dramatically. "We have been expecting you."

No one replied. Riley gripped the wand tightly and felt it heat up in his hand. It wanted to kill Lekiah immediately, but Riley knew that would be a mistake to be the first to attack.

"We would like to form a truce," Avestan said formally. "For your protection as well as ours."

A stunned silence followed that ridiculous statement for a moment.

"Wow," Marcus said with a small chuckle. "I thought you guys were supposed to be scary. Seems like we've been worried about a bunch of cowardly puppies who are afraid that seven people will beat them. How stupid of us."

"Tread carefully, my son," Carvolo said with a sneer. "The ancients have short tempers and no sense of humor."

"Don't you dare call me that," Marcus said almost lazily.

Carvolo's sneer deepened and he drew two medieval swords from the wall. Avestan stepped forward and took both of them and set them down on a wooden table. Carvolo then drew two knives and placed them next to the swords. The rebels stared at the werewolves in confusion.

"Since you all had the nerve to come here," Lekiah said quietly. "We will begin with offering you a trial by combat. Your greatest fighter against ours. If you win, we will gladly give up our plans of domination over humanity. If we win, you will leave Riley Hanson and Rebecca Singer with us. The rest will be allowed to leave."

"Wow," Gabriel said with a smirk. "You guys are desperate."

"Why don't we just use the wand and our tamer and take you out now?" Riley asked. "Why even bother with a trial by combat?"

"You would lose," a dark voice came from behind the large group of werewolves.

The crowd stirred and the werewolves moved aside to allow a blond haired young man to come to the front. He was average height and skinny. He looked as though he hadn't seen the sun in years.

"I am Broden the son of Arothor. Brother of Arodia, the one that escaped."

Broden said the whole introduction without an ounce of emotion in his voice.

"Wow," Riley said with a smirk. "How many kids did Arothor have? I killed him by the way. What makes you think you can beat me?"

Broden's facial expression didn't change, but Riley saw a flash of anger cross his eyes.

"We'll agree to a trial by combat," Marcus said with a thoughtful nod. "As long as you promise that you won't kill any of them if I lose."

Avestan gave him a curt nod and grinned hungrily.

"Marcus," Gabriel whispered incredulously. "What are you doing?"

Marcus turned to all of them before replying.

"Carvolo is their best fighter," Marcus whispered. "I've been itching to fight him one on one."

"How do you know he's their best fighter?" Gabriel asked incredulously.

"I just do," Marcus said with a shrug, Gabriel glared at him in annoyance.

"Since we are the ones that challenged you," Avestan said formally, interrupting their side conversation. "You may decide between a sword or knife as weapon of choice."

"I choose sword," Marcus said calmly as he turned to face their enemies.

"Are you sure?" Carvolo said with an evil smile. "Do you remember who taught you the art of swordplay?"

"Demian did, you idiot," Marcus replied with venom in his voice.

"And I taught Demian," his werewolf father said with a smirk.

"And who taught you, your mom?"

Lekiah's eyes flashed angrily when Marcus brought her into it. Riley would've laughed if he didn't have an awful feeling

337

in the pit of his stomach. He gripped the wand tightly in anticipation.

Marcus rolled his eyes and ignored Carvolo's attempt at taunting. Avestan stepped into the middle of the room and picked up the knives and slid them into their sheaths.

"The rules are as follows: the contestants will receive no help including their powers. They will be given welhum at the beginning of the fight. This is a fight to the death. Yielding is not an option. Once the fight is won there will be no more bloodshed. If Carvolo wins, we keep the chosen witch and wizard along with the wand. If Marcus wins, the ancients will abandon their goal of world domination. If there is a failure to comply to these terms I will exact judgment on the offenders."

Riley didn't buy it. There was no way that the ancients would stop trying to conquer the world and there was no way that they'd ever trust Avestan to do what he promised. There was no honor among their enemies.

"The contenders have five minutes to prepare," Lekiah said in a loud voice.

Marcus turned to their group and they stared at him worriedly. Gabriel looked at his brother as though he had lost his mind. Aurora started shivering and Riley held her more firmly to his side. If Samantha were there she would probably kill them all for allowing her husband to do this. Not that there was much they could do to stop him.

"Are you sure about this, Marcus?" Gabriel asked in a strained voice.

"I've never been more sure about anything in my life," he replied sternly. "This guarantees that Carvolo dies today. Right here, right now."

"Or it could guarantee the opposite," Aurora said quietly.

Marcus stepped toward her and took her hand in his big one. Then he bent down and rested his forehead against hers.

"I'm done watching that monster hurt the ones I love," he whispered. "I'm done watching him hurt you. I'm so angry right now that he doesn't stand a chance against me."

"Marcus…"

338

"I'm going to end this, Aurora. I promise you, I'll win."

"You better," she said as she hugged him.

Marcus held her for a moment and kissed the top of her head before giving her back to Riley.

"Marcus," Riley whispered as he wrapped his arm around Aurora's waist. "The protective barrier the wand gave you disappeared when you agreed to this. I just wanted to let you know that."

The skinwalker nodded in understanding and took a deep breath.

"When this fight is over be prepared for anything," Marcus told the group in a quiet whisper. "These guys aren't planning on just letting us leave."

Everyone nodded in agreement. They all wished Marcus good luck and watched him walk to the center of the room where Carvolo was waiting. They both removed their shirts and faced each other. Marcus was tall and very muscular whereas Carvolo was slender and toned. Riley couldn't see a family resemblance between them at all. He hoped that Marcus's obviously stronger physique would help him win the match against his father.

Avestan injected a needle into Carvolo's wrist and then did the same to Marcus. They each picked up a sword and stared each other down.

"It is custom for the opponents to bow respectfully before the match," Avestan said with a smile.

"Forget it," Marcus growled.

"Then you forfeit," the ancient werewolf replied slyly.

Marcus grimaced as he began to bow. In one swift movement Carvolo jumped into the air with his sword raised. He jumped so high that it was obvious Avestan didñ't actually give him any welhum.

Luckily, Marcus was ready and he rolled out of the way before the blade cut through his neck. He got nicked on the shoulder instead. Fresh blood dripped from the deep slice. Aurora's hand tightened around Riley's and a violent tremble rolled through her.

"Cheating, huh?" Marcus asked in amusement. "Can't say I'm surprised. I must scare the crap out of you."

Carvolo sneered triumphantly and attacked with werewolf strength. Marcus blocked the blow with his sword, but he couldn't compete with Carvolo's power since he'd been weakened by welhum. The sword fell from his hand and he did a body roll out of the way of Carvolo's next attack.

Without a weapon Marcus's only option was to continue dodging. Carvolo kept attacking him with such speed that Riley's eyes had a hard time keeping up. Some of the blows connected and Marcus bled freely from cuts left by his father's sword.

"Just give up, Marcus," Carvolo taunted him. "Show your brother and sister how weak you really are."

Finally, Marcus got close enough to grab his fallen sword and he stood up swinging. A large gash appeared on Carvolo's chest and he let out a small whine. Marcus put a little more space between them and took a shaky breath.

Marcus had a few serious injuries that were slowing him down, but that one gash he gave Carvolo was deep. It wouldn't heal as quickly because it was made by a silver blade. Riley hoped that it would slow the werewolf down too. So far the match had been extremely one sided. Marcus was lucky to get a hit in at all.

With a yell of fury, Carvolo surged forward and swung his sword. Marcus jumped back at the last second but still received a shallow cut across his abdomen. That one made Marcus cry out in agony and Riley stiffened. Marcus hardly ever reacted to pain that way. Something was terribly wrong.

"If you haven't guessed yet," Carvolo said as he walked up to Marcus with his sword held out. "There's begraw on my blade. You're chances of winning have been nonexistent this whole time."

Marcus let out a shaky moan of pain, but met Carvolo's triumphant sneer with a hard glare.

"It's going to be hilarious when I beat you," Marcus said with a hint of a smirk. "And you did nothing but cheat."

"Get over it," Carvolo said with a maniacal laugh. "Life has never been fair to you, Marcus Ryder. Why should it start being fair now? Embrace your inevitable death and just submit."

Carvolo attacked again and Marcus blocked the blow a little slower than Riley would've liked. He stumbled backwards, but caught his footing before he fell down. Carvolo took advantage of the misstep and lunged forward again. Their blades hit so hard that sparks flew from the force of it and Marcus stumbled. He was past the point of exhaustion and was running on pure adrenaline.

Aurora's grip on Riley's hand seemed to get tighter with each injury her brother sustained. It was getting harder to believe that Marcus would win this one with each hit he took from Carvolo's poisoned blade.

Marcus took a swing at Carvolo's fighting arm, but missed. He barely got his blade up to block another one of Carvolo's werewolf strength blows. The hit caused his arms to tremble and his joints to crack. Marcus grimaced in agony, but kept a grip on his sword.

They kept taking turns swinging at each other. Marcus would miss every time he went on the offensive. Carvolo would swing at him and either cut him again or hit Marcus's blade so hard that the sharp clank hurt Riley's ears. He wasn't sure how long Marcus could keep this up. His knees wobbled and his hands shook so hard he couldn't grip his sword correctly.

Suddenly, Carvolo swung his blade at Marcus's head and he ducked under it. With speed that surprise everyone in the room, Marcus lunged forward and stabbed Carvolo through the stomach. The werewolf's eyes grew wide with pain and shock. He let out a small whimper and blood trickled from his open mouth. His sword fell from his hands with an echoing clank on the stone floor.

Marcus left his sword lodged in Carvolo's stomach and grabbed the werewolf's blade off of the floor. He brought it up to deliver the final blow when Carvolo held out his hands in submission.

"Respite," he said through a gurgling gasp.

341

"Seriously?" Marcus said tiredly. "Just take it like a man, Carvolo. You're done."

"Respite," he whispered again.

Marcus ignored him, and was about to stab him in the heart when the sound of a gun being cocked echoed through the room. The skinwalker froze and glanced over to see Tomas holding a gun to his head.

"He called for a respite," Tomas said with a smirk. "He gets one or you die before your blade touches him. Your choice."

Aurora shivered next to Riley when Tomas spoke. He gently rubbed her arm with the tips of his fingers as he watched Marcus back away from Carvolo with the sword still in his hand. Tomas lowered the gun with a triumphant smile. He hurried forward and pulled the blade from Carvolo's abdomen. The werewolf snarled and slowly stood up.

Marcus collapsed on the ground and Gabriel knelt next to him to check over his wounds. He wasn't in good shape. He was shaking so badly that Riley didn't know how he was able to lift the sword at all. Rebecca hurried over to use her magic to get the begraw out of his system, but Avestan yelled at her to stop.

"He mustn't have any help!" the ancient werewolf exclaimed. "It is against the regulations!"

Rebecca growled and stood in front of Marcus protectively.

"What a load of crap! You guys have been cheating this whole time!"

"You have no proof of that," Avestan sneered at her triumphantly. "No proof that I will recognize."

Marcus grabbed a hold of Rebecca's hand when it looked like she would lunge at Avestan. He was too weak to stop her, but he gave her arm a light tug anyway. She tore her angry glare from Avestan and glanced at her brother-in-law.

"It's fine," Marcus said breathlessly. "Let them have their cowardly moment. The match isn't going to last much longer anyway."

Rebecca stared at him in shock, but didn't reply.

Riley itched to use the wand against them all, but something stopped him. Even though the situation seemed impossible the wand suddenly gave him a feeling of peace. The wand trusted Marcus to win. That realization gave him the fortitude to resist attacking their enemies in that moment.

Gabriel gave Marcus a bottle of water. He took a small sip and dumped the rest over his head. Rebecca examined his wounds, but didn't use her magic to help no matter how much she wanted to. Marcus closed his eyes and waited for the five minute break to be over.

Jeremy put a hand on Marcus's shoulder when Avestan gestured for the opponents to return to the middle of the room. The werewolf helped him stand up and put a steady hand on his arm.

"You've got this, man," Jeremy said encouragingly. "Do what you do best. Tick him off."

Marcus grinned weakly and gave Jeremy a pat on the shoulder before walking slowly to the middle of the room. Blood covered the stone floor where Carvolo was stabbed. Riley hoped Marcus was sure footed enough not to slip in it. He held up his sword…

Carvolo's sword.

Riley had to hide his smirk from their enemies.

Carvolo's face was pale when he walked to the middle of the room. He squatted down stiffly and picked up the bloody sword that Marcus had used to stab him. The wound in his stomach was terrible and still bleeding. Because he had no welhum he was still healing normally for a werewolf. But since he no longer had the poisoned blade things were looking up for Marcus.

"Begin," Avestan's voice echoed through the room.

Carvolo attacked first, but Marcus was ready. He dodged the blow and gave Carvolo a nasty cut on his hip.

"I hope your heart is pumping nice and strong," Marcus said with a smirk. "Wouldn't want the weapons switch to be for nothing."

"Begraw affects skinwalkers more than it does werewolves," Carvolo sneered.

"Yeah, just keep telling yourself that."

Marcus gave him another gash on his fighting arm and Carvolo howled angrily.

"Are you sure you're the one who taught Demian swordplay? Because I have to admit I'm a little disappointed."

Carvolo yelled furiously and swung his blade at Marcus. He barely got out of the way before it struck him. Marcus pulled off a somersault and managed to slice through Carvolo's calf muscle as he rolled. The werewolf fell to one knee and swore angrily.

"What's wrong, Carvolo?" Marcus asked in that annoying tone he often used. "Am I frustrating you?"

Marcus hit Carvolo in the face with the hilt of his sword. Blood spurted from his nose and he hissed in pain.

"Jeez," the skinwalker said with a tsk tsk. "You're really bad at this. I almost feel sorry for you."

Marcus kicked Carvolo to the ground with strength borrowed from adrenaline and hit the sword out of his hand. When Carvolo coughed Riley could hear fluid in his lungs.

"You can kill me," Carvolo gurgled breathlessly. "But my followers will never stop hunting your daughters. You'll never have a moment of peace-"

Carvolo's last word caught in his throat as Marcus inserted the blade into the werewolf's heart. The life left his eyes and his head hit the stone floor.

Marcus let out a shaky breath and staggered backwards. Time seemed to stand still as everyone stared at Carvolo's still form.

He was finally dead.

There was a moment of silence before the whole room burst into chaos.

It all happened so quickly that Riley didn't have time to replace their protective barriers that faded while they watched the fight.

Lekiah screamed angrily and a loud boom echoed through the large room. Marcus saw it coming and he was able to move out of the way so the bullet wouldn't enter his heart. Instead he got shot in the stomach. Lekiah held the pistol in shaking hands as she screamed at Marcus for killing her last child.

Everyone burst into action a split second after Marcus's body hit the floor. Aurora rushed over to her brother with Riley close behind her. He didn't want anyone attempting to hurt her. When she touched Marcus with her hands Riley muttered the protection spell. The silvery mist enveloped both of them a second later.

It was then that Riley noticed that Marcus was struggling to breath. He knew there was nothing he could do to help him at the moment, so he pushed it to the back of his mind.

"Stay with him," Riley told Aurora. "You'll both be safe."

She nodded as she took out her gun and started firing at the werewolves that tried to approach her and Marcus. Even though it was hard to leave them, Riley hurried to help fight off the werewolves.

In his wolf skin, Gabriel was locked in a battle with Lekiah and Avestan. They were both taking turns lunging at him with knives. Gabriel had no problem dodging them, but he wasn't able to attack them effectively. The rest of the ancient ones stood back and watched the fight. Some had the nerve to looked amused.

Jeremy and Raya fought off werewolf leaders side by side. It seemed that most of the old leaders were attacking them simultaneously. It was at least ten to two. They were soon over run and Riley could no longer see them in the crowd of vicious werewolves. He had a surge of adrenaline as he raised his wand to help them, but a flash of yellow magic caught his eye.

Rebecca was blocking attacks from Broden, but every time she tried to throw a spell it ran over him like water. Nothing she did slowed Broden down. Before Riley could replace their faded protective barriers he got hit in the side by what felt like a boulder.

The wand flew out of his hand and skidded across the floor. He mentally cursed himself for not acting quicker as pain erupted above his hip.

He glanced down and saw a long deep gash oozing blood through his shirt. He pulled out his throwing knife and faced the werewolf that attacked him.

Tomas watched him with amusement in his eyes as he brandished his bloody blade casually.

"Now that Carvolo is dead," the werewolf leader said excitedly. "I get to be the one to turn you this full moon. I'm looking forward to it."

Riley was so angry that he couldn't speak. He didn't think he could hate anyone more than he hated Carvolo, but this psychopath brutalized Aurora. More than Carvolo ever had. The fact that Tomas was still breathing bothered Riley…a lot.

"Craticas electios!"

Riley's blue ball of energy raced toward Tomas. The werewolf jumped through the air in a graceful maneuver. The energy ball hit one of the ancient werewolves that was watching the commotion from the side lines.

Riley had to stop himself from gaping. The ancient werewolf didn't even flinch from the electrical shock. He just fixed Riley with an angry glare and growled in annoyance.

Yeah, they were definitely in trouble if a craticas spell had no effect on the ancient ones.

Tomas chuckled from where he landed a few feet away.

"You aren't so powerful without the wand," Tomas said as he took a moment to glance at the ancient werewolf that Riley electrocuted. "Are you ready to surrender or do you want to watch us kill all your friends?"

Riley threw his knife at Tomas's heart and held his hand out toward the wand. He didn't look to see if his knife connected with it's target, but he still wasn't surprised when Tomas tackled him to the ground. Unfortunately, the wand didn't have a chance to reach his outstretched hand before he hit the stone floor.

The air rushed out of Riley's lungs when Tomas landed on top of him. His fingers were just inches from the wand. He

346

struggled to use his magic to make the wand come to him, but Tomas flipped him over onto his back. Riley's knife gleamed in his hand as he brought it to Riley's throat.

"You missed," Tomas said with a smirk. "Has Aurora told you about our time together yet?"

All the pain from being tackled fled to the back of his mind as he stopped struggling against Tomas. He couldn't believe the sadistic werewolf had the audacity to say her name. He was so angry he stopped trying to breathe. All he could feel was rage.

"I found her very amusing."

Riley threw the werewolf off of him with his magic and pinned him to the floor. He ignored the black spots that clouded his vision and the immediate fatigue that plagued him. He stood up and staggered over to Tomas. The werewolf glared at him, but couldn't speak since Riley's magic cut off his oxygen.

He was so angry he didn't even think about the wand as he approached the struggling werewolf.

He took his knife out of Tomas's hand and squatted down next to him.

"You'll never say her name again," Riley whispered angrily. "You'll never hurt her again."

Riley killed him quickly and held his hand out for the wand. When it didn't immediately come to him, Riley glanced around for it.

Unfortunately one of the werewolf leaders had picked it up off the ground. The wand didn't budge since it was in some else's hands. The female werewolf with very white teeth snarled at him as she brandished the wand. He ignored her threatening facial expression and threw his knife at her with record speed. She dropped to the ground the second the knife entered her heart.

The wand rolled out of her limp hand.

Riley couldn't use his magic anymore without passing out. He lunged for it, but was a second too late. An ancient one picked it up off of the floor and immediately tucked it into his sleeve.

347

Riley yanked his knife out of the dead female leader and threw it. The ancient one merely held out his hand and the knife stopped in midair. It fell to the ground and the ancient one stared at Riley with icy blue eyes.

"Riley Hanson," he said in a patient tone. "A few of the ancient ones have some magical ability and I am one of them. It would be foolish to try to kill me in such a way again."

Riley pulled out his gun. The ancient one flicked his fingers and the gun burned hot in his hand. He had to drop it before his skin blistered.

"You will accept your fate," the ancient werewolf said quietly. "And you will watch your friends die."

Suddenly, the ancient werewolf was standing next to him with a hand on the back of his neck. His grip was so tight that Riley blacked out for a moment from the pain. He was forced down to his knees by the strong ancient one. When Riley's vision cleared he saw his friends struggle to keep fighting.

Rebecca looked furious as she continued blocking the yellow magic that Broden threw at her. Gabriel was now in his human skin and had sustained multiple knife wounds. By the looks of it, the blades that struck him had been poisoned with begraw. He looked like he could barely stay upright let alone continue fighting.

Jeremy and Raya were struggling to keep the old leaders from killing them with every blow they blocked. Jeremy was covered in blood and the bodies of his opponents littered the floor. Raya didn't have a scratch on her, but she had lost her weapons in the fight. Jeremy had been doing a good job making sure no one touched her.

Aurora was out of bullets, but there were werewolf leaders scattered on the ground around her. Riley assumed they had tried to touch her, or Marcus, and received an electrical shock. At least they were still safe until the magical shield wore off.

Riley wasn't going to accept the fate that the ancients had planned for him. He definitely wasn't going to watch his friends die.

He let his body go limp under the ancient one's tight grip. He used his fingers to grab his gun that sat on the ground next to him. The metal was so hot that he could feel his skin blister immediately, but he held on as he let the burning pain roll through him.

He lifted his arm and quickly fired a silver bullet into the ancient werewolf's heart. The werewolf gasped before lifelessly dropping to the ground. Riley shot to his feet and grabbed the wand from the dead werewolf's sleeve. By the time he turned around Gabriel had collapsed to the ground.

He pointed the wand at Gabriel and muttered the protection spell under his breath. The silvery mist floated through the air quickly. It wrapped itself around Gabriel right before Lekiah brought her knife toward Gabriel's exposed chest. Lekiah shrieked as the protective barrier zapped her. She flew backwards and landed on the ground in front of the group of werewolf spectators.

Riley quickly pointed the wand at Rebecca and gave her a protective barrier before a yellow electrical bolt from Broden's fingertips could reach her. There was a small magical explosion of yellow and blue as the bolt hit the shield that surrounded Rebecca.

Just as Riley was about to do the same for Jeremy and Raya, Avestan shot a bullet straight at Raya's chest.

Things seemed to happen in slow motion.

Riley sent the silvery protection barrier toward her, but he knew it wouldn't get there before the bullet killed her. Within the same second, Jeremy hurled his body in front of Raya's. For a moment all Riley could see was blood squirt from Jeremy's chest as the magical shield wrapped itself around Raya.

She screamed in despair as Jeremy's body hit the ground.

Avestan smiled triumphantly as he watched Raya kneel down next to Jeremy's still form. It looked as though the bullet went straight into his heart. Grief ripped through Riley and it blinded him for a moment. He had to stop himself from bending over and vomiting.

Riley had only known Jeremy for a few weeks, but he'd become a close friend. Seeing him die threatened to force him to his knees.

Tears streamed down Raya's cheeks as she held Jeremy's lifeless face in her hands. The sobbing sounds that came from her matched that of a girl who had lost too many people in her short life.

Another bullet exploded from Avestan's gun that he had aimed at Raya. She didn't even flinch as her eyes glowed yellow. The bullet bounced off of her magical shield as she glared at Avestan, but she quickly looked back down at Jeremy with shocked wide eyes.

Suddenly, Jeremy coughed as his chest heaved. Riley stared at him in utter disbelief. He could've sworn that the bullet hit his heart.

Riley didn't waste anymore time getting a protective shield around Jeremy. The werewolves figured out quickly that they couldn't touch them. The fighting slowly died down and Riley was able to take in the destruction of the room. All that was left of their enemies were nineteen ancient ones and Broden. All the rest of the leaders were either dead or unconscious.

Rebecca hurried over to Jeremy and used her magic to extract the bullet from his chest. The berserker immediately jumped to his feet and growled at Avestan. The ancient one was still standing over Gabriel; who was deeply unconscious. At least Avestan couldn't touch him again, but he needed Rebecca to help him before he bled out.

Suddenly, the triumphant look on Avestan's face faltered. He staggered back and slowly sank to his knees. Riley stared at the ancient one in confusion. Then he heard gasps coming from the rest of the werewolves in the room. It took Riley a moment to notice that Raya had stood up with her eyes glowing bright blue.

Riley could almost see the calming waves flow from her to the ancient ones. Some snarled and some collapsed to the

350

floor on their knees. It was almost immediate. The only one of their enemies that didn't seem to be effected by it was Broden.

Broden growled and glared at Raya with rage in his yellow eyes.

"You are an abomination," he snarled angrily. "You must be destroyed before you ruin us all."

Riley shakily aimed his gun at Broden and fired a single shot. It went a little wide and he missed his heart. The bullet hit him in the shoulder and he howled furiously. Riley was about to shoot him again, but the werewolf disappeared.

One moment he stood there, bleeding; then he was just gone.

Riley was too tired to care about where he could've gone, or how he was able to just disappear like a fairy.

He turned his attention back to Raya. She was slowly walking toward the ancient ones and the closer she got the more terrified they looked. Her tamer abilities made the most powerful werewolves to ever exist submit to her against their will. Riley had no idea that she was that powerful. He doubted she knew she was either.

"Avestan," Raya said in her soothing voice. "When I thought you killed Jeremy you made me realize my full potential. Something inside me roared to life. Now I realize what I can do and now I know what my true purpose is."

Raya turned away from Avestan and looked at the rest of the ancient ones. They were all on their knees now. They didn't look at her or move, but some of them snarled angrily. She walked past each of them with a sad look on her face. The blue glow in her eyes seemed to get brighter as she walked.

"You say that I'm an abomination," Raya said in a disapproving tone. "And that Jeremy is an abomination. But that is because you didn't want us to realize what our true purpose is. You have killed all the tamers that you have come across because you fear us. You imprisoned and tortured berserkers because you want to create mindless killers. You wanted to kill or change humans because you think they are inferior to you.

351

You imprisoned and abused your skinwalker children because you wanted obedient soldiers."

Raya stopped pacing and stood in the middle of the room to glare at their enemies. Even though she was angry she still exuded a calmness that Riley had never seen from her before. He still couldn't feel it, but he could tell the difference in her just by watching.

"You are the real monsters," she continued. "You get your joy and your purpose from death and destruction. You all have lived so long that you have literally gone insane. We can't in good conscious allow you to continue living."

Raya glanced at Riley and nodded. Riley lifted the wand and muttered the incantation that came to his mind. Once again the terrifying power that the wand possessed amazed him. Blue light flooded the room and blinded everyone. The only one the light didn't affect was Riley. He watched as the light pierced through each of the ancient werewolves. One by one they collapsed to the ground as the wand's magic overtook them.

It didn't take long for the ancients to die. It was a quick and painless death. With all the evil things the ancients caused and all the lives they had taken and destroyed…it was more than they deserved.

When it was over Riley gripped the wand tightly in his hand. It was warm and oddly comforting. He glanced over at Aurora and the look on her face caught him off guard. She was terrified as she stared at him. When she finally noticed him looking back at her she seemed to relax. He hurried over to her and knelt down next to Marcus.

"Are you okay?" she asked in a quivering voice.

"Yeah," he said as he kissed her forehead. "Everything is okay now. It's over."

She stared at him with wide eyes. There was so much pain in that look that he couldn't take it anymore. He tore his eyes away from her and looked down at Marcus.

He used the wand to get the begraw out of Marcus's system.

Chapter 23

Riley watched the flames grow higher and higher in the semi darkness. Naomi and Drake stood on the other side of the inferno that served as the burial for their enemies. He still had a hard time believing that the war was finally over. The thought was so overwhelming that he had a hard time staying upright. He thought that he would feel more content, but in all reality he was just tired. He was afraid he'd go into a deep sleep if he put the wand down, so he didn't.

Demian had arrived with a small army an hour ago. Marcus and Gabriel were given healing elements and were helping with cleanup. They had received word from Samantha that they were still safe and hidden from any werewolves that might still try to take the babies. Jackson, Rachel, and Karven were still with them.

Aurora was given guresh, but was still very weak and sick. Riley had insisted that she rest, so she was asleep in a tent that Demian had brought. He wanted to join her, but he still had adrenaline coursing through him even though it had been hours since the fighting stopped. She didn't need to see him like that right now. She'd been through enough as it was.

Someone touched his shoulder and he jumped. Small hands grabbed his arms to steady him and he trembled slightly. He glanced down and saw that it was Veronica. She looked a lot better than the last time he saw her.

"I'm sorry, Ry," she said in concern. "I didn't mean to startle you."

Riley didn't say anything. He just hugged her. He honestly didn't know if he would ever see her alive again. He was so grateful that Karven got to her in time to save her.

"Are you okay?" she asked as she pulled away from him to look in his eyes. He didn't know how to answer that so he asked his own question.

"So, what's your plan now? Demian said something about fixing up the Ancients Den."

353

"Yeah," she said with a small smile. "He said that when he was a child werewolves would come to the Ancients Den for refuge when they needed it. He wants to do that again. Now that most of the old leaders are dead there's going to be a lot of followers that will need a place to be. To feel like they belong."

Riley nodded and looked back at the flames that Naomi and Drake controlled. Nothing around them burned but the bodies of the dead werewolves.

"It sounds like he wants to fix the werewolf hierarchy. Make the world a safe place for humans and werewolves alike."

"Yeah," Veronica said with a nod. "I think he can do it."

"He can do anything with you by his side," Riley said as he kissed his sister's cheek. "Have you seen Raya and Jeremy? I haven't talked to them since he was shot."

Veronica nodded and pointed toward the trees. Riley couldn't see them, but he thanked her and walked toward the trees. He waded through the brush, not caring about he noise he was making. He didn't want to try to sneak up on a berserker anyway.

When he walked around a cluster of trees he spotted Jeremy and Raya huddled on the ground next to each other. He immediately felt guilty for intruding, but he just needed to make sure they were alright.

"Hey, Riley," Raya said. Her small smile quickly vanished when she saw his face. "Are you okay?'

"I just came to see how you two are doing," Riley said with a shrug. "I could've sworn that Jeremy…"

Riley's voice trailed off when he noticed Raya wince.

"I thought I was a goner too," Jeremy said with a nod. "I felt the bullet scrape against my heart. Close call."

Raya's arm tightened around his waist as she shivered. Jeremy kissed the top of her head and ran his hand down her arm.

"Well, you definitely look better," Riley said. "What are you guys planning on doing now?"

"I think we are going to go back to the Washington community," Jeremy said with a shrug. "Demian asked us to

354

stay there for a few years until the younger skinwalkers become legal adults."

"I'm technically not a legal adult yet," Raya said in amusement.

"You made it possible for the wand to take out all the ancient werewolves at one time," Riley said incredulously. "I don't think you count. You're more than capable of helping skinwalkers find their place in life."

"I was also thinking about finishing school," Raya said with a shrug. "It seems more relevant now that the war is over."

Riley waited for the relief to come, but it didn't. He was still on edge. He still felt like they could be attacked at any moment. He knew that it showed on his face because Raya kept looking at him with concern. He was surprised that her eyes hadn't gone blue yet.

"Where's Aurora?" Jeremy asked him. Riley knew it was a rhetorical question since Jeremy already knew exactly where she was, but he answered anyway.

"She's resting."

"You should be with her, man."

"I know," Riley said with a nod. "I just wanted to check up on you guys."

"What's wrong, Riley?" Raya asked as she continued studying his expression.

"I'm just having a hard time," he said through a small breath. "Calming down from everything. That's the last thing Aurora needs to deal with right now."

"I am too," Raya said. "I think we all are, but you need Aurora right now. So stop being the amazing friend that you are and go take care of yourself. We'll all be fine."

Jeremy nodded in agreement.

Riley gave them a small smile and walked the short distance to Aurora's tent. He should've known that Jeremy wouldn't be too far away from her while she was recuperating. He was the kind of man that took care of the people he cared about, even ex-girlfriends.

355

He unzipped the door as quietly as he could and kicked his shoes off. He was covered in dried blood and sweat, but he knew it didn't matter. No one had bothered to clean up or get changed yet. They probably wouldn't be able to until they found a shower somewhere. Still, he peeled off his disgusting shirt and threw it in the corner of the tent.

He was careful not to disturb his bandages while he undressed. He'd insisted that Demian use the limited amount of guresh that he had on the Ryders since they had been the most injured during the battle today. It still amazed Riley that Marcus hadn't died from his wounds. Marcus Ryder was one tough guy.

Gabriel had been barely alive by the time Rebecca was able to tend to his wounds. Riley would never forget his sister's panicked pleas for Gabriel to wake up when he'd passed out. Raya had been too exhausted after using her powers against the ancient ones to be of much help to Rebecca at that moment. Surprisingly it had been Jeremy that took charge of the situation despite almost dying himself. He'd gotten Rebecca calmed down enough so that she could perform the spell to get the begraw out of Gabriel's system. He had even clamped down on Gabriel's radial artery that had been nicked in the fight so he wouldn't bleed out.

Riley knew he'd have nightmares about Marcus and Gabriel dying for the rest of his life. He was so relieved that they were alive, but he still felt paranoid despite all the bad guys being killed or imprisoned in the Ancients Den dungeons.

Riley shoved his thoughts to the back of his mind and concentrated on the beautiful angel laying down in front of him.

Aurora was sound asleep on top of a sleeping bag. He was worried about startling her. The last time he woke her up she almost beat the crap out of him. He wouldn't blame her if she did it again. But when she opened her eyes she gave him a small smile and patted the ground beside her. He lowered himself onto the sleeping bag and wrapped an arm around her waist.

"How are you feeling, sweetie?" he asked softly.

"I'll feel much better when I can eat normally again."

356

Demian had given her some raw meat when he arrived, but she was also battling a fever. Which was normal after living in a werewolf dungeon for as long as she did. Riley kissed her forehead and nuzzled his nose into her hair. Usually she calmed him, but it wasn't working this time.

She ran a weak hand over his arm and then rested it on his cheek.

"Are you okay, Riley?"

He balked at the question.

"I'm pretty sure that I should be asking you that."

"You look like you're on edge," she said weakly.

Riley took a deep breath and pulled her closer to him. He knew she was probably in pain, but he couldn't help it. He needed her body next to his, to feel her touch. He had missed her for far too long.

"I'm still hyped up on adrenaline," he said shakily. "I can't calm down and I don't know why."

"I can tell," she said as she smoothed her thumb over his cheek. "Do you realize how badly you're shaking?"

He hadn't until she mentioned it. Now that he noticed he tried to make it stop.

"When I found out that Carvolo took you to the Ancients Den," he said in a quivering voice. "I thought I lost you forever."

"I know," she whispered as she ran her fingers through his hair.

"I didn't know if you were dead or alive and it broke me."

"I know," she said again.

Riley loathed himself in that moment. She was the one who thought he had been dead. She was the one who suffered. She was starved and shut in a dark cell alone for who knows how many days. He wanted to be the one to comfort her. He shouldn't need to be comforted, but he did and he hated it.

But he knew that if he was going to talk to her he should tell her everything.

"I almost tortured my own mother," he whispered into her hair. Tears stung his eyes as he said it. "She knew where you were and I was willing to do anything to get to you. If Marcus,

357

Gabriel, Jeremy, Raya, and Naomi hadn't been there to stop me-"

His voice broke and he couldn't talk anymore. Tears fell from his eyes and dampened her skin. She continued running a comforting hand through his hair. They held each other for a while until his tears stopped.

"Riley," she whispered to him. "The first thing you need to realize is that Jenna doesn't deserve the title of *mother*. As the world's leading expert on dealing with a crappy parent... trust me when I say you have to stop thinking of her that way. Rachel is your mother...not her. Never her."

"Just like Demian is your father."

"Always has been in my eyes," she said with a nod. "He deserves the title and Carvolo never did."

Riley nodded and buried his face in her hair again. His shaking hadn't subsided and he was beginning to wonder if it ever would.

"The second thing you need to realize," she said quietly. "You may have been prepared to torture Jenna, but you didn't."

She pulled away from him slightly to look him in the eye. "You didn't."

"I would have," he said with a shudder.

"That's not the point. You and I both know that no one would've been able to stop you if you really wanted to hurt Jenna."

Riley knew she was right, but he still couldn't accept that. He didn't know if he ever would. He had gone down a dark path that night and it scared him. He didn't want it to change him, but he knew that it did a little bit.

"What can I do to help you?" she asked. "I think you'd feel better if you were calmer."

"I don't know." His voice cracked. "I just want you."

"I'm here," she said as she planted a kiss on his nose. "And I'm not going anywhere."

He nodded and buried his face into her neck. He kissed her there and left a trail of smaller kisses up to her jawline.

358

When his lips met hers the last of his adrenaline washed away. He sighed as he tried again to calm his shaking body.

"I'm going to put the wand down," he said in a tight whisper. "Don't freak out if I pass out, okay? Sometimes when the connection breaks I have to sleep for a while."

"Seriously?" Aurora asked in mild surprise.

"Is there anything you want to talk about before I do?"

"No," she said with a small shake of her head. "We have the rest of our immortal lives to talk. Right now we could both use the rest."

"I love you," he said as he kissed her once more.

"I love you too."

Riley set the wand in it's accustomed place on the dresser in his and Aurora's room. They had been helping the Singers repair their house in Palmer, so he had been learning to use the wand to create things and repair broken objects. It helped the construction go by more quickly with less expense. Not that money had ever been an issue.

Being back in Alaska had been surprisingly therapeutic for Riley. Helping repair the house that had been his safe haven as a young boy had done wonders for his mood. It had been a difficult few weeks of trying to recover from everything that had happened over the past few years.

The hardest part for Riley was feeling safe again. After the constant danger that they lived in and the never ending fear that the ones he loved would die it was hard to believe that it was all truly over. The Ryders were having a hard time with it as well. Especially Marcus, which Riley thought was surprising.

Rachel still tried to get him to talk to a therapist, but he would forever fight her suggestions. Being with Aurora was all the therapy he needed. She was his lifeline and always would be.

Riley hadn't heard from Veronica for a while, but he knew that she and Demian were busy helping the werewolves find their place in the world. They were repairing the dens that the rebellion destroyed to give homes to the followers that needed them. Minus the dungeons and prisons as Demian had promised. With the right werewolves in charge things were going to be a lot more peaceful for everyone.

Gabriel, Rebecca, Marcus, and Samantha had all moved to Alaska permanently. Marcus and Samantha wanted to raise their girls there and were looking into buying a house. All normal things that Riley thought wouldn't ever be possible for them. But it was and it was happening. Riley was happy for them. Gabriel and Rebecca planned on living with the Singers until they found a more permanent place to stay.

After a week since her rescue Riley had finally insisted that Aurora tell him about her ordeal. She had been hesitant after seeing how damaged he'd been when everything was over. She didn't think that telling him all that she had gone through would help him. She had been right, but he knew that he needed to know. She also needed to have someone to tell. The things she went through wasn't something that could be bottled up. It needed to be aired out so the healing process could begin. She still wasn't healed and neither was he, but they were well on their way. Coming together had made them even stronger as a couple and Riley had been surprised by that.

There was a knock at the door before it opened. Pearl stood in the doorway with a smile on her face. She had changed the most since the war ended. She was actually happy now most of the time. She still had a sardonic sense of humor that colored her personality, but that's what he loved most about her.

"Mom told me to get you," she said. "Dinner is ready."

Riley nodded and followed her out the door.

"Are you and Aurora going to leave now that the house is finished?"

"I don't think so," Riley said with a grin. "We've been talking about tearing down the old house I grew up in and building a new one. We've got to have a place of our own."

"You're not moving back to Washington?" she asked with a hopefulness in her tone that Riley had never heard before.

"Most of our family is here," Riley said as he ruffled her hair. "Why would we leave?"

She smiled and hurried down the stairs. He followed her and saw Jasmine and Tanya trying to corral the crawling babies in the living room. Leigh and Elizabeth laughed as the two girls chased them around. The adorable scene made Riley smile.

Jasmine had taken the news of Teresa's death very well; all things considered. She had times when she was very sad, but Jackson and Rachel made sure she got the emotional support she needed. They were in the process of adopting her so that Veronica wouldn't have to. They thought it best that Veronica just be a sister to her and not a mother. So far the arrangement seemed to be working.

When he made it to the dining room he sat next to Aurora. The meal they had together was so normal it made Riley's head spin. He didn't eat much as he listened to the different conversations. He'd done a good job putting on a face that told everyone he was okay. He wasn't, but maybe someday he would be. The ones he didn't think he ever fooled were Aurora and Rebecca. And of course, Gabriel, but he never commented on it.

Aurora squeezed his hand under the table. He closed his eyes for a moment to enjoy the feel of her fingers entwined with his. He kissed her cheek and she gave him a sweet smile. She was having a good day and it made him happy. He couldn't get enough of her these days, or ever. There were times that he still couldn't believe that she was his and he was hers.

After they all pitched in to clean the kitchen Riley snuck outside for some fresh air. The leaves were beginning to turn yellow as autumn crept up on them. It was one of his favorite seasons in Alaska. The crisp air cleared his head and he felt like he could finally take a deep breath. He loved his family, but he realized that he craved the quiet sometimes.

The front door opened and Rebecca walked onto the porch. He smiled at her as he leaned against the railing. She gave him a small punch on the arm before resting her head against his shoulder.

"You're having a hard day," she said it as an observation and not a question.

"I am not."

"Sure you are," she said as she looked up at his face. "But that's okay."

"No, it's not," he grumbled with a shake of his head.

"It is," she said with a nod. "I have them too. I'm just more vocal about it."

Riley couldn't help but chuckle at that.

"Have you thought about moving on to the next thing?" she asked him. "Like college or something?"

"I don't think I'm there yet, sis," he said gruffly. "But I definitely will someday. What about you?"

"I'm thinking of college, but I'm not sure when," she said with a small smile. "I still want to study psychology."

"That is awesome," he said with a real smile. "You'll be great at that."

There was silence between them for a while as they watched the sunset.

"How long to do you think it'll take?" she asked solemnly.

"For what?" he asked with a raised eyebrow.

"For things to feel normal again? Is that even possible?"

"I don't know," Riley replied. Truthfully, he didn't even know what normal was. He didn't think he ever had. The thing that brought him normalcy was his family.

"Do you still have nightmares?" she asked in a whisper.

Every night. But Riley wasn't about to tell her that. They were concerned enough for him as it was.

"Sometimes," he lied. "They don't bother me as much as they used to. At least the danger is gone now."

Rebecca smiled and watched the rest of the sunset with him in silence. Aurora joined them on the porch and Rebecca smiled at her before giving Riley another punch on the arm. She hurried into the house to give them some much needed time alone.

Aurora pulled his head toward hers and kissed him. He didn't know what it was about that kiss, but all of his anxiety washed away the moment her soft lips touched his. His hands went to her back and he pulled her in closer. Her touch sent chills up his spine and he had to remember not to hold her too tightly. Her pain was almost completely gone, but some of her burns were still a bit tender.

She made an irritated noise and pulled his arms tighter around her. He broke off the kiss and smiled at her.

"Is that your way of telling me that I don't need to be careful with you anymore?"

"Sure is," she said with a smirk. "It's more painful for me when you hold back."

"I think I can do something about that," he said with a flirty smile.

He kissed her again with such passion that tears formed in his eyes. For the first time in a long while he felt at ease. He could get used to this feeling. Being with Aurora made that happen. She was everything that was good about him and he hung onto her for dear life. He would never lose her again and she was his forever. He was more than okay with that.

The End

The Skin Series *by Mariah Dyer*

SKIN book 1

SHED book 2

SCRAPE book 3

SCORCH book 4

SCAR book 5

367

Made in the USA
Columbia, SC
19 February 2025

53901276R00221